ANIMAL FARM

George Orwell

Animal Farm

Illustrated
by **Odyr**

Houghton Mifflin Harcourt
Boston • New York
2019

First U.S. edition 2019

First published with the title *A revolução dos bichos* in Brazil by
Editora Schwarcz s.a. in 2018.

hmhco.com

Library of Congress Cataloging-in-Publication Data
Names: Odyr, illustrator, adapter. | Orwell, George, 1903–1950. Animal farm.
Title: Animal farm : the graphic novel / George Orwell ; illustrated by Odyr.
Other titles: A revolução dos bichos. English
Description: First U.S. edition. | Boston : Houghton Mifflin Harcourt, 2019. |
First published with the title A revolução dos bichos in Brazil by
Editora Schwarcz s.a. in 2018.
Identifiers: LCCN 2019006380| ISBN 9780358093152 (hardback) |
ISBN 9780358093022 (ebook)
Subjects: LCSH: Totalitarianism—Comic books, strips, etc. | Fables, English. |
Graphic novels. | BISAC: COMICS & GRAPHIC NOVELS / Literary. |
FICTION / Classics.
Classification: LCC PN6790.B73 O3713 2019 | DDC 741.5/981—dc23
LC record available at https://lccn.loc.gov/2019006380

The illustrator's handwriting was digitized and specially developed for this book
and is of exclusive use from Editora Schwarcz s.a. Used by permission.

Printed in China

IMO 10 9 8 7 6 5 4 3 2 1

I

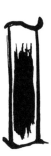

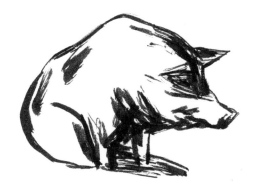

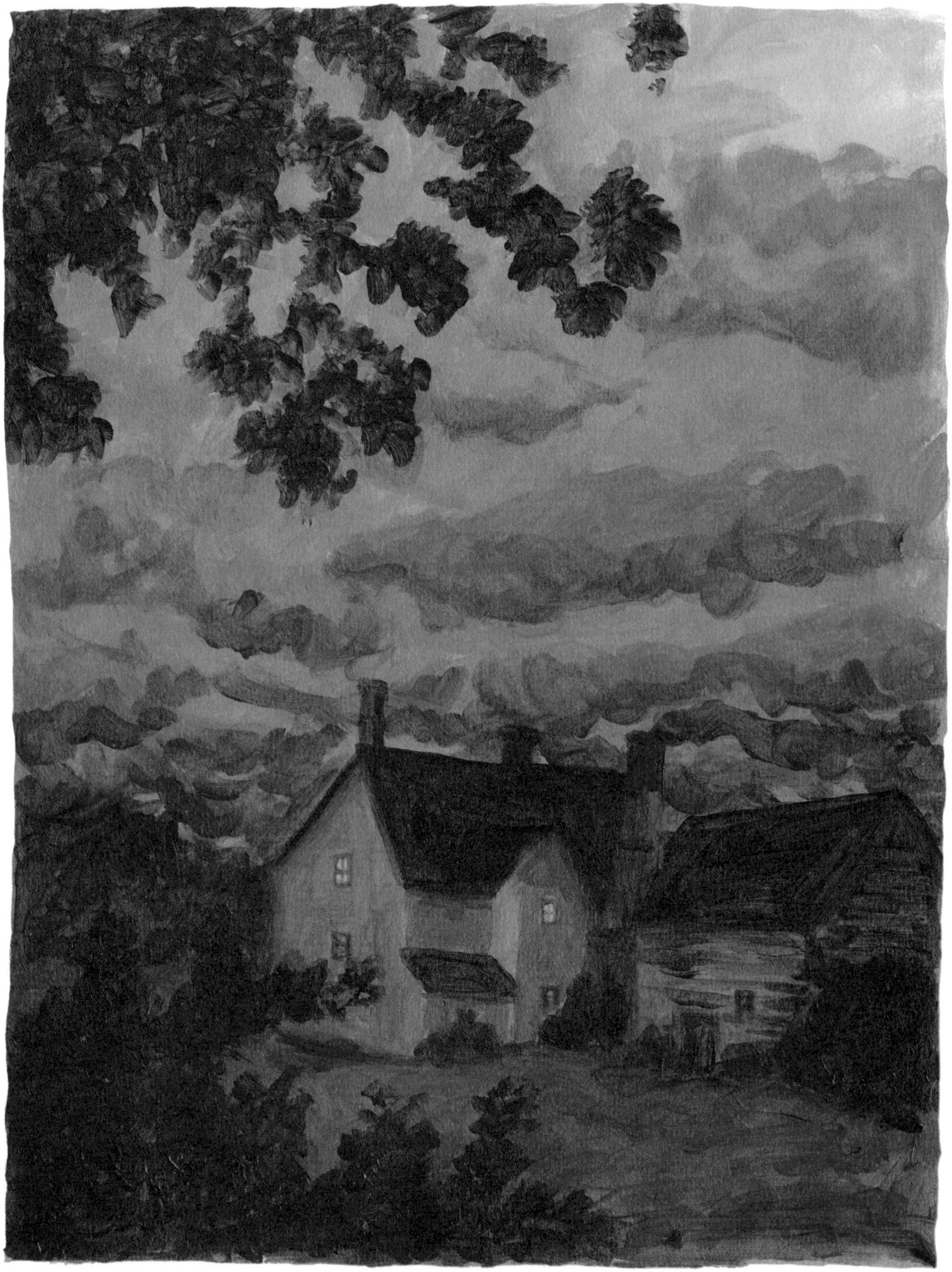

Mr. Jones had locked the hen-houses
but was too drunk to remember
to shut the popholes.

The light from his lantern
danced from side to side.

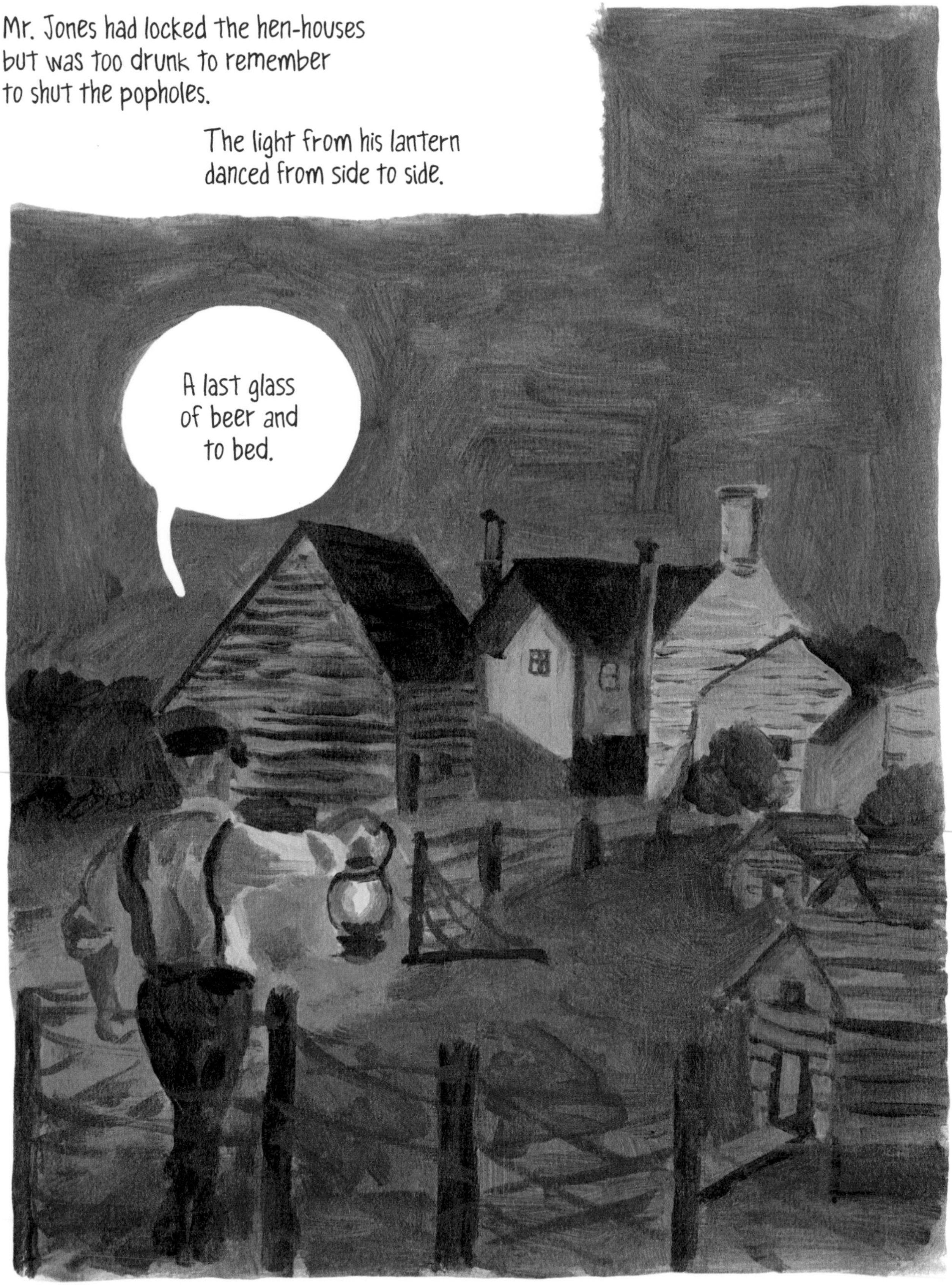
A last glass of beer and to bed.

As soon as the light in the bedroom went out there was a stirring and a fluttering through the farm buildings.

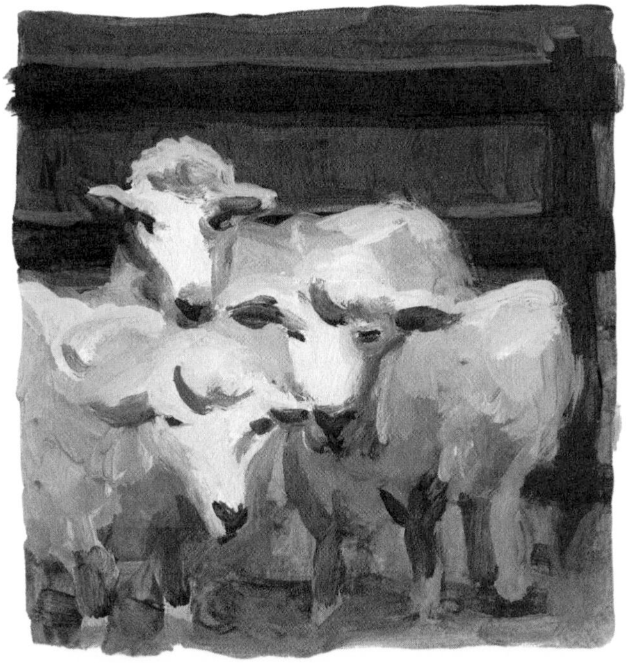

Old Major had had a strange dream on the previous night and wished to communicate it to the other animals.

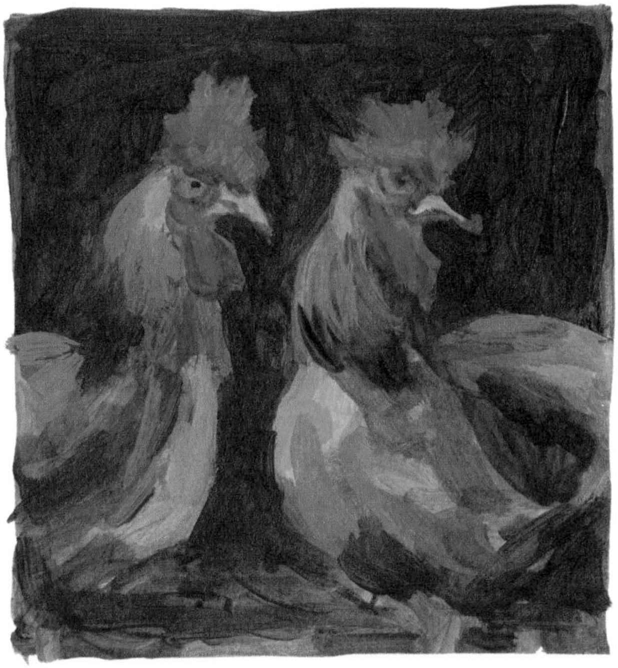

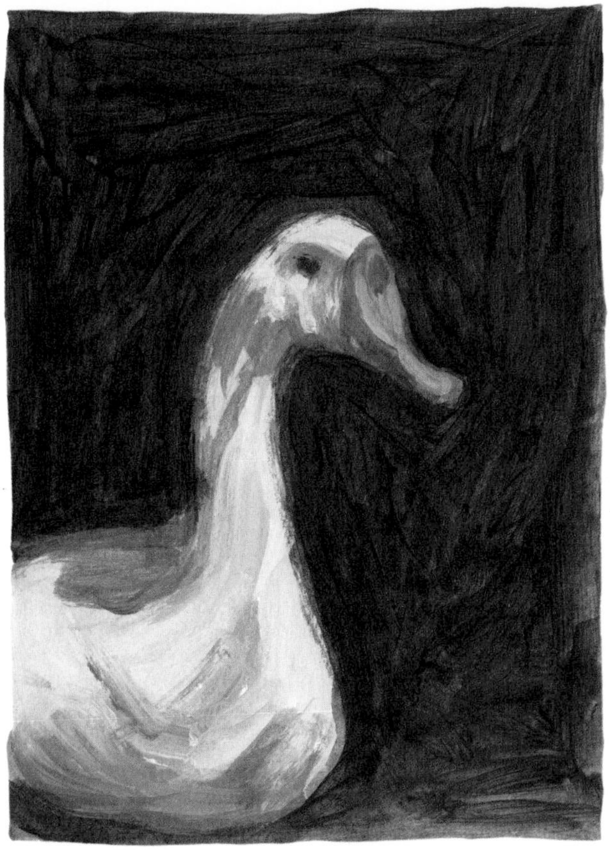

It had been agreed that they should all meet in the big barn.

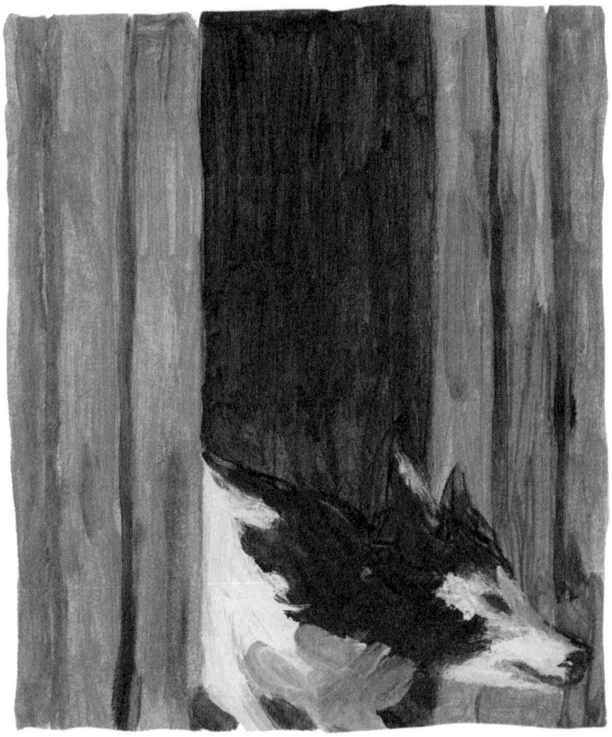

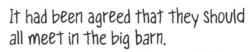

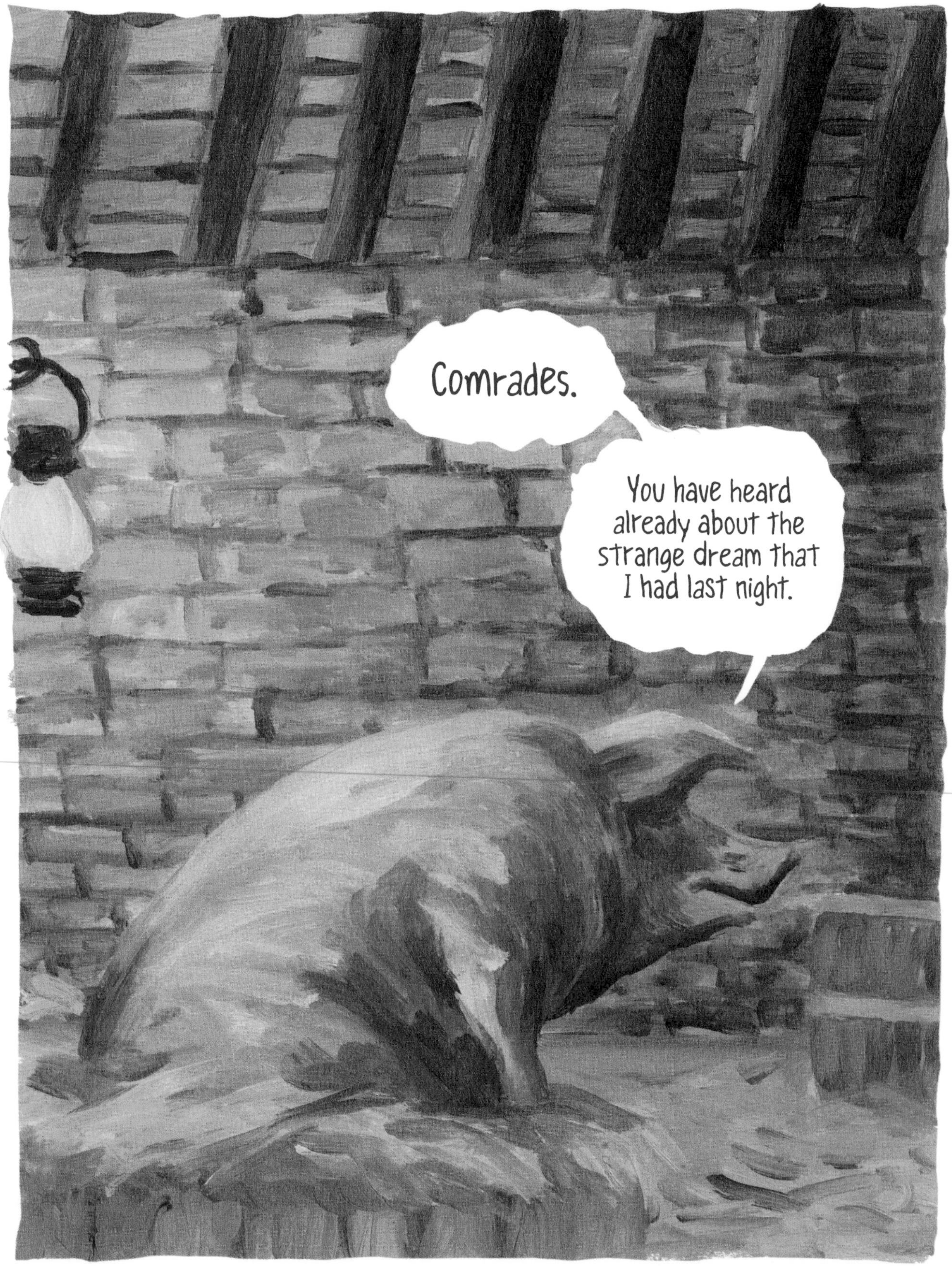
Comrades.
You have heard already about the strange dream that I had last night.

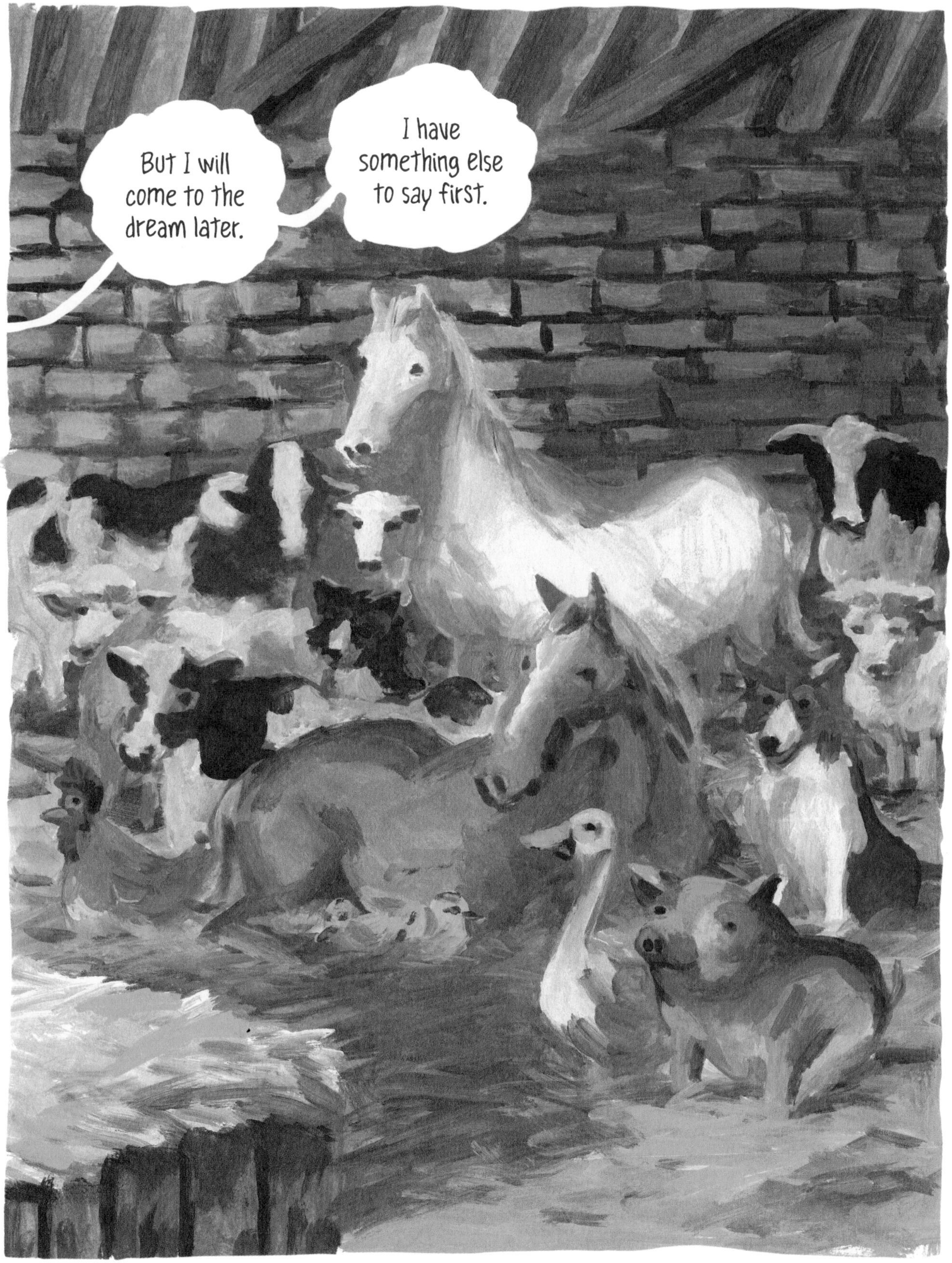
But I will come to the dream later.
I have something else to say first.

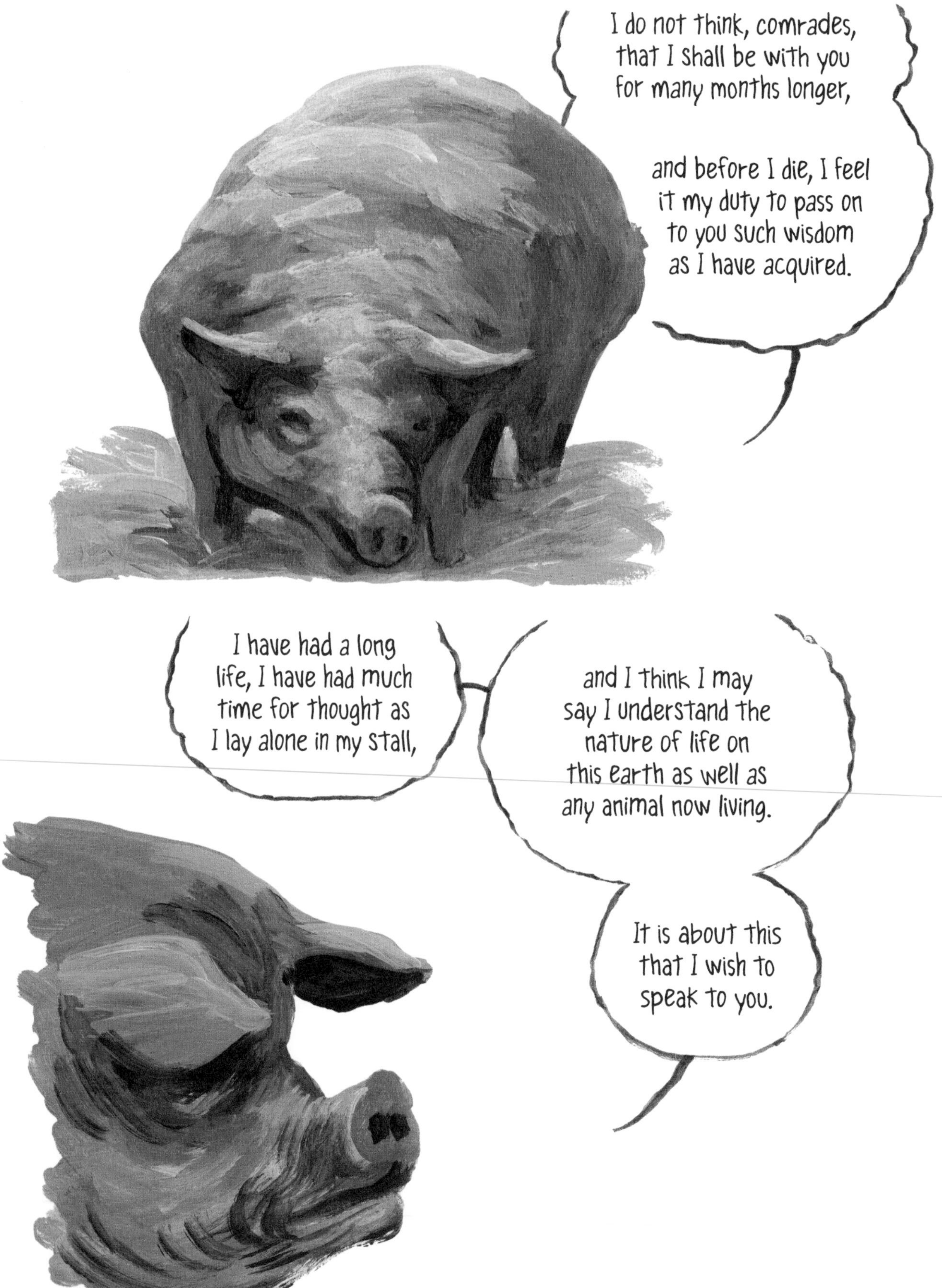
I do not think, comrades, that I shall be with you for many months longer,
and before I die, I feel it my duty to pass on to you such wisdom as I have acquired.
I have had a long life, I have had much time for thought as I lay alone in my stall,
and I think I may say I understand the nature of life on this earth as well as any animal now living.
It is about this that I wish to speak to you.

Now, comrades, what is the nature of this life of ours?

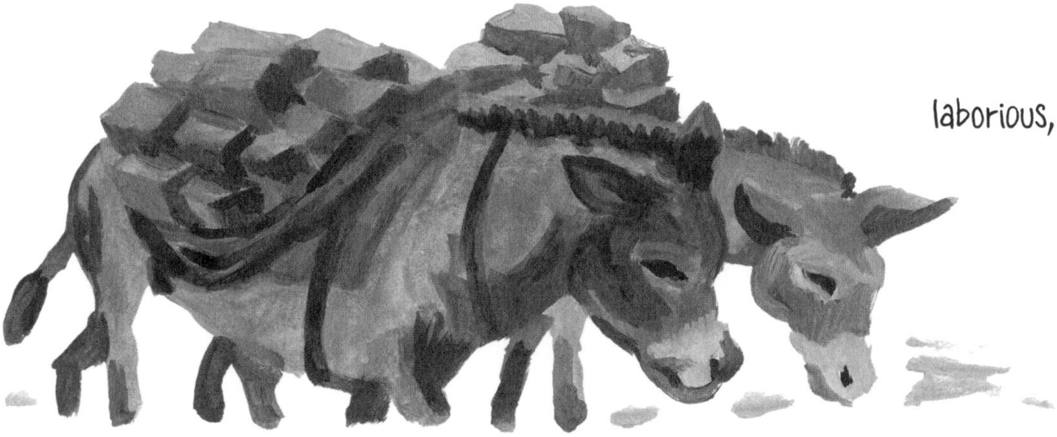

Miserable, laborious, and short.

We are born, we are given just so much food as will keep the breath in our bodies, and those of us who are capable of it are forced to work to the last atom of our strength; and the very instant that our usefulness has come to an end we are slaughtered with hideous cruelty.

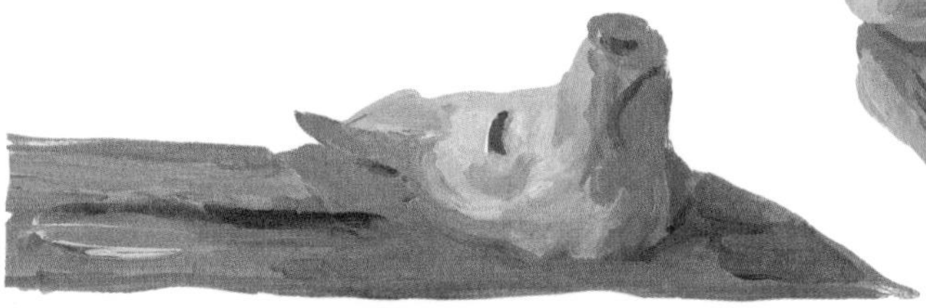

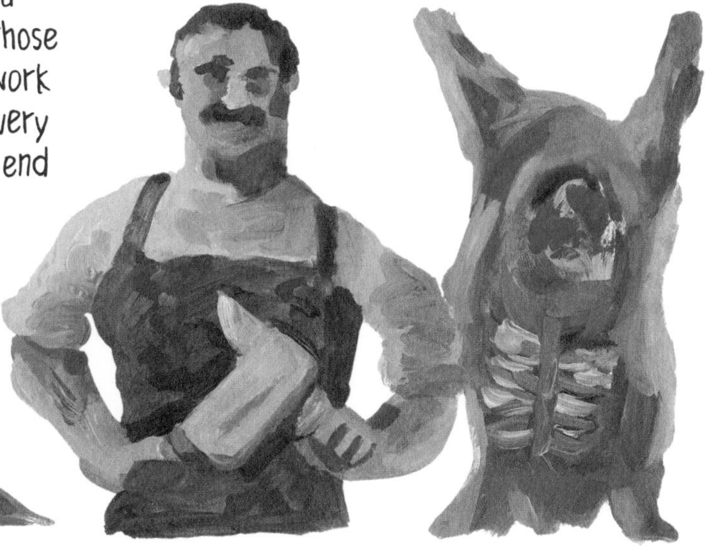

No animal in England is free. The life of an animal is misery and slavery: that is the plain truth.

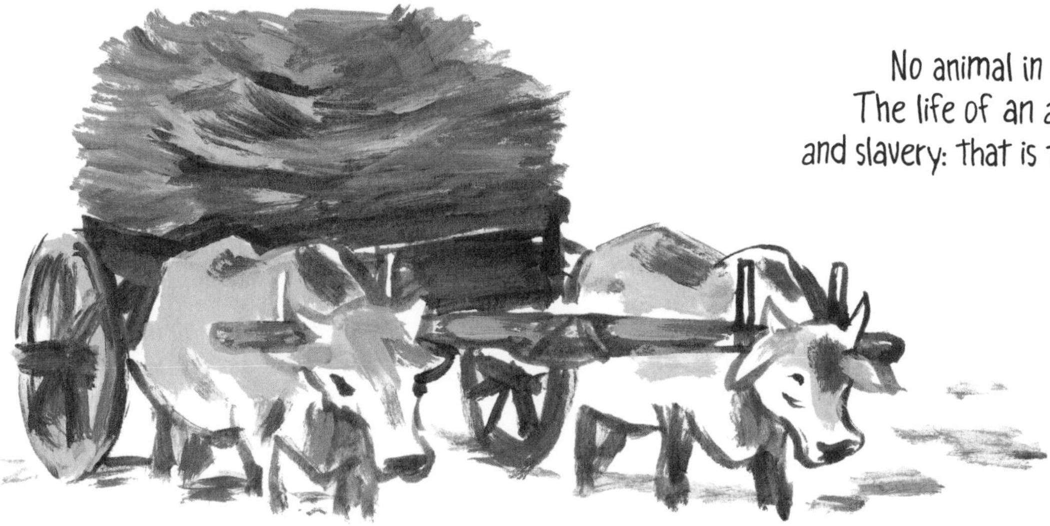

But is this simply part of the order of nature? Is it because this land of ours is so poor that it cannot afford a decent life to those who dwell upon it?

No, comrades, a thousand times no!

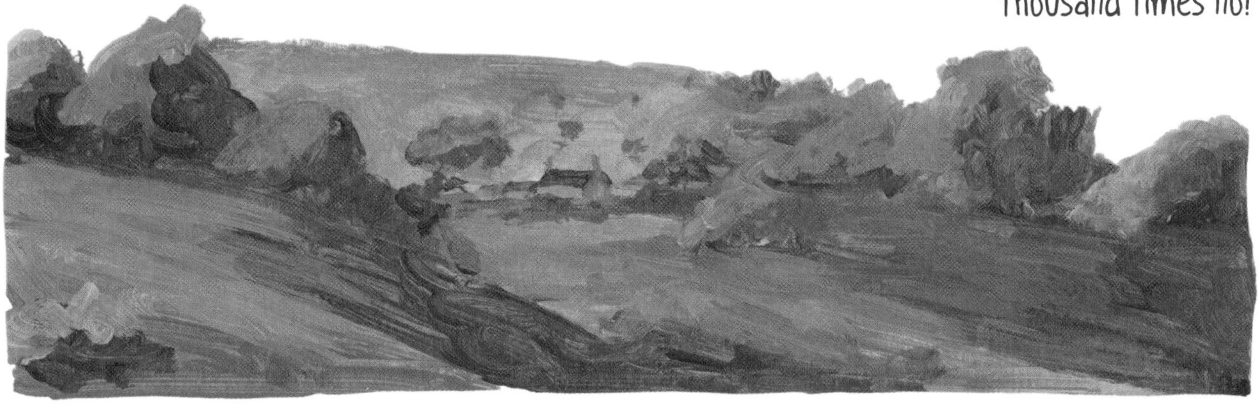

The soil of England is fertile, its climate is good, it is capable of affording food in abundance to an enormously greater number of animals than now inhabit it.

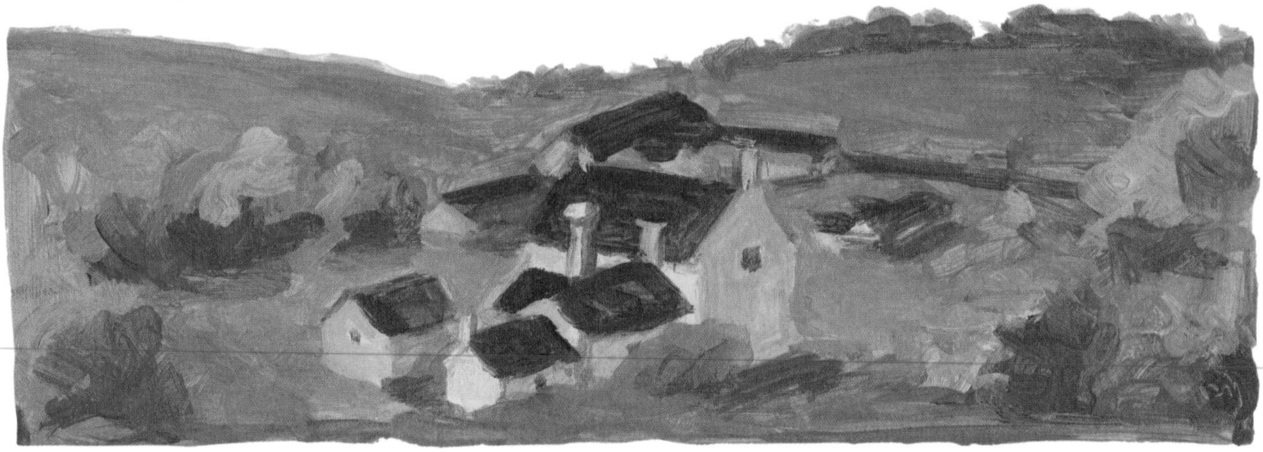

The answer to all our problems, it is summed up in a single word—Man.

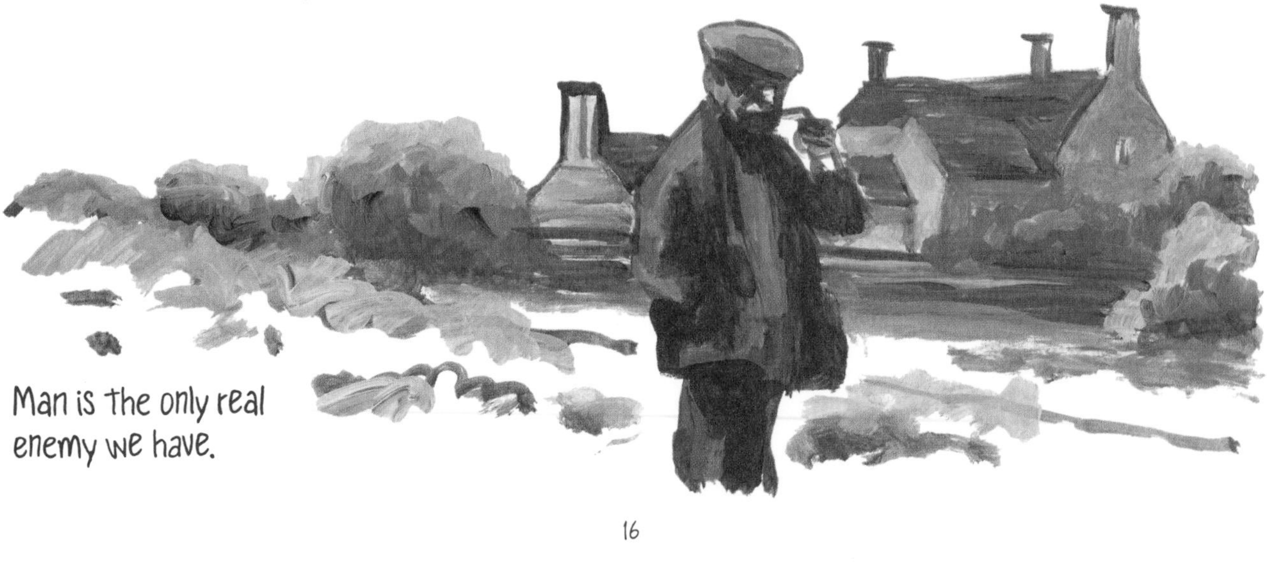

Man is the only real enemy we have.

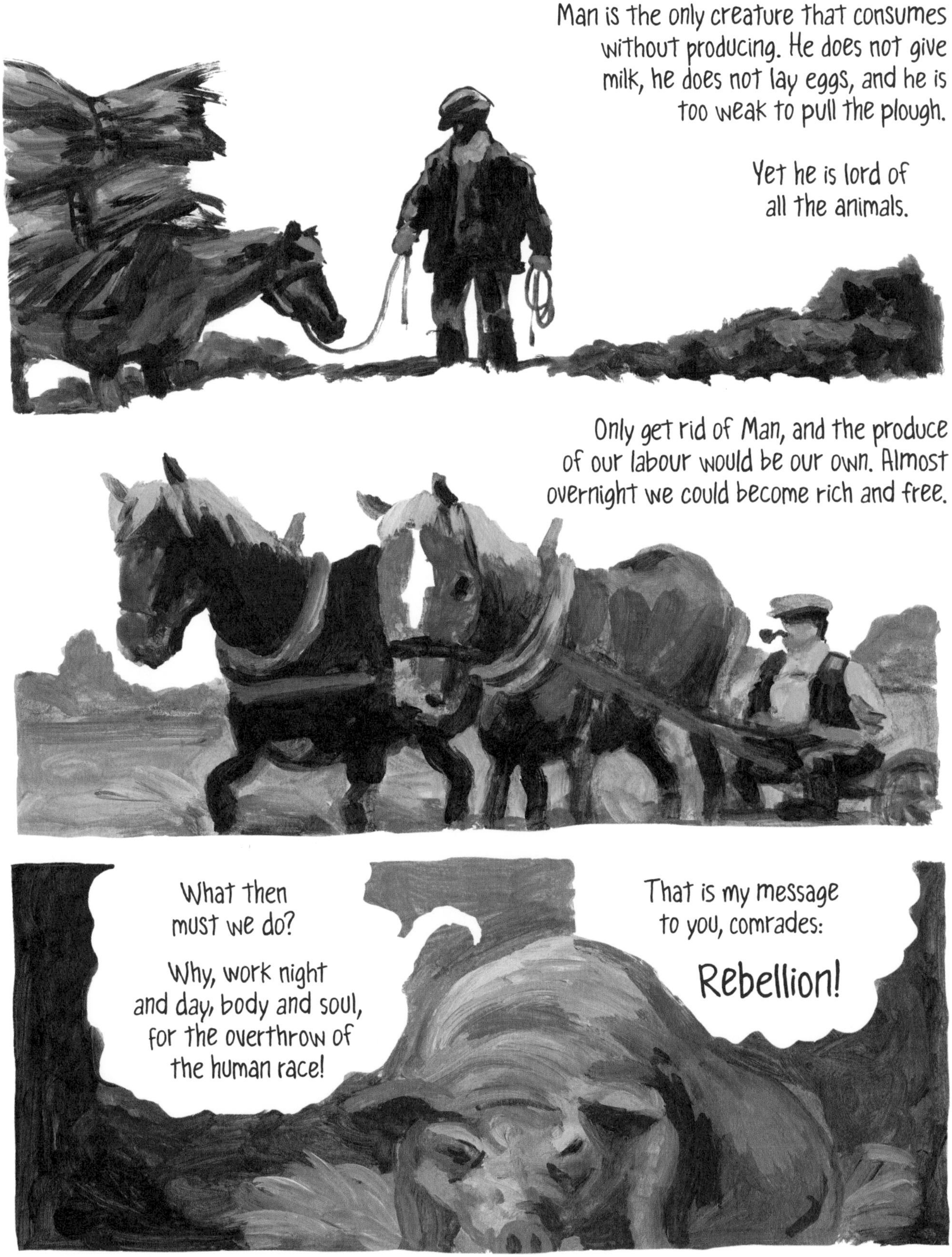
Man is the only creature that consumes without producing. He does not give milk, he does not lay eggs, and he is too weak to pull the plough.
Yet he is lord of all the animals.
Only get rid of Man, and the produce of our labour would be our own. Almost overnight we could become rich and free.
What then must we do?
Why, work night and day, body and soul, for the overthrow of the human race!
That is my message to you, comrades:
Rebellion!

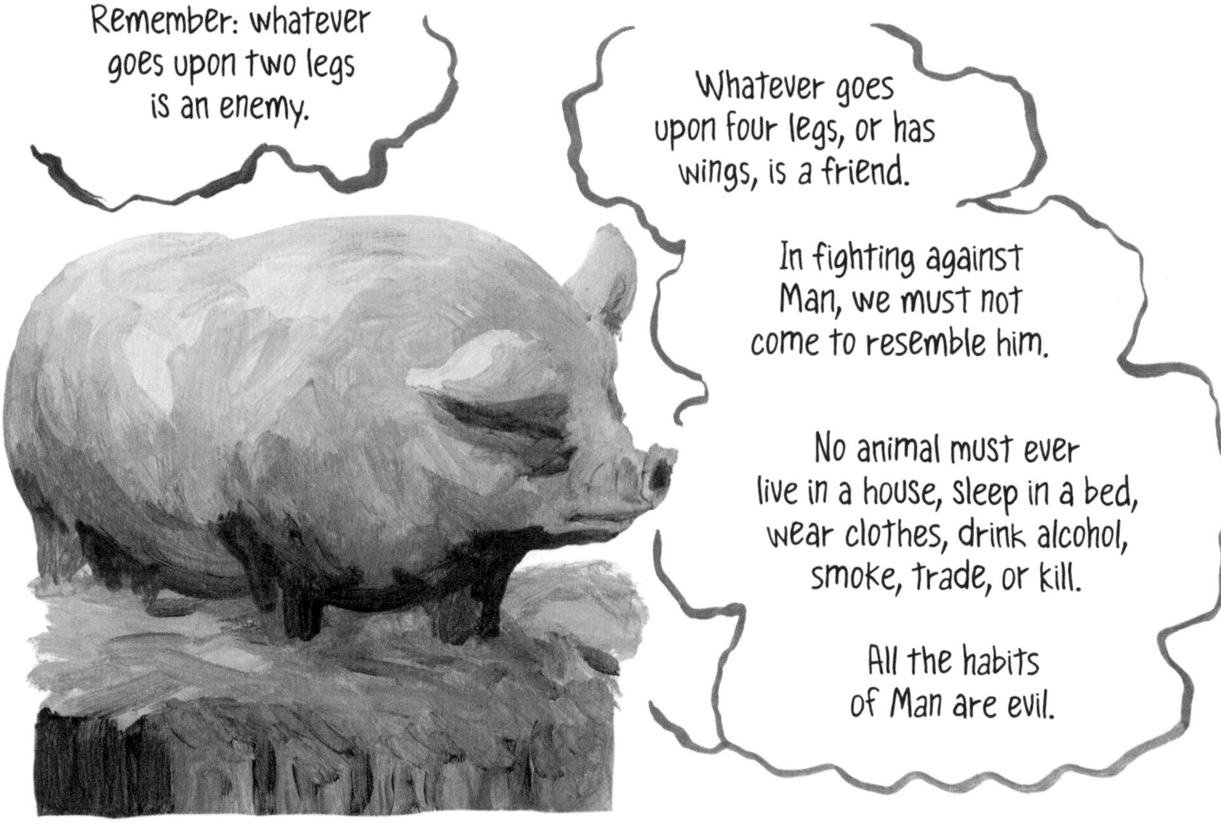
Remember: whatever goes upon two legs is an enemy.
Whatever goes upon four legs, or has wings, is a friend.
In fighting against Man, we must not come to resemble him.
No animal must ever live in a house, sleep in a bed, wear clothes, drink alcohol, smoke, trade, or kill.
All the habits of Man are evil.

And, above all, no animal must ever tyrannise over his own kind.

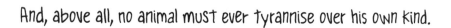

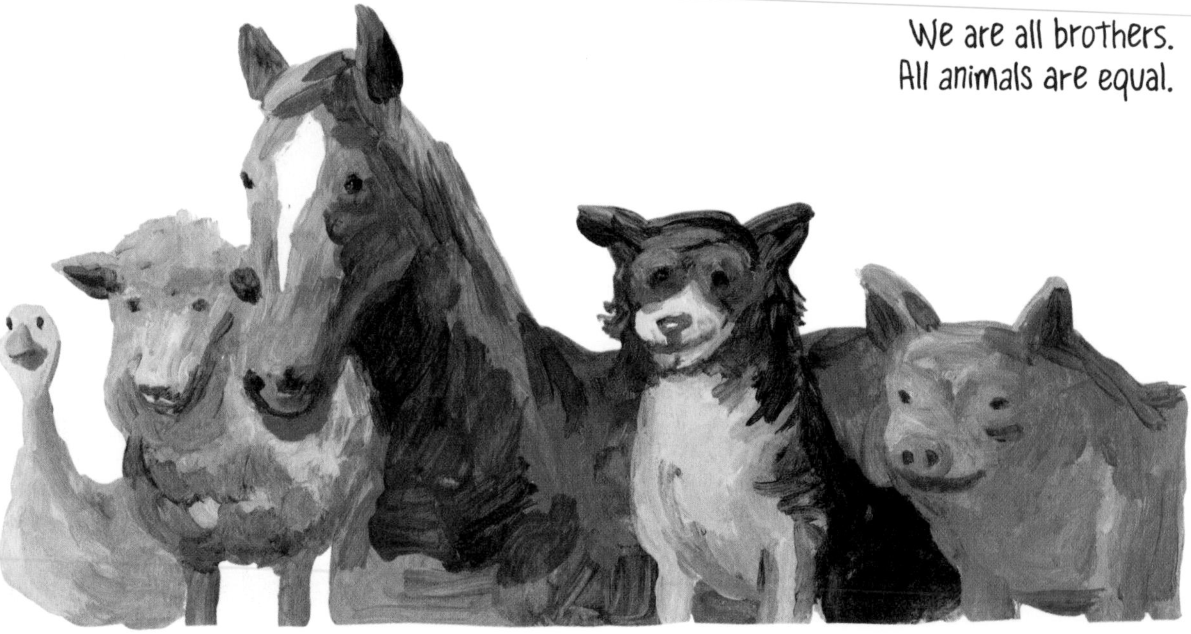
We are all brothers.
All animals are equal.

My dream of last night was a dream of the earth as it will be when Man has vanished. I cannot describe it to you.

But it reminded me of an old song my mother used to sing and words of the song came back — which were, I am certain, sung by animals of long ago.

Beasts of England, beasts of Ireland,
Beasts of every land and clime,
Hearken to my joyful tidings,
Of the golden future time.

Soon or late the day is coming,
Tyrant Man shall be o'erthrown
And the fruitful fields of England
Shall be trod by beasts alone.

Bright will shine the fields of England,
Purer shall its waters be,
Sweeter yet shall blow its breezes
On the day that set us free.

For that day we must all labour,
Though we die before it break;
Cows and horses, geese and turkeys,
All must toil for freedom's sake.

Beasts of England, beasts of Ireland,
Beasts of every land...

The singing of this song threw the animals into the wildest excitement.

They had the entire song by heart within a few minutes. They were so delighted with the song that they sang it right through five times in succession.

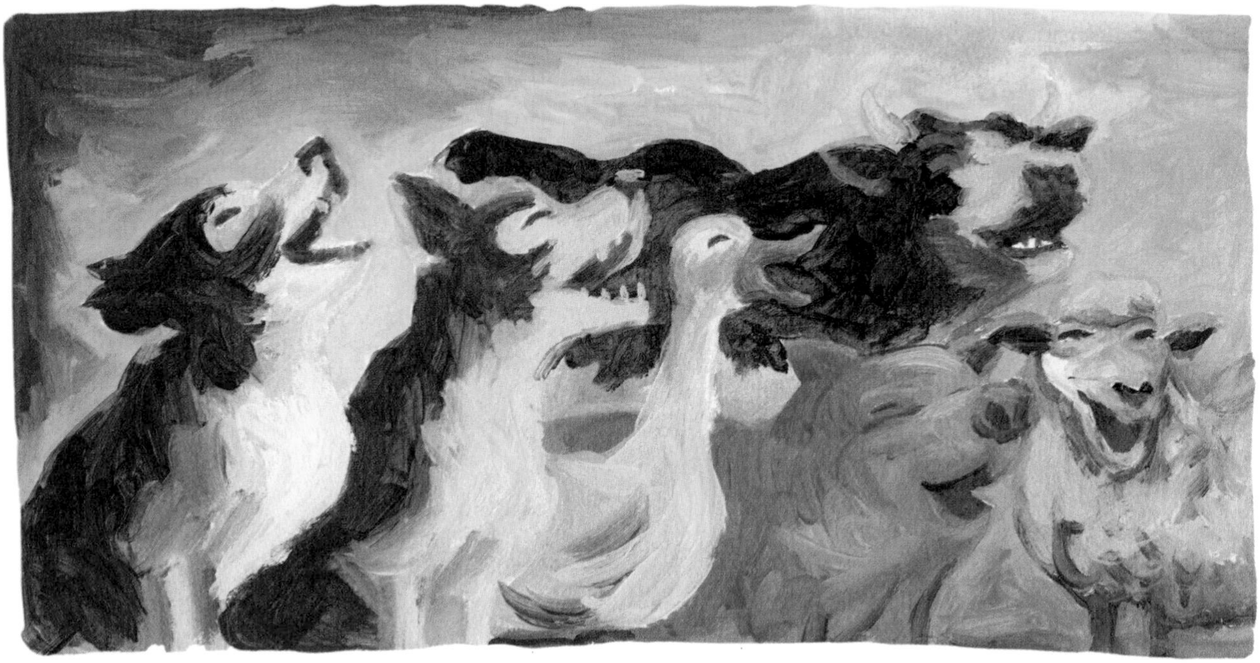

They might have continued singing it all night, but unfortunately the uproar awoke Mr. Jones.

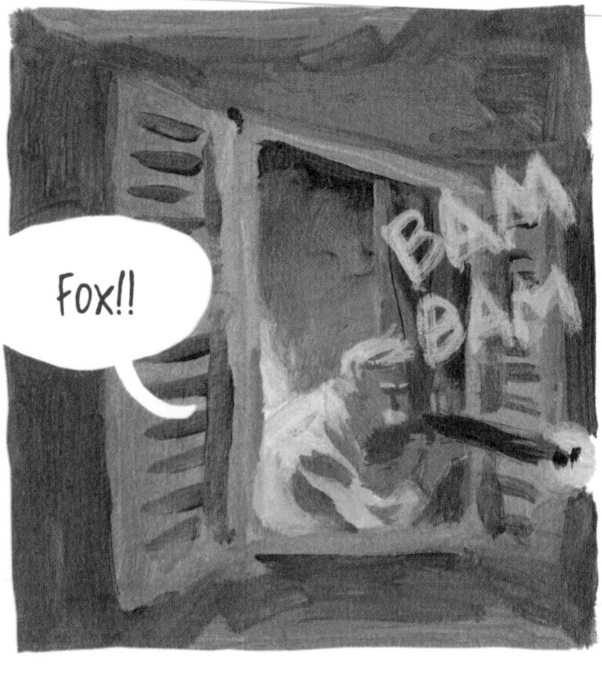
Fox!!
BAM
BAM

Everyone fled to his own sleeping-place and the whole farm was asleep in a moment.

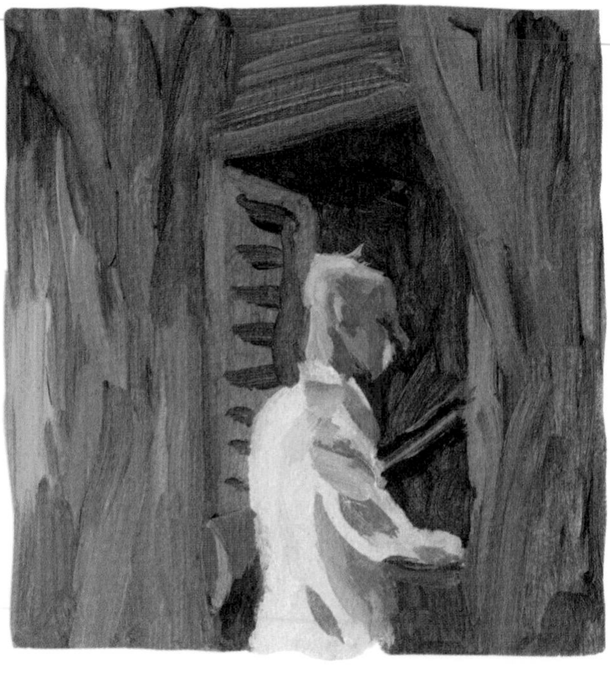

II

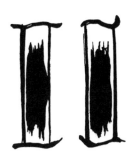

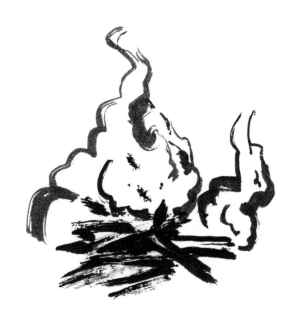

Three nights later old Major died peacefully in his sleep.

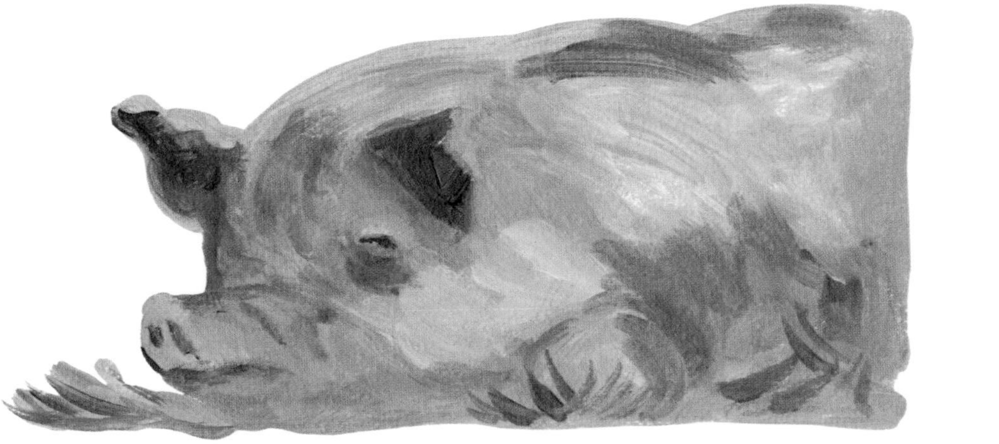

During the next three months there was much secret activity.

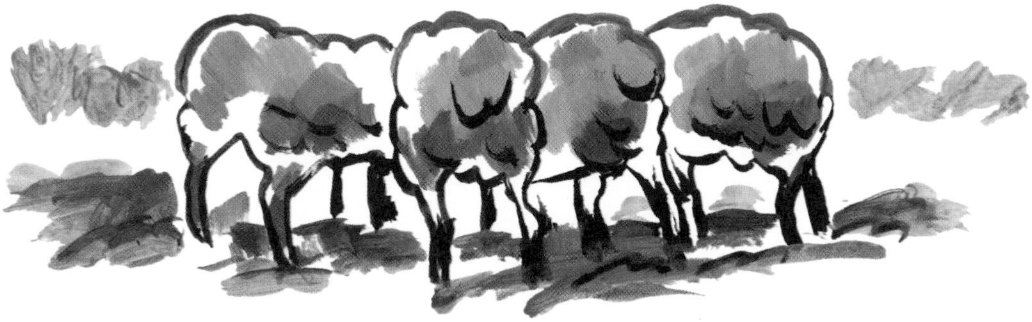

Major's speech had given to the more intelligent animals on the farm a completely new outlook on life.

They did not know when the Rebellion would take place, they had no reason for thinking that it would be within their own lifetime, but they saw clearly that it was their duty to prepare for it.

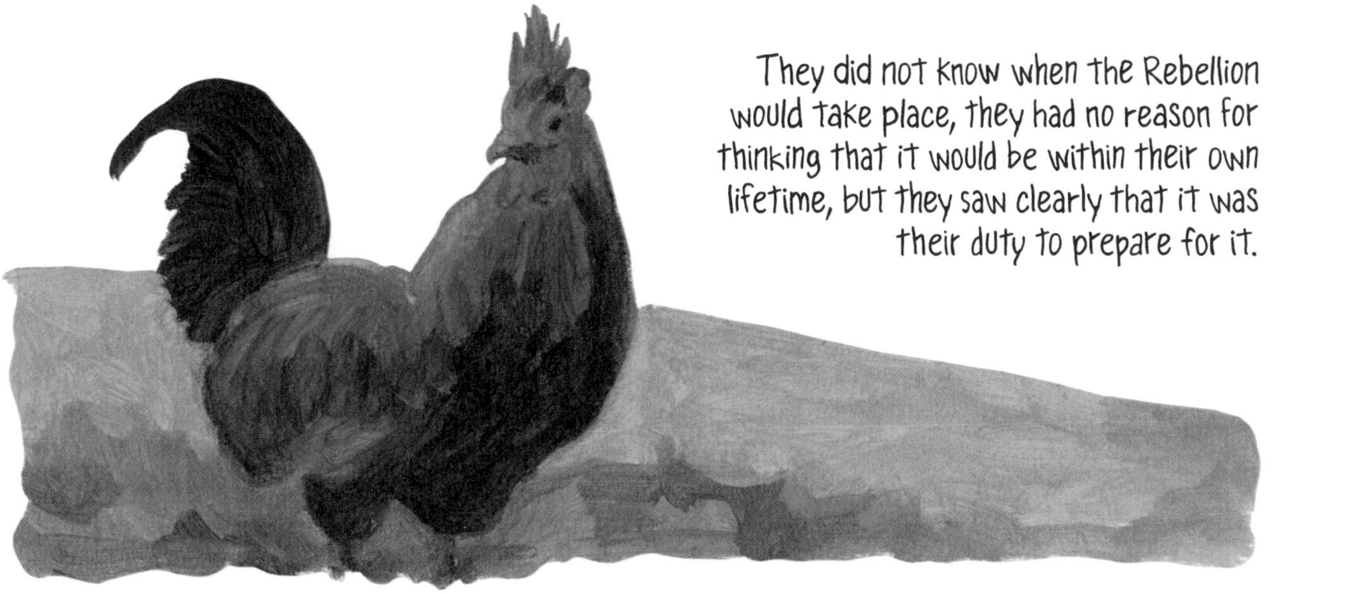

The work of teaching and organising the others fell naturally upon the pigs, who were recognised as the cleverest of the animals.

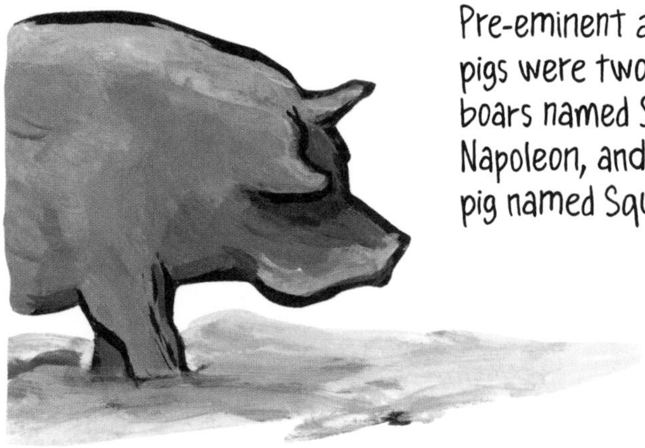

Pre-eminent among the pigs were two young boars named Snowball and Napoleon, and a small fat pig named Squealer.

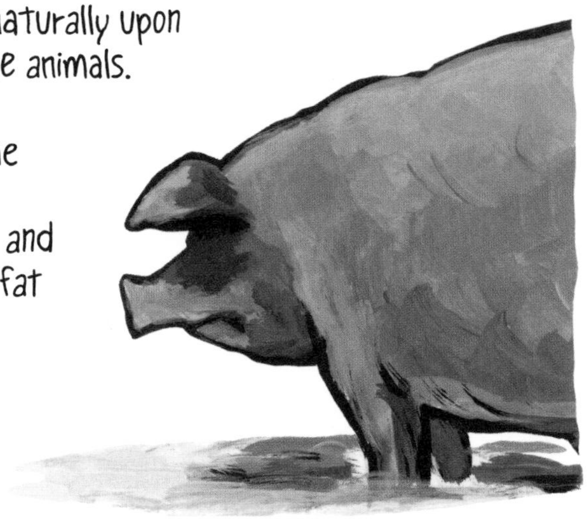

They had elaborated old Major's teachings into a complete system of thought, to which they gave the name of...

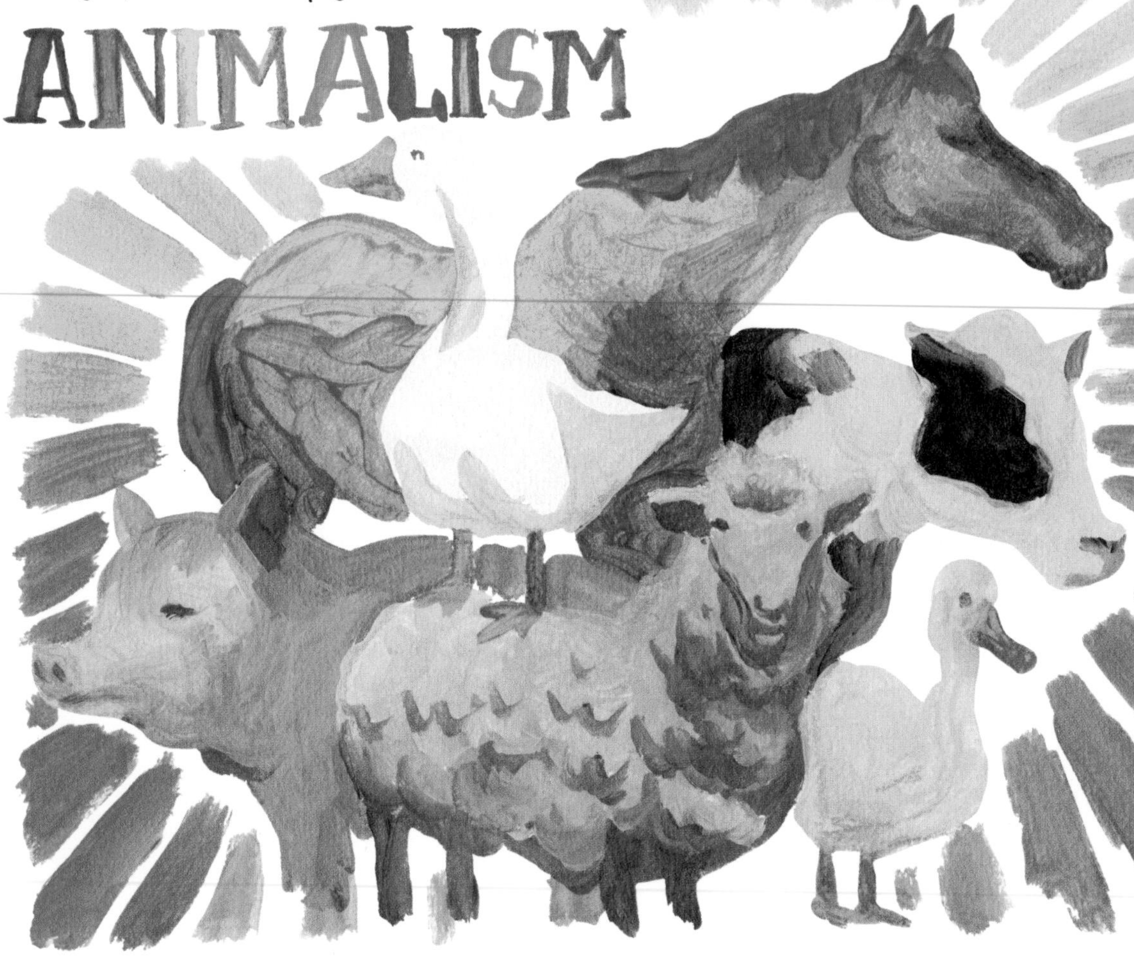
ANIMALISM

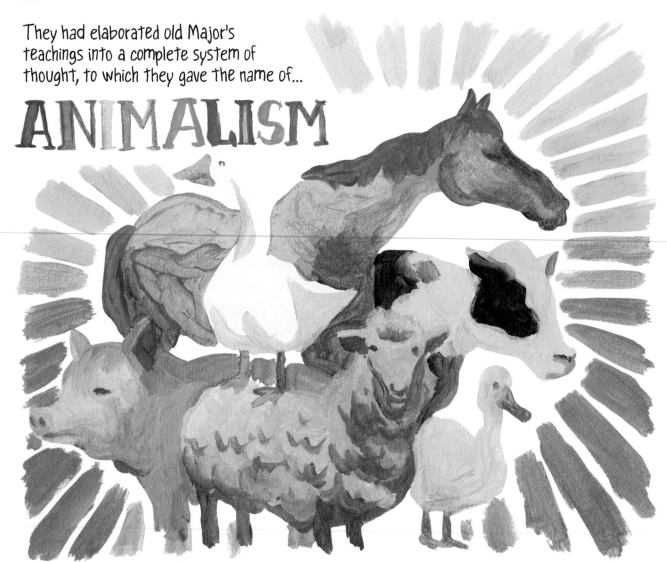

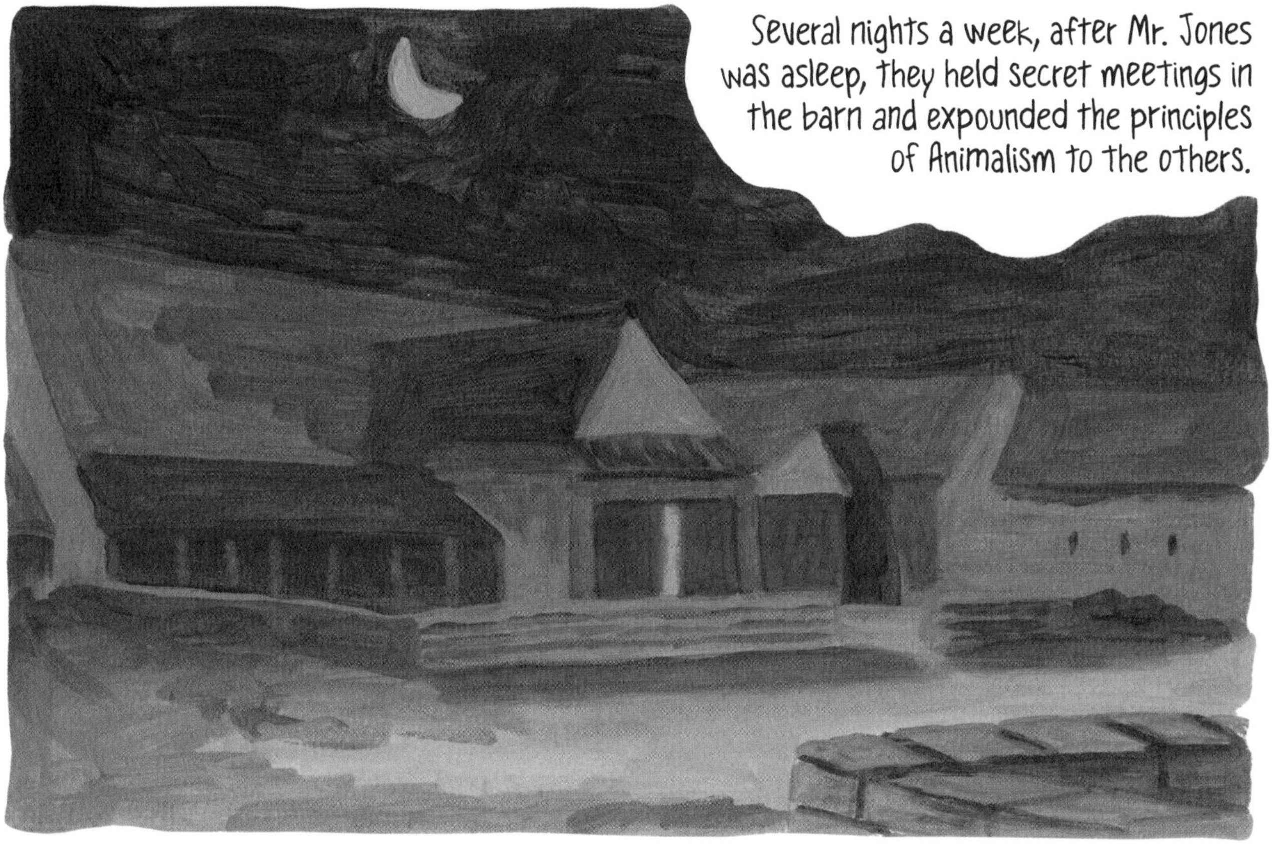
Several nights a week, after Mr. Jones was asleep, they held secret meetings in the barn and expounded the principles of Animalism to the others.

At the beginning they met with much stupidity and apathy.

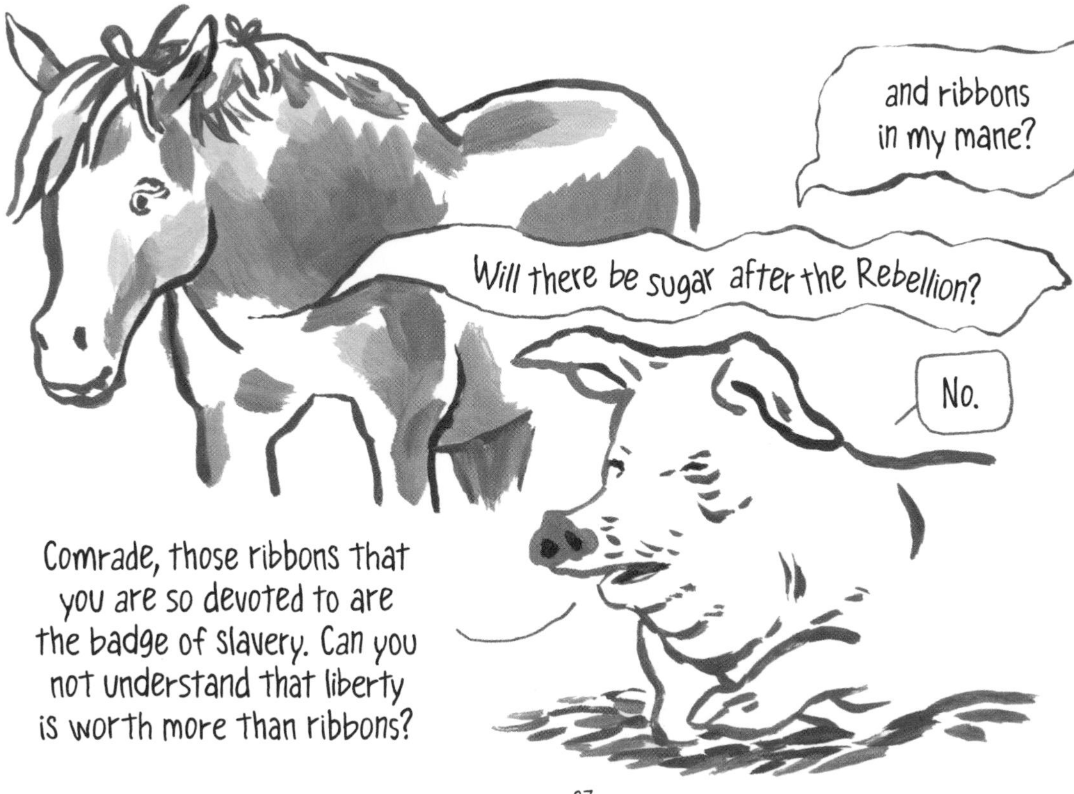
Will there be sugar after the Rebellion?
No.
and ribbons in my mane?
Comrade, those ribbons that you are so devoted to are the badge of slavery. Can you not understand that liberty is worth more than ribbons?

The pigs had an even harder struggle to counteract the lies put about by Moses.

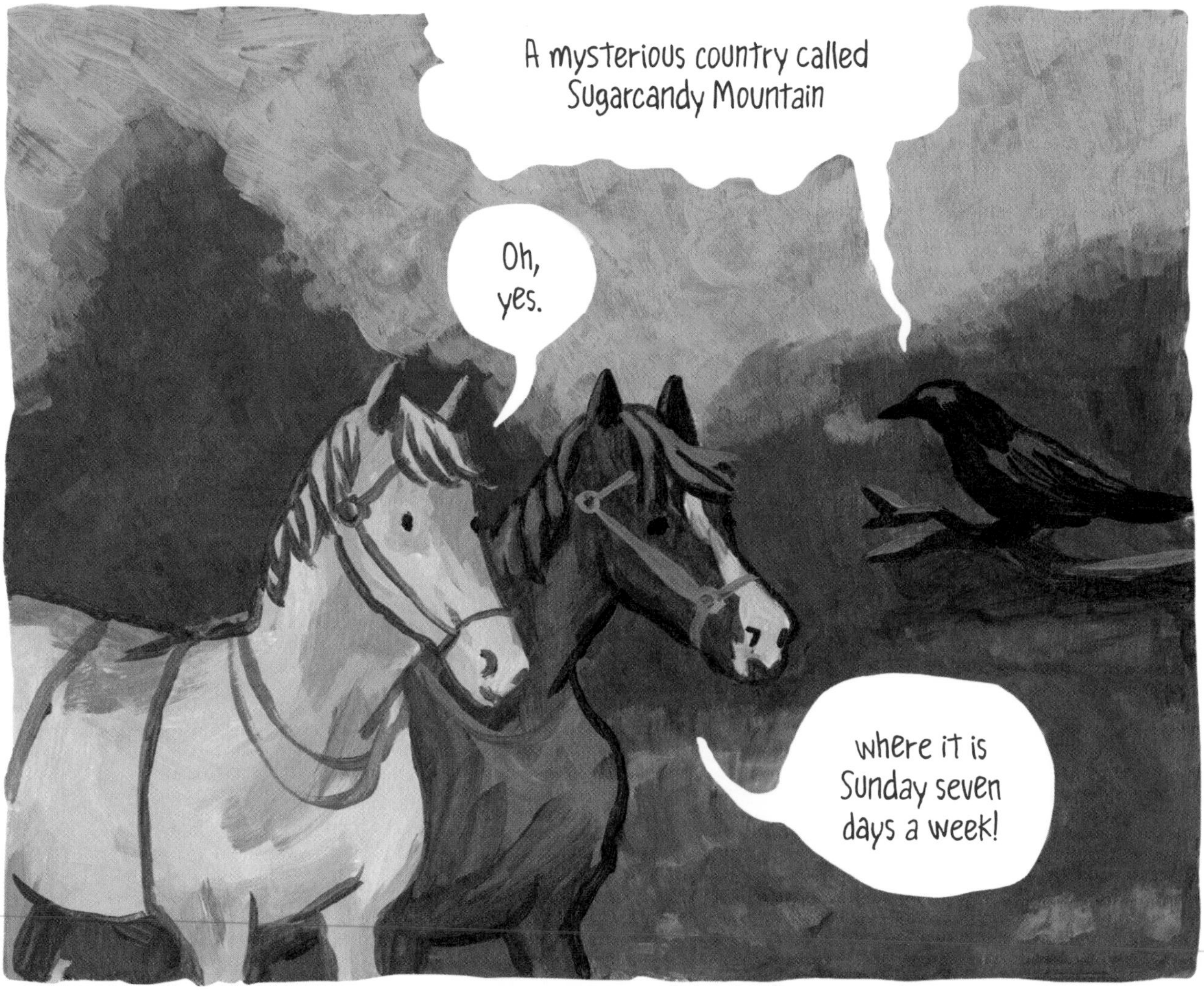
A mysterious country called Sugarcandy Mountain
Oh, yes.
where it is Sunday seven days a week!

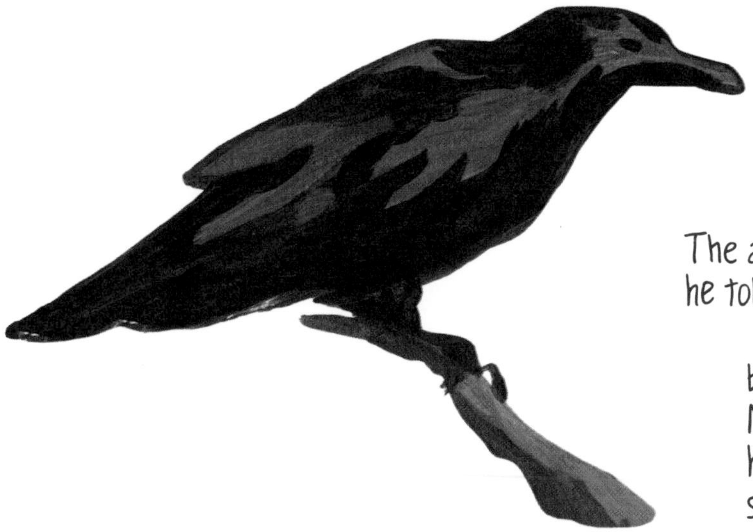

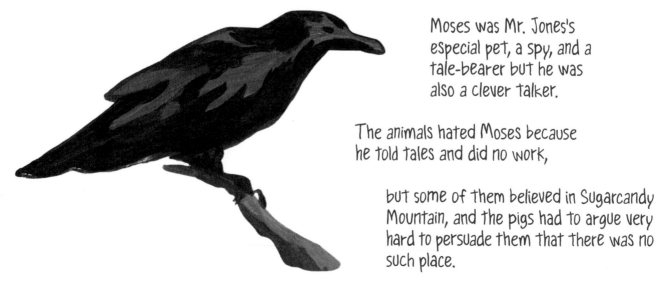

Moses was Mr. Jones's especial pet, a spy, and a tale-bearer but he was also a clever talker.

The animals hated Moses because he told tales and did no work,

but some of them believed in Sugarcandy Mountain, and the pigs had to argue very hard to persuade them that there was no such place.

Now, as it turned out, the Rebellion was achieved much earlier and more easily than anyone had expected.

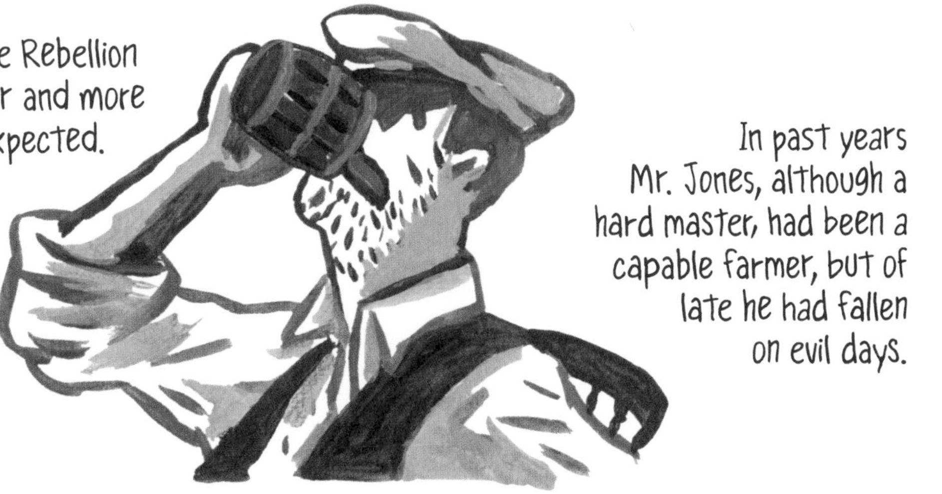

In past years Mr. Jones, although a hard master, had been a capable farmer, but of late he had fallen on evil days.

He had become much disheartened after losing money in a lawsuit, and had taken to drinking more than was good for him.

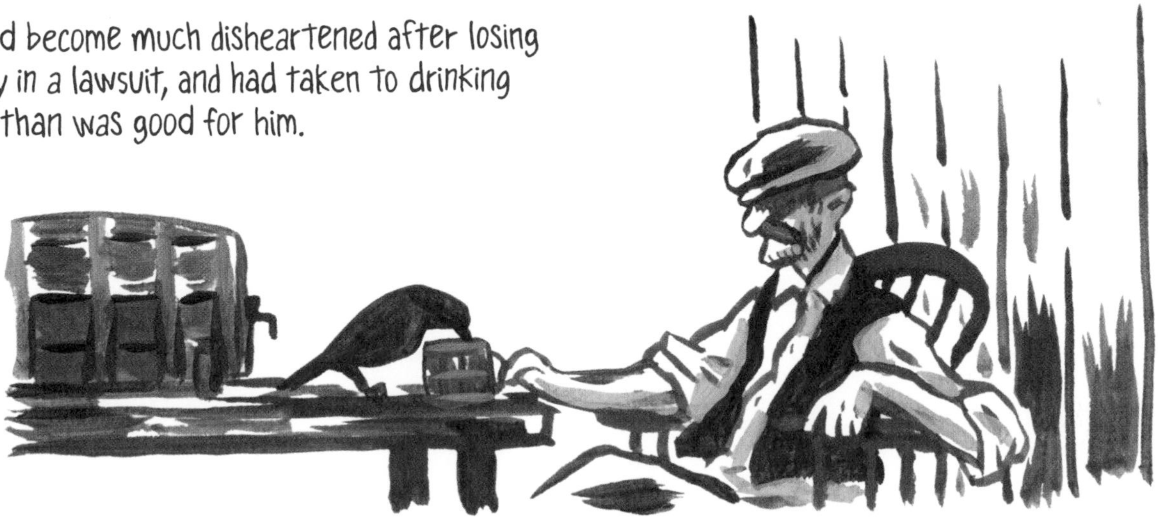

His men were idle and dishonest.

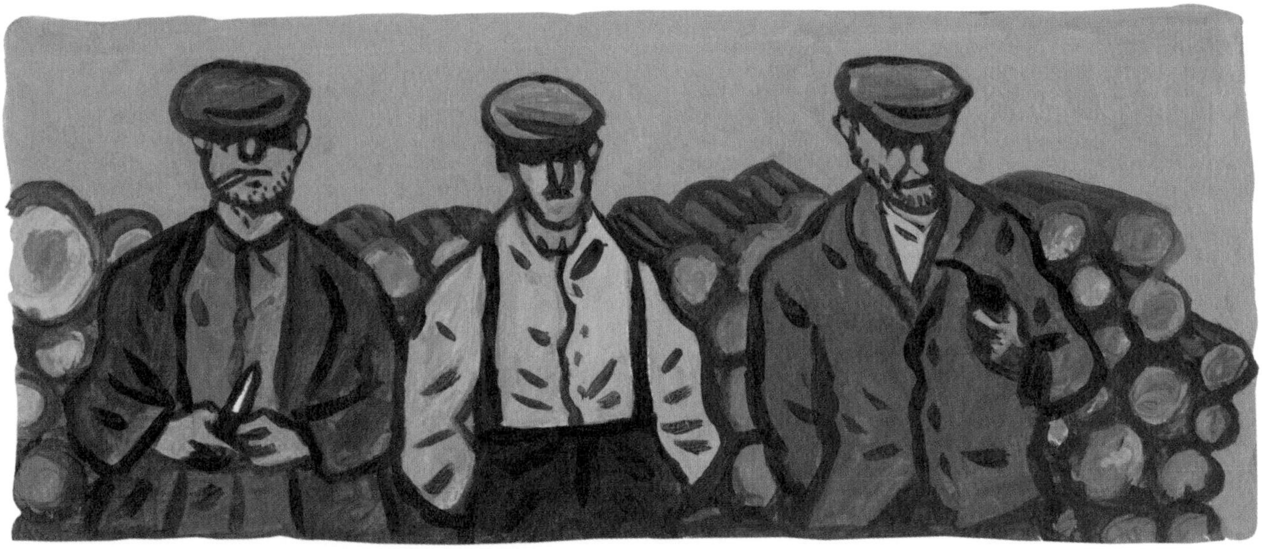

The fields were full of weeds, the animals were underfed.

June came and the hay was almost ready for cutting. On Midsummer's Eve, which was a Saturday, Mr. Jones got so drunk at the Red Lion that he did not come back till midday on Sunday.

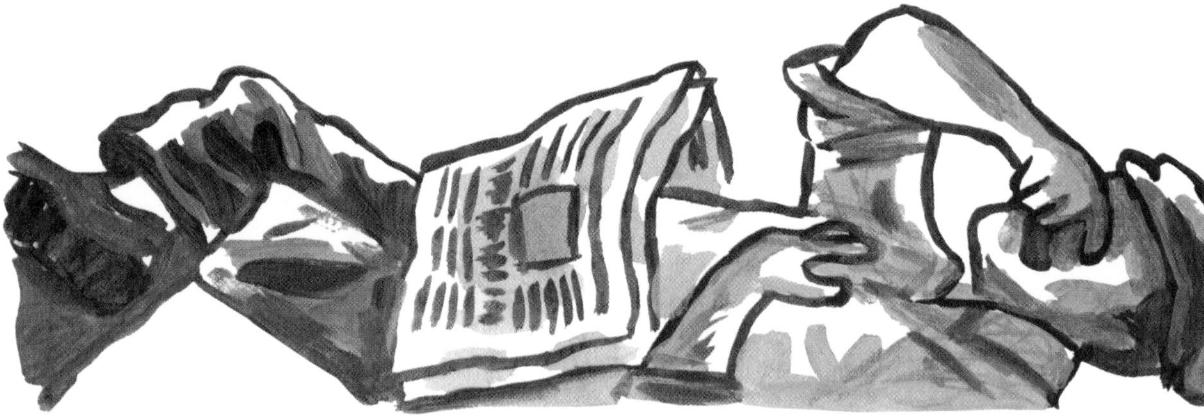

The men had milked the cows in the early morning and then had gone out rabbiting without bothering to feed the animals.

At last, they could stand it no longer.

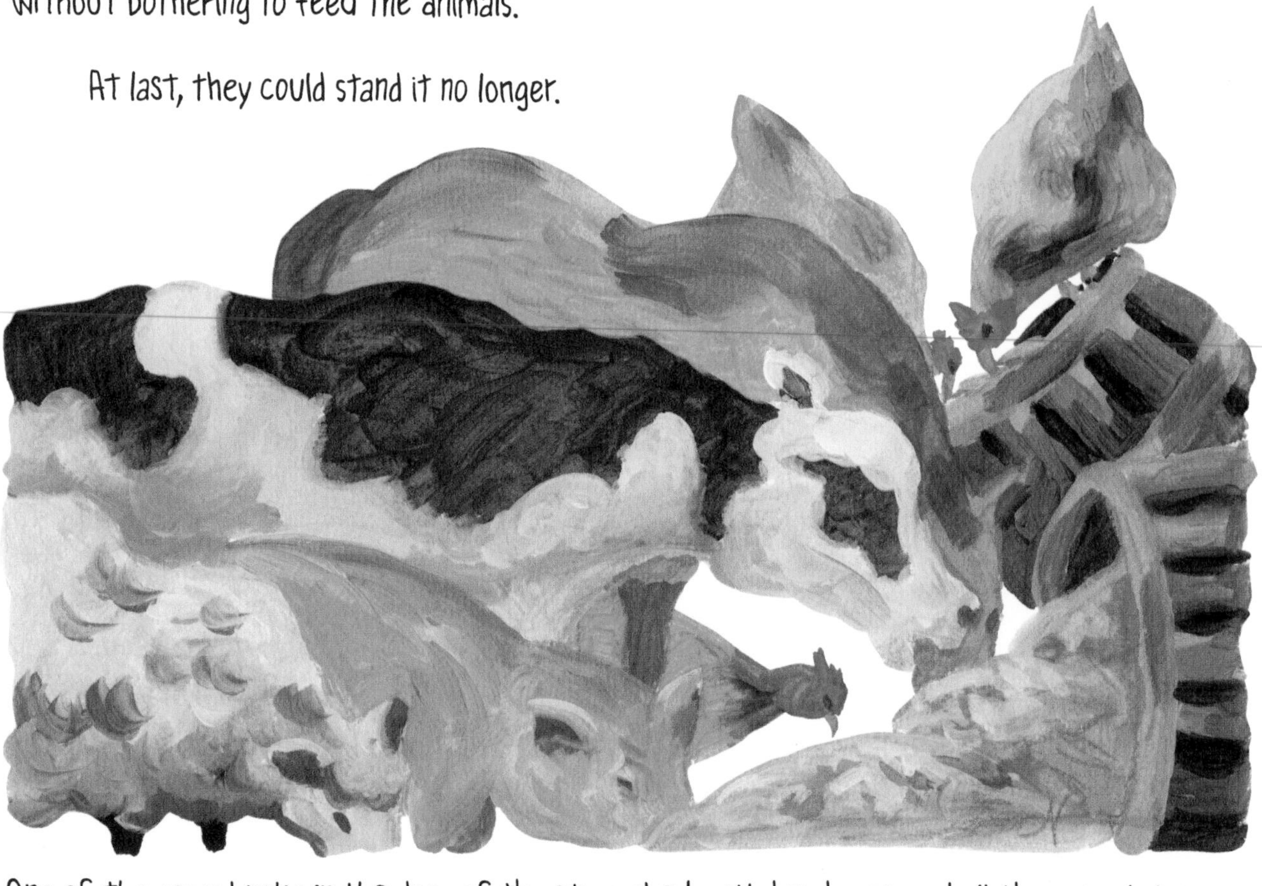

One of the cows broke in the door of the store-shed with her horns and all the animals began to help themselves from the bins.

It was just then that Mr. Jones woke up.

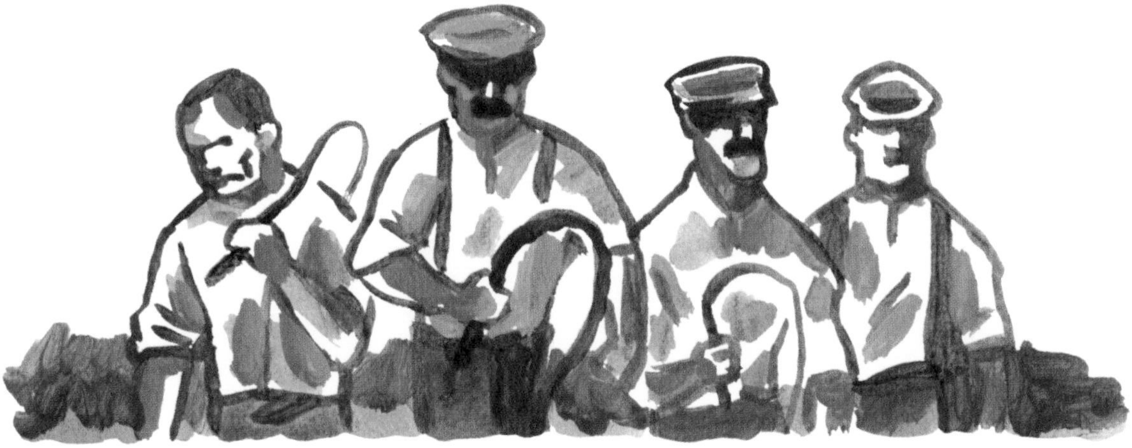

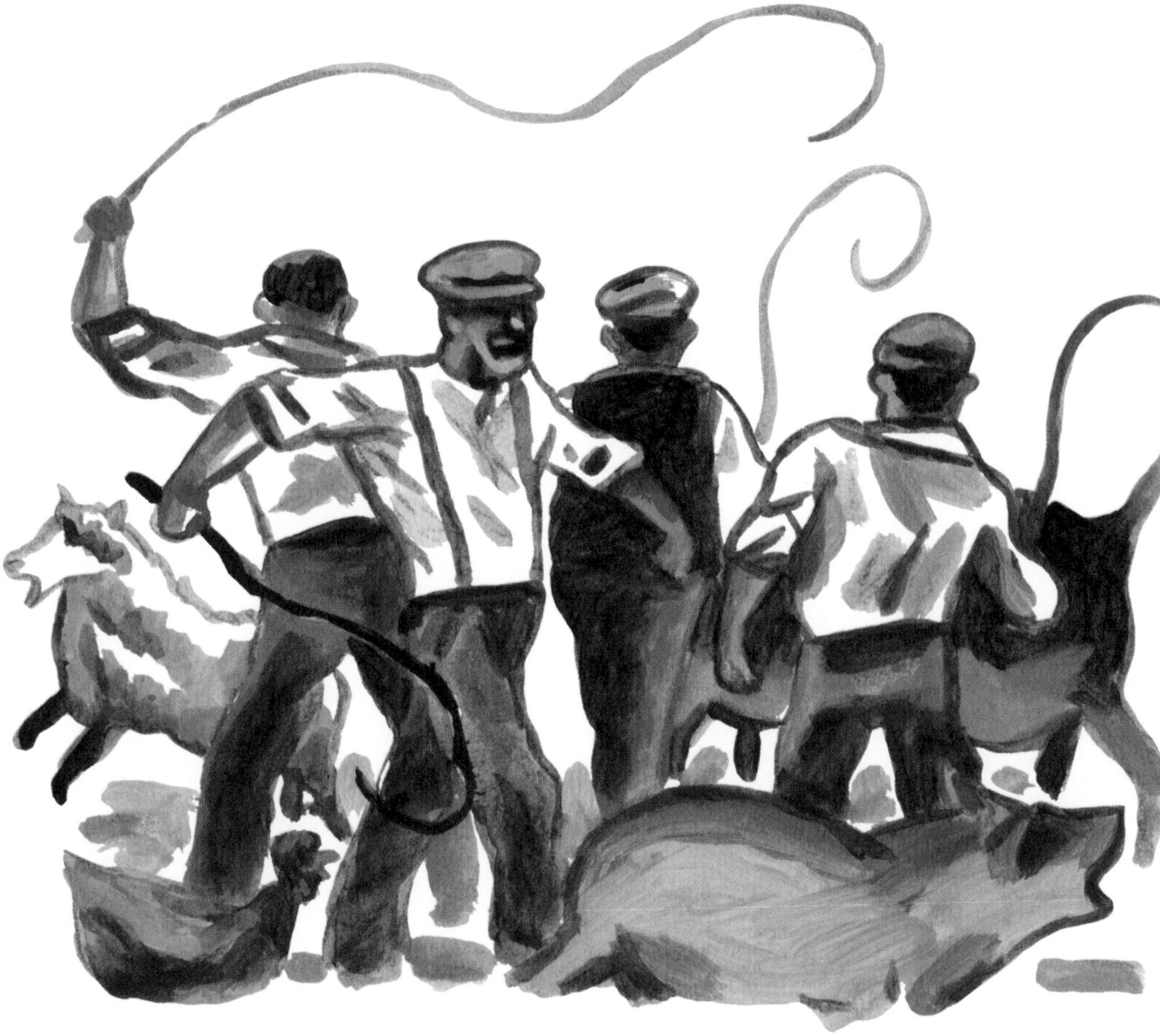

This was more than the
hungry animals could bear.

The situation was quite
out of their control.

They had never
seen animals behave
like this before,

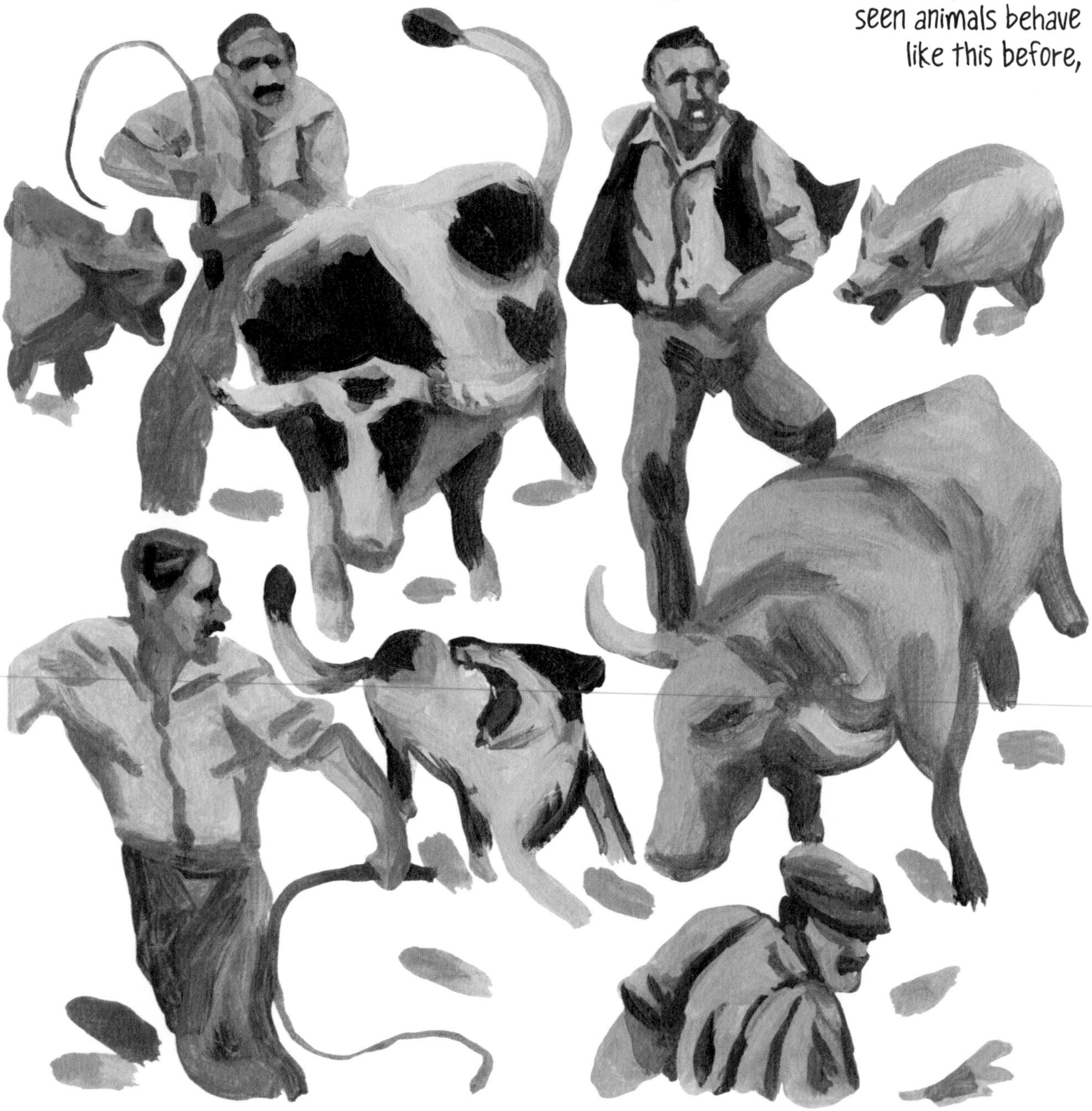

and this sudden uprising of creatures whom they were used to thrashing and maltreating just as they chose, frightened them almost out of their wits.

A minute later all five of them were in full flight, with the animals pursuing them in triumph.

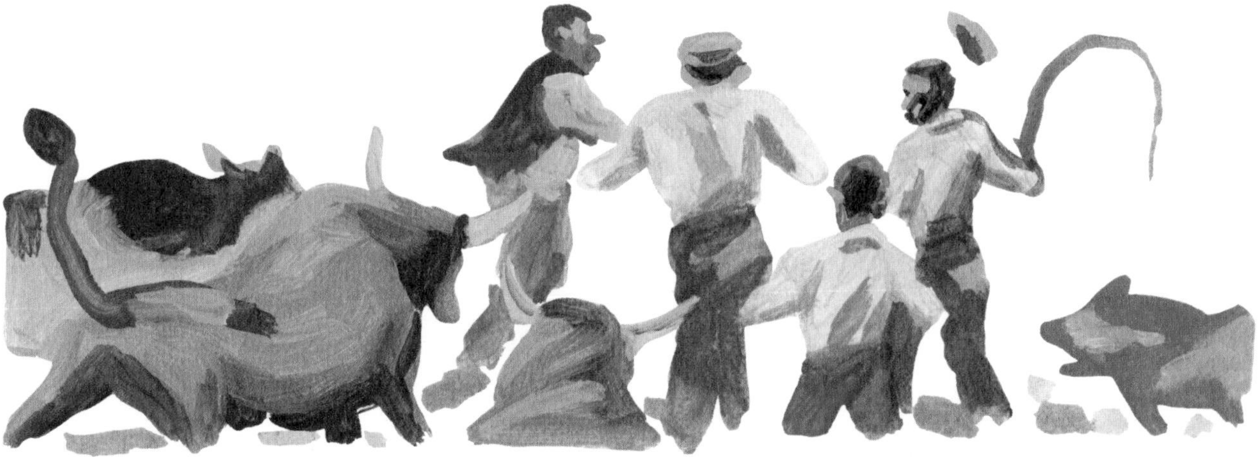

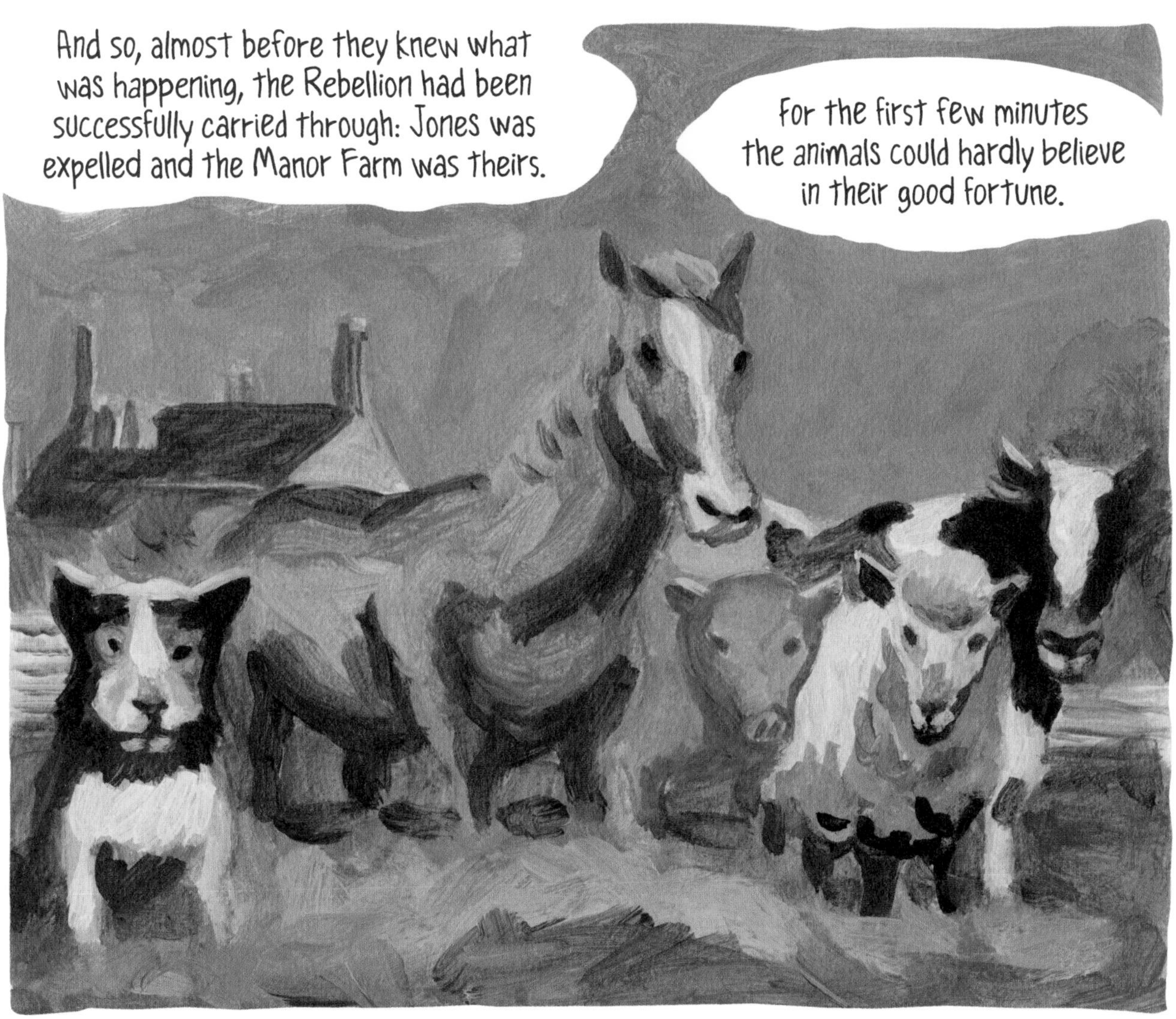
And so, almost before they knew what was happening, the Rebellion had been successfully carried through: Jones was expelled and the Manor Farm was theirs.
For the first few minutes the animals could hardly believe in their good fortune.

Their first act was to gallop in a body right round the boundaries of the farm, as though to make sure that no human being was hiding.

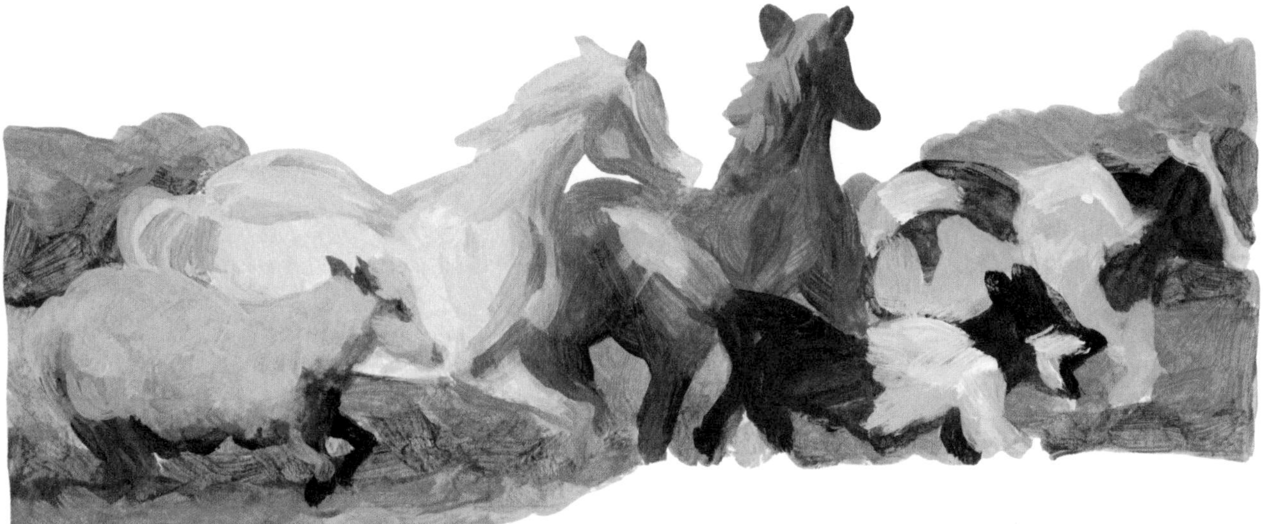

Then they raced back to the farm buildings to wipe out the last traces of Jones's hated reign.

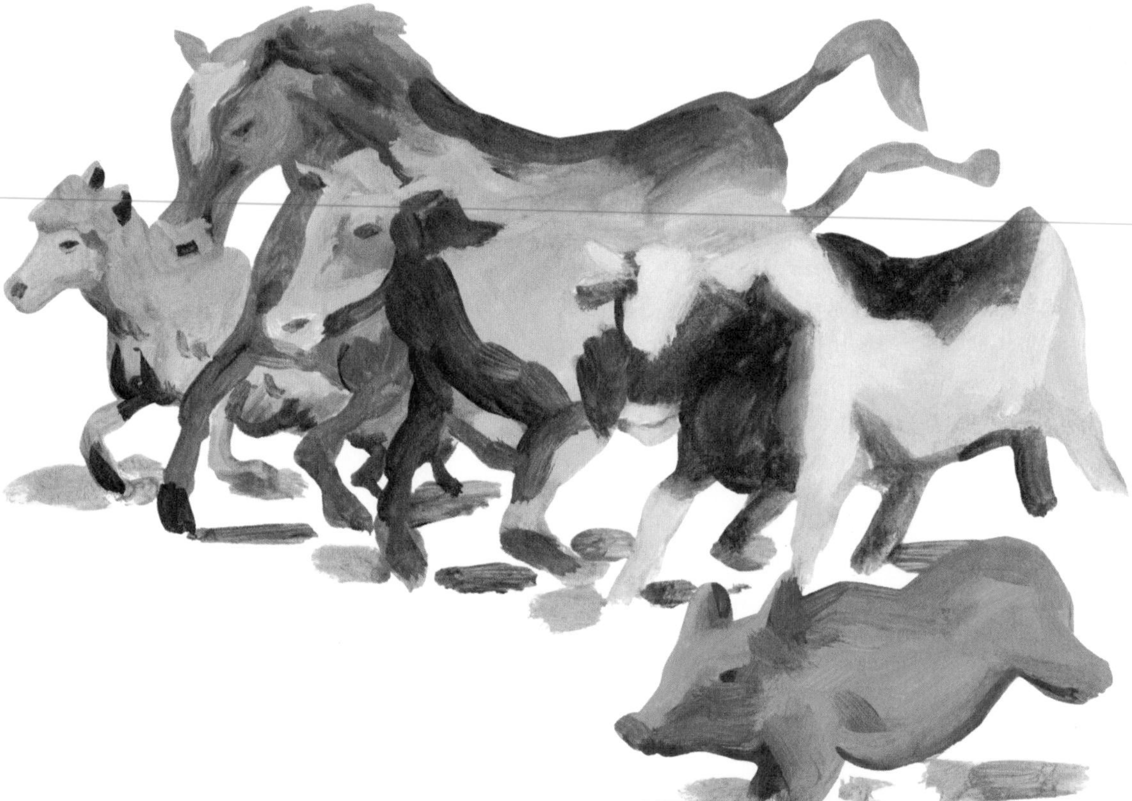

The harness-room!

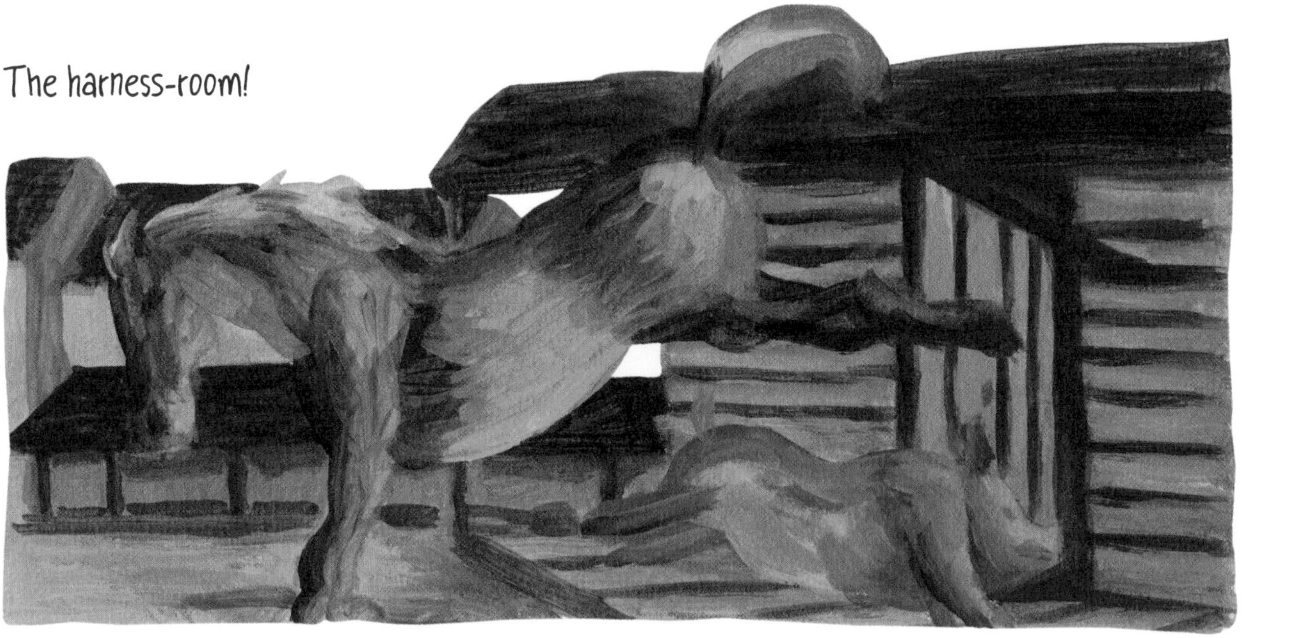

The nose-rings, the dog-chains, the cruel knives—flung down the well or thrown on the fire.

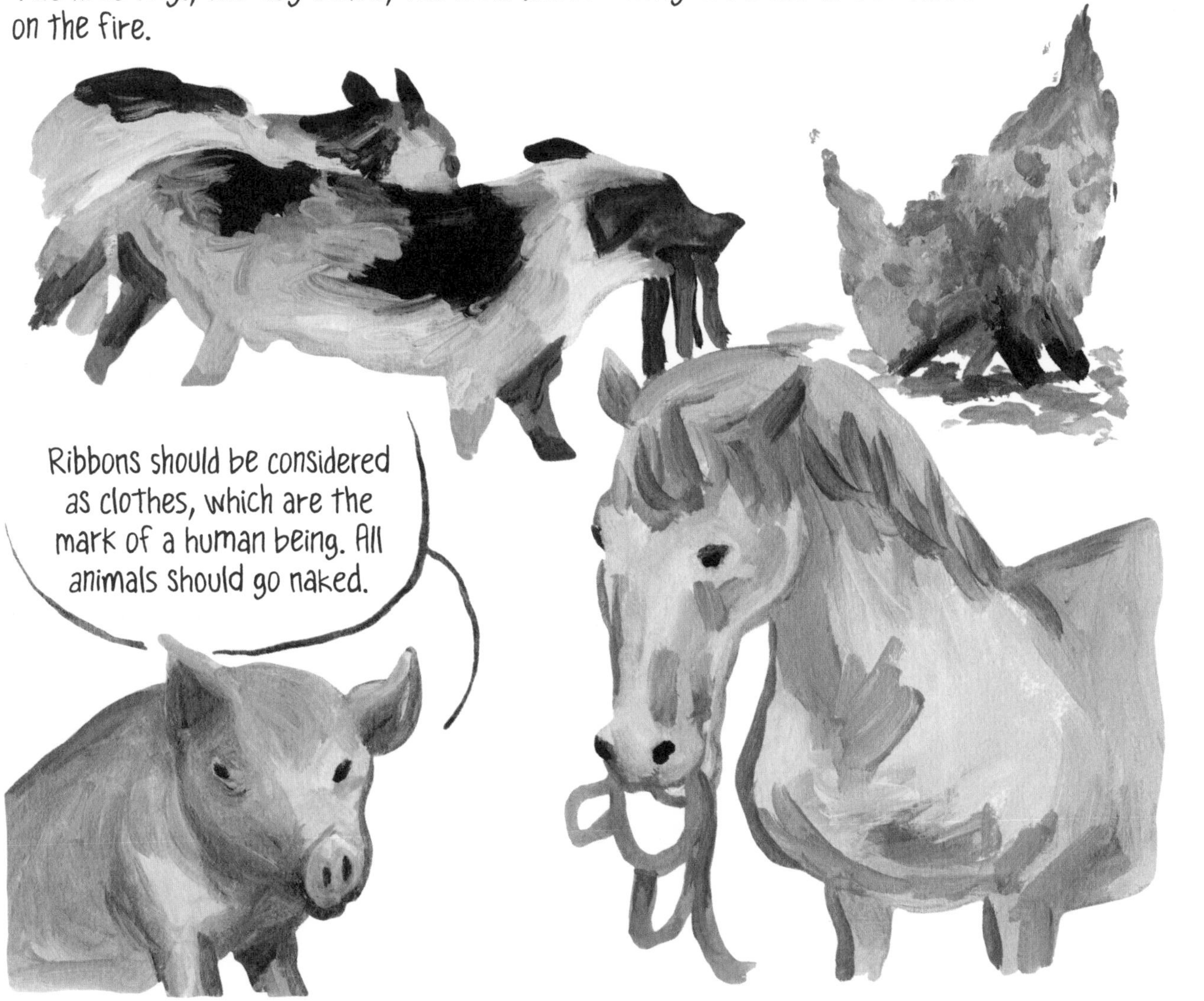
Ribbons should be considered as clothes, which are the mark of a human being. All animals should go naked.

In a very little while the animals had destroyed everything that reminded them of Mr. Jones.

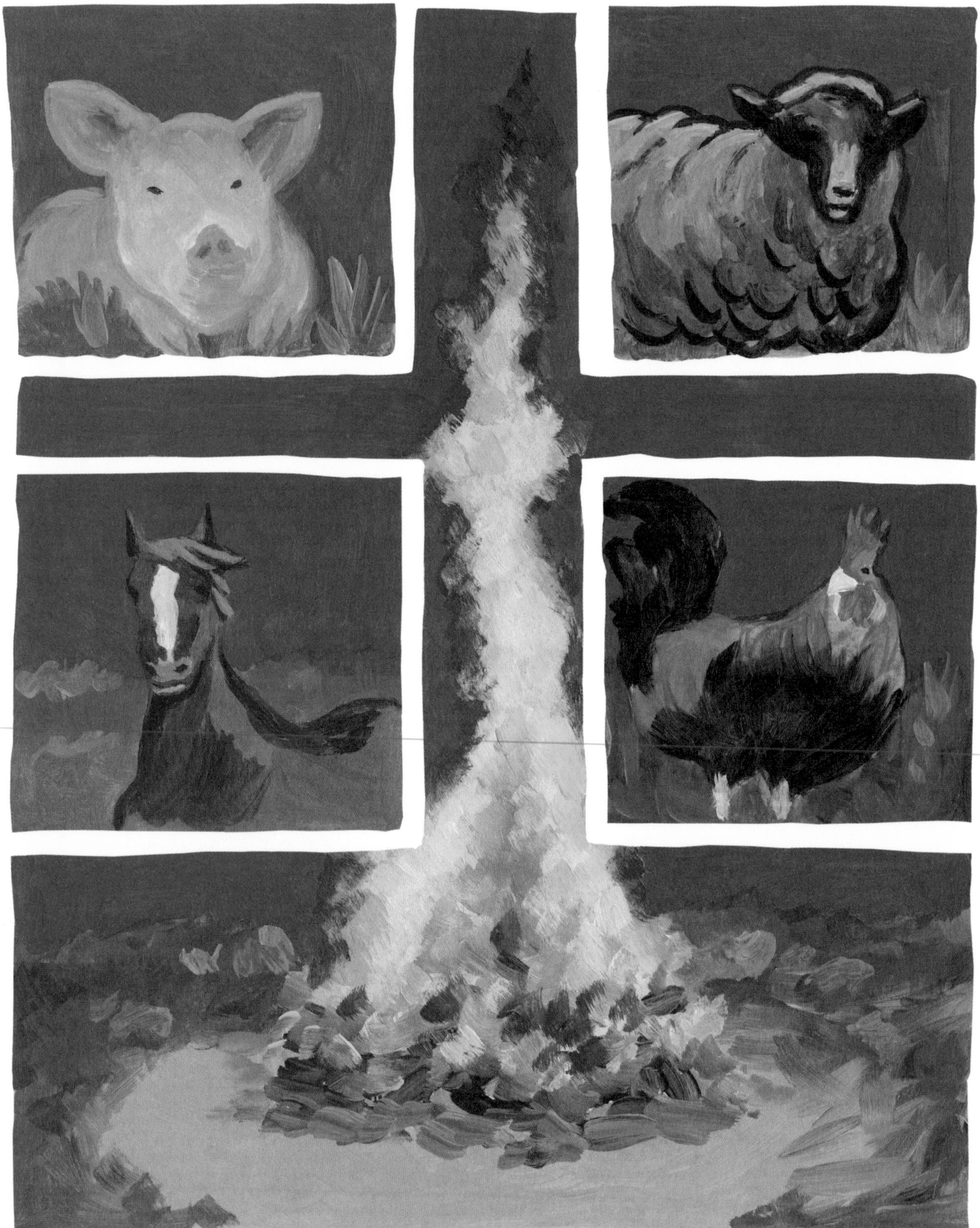

Napoleon then led them back to the store-shed and served out a double ration of corn to everybody, with two biscuits for each dog.

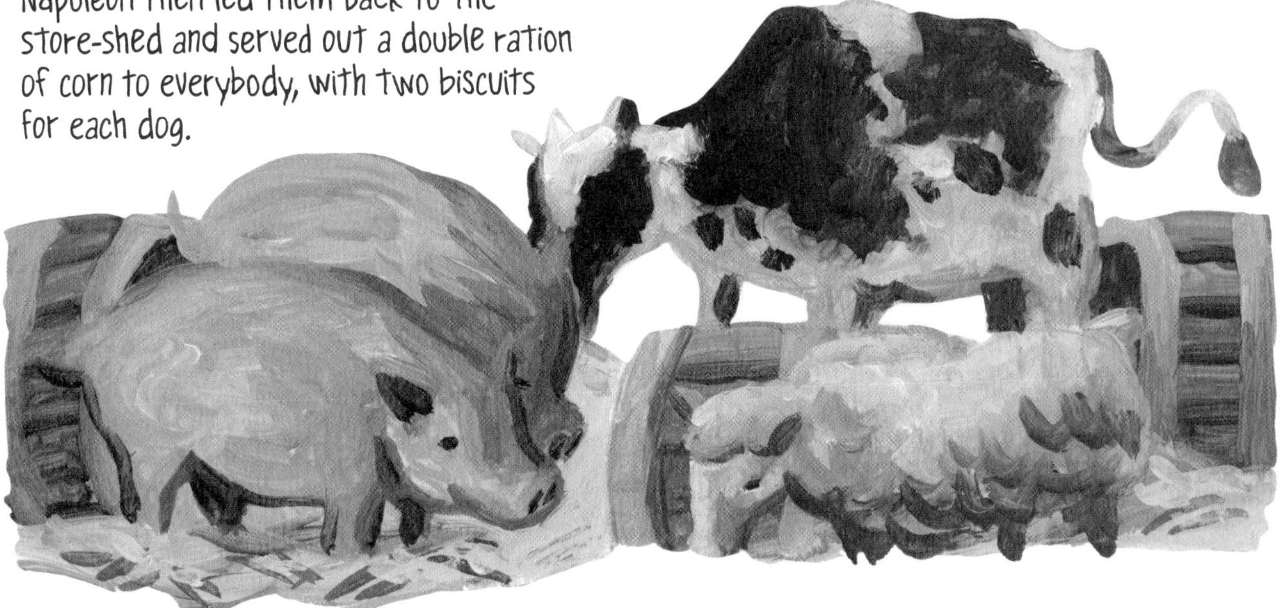

Then they sang "Beasts of England" from end to end seven times running.

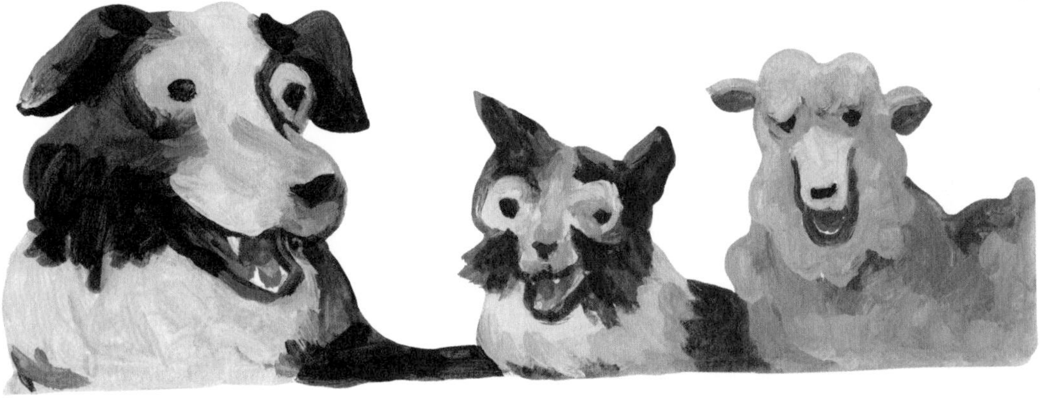

They settled down for the night and slept as they had never slept before.

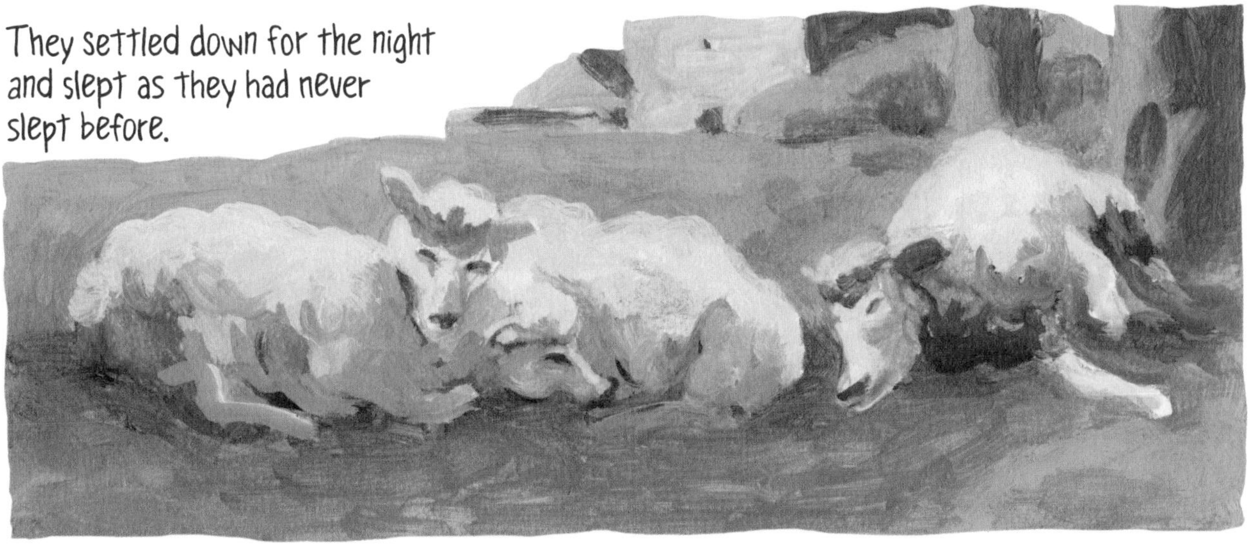

They woke up at dawn remembering the glorious thing that had happened.

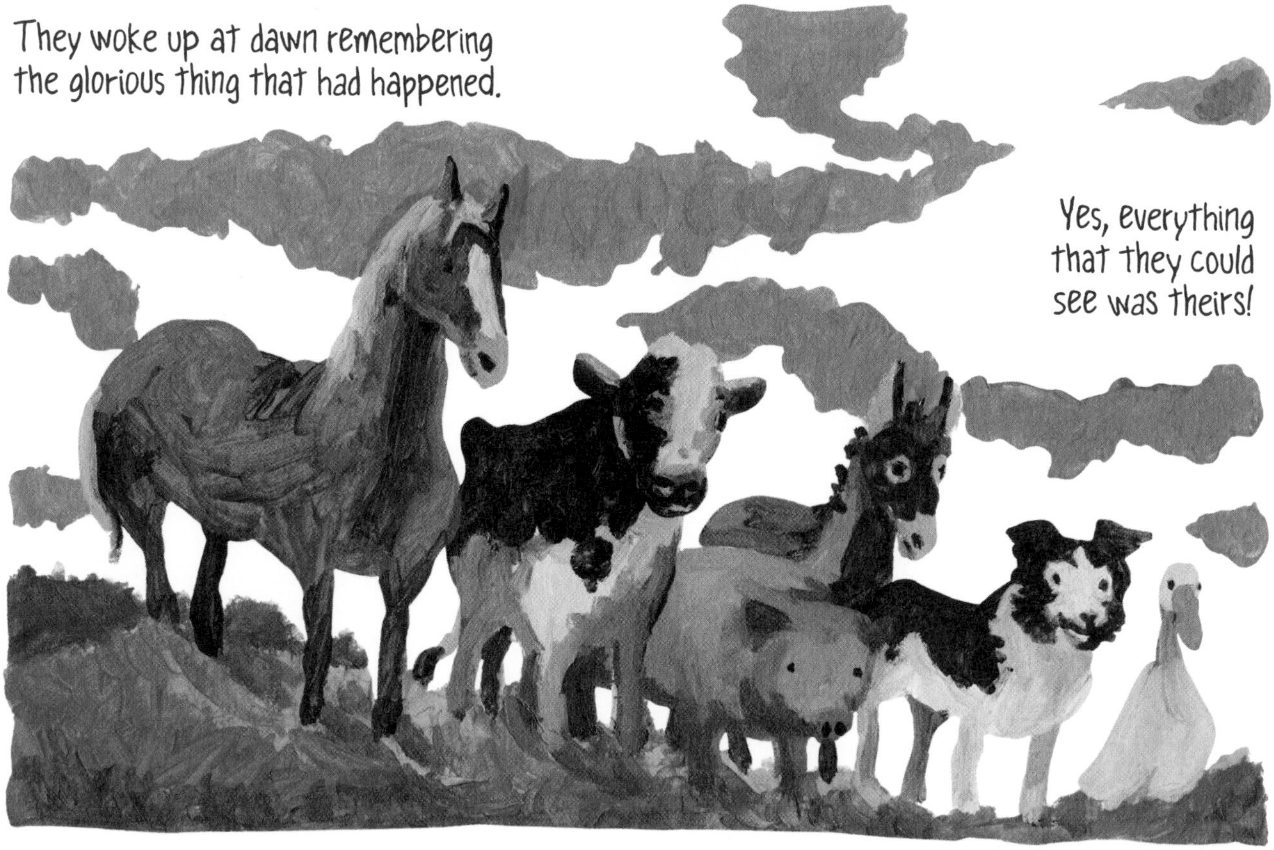

Yes, everything that they could see was theirs!

Then they halted in silence outside the door of the farmhouse.

That was theirs too, but they were frightened to go inside.

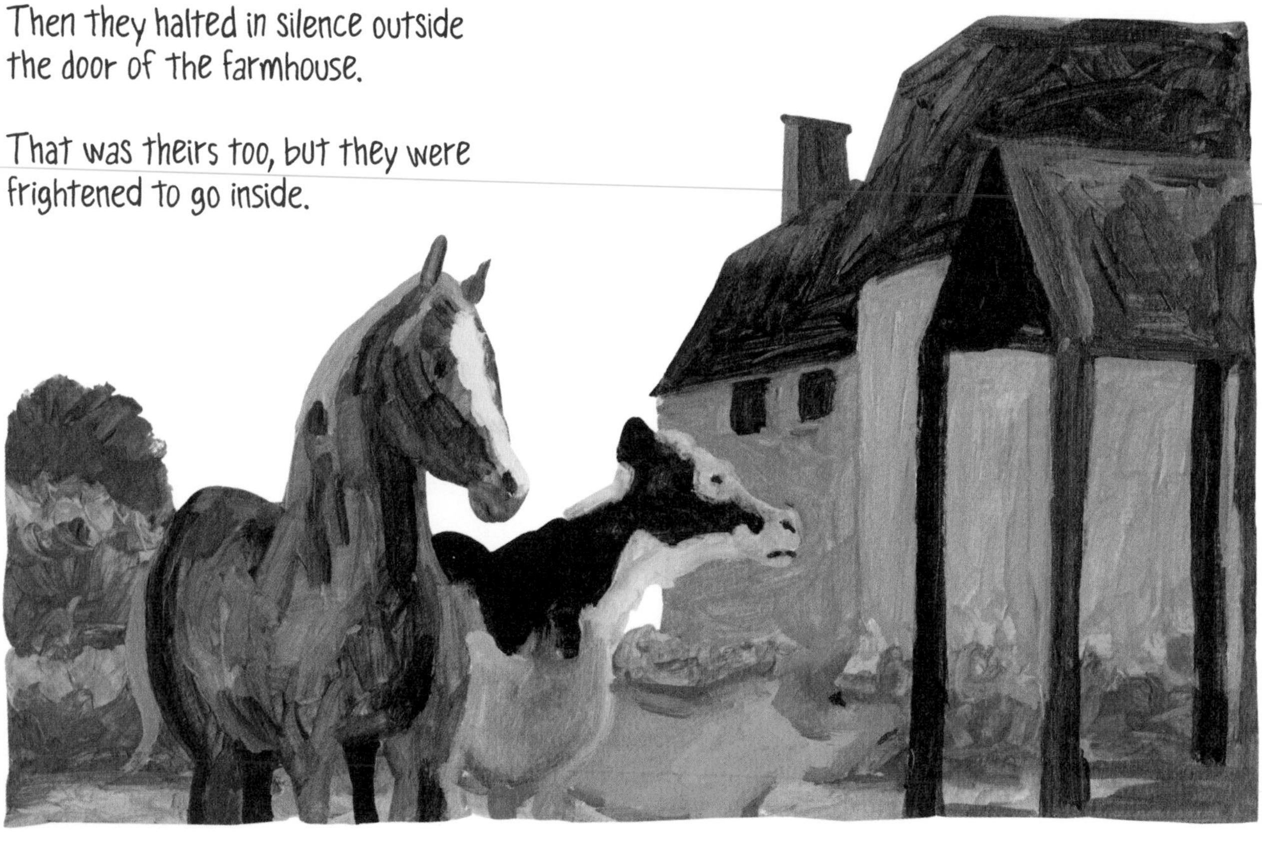

They tiptoed from room to room, afraid to speak above a whisper,

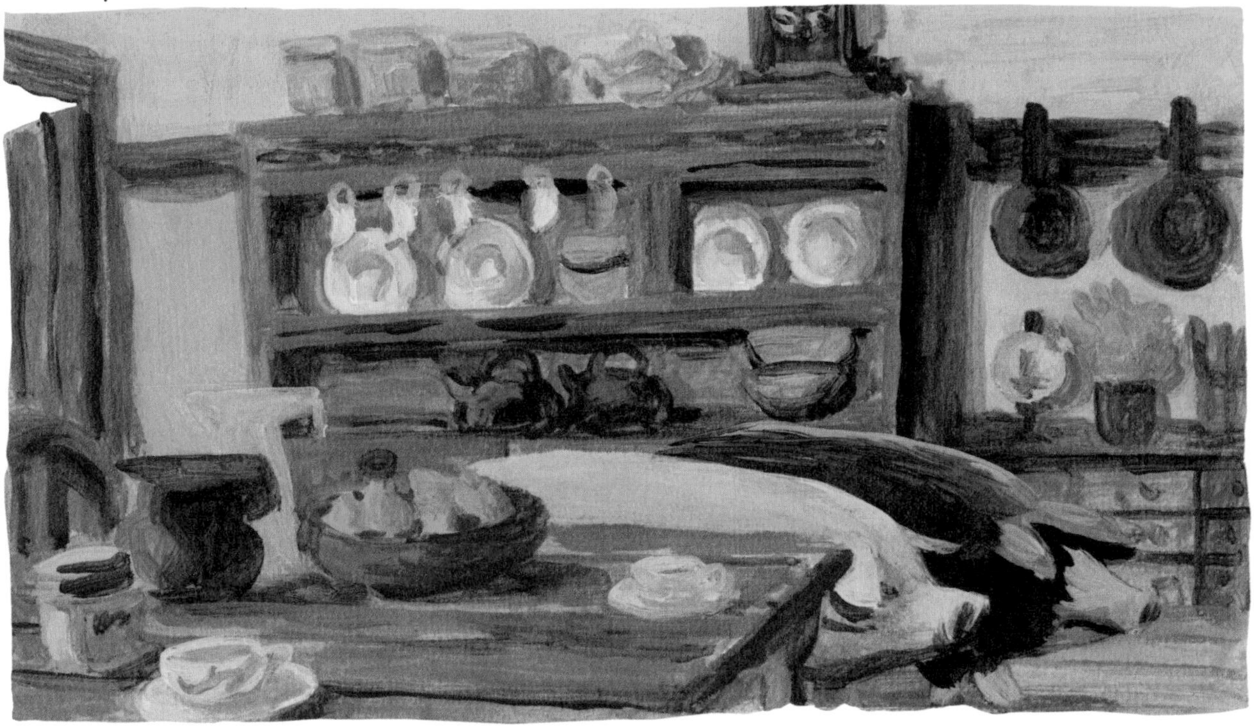

and gazing with a kind of awe at the unbelievable luxury.

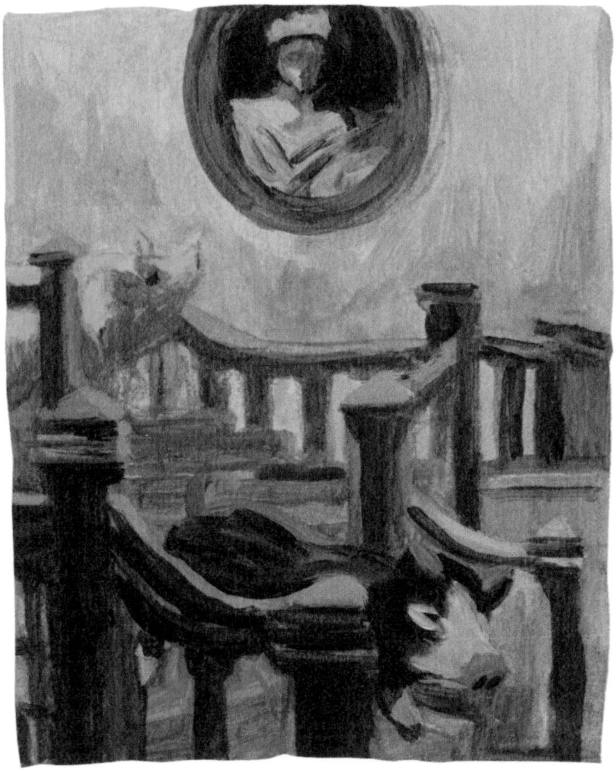

A unanimous resolution was passed on the spot that the farmhouse should be preserved as a museum. No animal must ever live there.

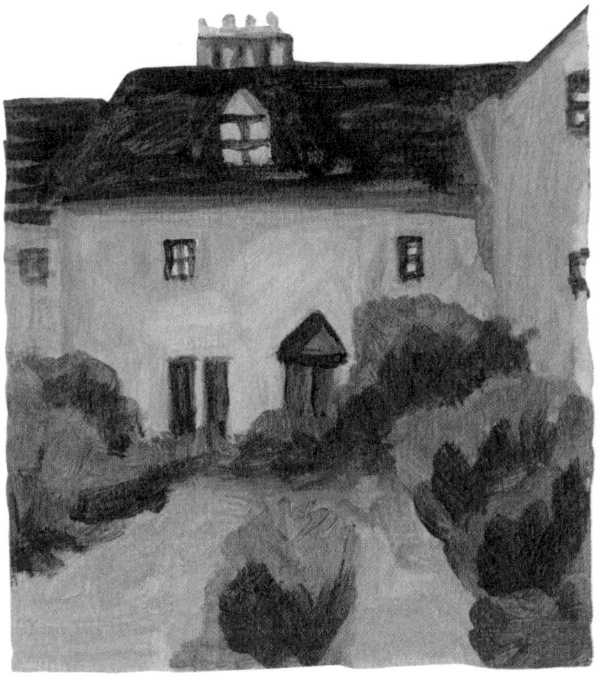

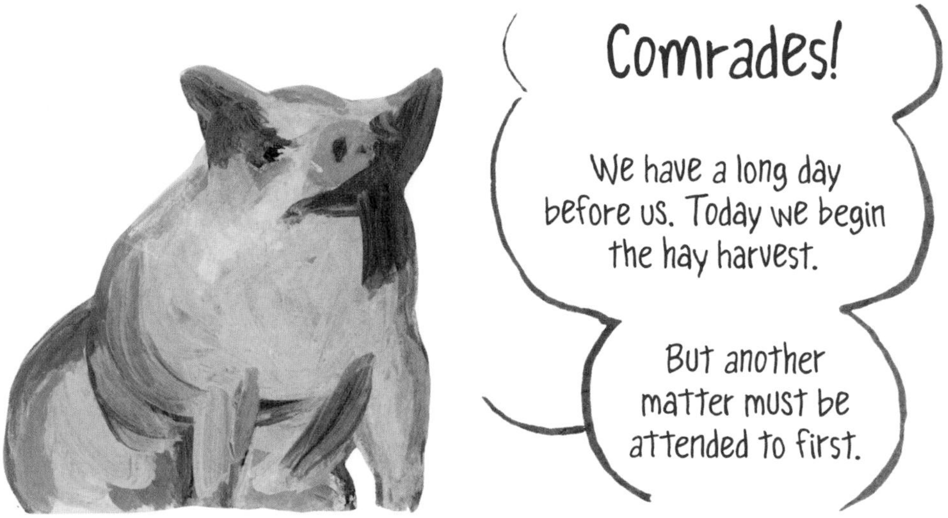
Comrades!
We have a long day before us. Today we begin the hay harvest.
But another matter must be attended to first.

The pigs now revealed that during the past three months they had taught themselves to read and write.

They had reduced the principles of Animalism to Seven Commandments, by which all animals on Animal Farm must live for ever after.

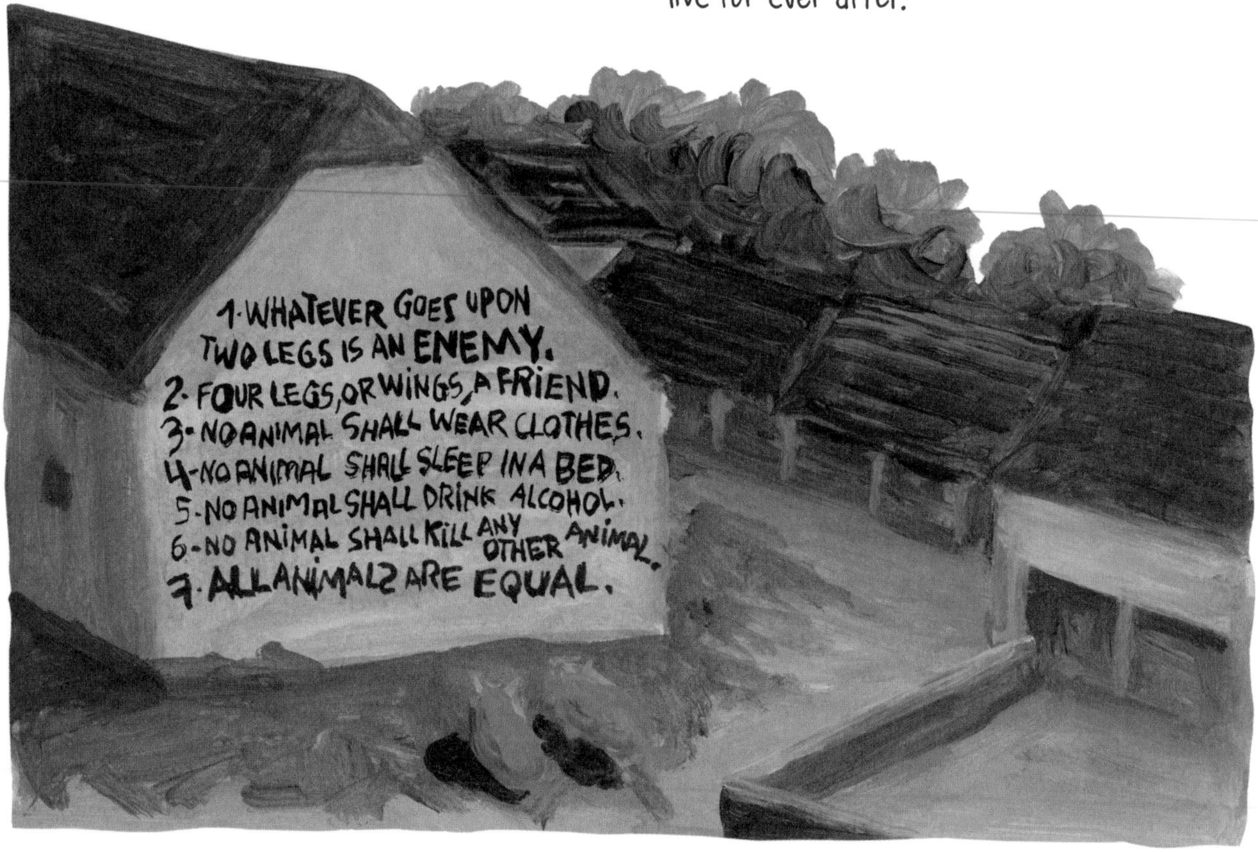
1·WHATEVER GOES UPON TWO LEGS IS AN ENEMY.
2·FOUR LEGS, OR WINGS, A FRIEND.
3·NO ANIMAL SHALL WEAR CLOTHES.
4-NO ANIMAL SHALL SLEEP IN A BED.
5-NO ANIMAL SHALL DRINK ALCOHOL.
6-NO ANIMAL SHALL KILL ANY OTHER ANIMAL.
7·ALL ANIMALS ARE EQUAL.

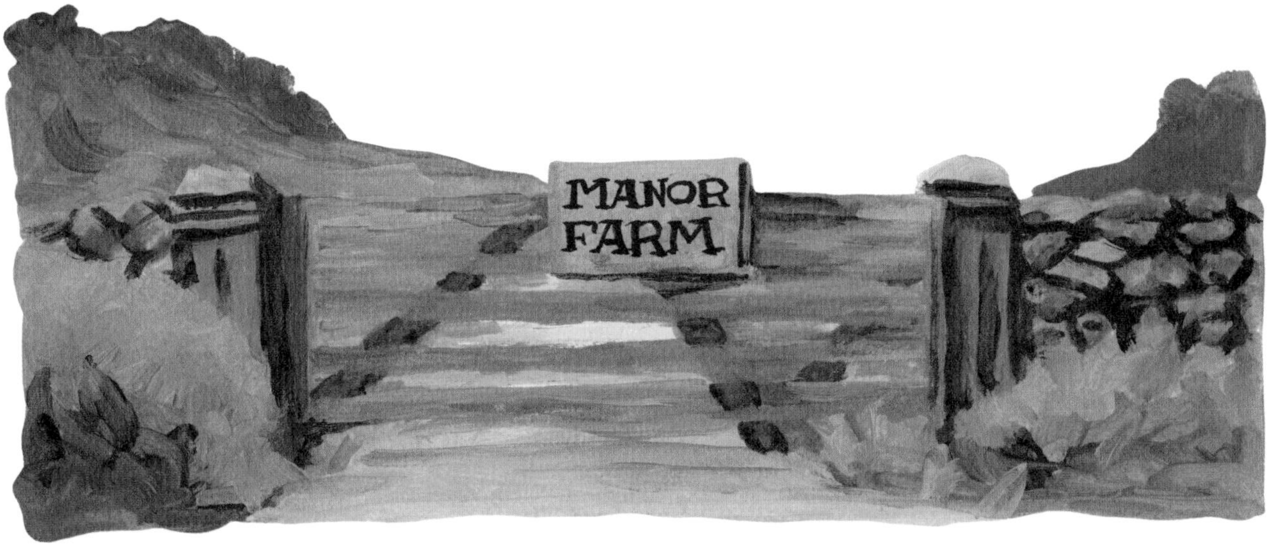
MANOR
FARM

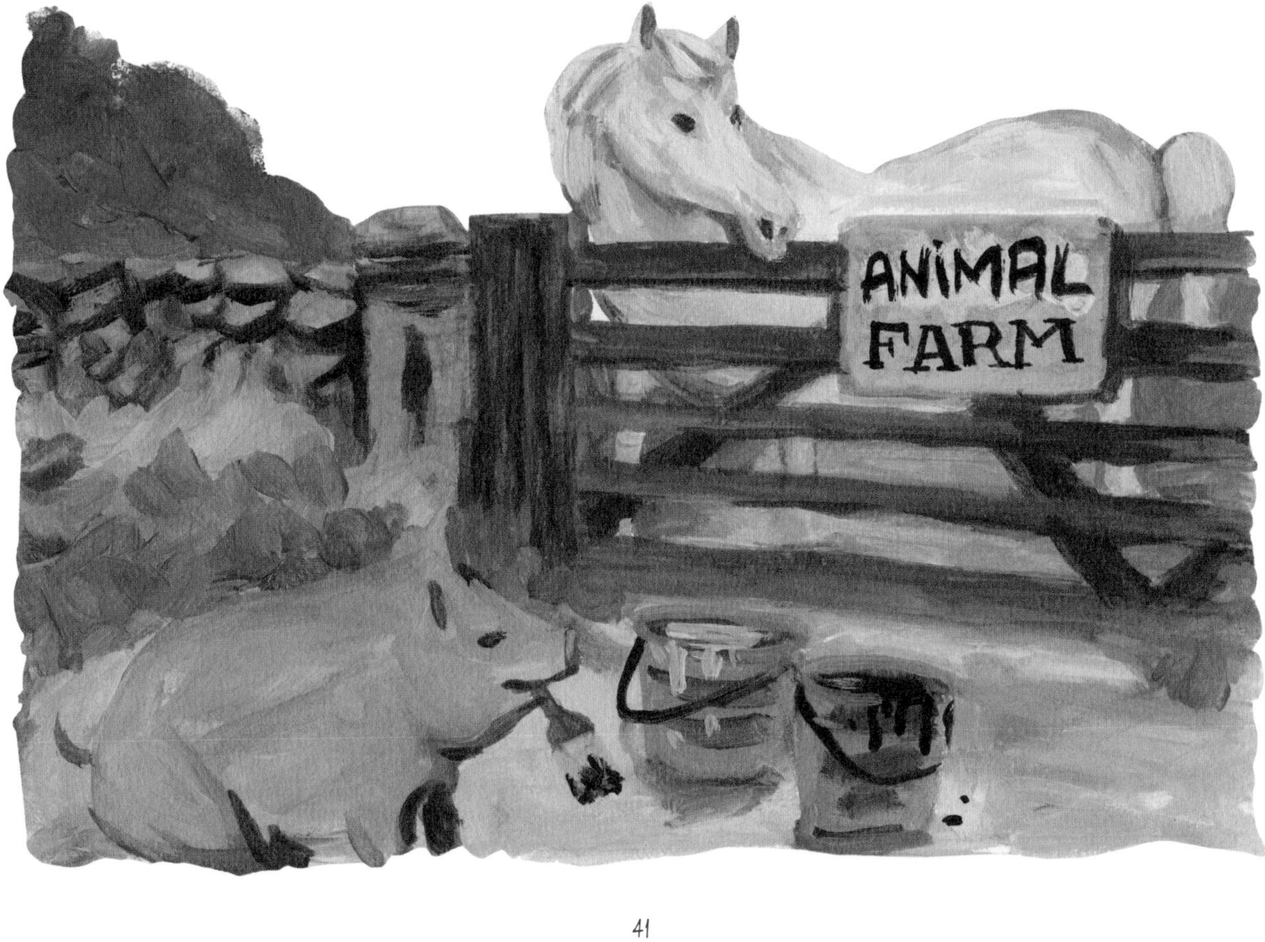
ANIMAL
FARM

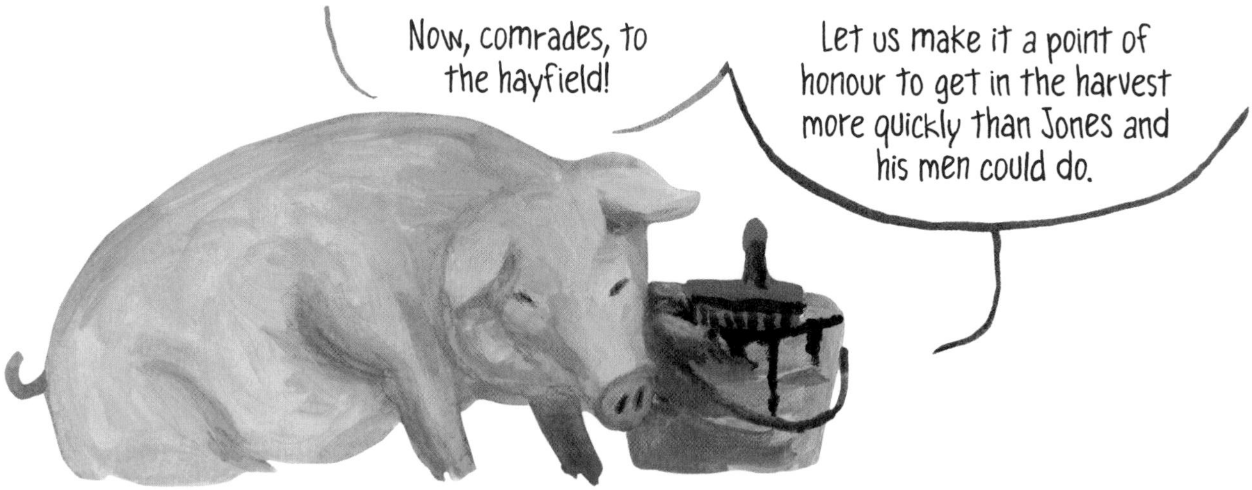
Now, comrades, to the hayfield!
Let us make it a point of honour to get in the harvest more quickly than Jones and his men could do.

But the cows had not been milked for twenty-four hours.

The pigs sent for buckets and milked the cows fairly successfully.

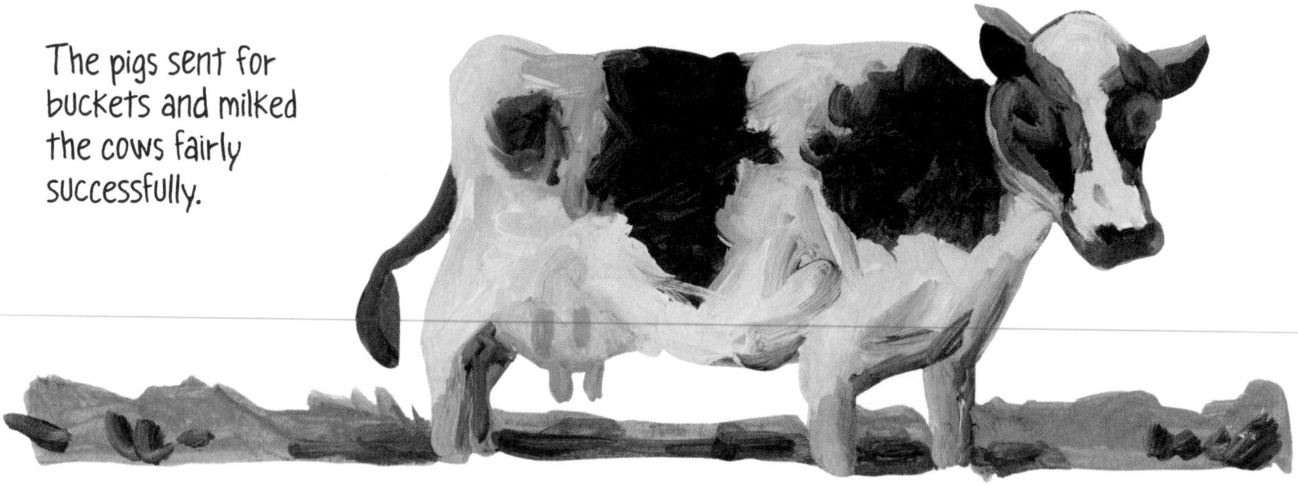

Soon there were five buckets of frothing creamy milk and many of the animals looked with interest.

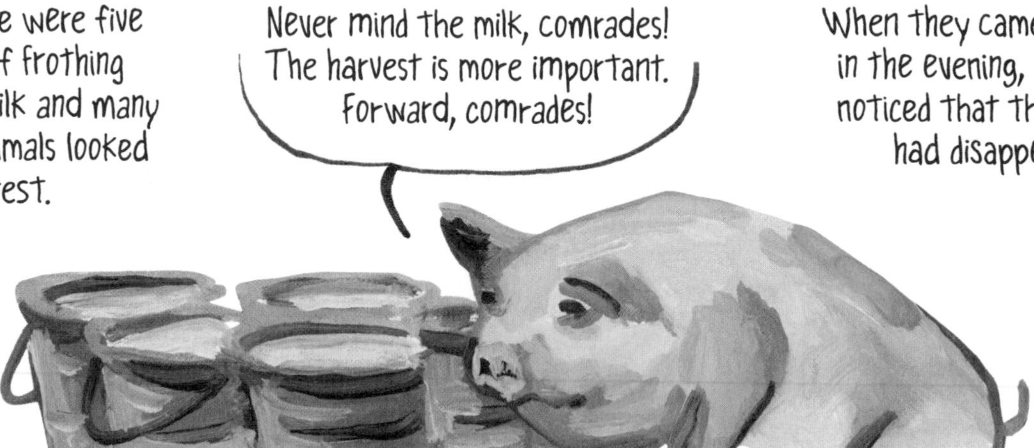
Never mind the milk, comrades! The harvest is more important. Forward, comrades!

When they came back in the evening, it was noticed that the milk had disappeared.

III

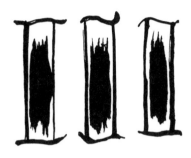

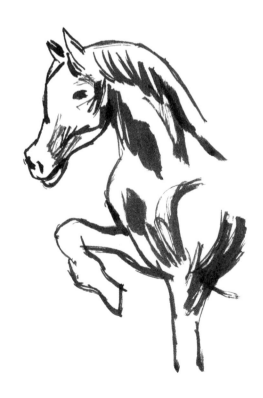

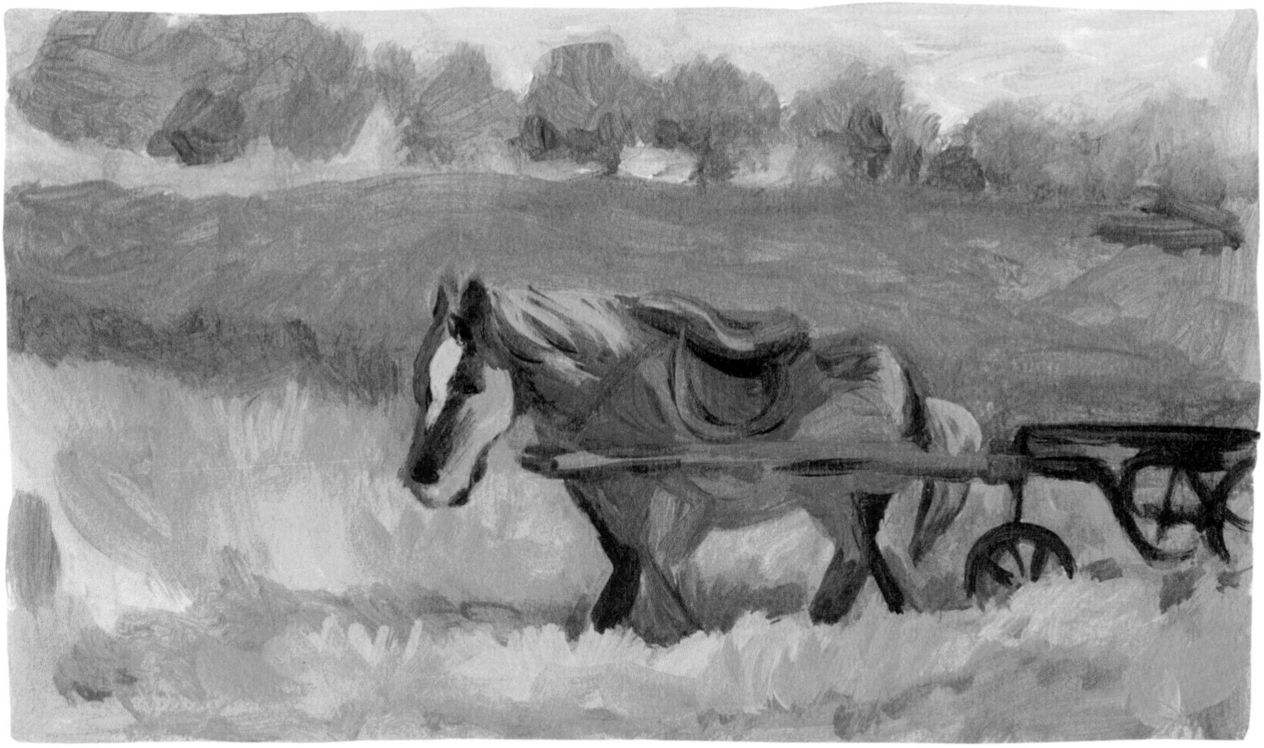

How they toiled and sweated to get the hay in!

The horses knew every inch of the field, and in fact understood the business of mowing and raking far better than Jones and his men.

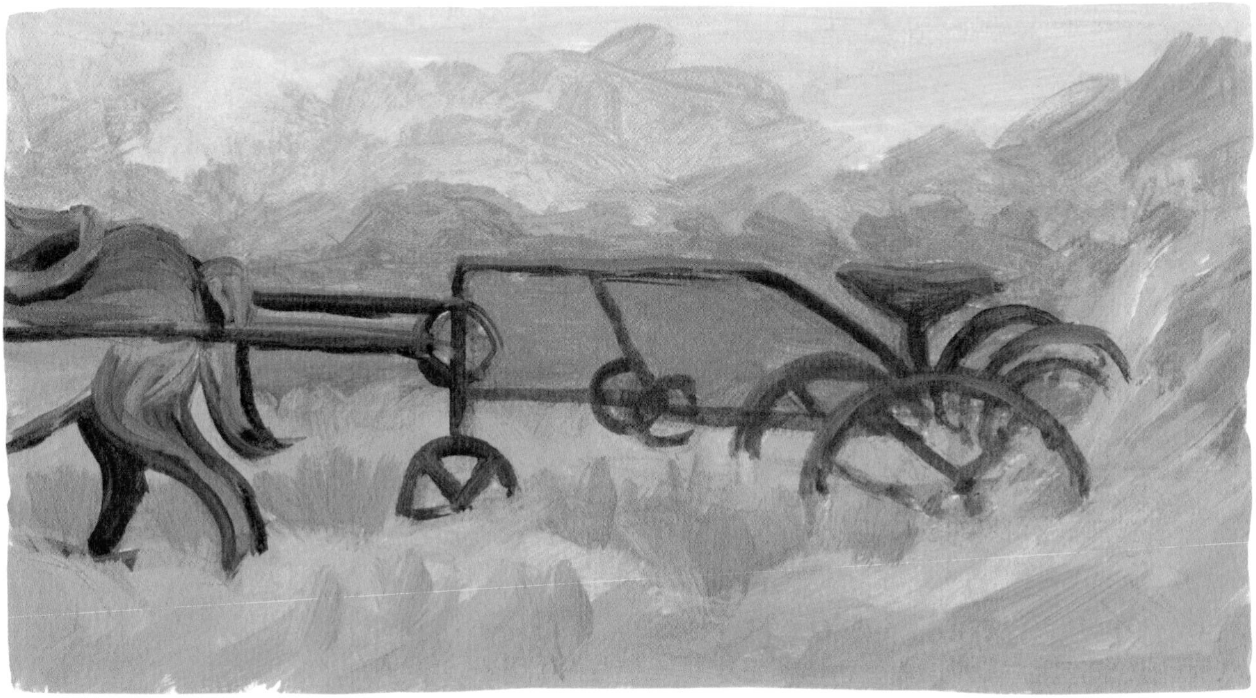

The pigs did not actually work, but they directed and supervised.

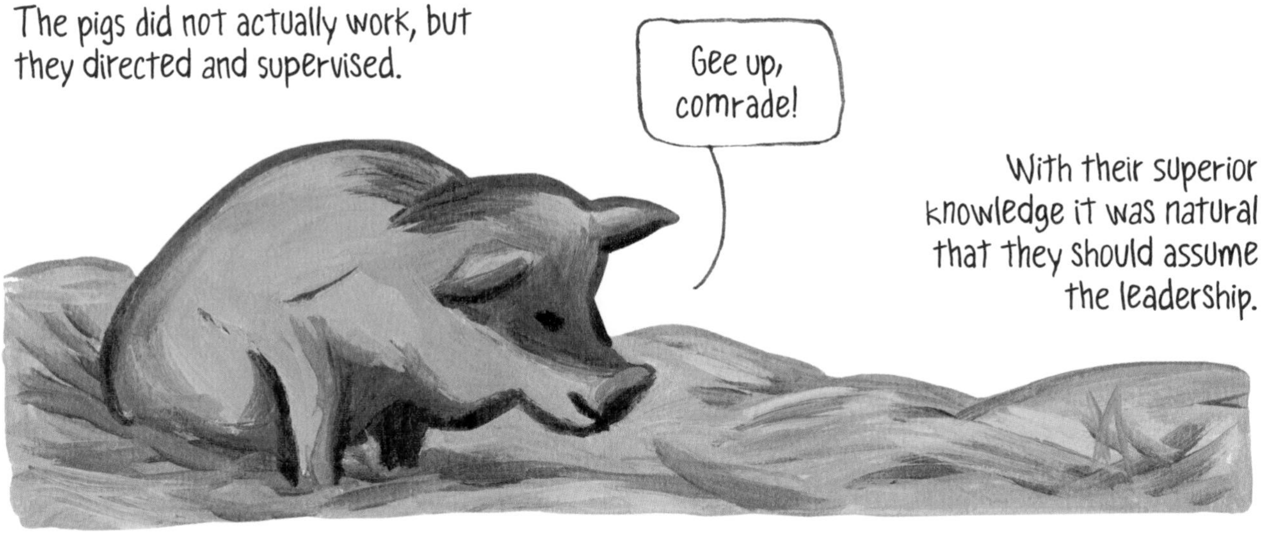
Gee up, comrade!

With their superior knowledge it was natural that they should assume the leadership.

And every animal down to the humblest worked at turning the hay and gathering it.

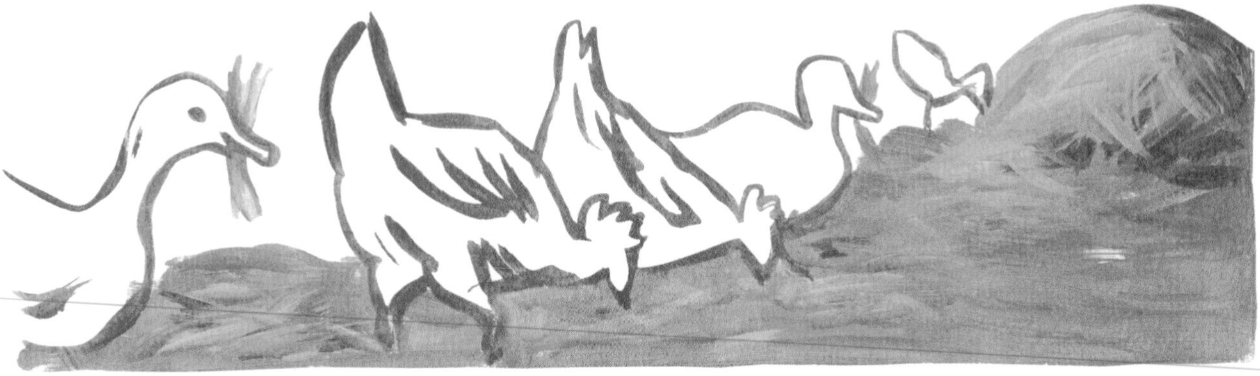

It was the biggest harvest that the farm had ever seen.

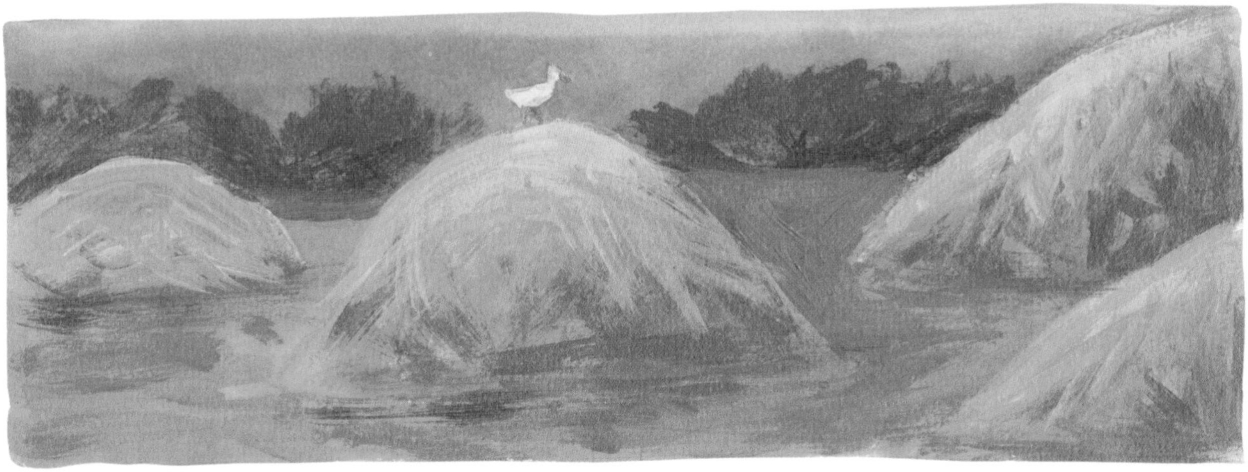

The animals were happy as they had never conceived it possible to be.

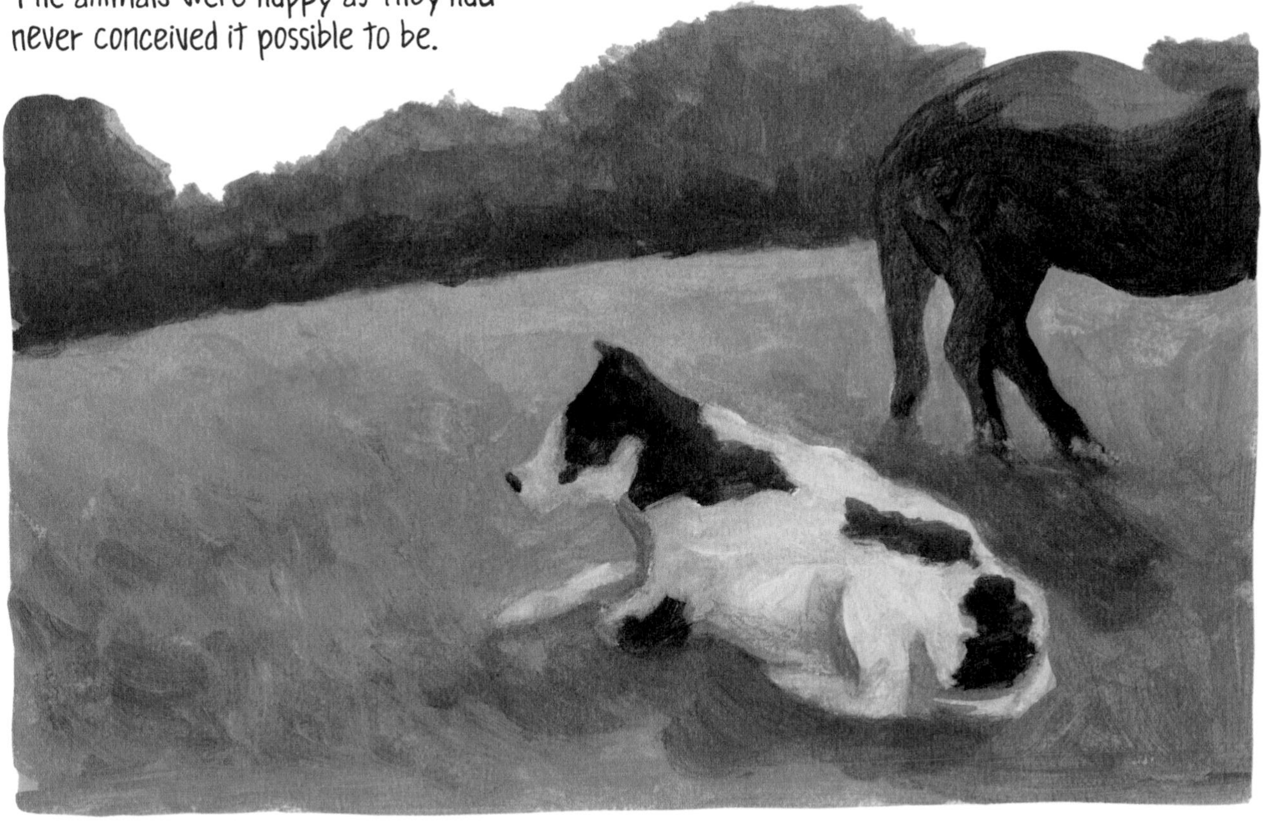

With the worthless parasitical human beings gone, there was more for everyone to eat. There was more leisure too.

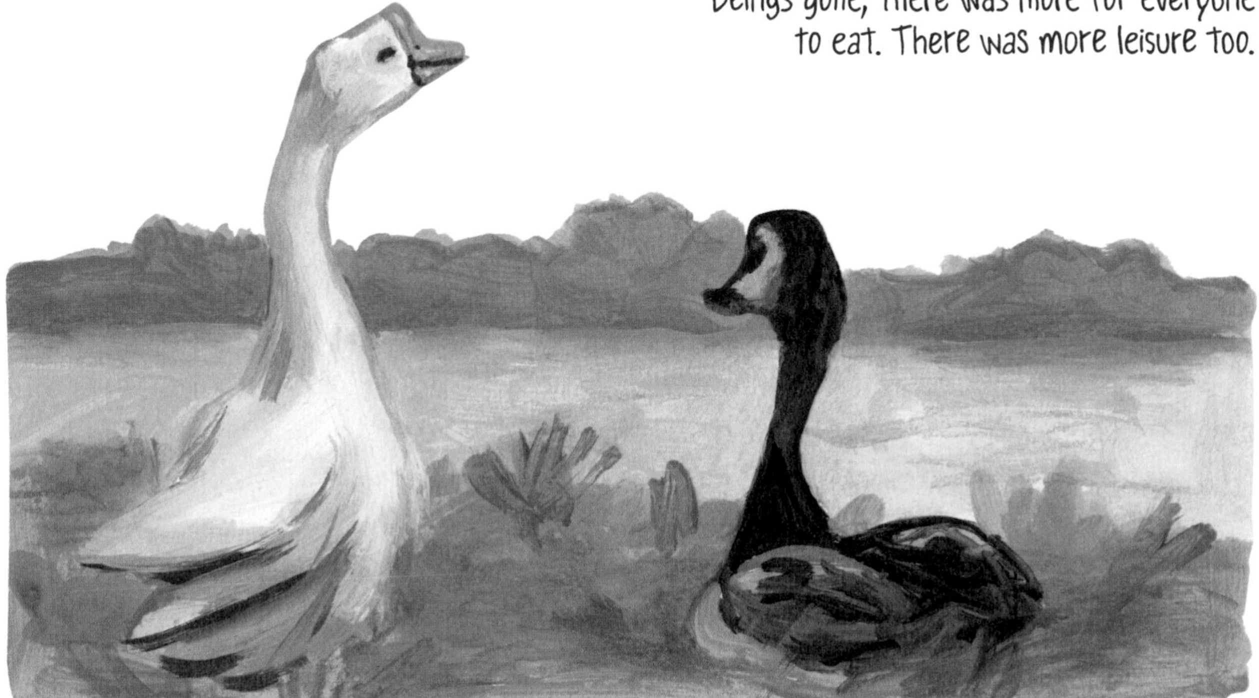

All through that summer the work of the farm went like clockwork.

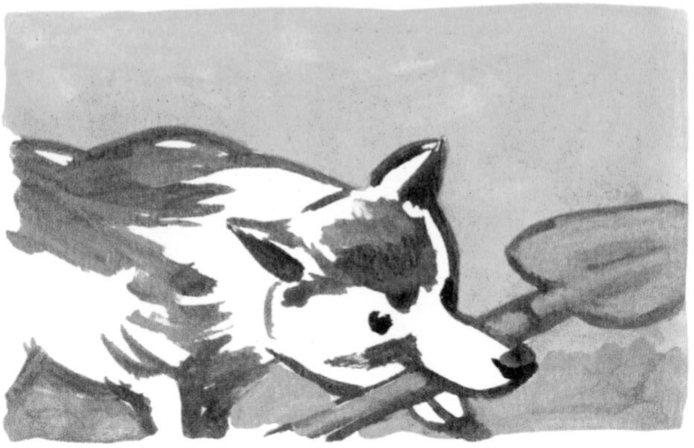

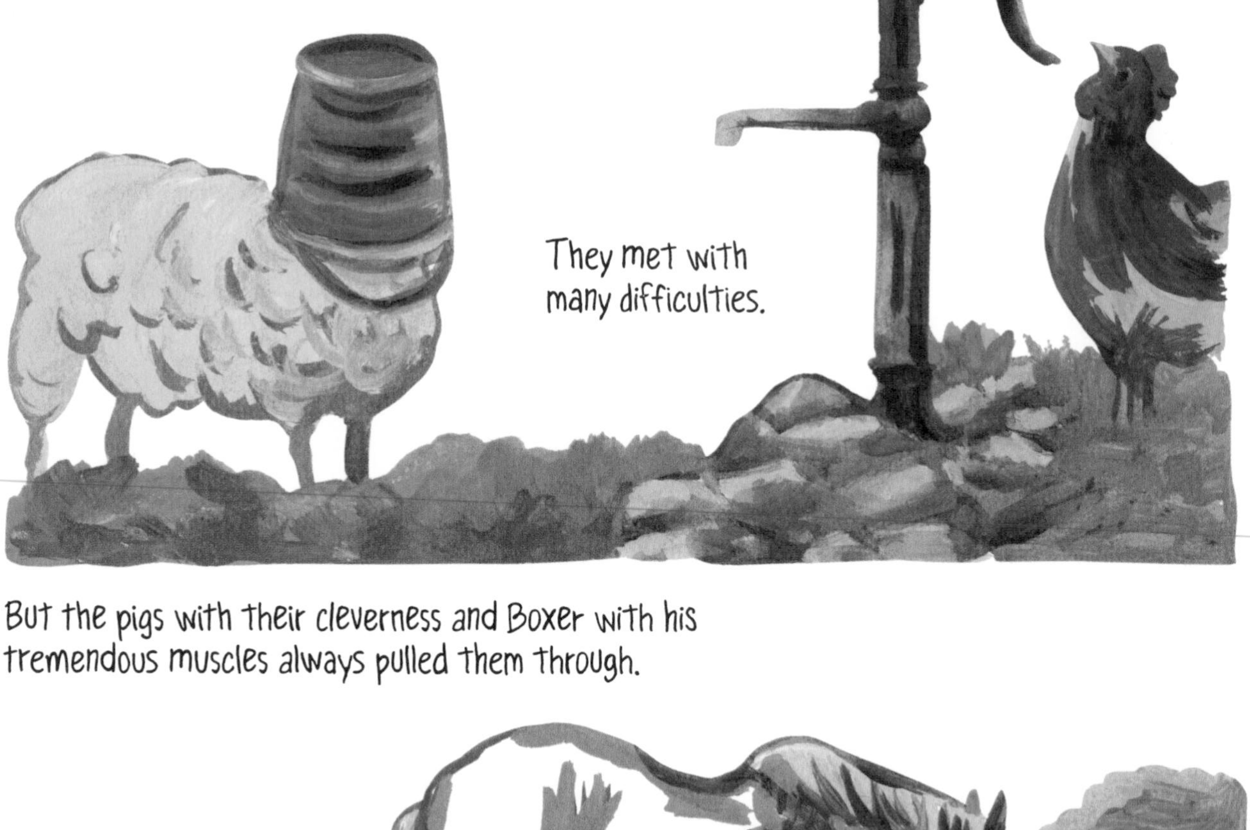

They met with many difficulties.

But the pigs with their cleverness and Boxer with his tremendous muscles always pulled them through.

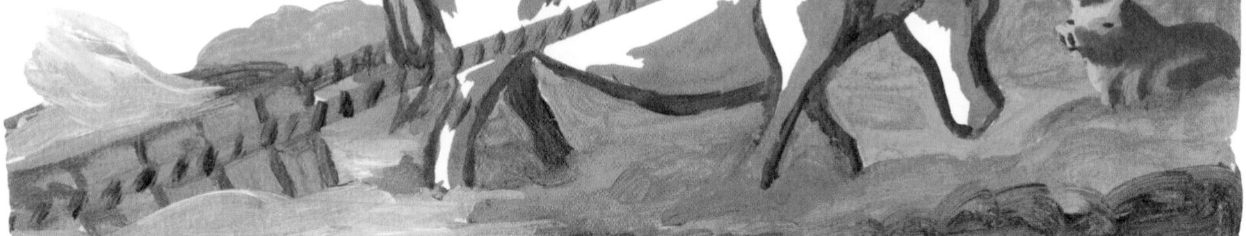

Boxer was the admiration of everybody.

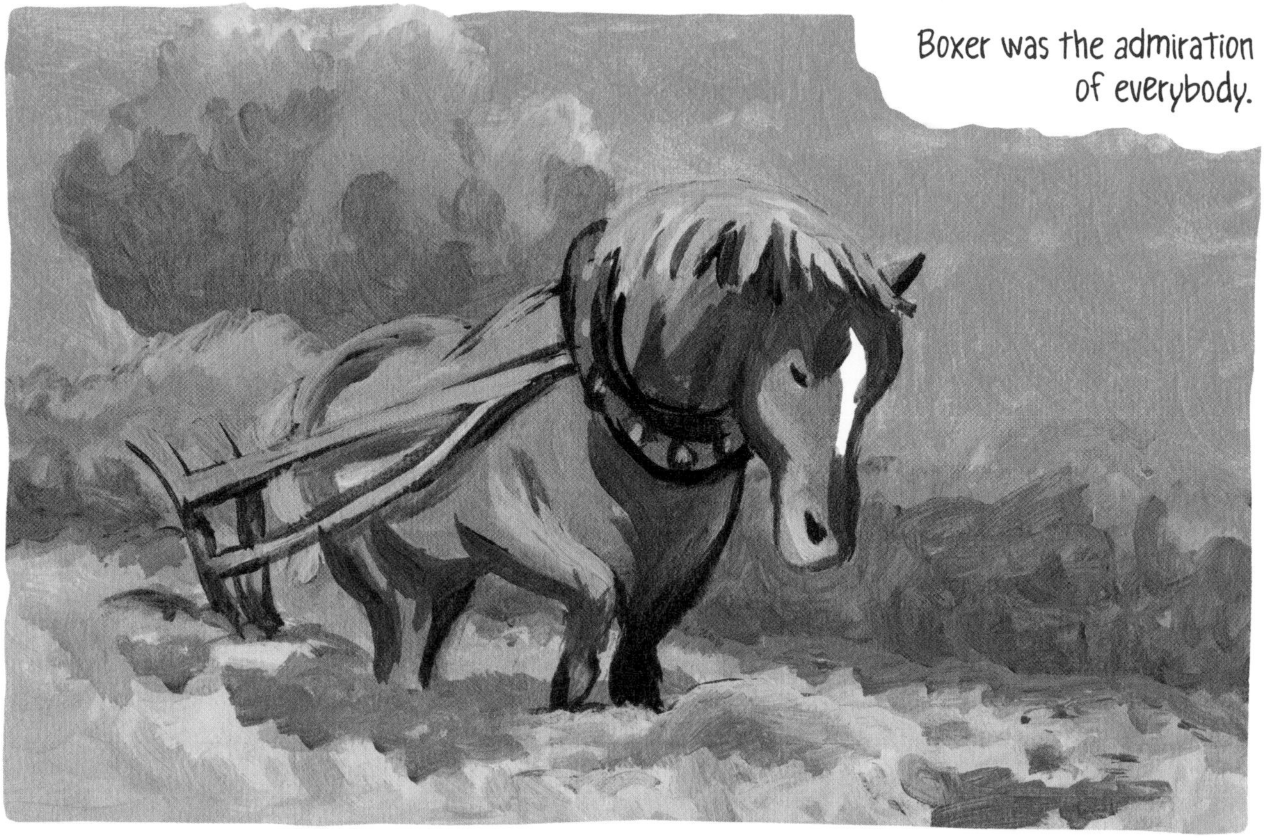

There were days when the entire work of the farm seemed to rest on his mighty shoulders.

From morning to night he was pushing and pulling, always at the spot where the work was hardest.

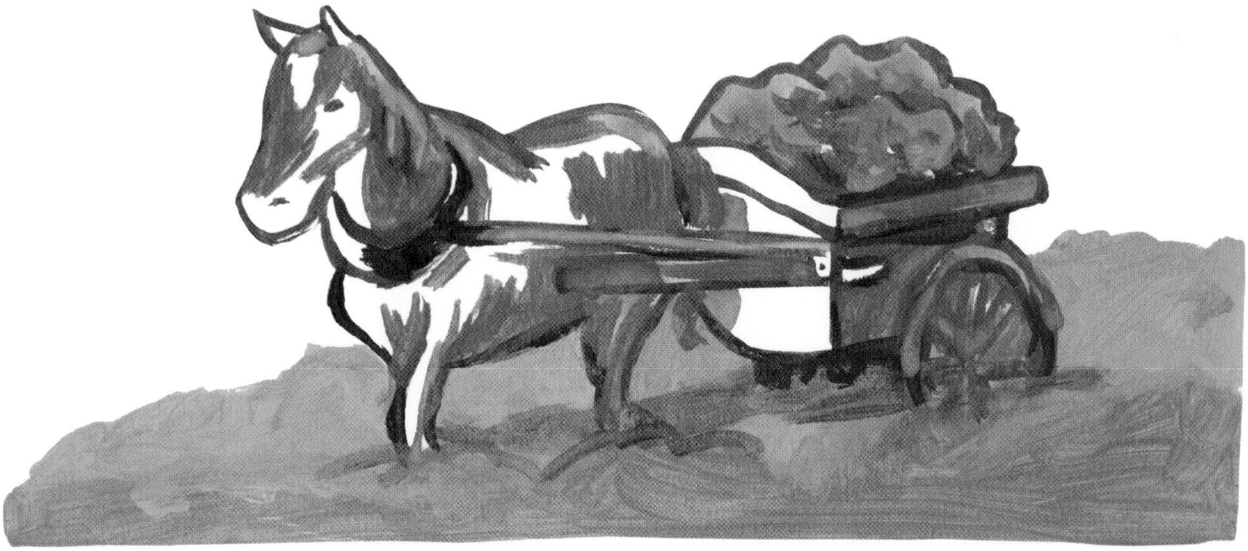

On Sundays there was no work.

Breakfast was an hour later than usual, and after breakfast there was a ceremony which was observed every week without fail.

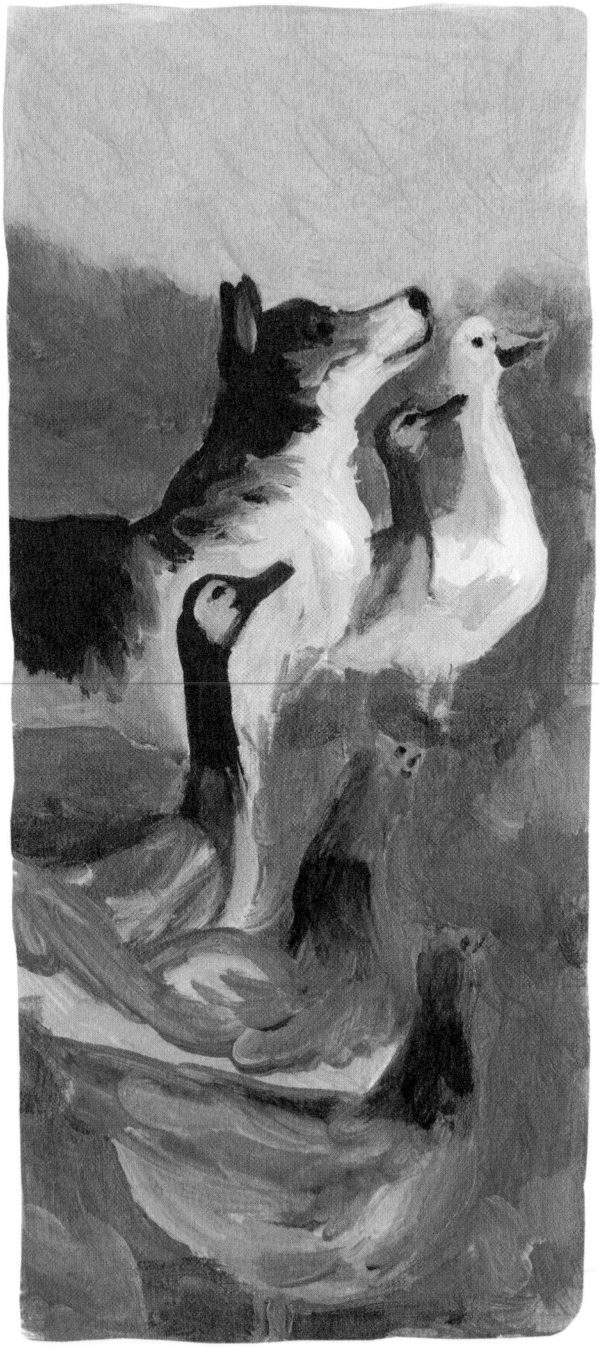

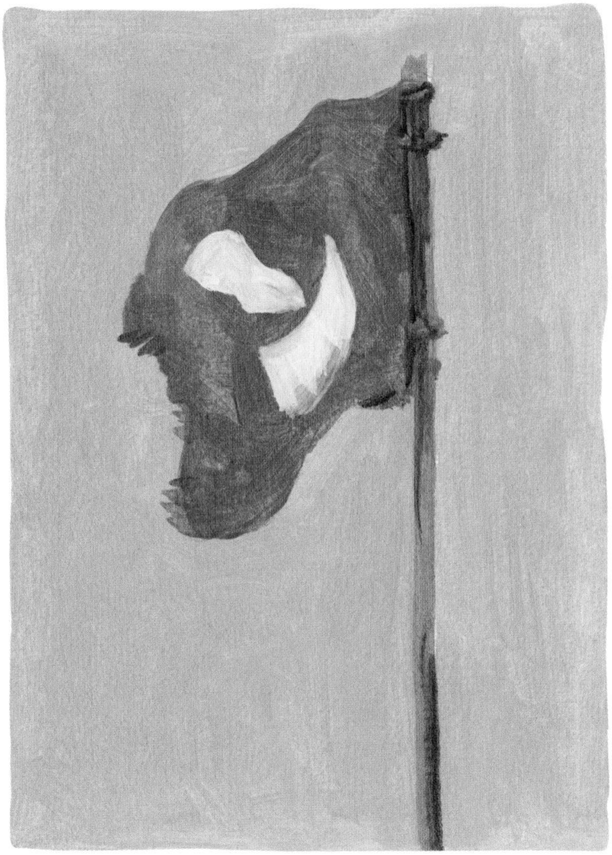

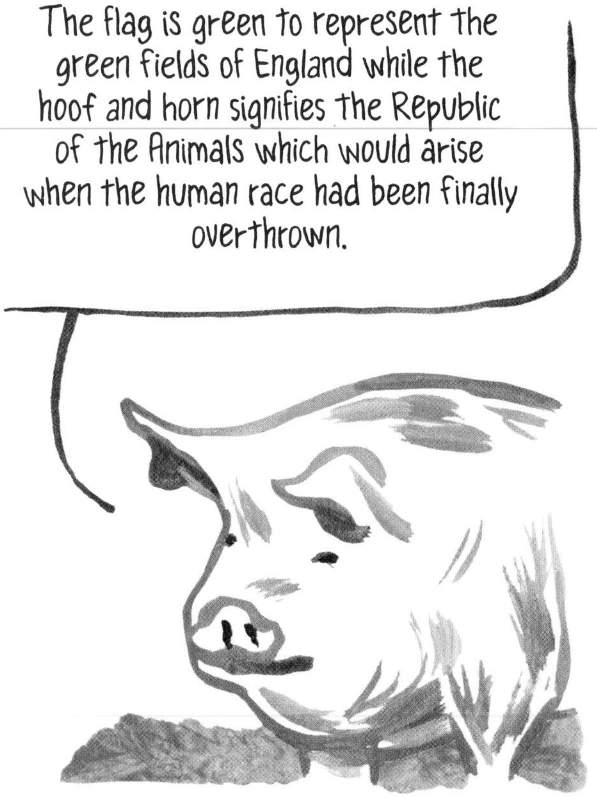
The flag is green to represent the green fields of England while the hoof and horn signifies the Republic of the Animals which would arise when the human race had been finally overthrown.

After the hoisting of the flag, all the animals trooped into the big barn for a general assembly called the Meeting.

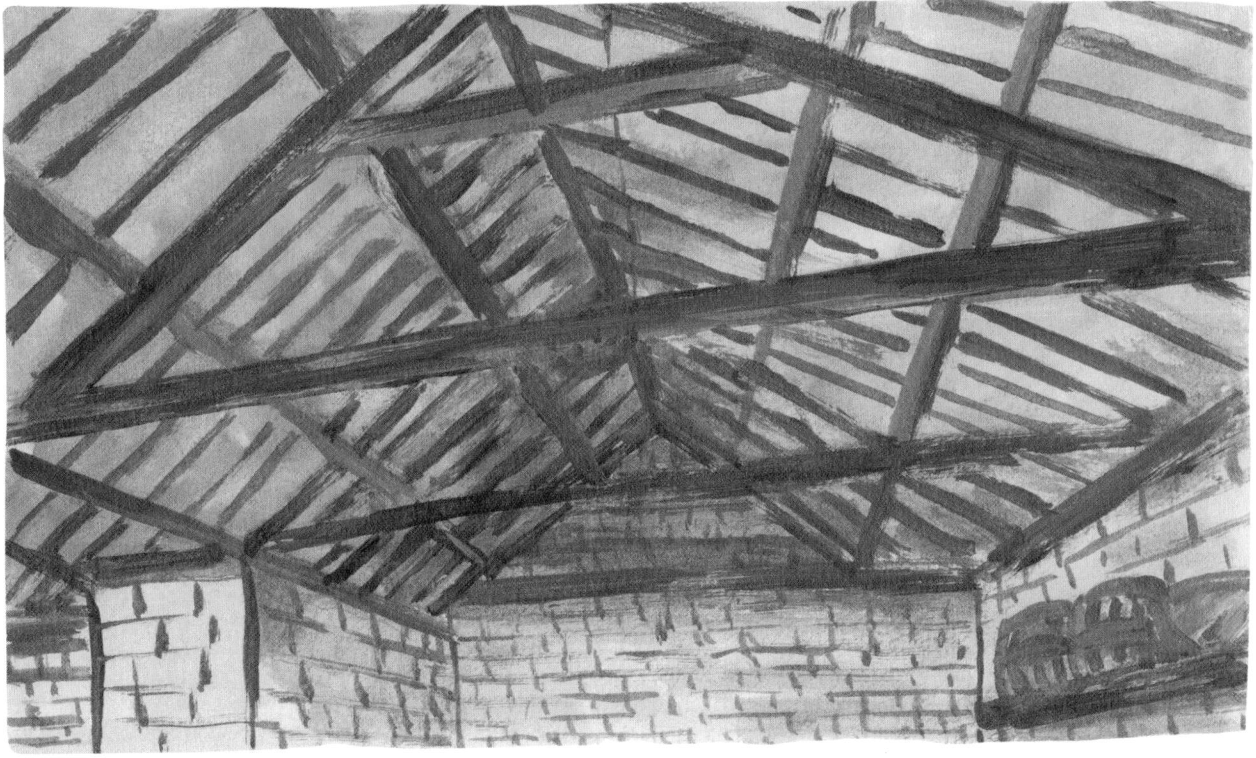

Here the work of the coming week was planned out and resolutions were put forward and debated.

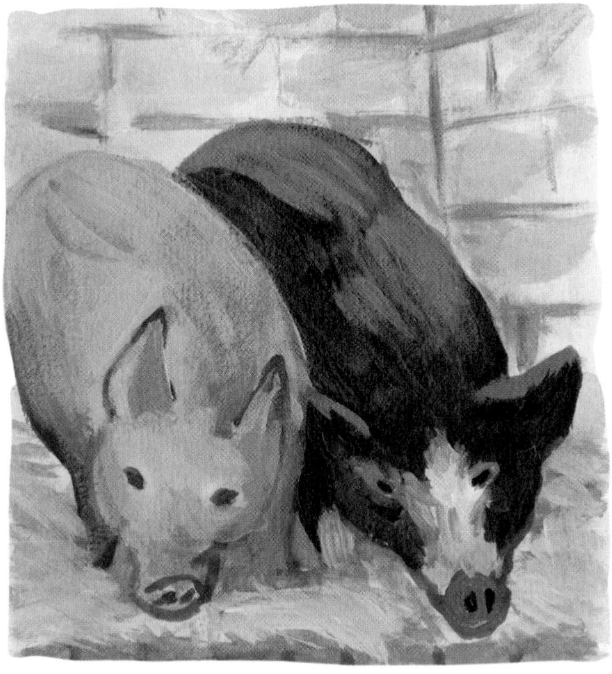

It was always the pigs who put forward the resolutions. The other animals understood how to vote, but could never think of any resolutions of their own.

The Meeting always ended with the singing of "Beasts of England," and the afternoon was given up to recreation.

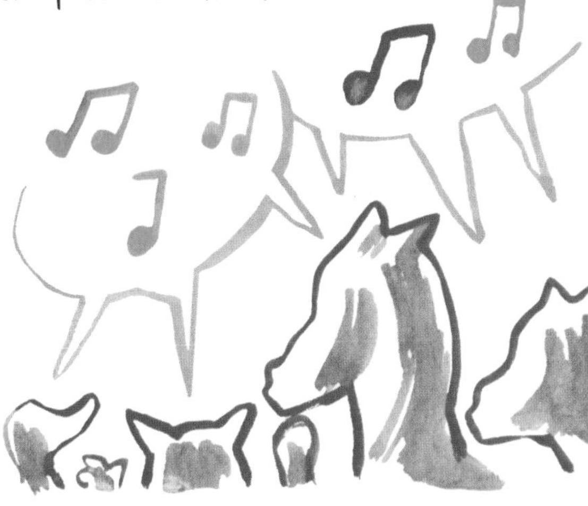

The pigs had set aside the harness-room as a headquarters for themselves.

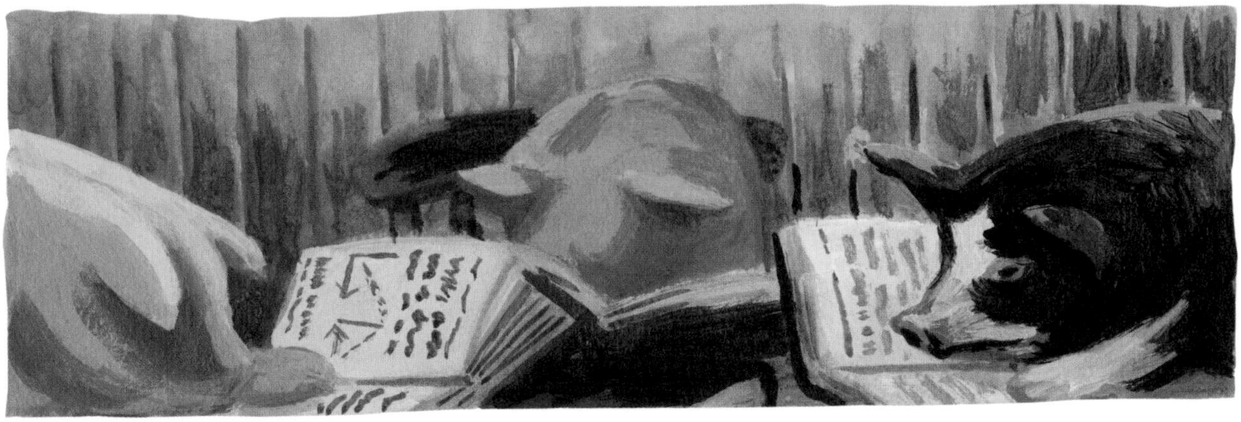

Here, in the evenings, they studied blacksmithing, carpentering, and other necessary arts from books brought out of the farmhouse.

Snowball busied himself with the organising of the other animals into Animal Committees.

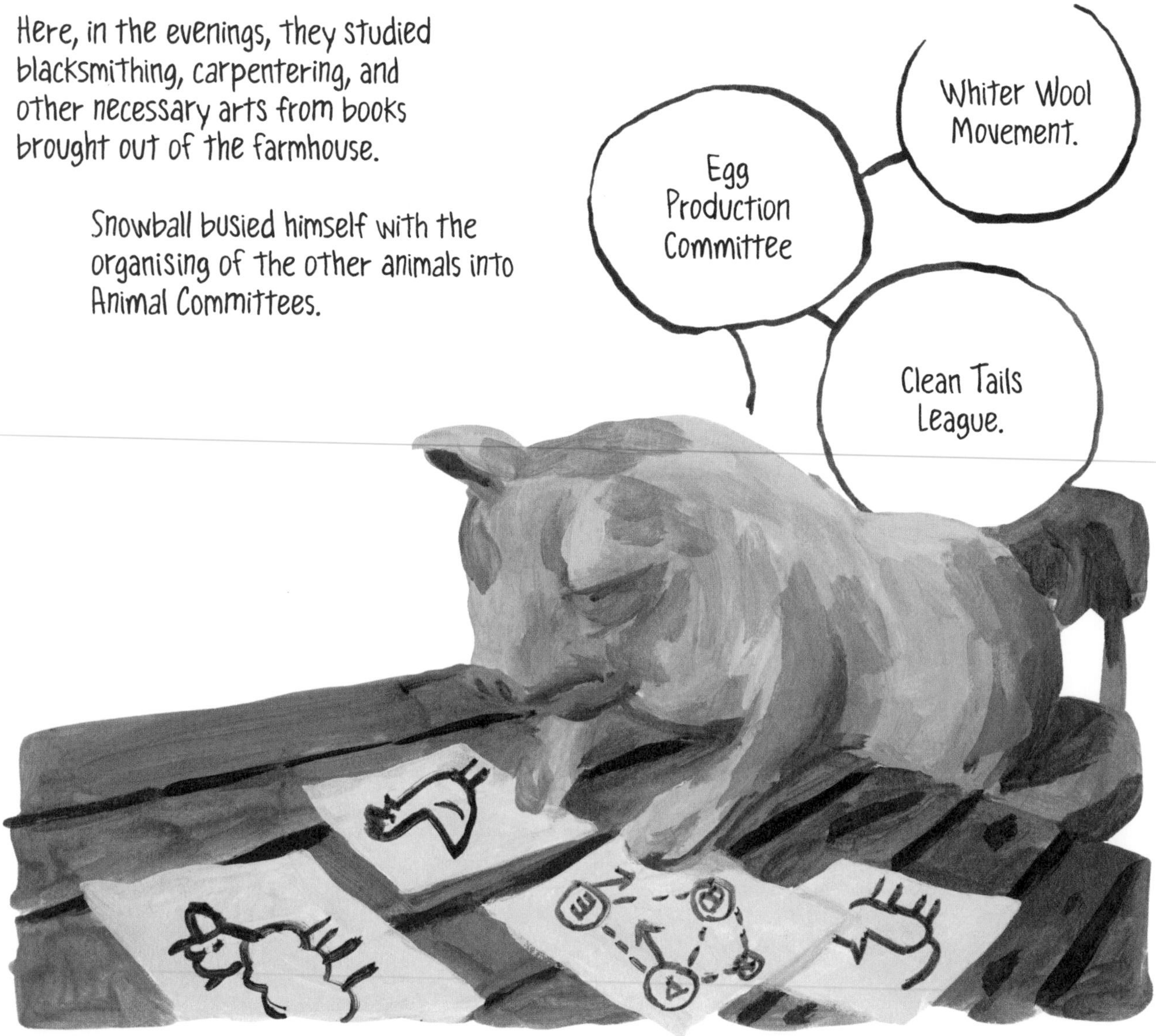

Egg Production Committee
Whiter Wool Movement.
Clean Tails League.

And the Wild Comrades' Re-education Committee. On the whole, these projects were a failure.

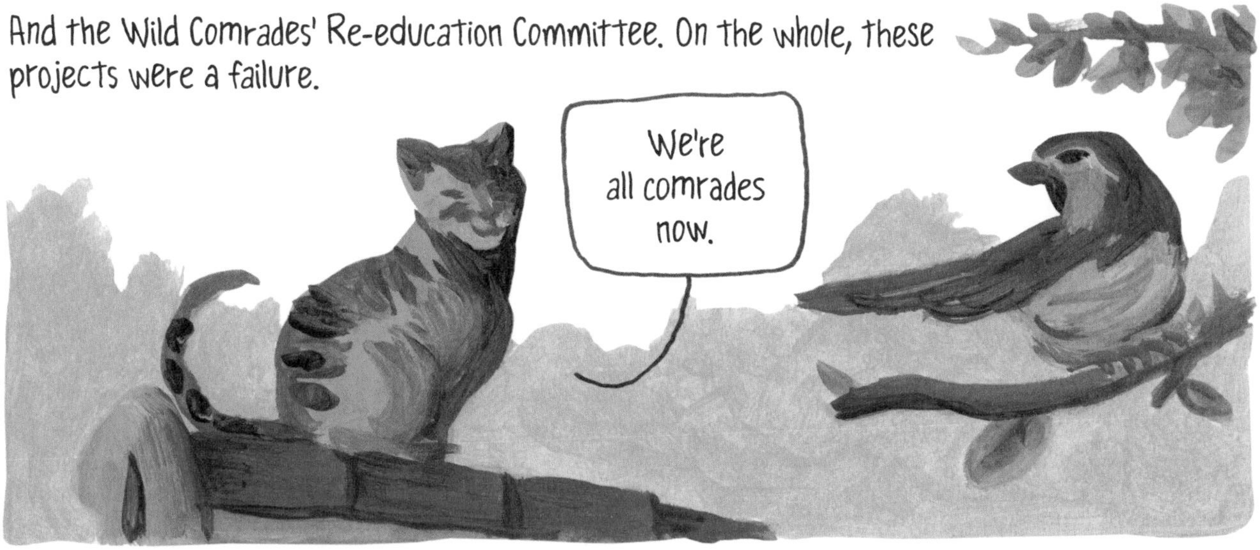
We're all comrades now.

The reading and writing classes, however, were a great success.

By the autumn almost every animal on the farm was literate in some degree.

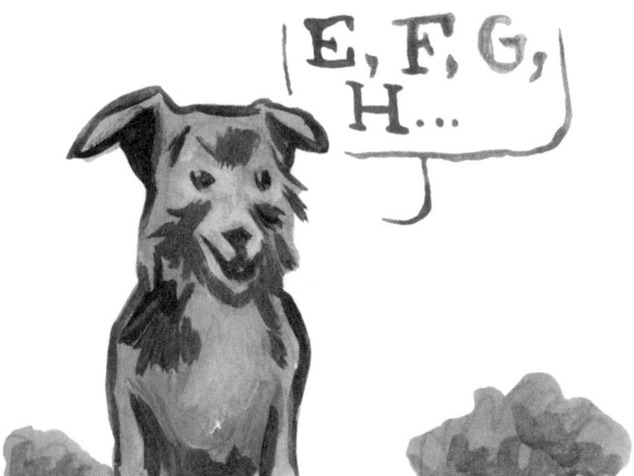
E, F, G, H...

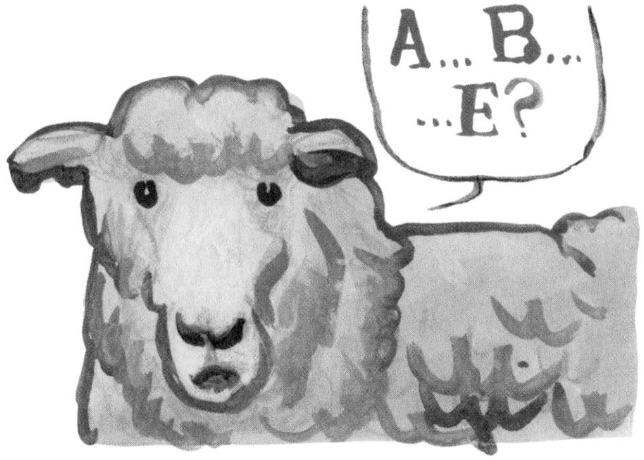
A... B... ...E?

It was found that the stupider animals, such as the sheep, hens, and ducks, were unable to learn the Seven Commandments by heart.

This contained the essential principle of Animalism.

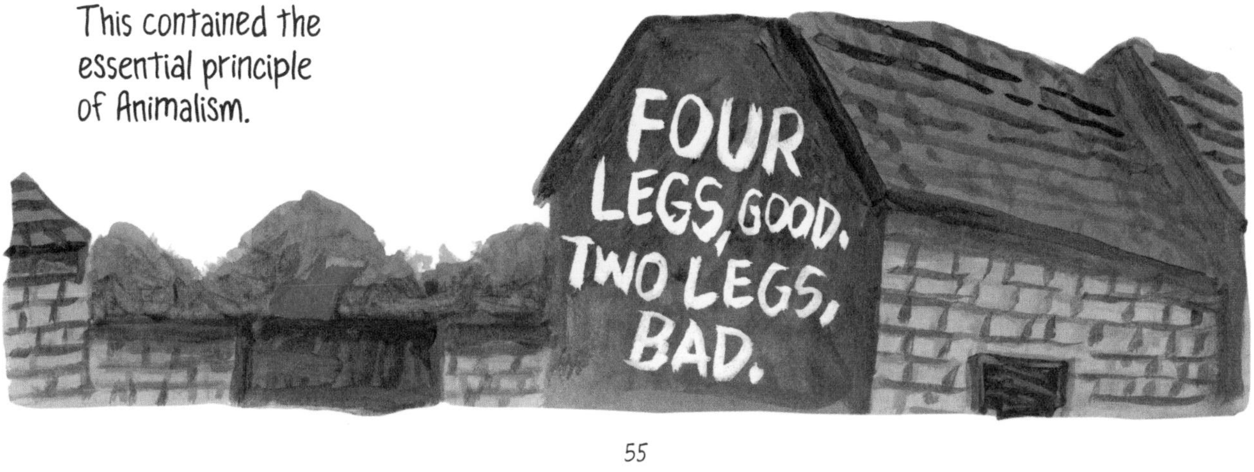
FOUR LEGS, GOOD. TWO LEGS, BAD.

Napoleon took no interest in Snowball's committees.

He took nine puppies from their mothers, saying he would make himself responsible for their education.

The education of the young is more important than anything that could be done for those who had already grown up.

He took them up into a loft which could only be reached by a ladder from the harness-room, and there kept them in such seclusion that the rest of the farm soon forgot their existence.

The mystery of where the milk went to was soon cleared up. It was mixed every day into the pigs' mash.

The early apples now ripening were to be collected for the use of the pigs.

"Our sole object is to preserve our health," said Squealer. "We pigs are brainworkers. What would happen if we pigs failed in our duty?

JONES WOULD COME BACK!"

When it was put to them in this light, they had no more to say. The milk and apples should be reserved for the pigs alone.

IV

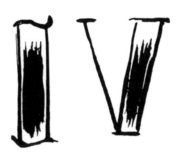

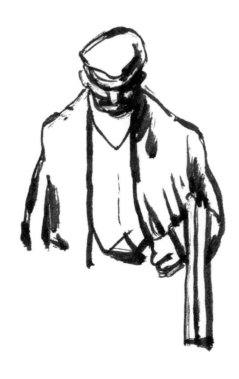

By the late summer the news of what had happened on Animal Farm had spread across half the county.

Every day pigeons were sent with instructions to mingle with the animals on neighbouring farms, tell them the story of the Rebellion, and teach them the tune of "Beasts of England."

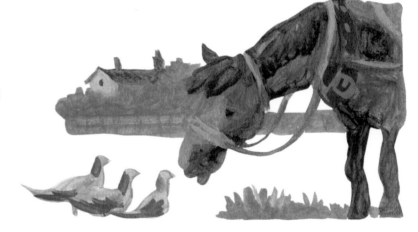

Most of this time Mr. Jones had spent sitting in the tavern, complaining to anyone who would listen of the monstrous injustice he had suffered.

The other farmers at first pretended to laugh to scorn the idea.

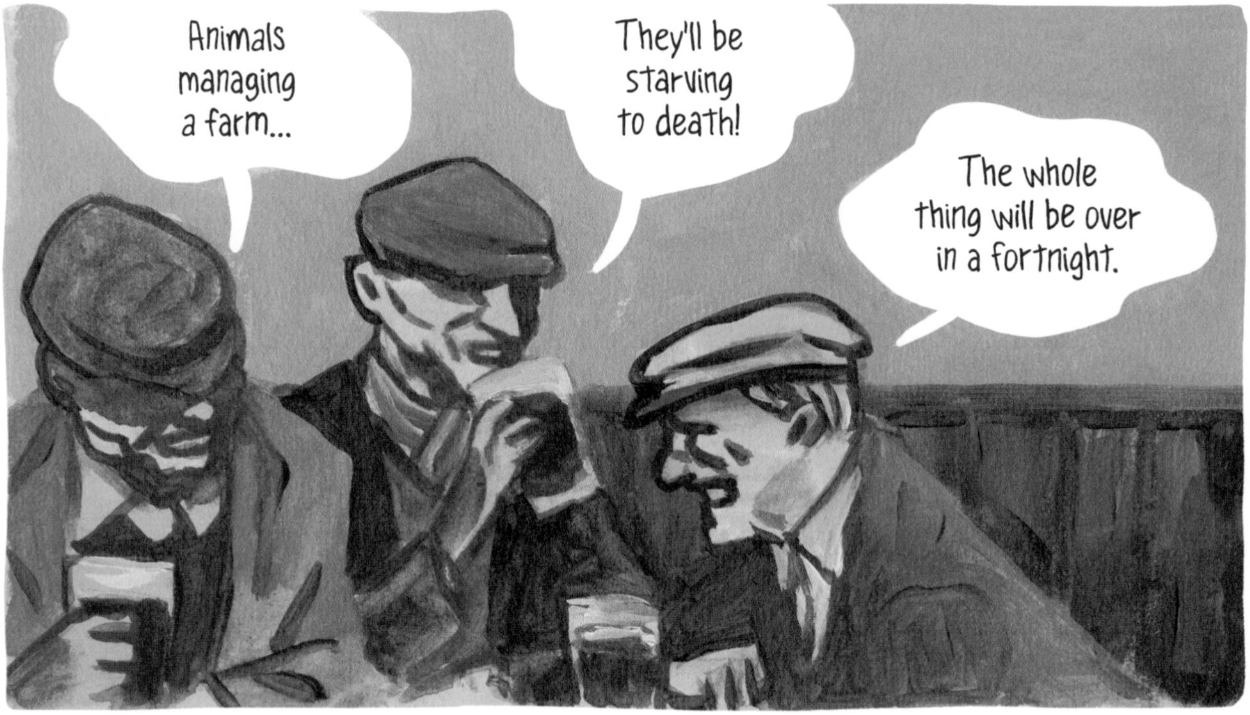
Animals managing a farm...
They'll be starving to death!
The whole thing will be over in a fortnight.

When time passed and the animals had evidently not starved to death, they began to talk of the terrible wickedness that now flourished on Animal Farm.

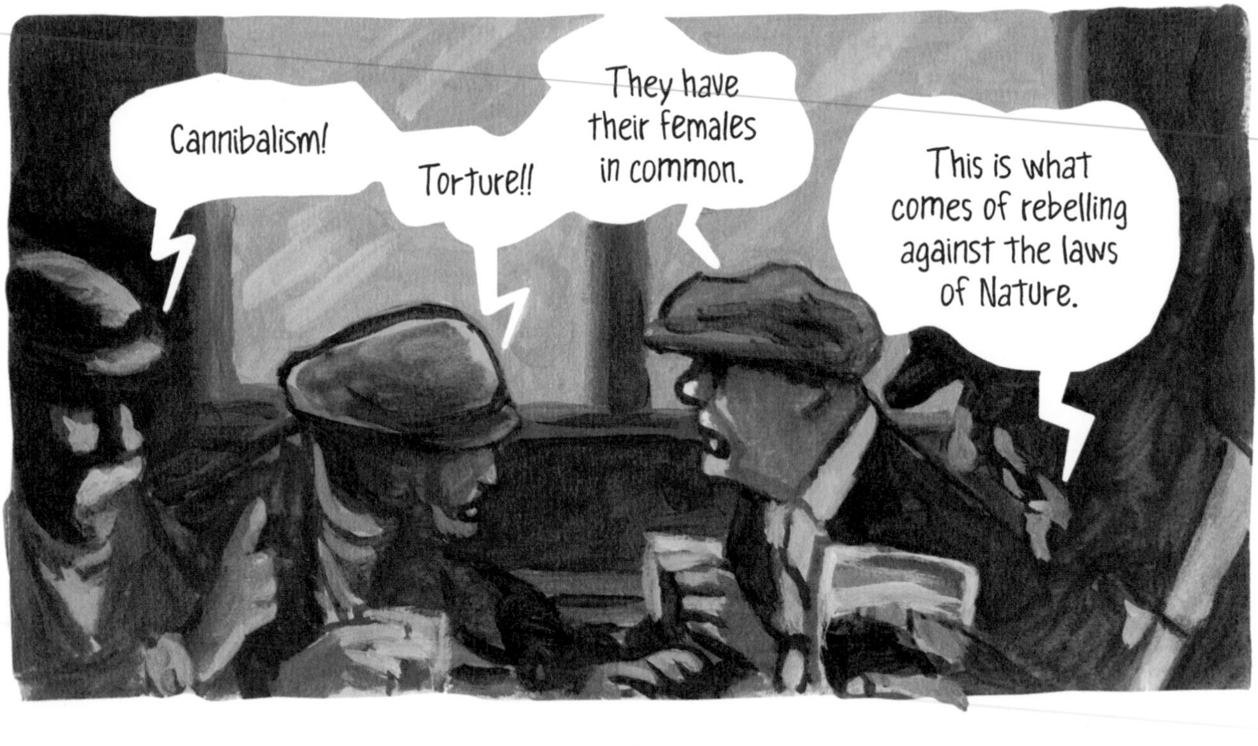
Cannibalism!
Torture!!
They have their females in common.
This is what comes of rebelling against the laws of Nature.

But rumours of a wonderful farm, where the human beings had been turned out and the animals managed their own affairs, continued to circulate.

Throughout that year a wave of rebelliousness ran through the countryside.

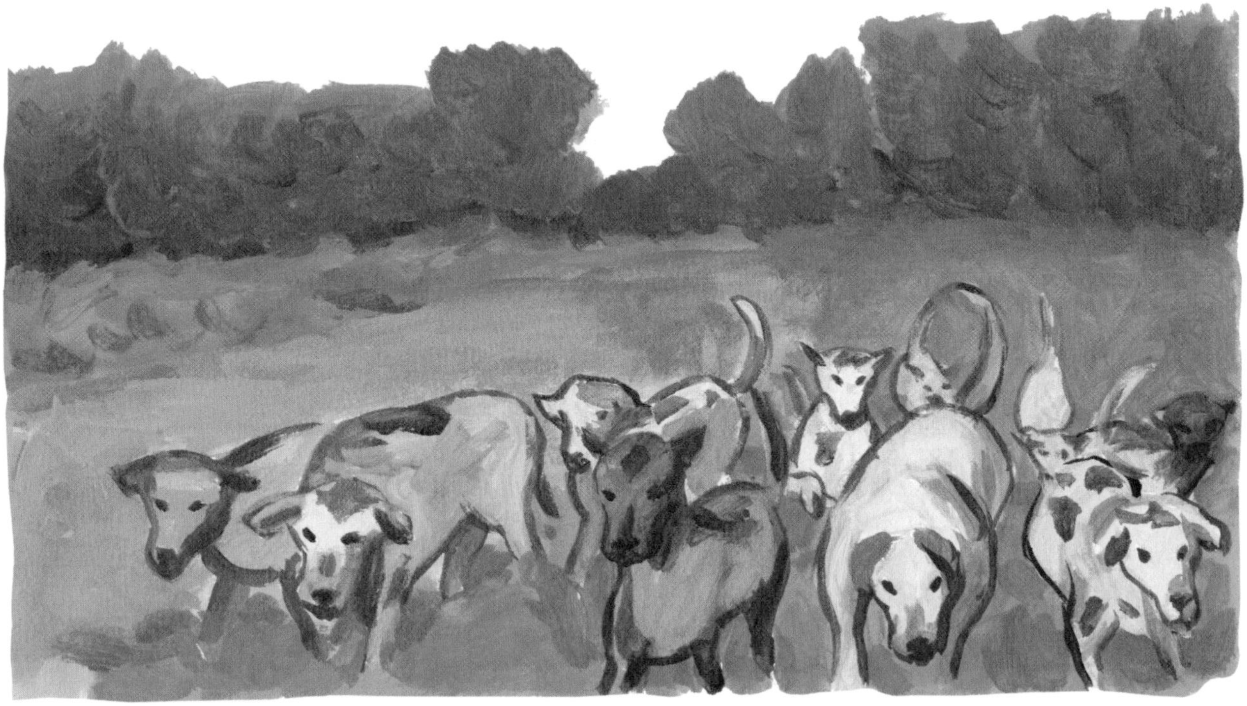

The tune and words of "Beasts of England" were known everywhere.

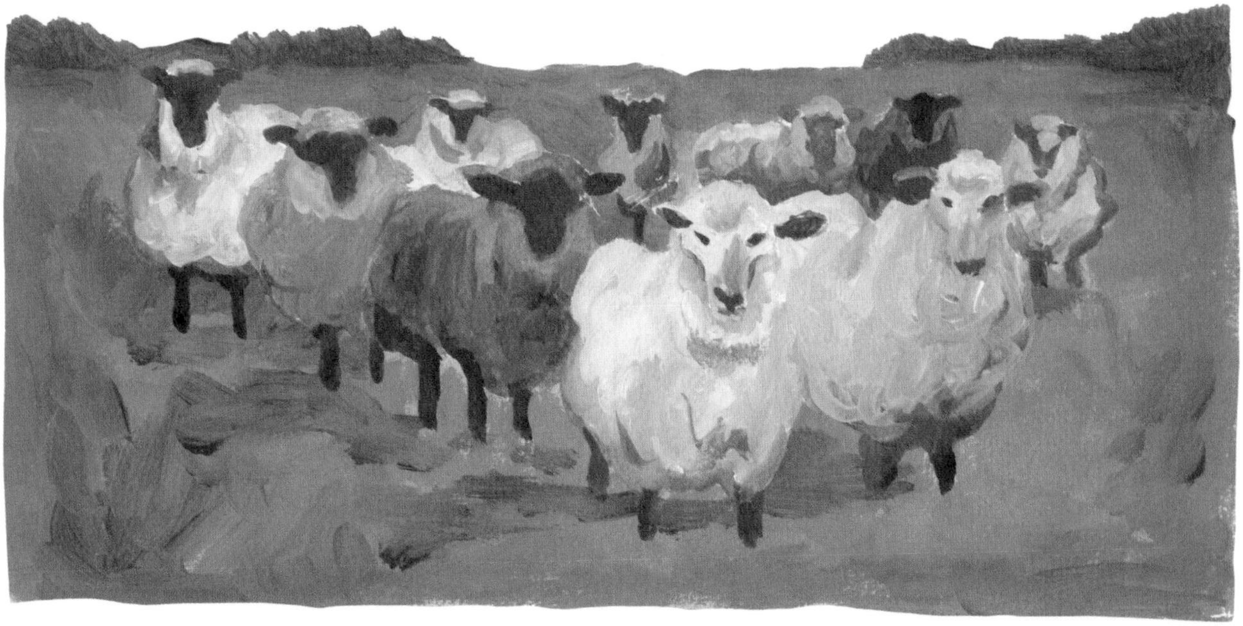

And human beings secretly trembled, hearing in it a prophecy of their future doom.

Early in October...

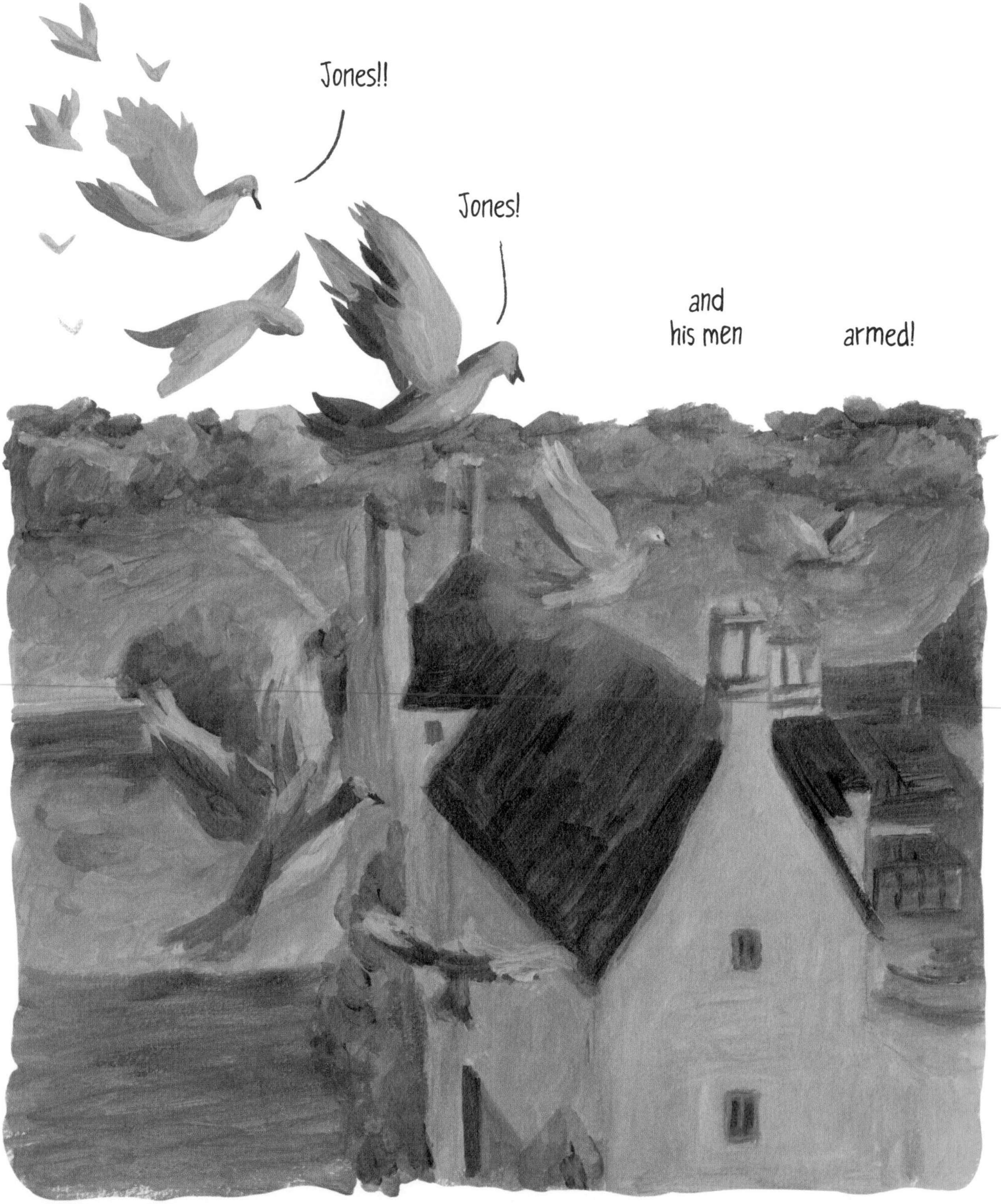
Jones!!
Jones!
and his men
armed!

Obviously they were going to attempt the recapture of the farm.

This had long been expected, and all preparations had been made.

Snowball had studied an old book of Julius Caesar's campaigns.

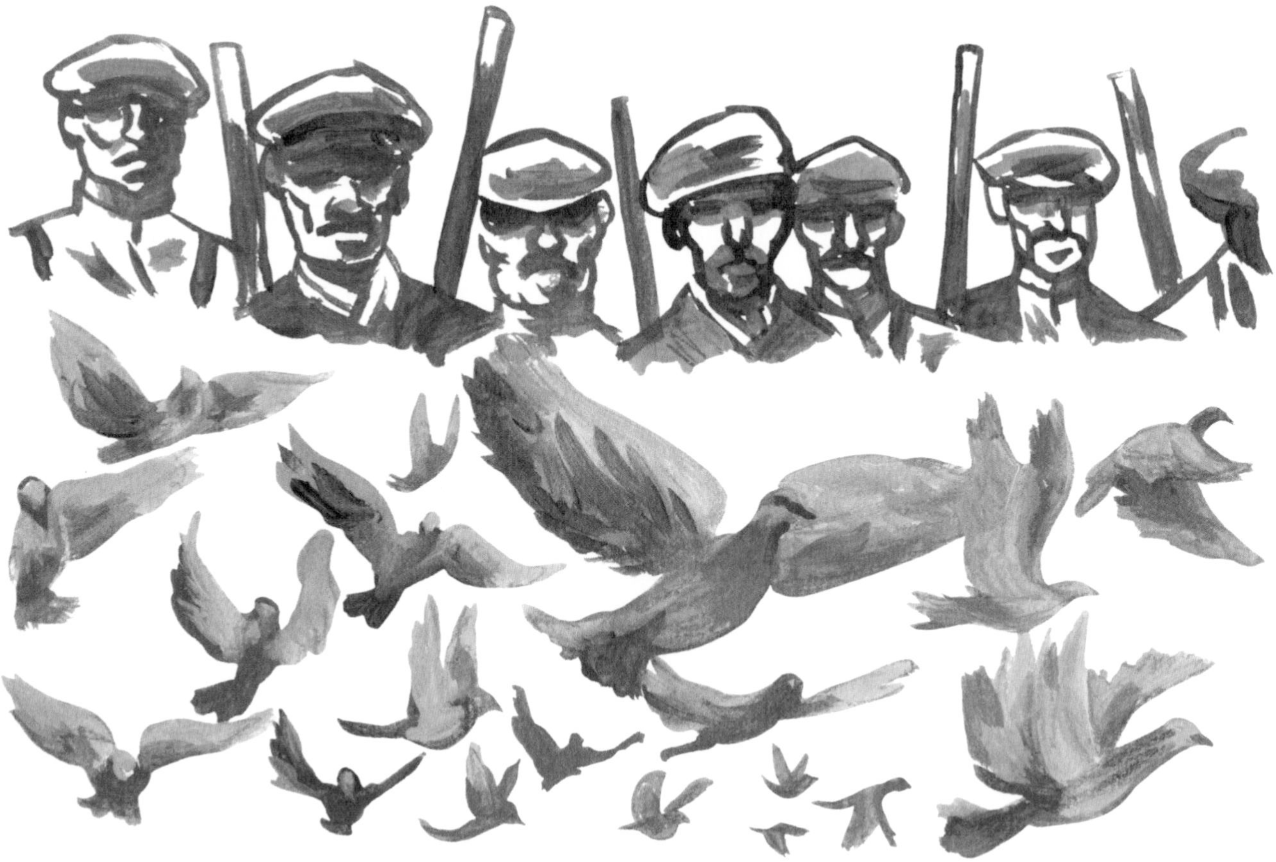

The first attack: all the pigeons.

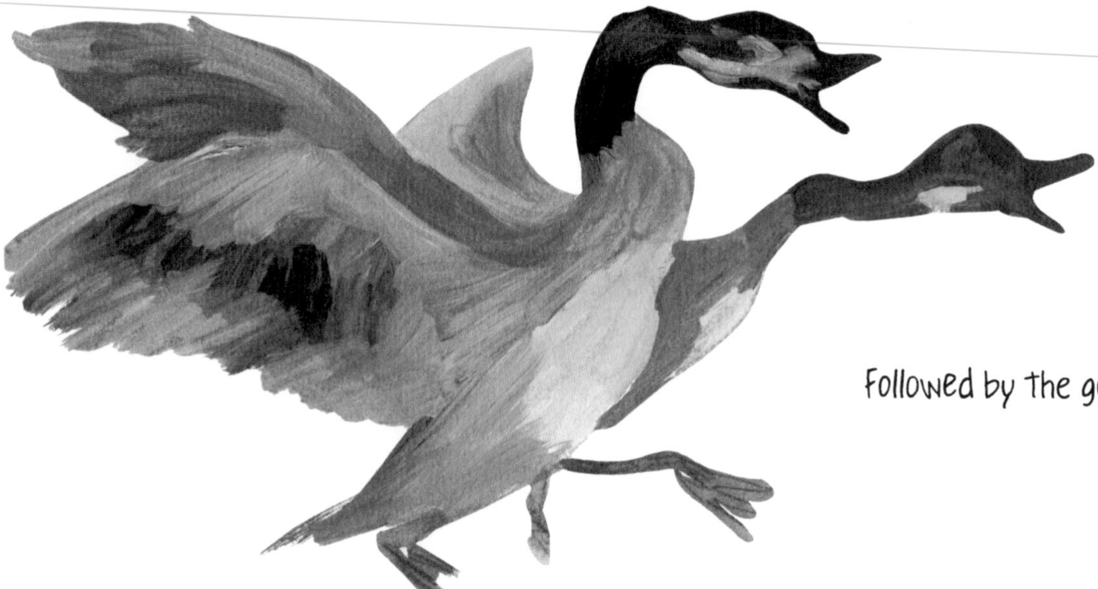

Followed by the geese.

A skirmishing manoeuvre intended to create disorder.

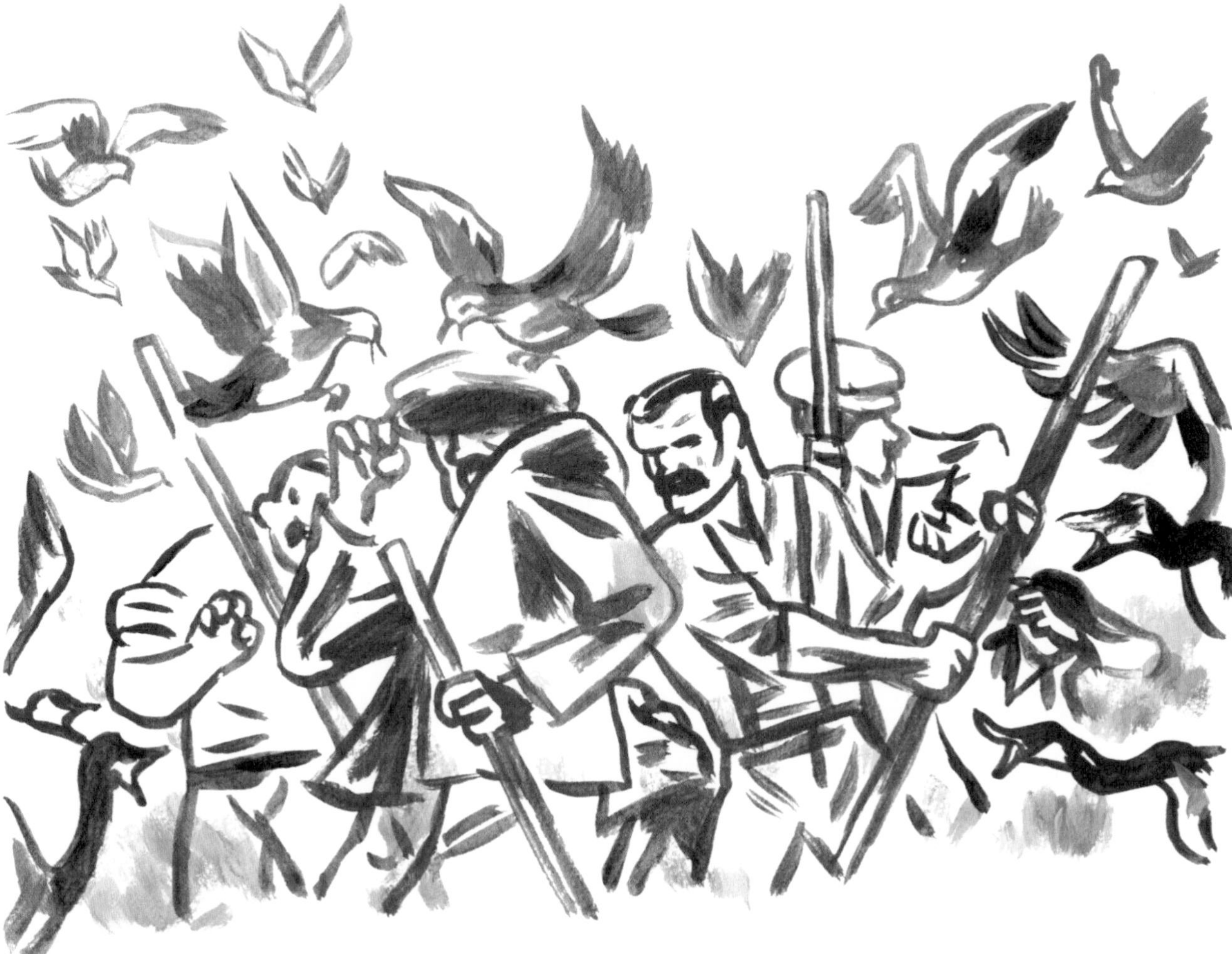

Then Snowball launched the second line of attack.

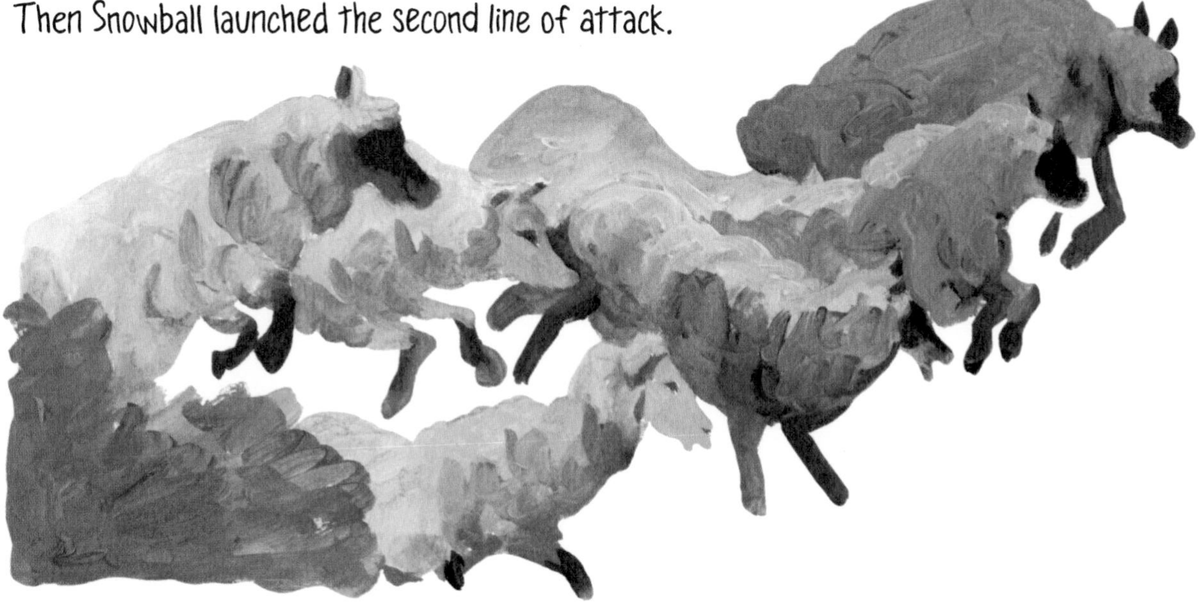

Suddenly a retreat.

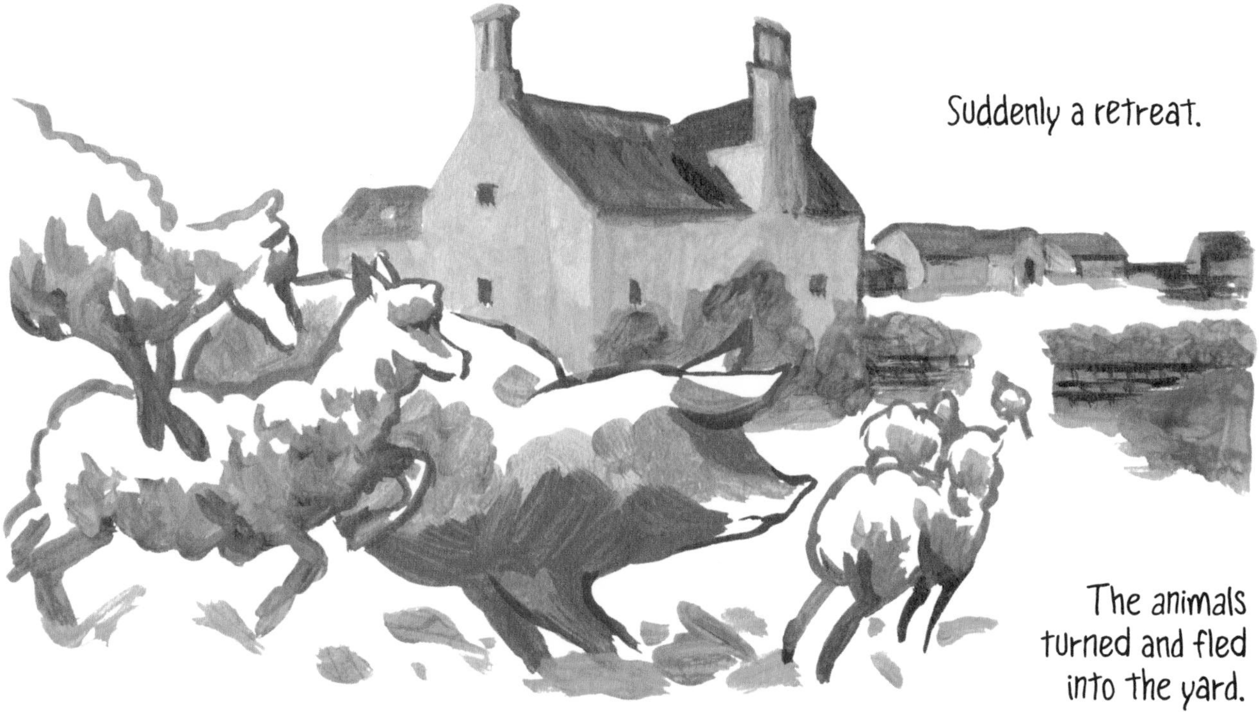

The animals turned and fled into the yard.

The men gave a shout of triumph. They saw their enemies in flight and rushed after them in disorder.

This was just what Snowball had intended.

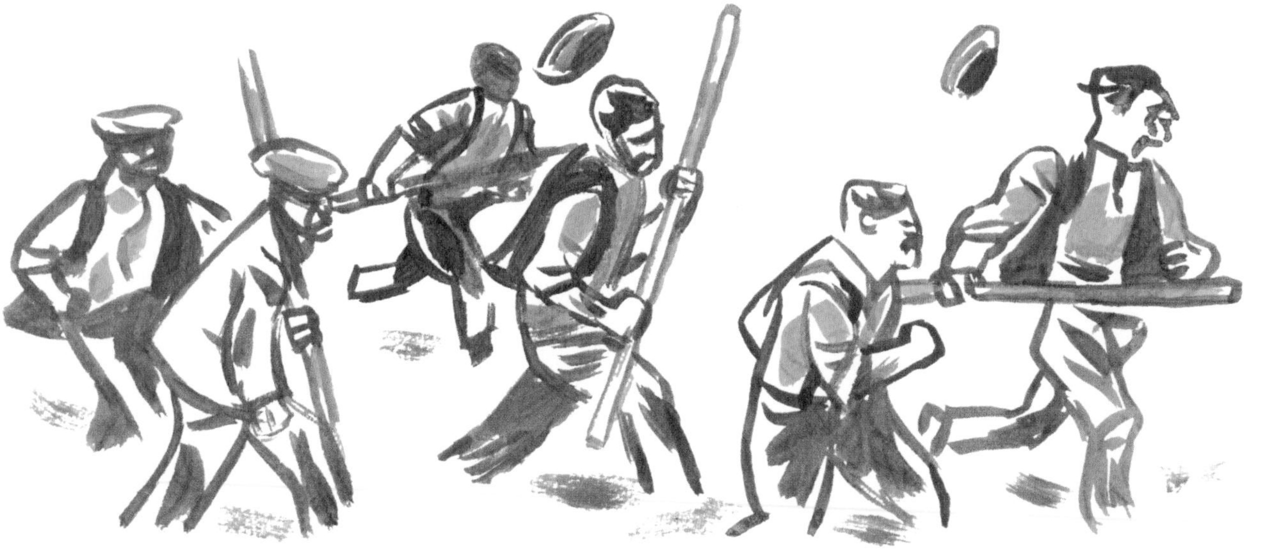

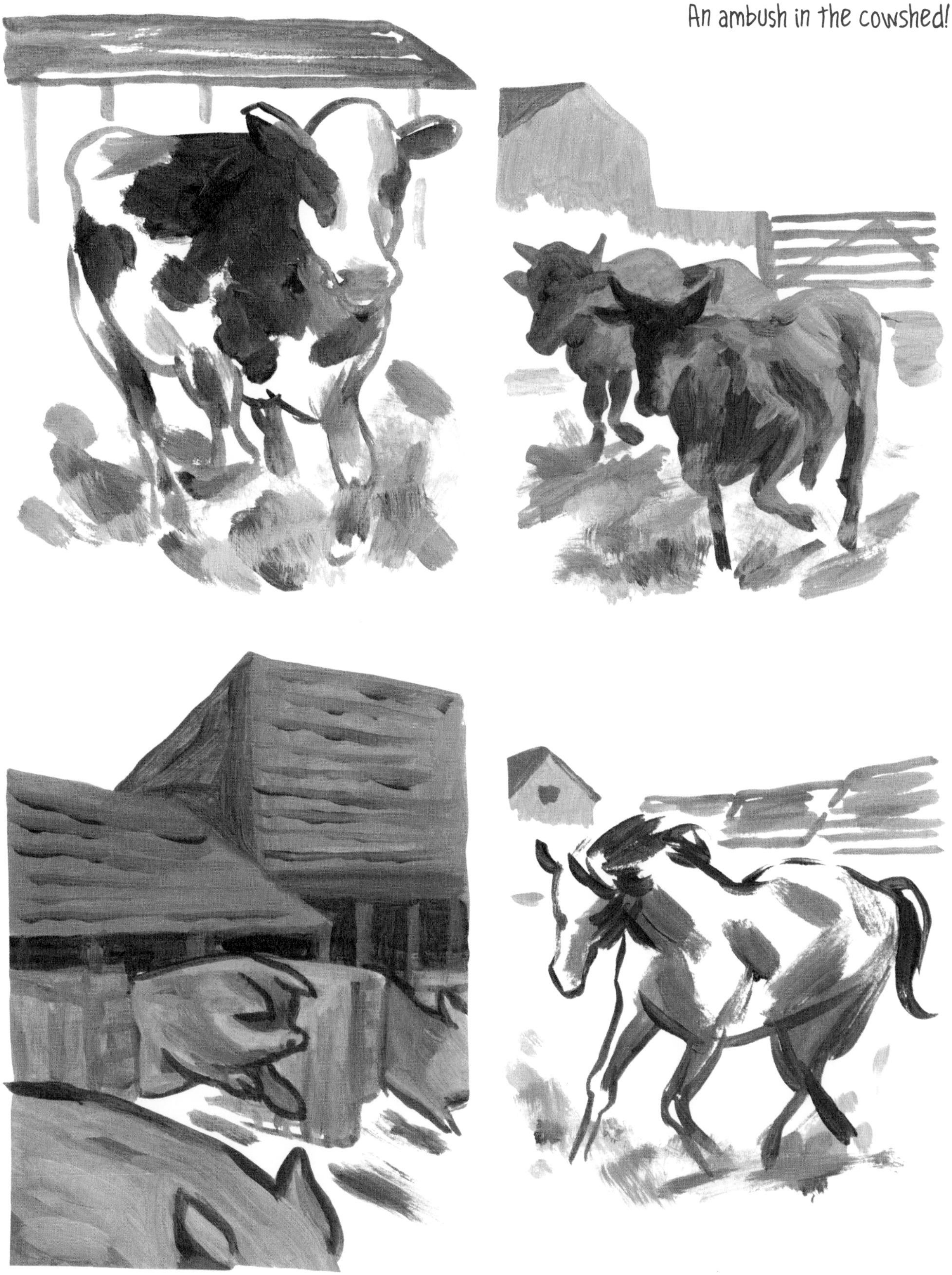
An ambush in the cowshed!

They were gored, kicked, bitten, trampled on. There was not an animal on the farm that did not take vengeance on them after his own fashion.

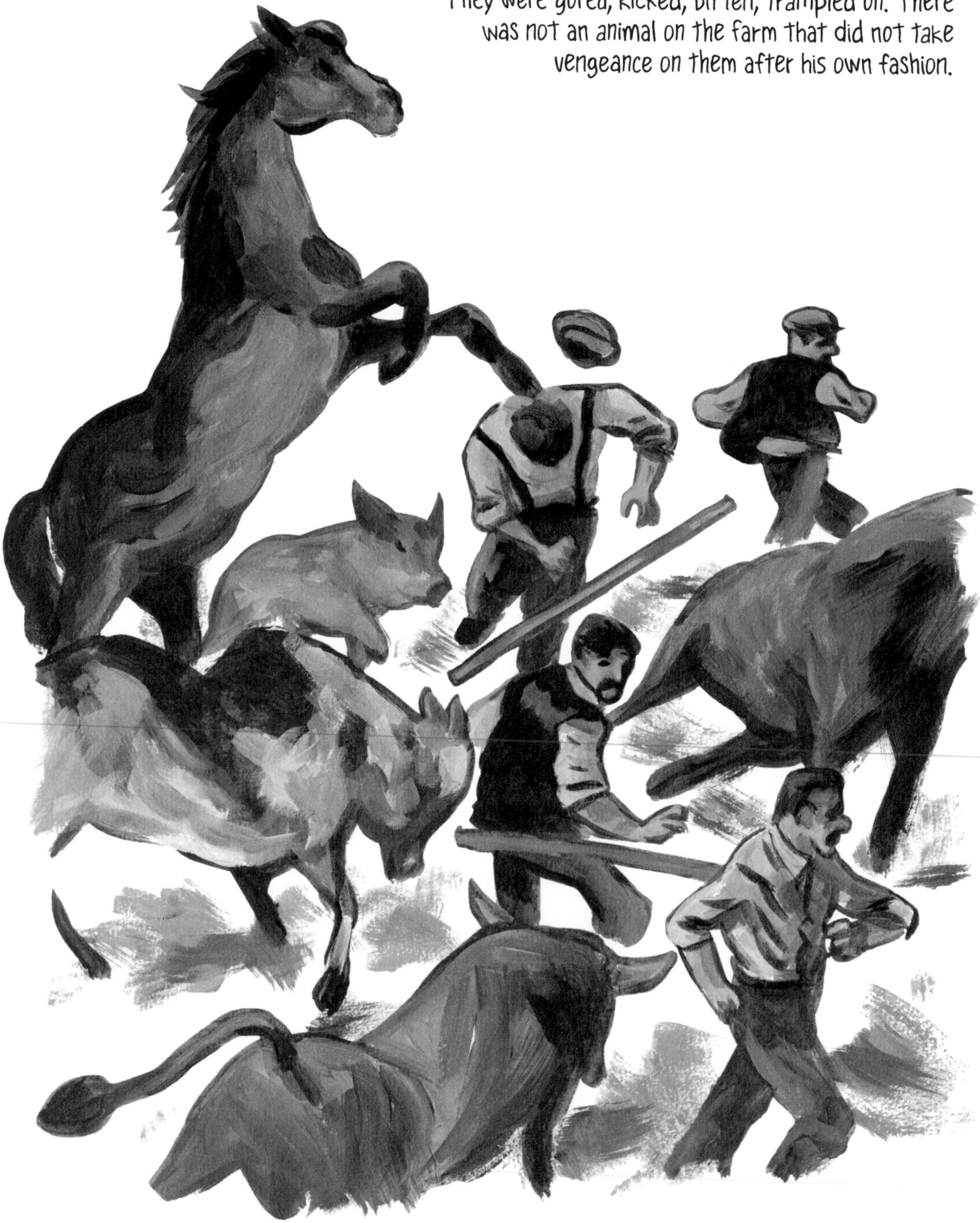

And so within five minutes of their invasion, they were in ignominious retreat.

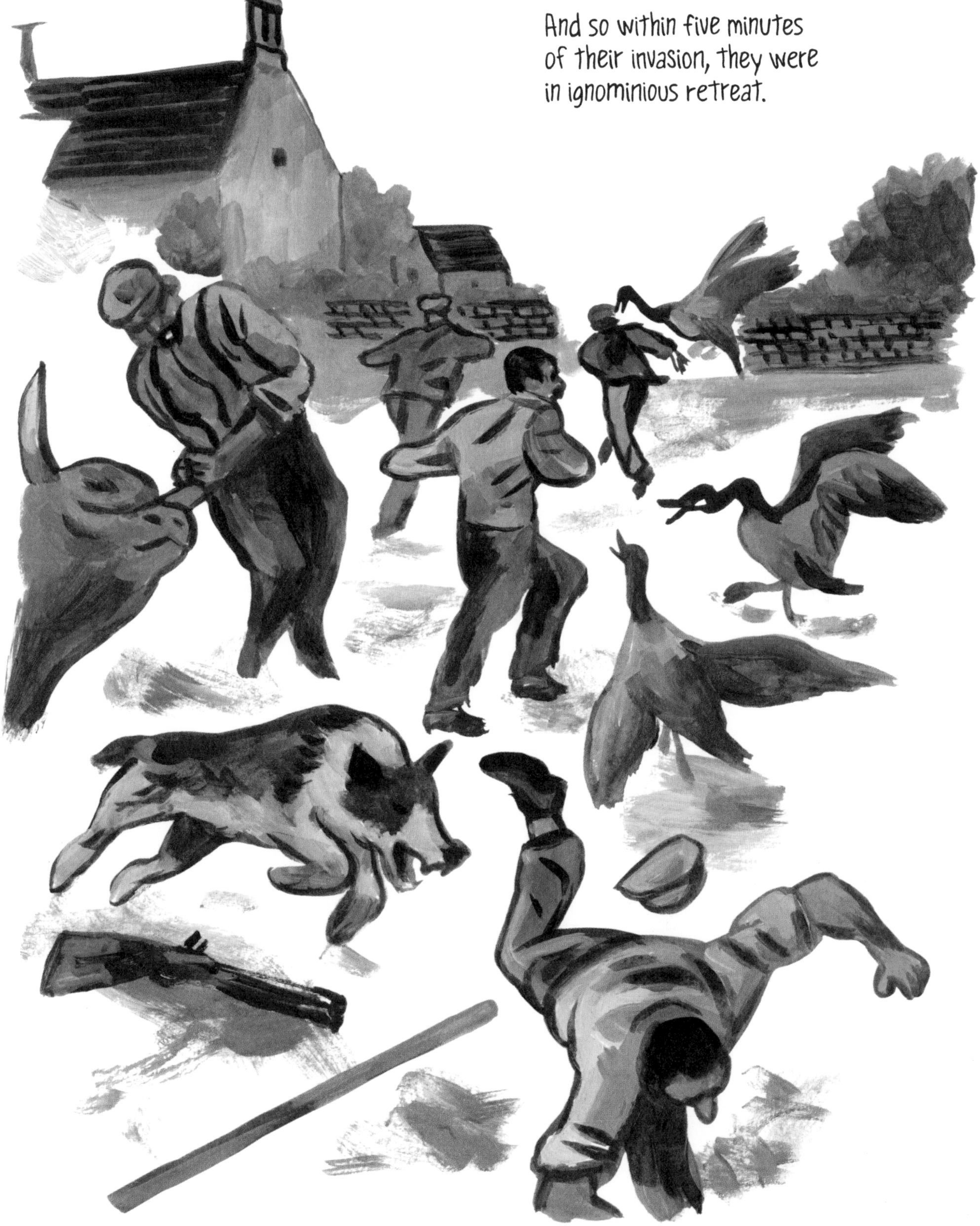

An impromptu celebration of the victory was held immediately. The flag was run up and "Beasts of England" was sung a number of times.

The sheep who had been killed was given a solemn funeral, and after much discussion, the battle was called the Battle of the Cowshed.

V

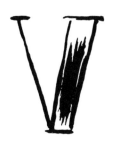

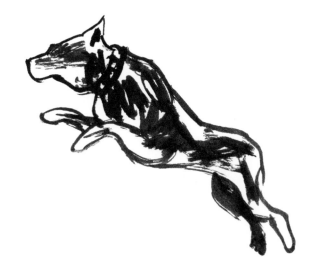

In January there came bitterly hard weather.

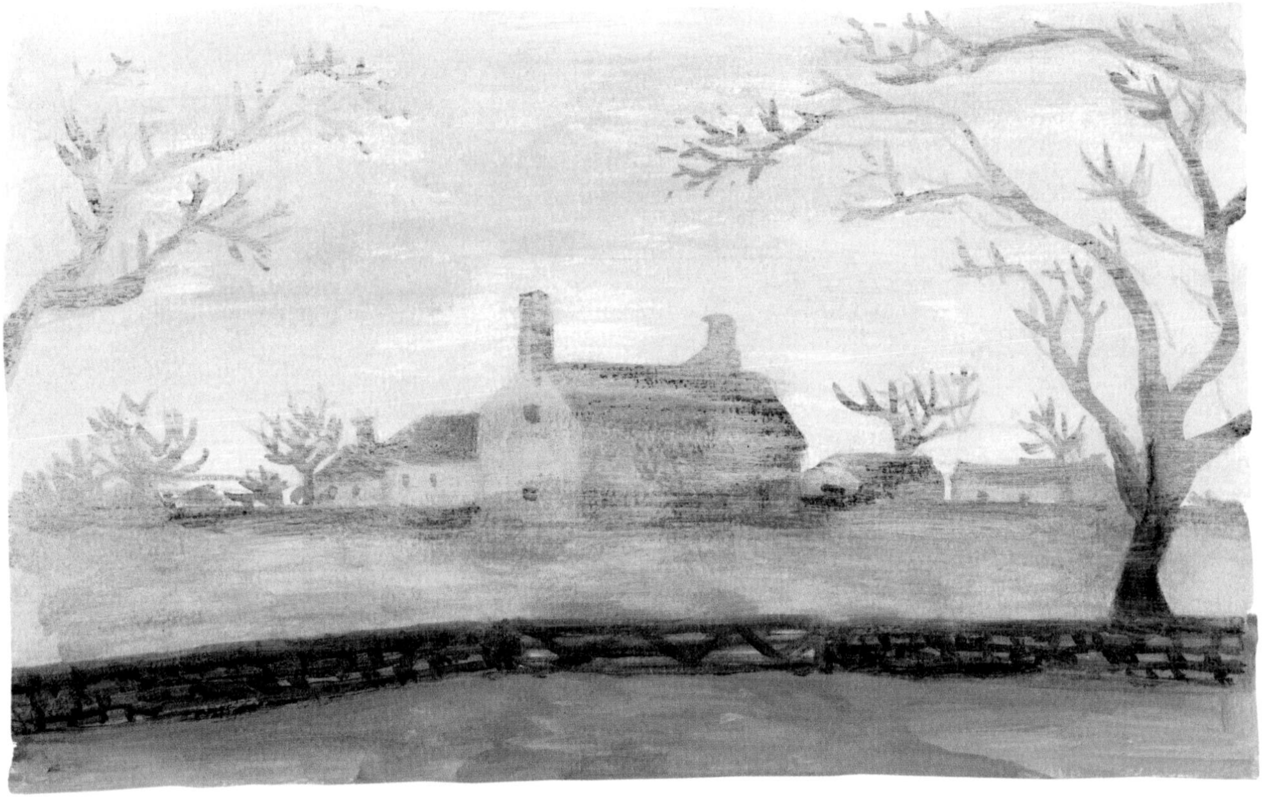

The earth was like iron, and nothing could be done in the fields.

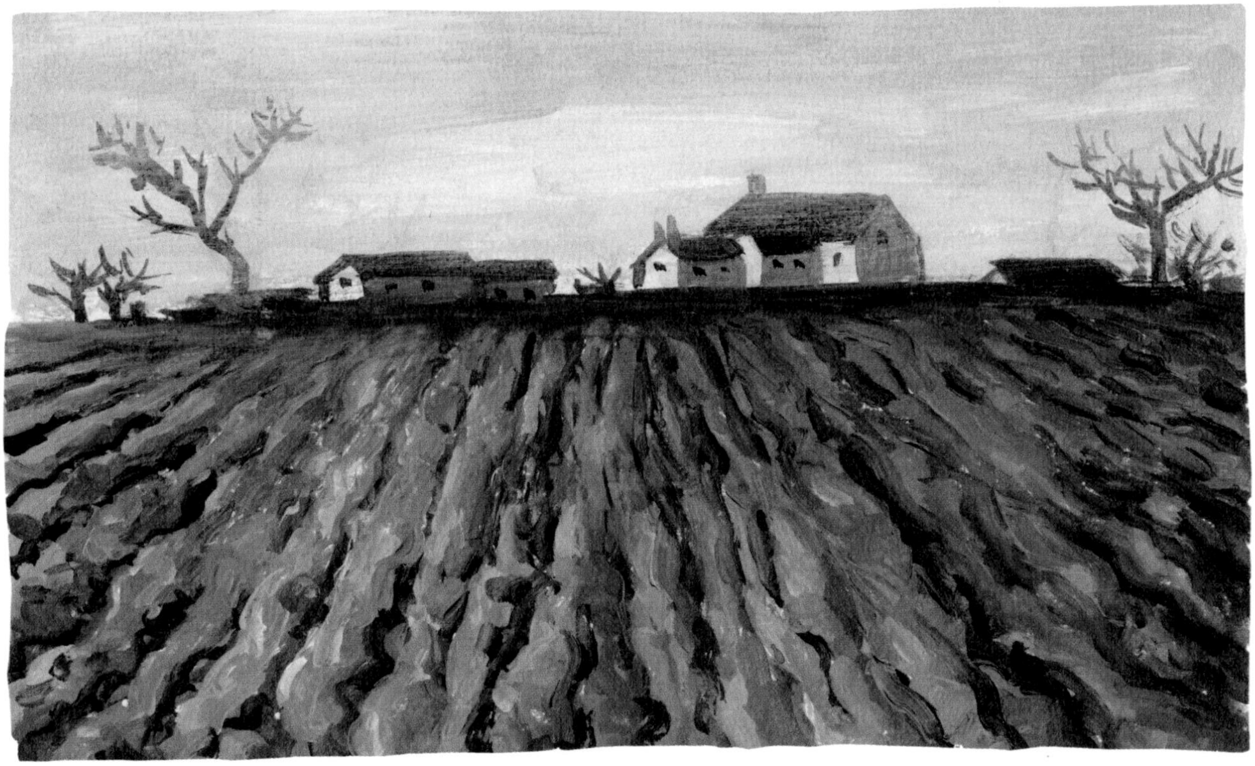

Many meetings were
held in the big barn.

The pigs occupied themselves
with planning out the work
of the coming season.

It had come to be accepted
that the pigs should decide all
questions of farm policy.

This would have
worked well enough
if it had not been
for the disputes
between Snowball
and Napoleon.
These two
disagreed at
every point.

Each had his own following and there were
some violent debates.

But none was so bitter as the one that took
place over the windmill.

In the long pasture, not far from the farm buildings, there was a small knoll which was the highest point on the farm.

After surveying the ground, Snowball declared that it was just the place for a windmill,

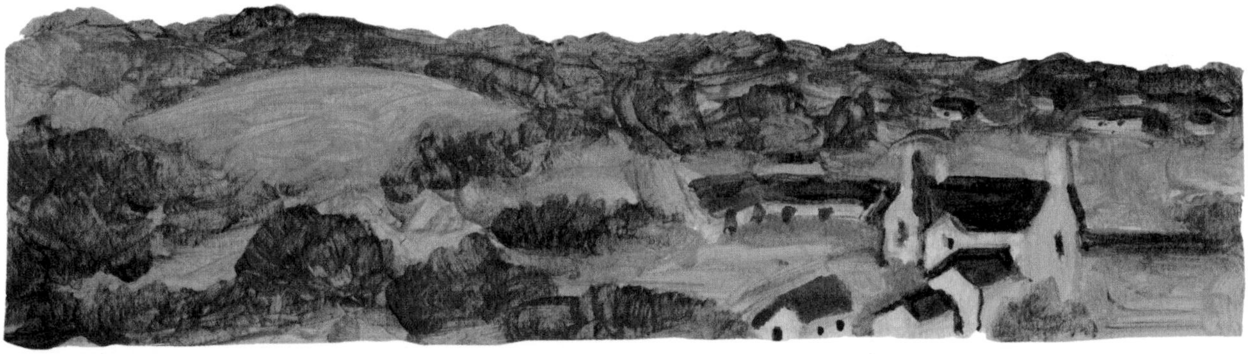

which could be made to operate a dynamo and supply the farm with electrical power.

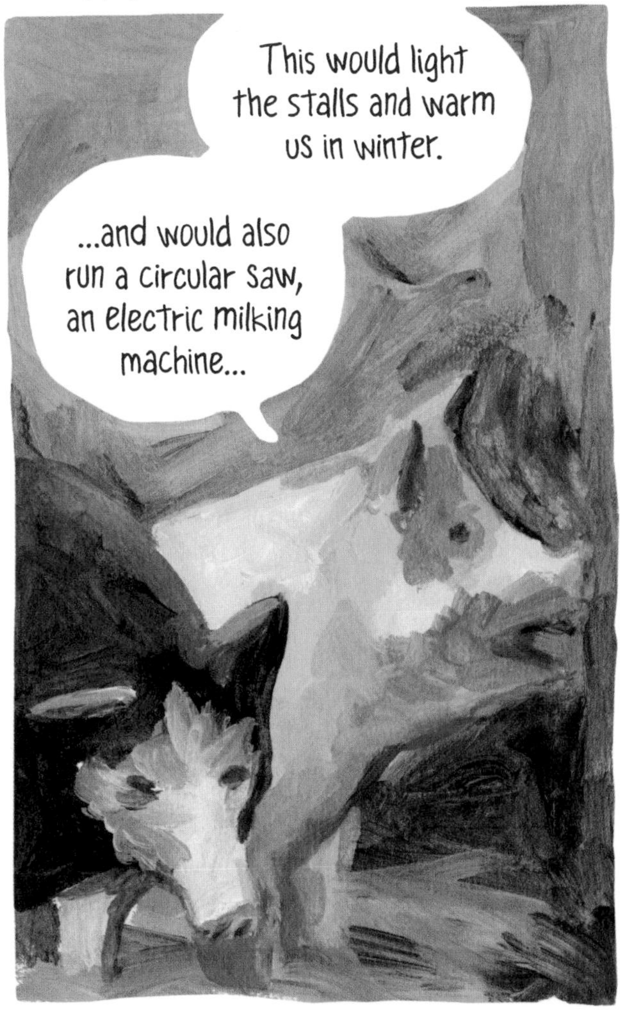
This would light the stalls and warm us in winter.
...and would also run a circular saw, an electric milking machine...

The animals listened in astonishment while Snowball conjured up pictures of fantastic machines which would do their work for them.

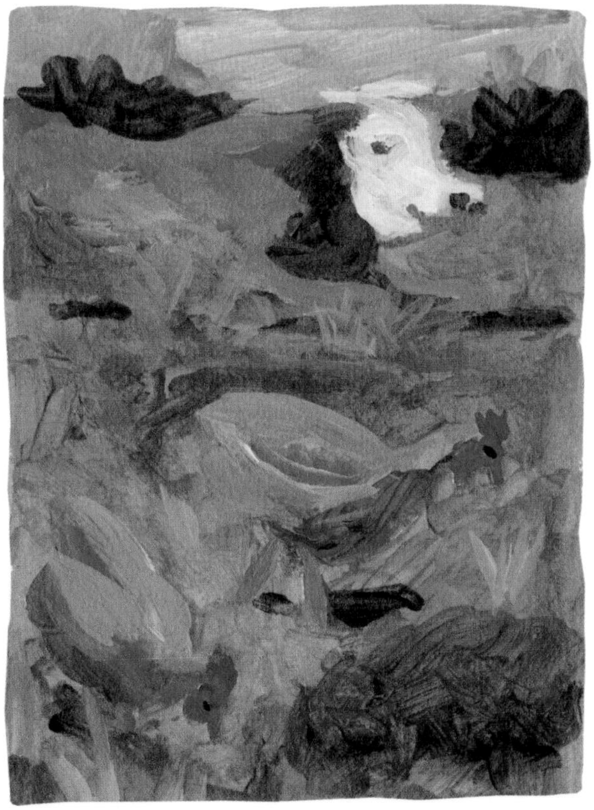

Snowball used as his study a shed which had once been used for incubators and had a smooth wooden floor, suitable for drawing on. He was closeted there for hours at a time.

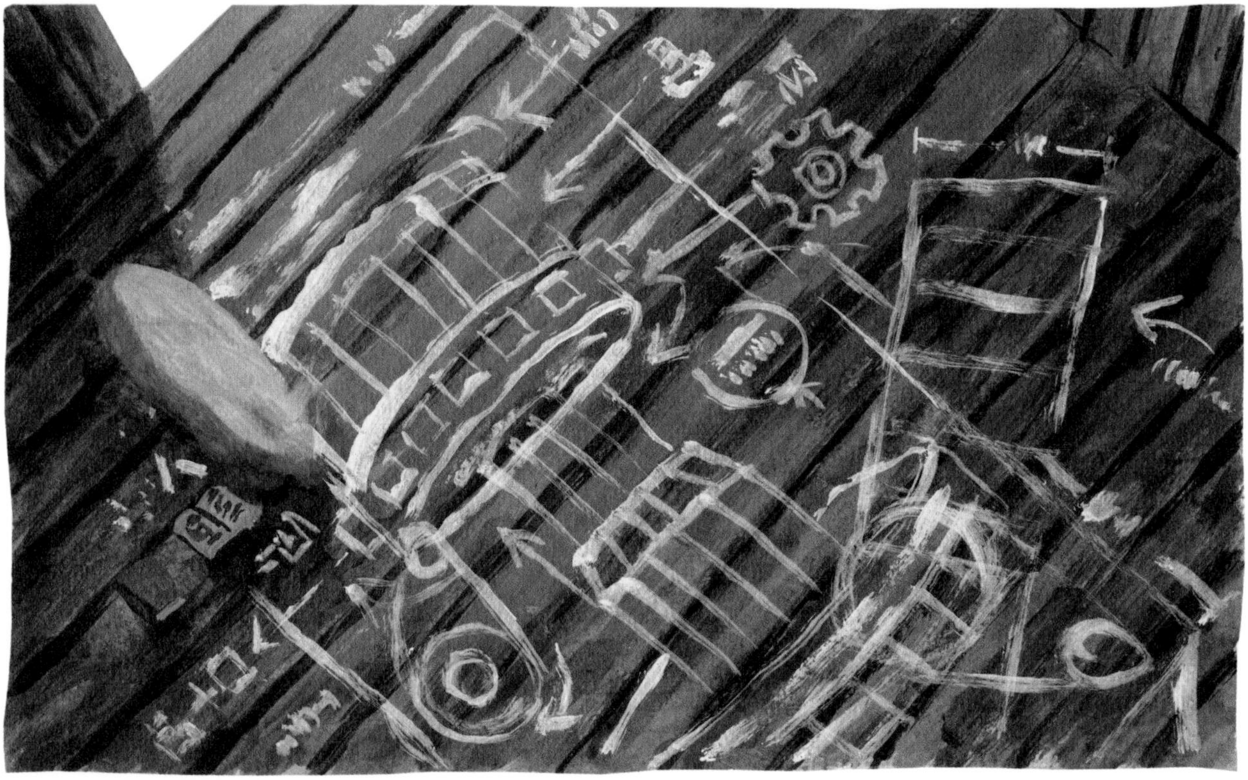

Gradually the plans grew into a complicated mass covering more than half the floor, which the other animals found completely unintelligible but very impressive. All of them came to look at Snowball's drawings at least once a day.

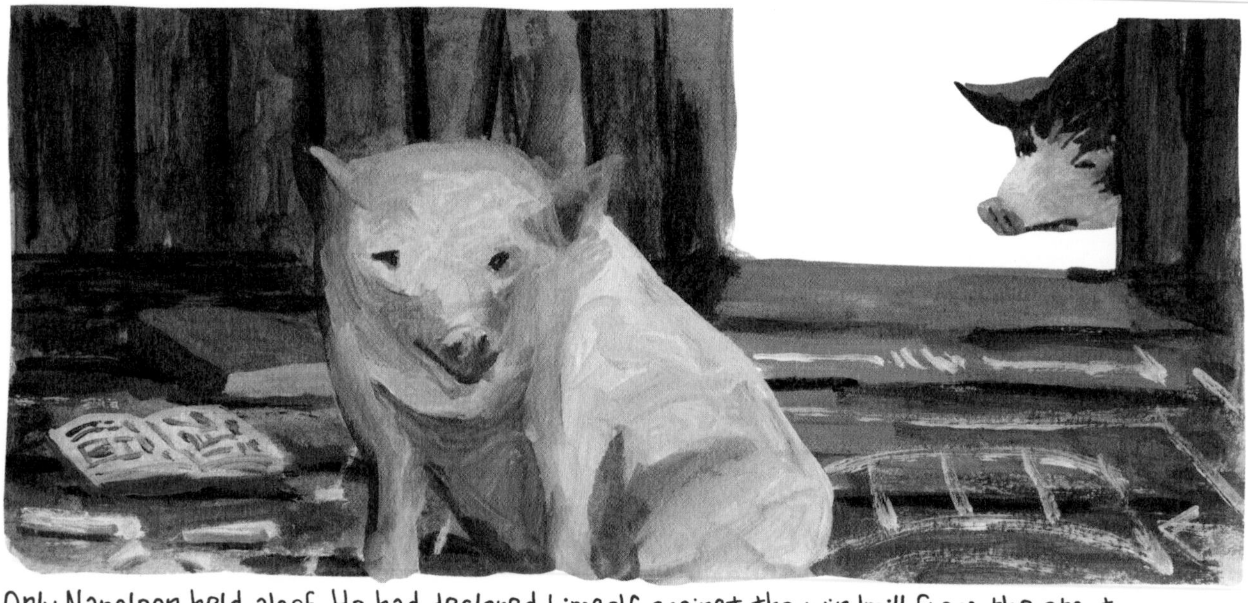

Only Napoleon held aloof. He had declared himself against the windmill from the start.

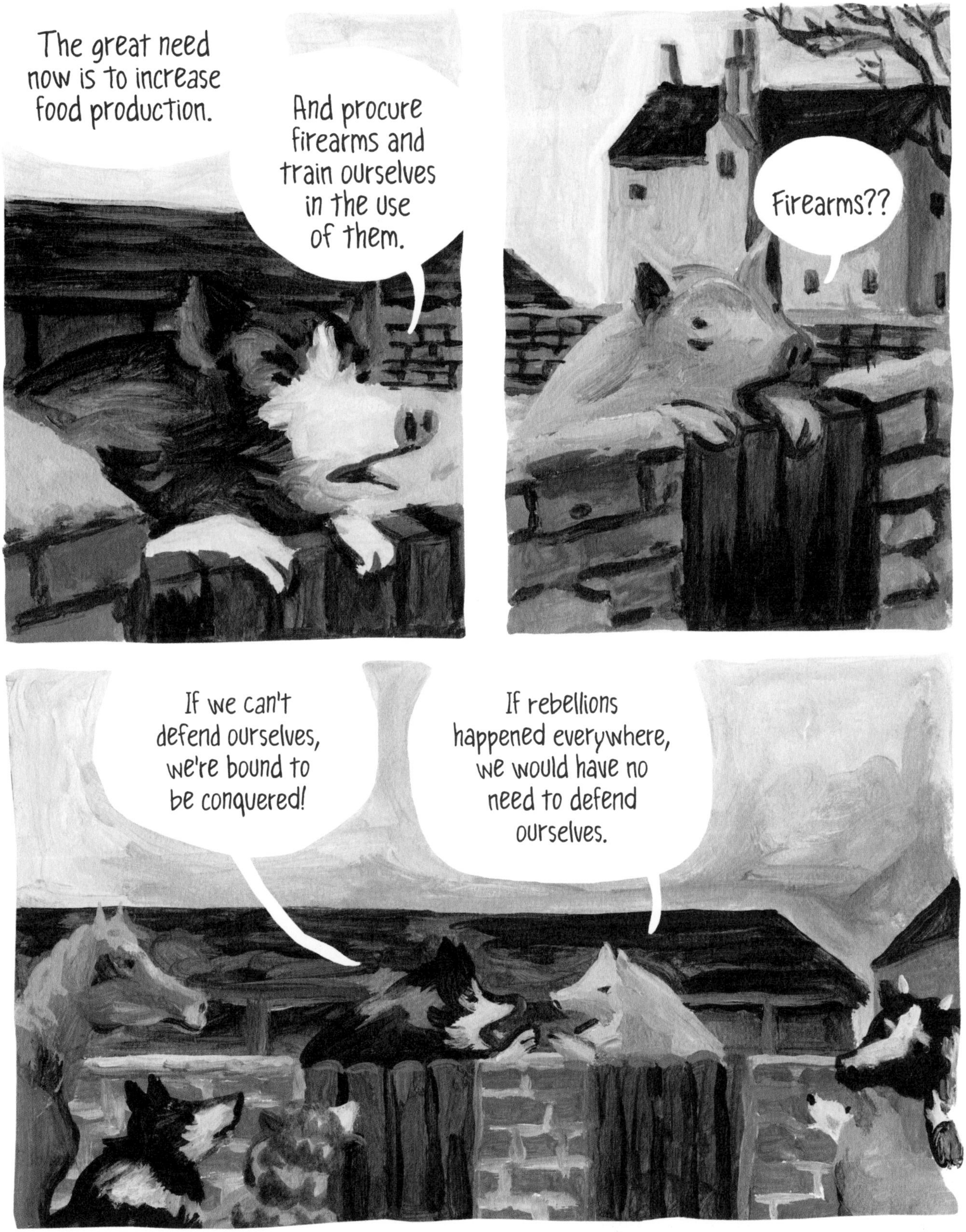
The great need now is to increase food production.
And procure firearms and train ourselves in the use of them.
Firearms??
If we can't defend ourselves, we're bound to be conquered!
If rebellions happened everywhere, we would have no need to defend ourselves.

The whole farm was deeply divided.

At last the day came when Snowball's plans were completed. At the Meeting on the following Sunday the question of whether or not to begin work on the windmill was to be put to the vote.

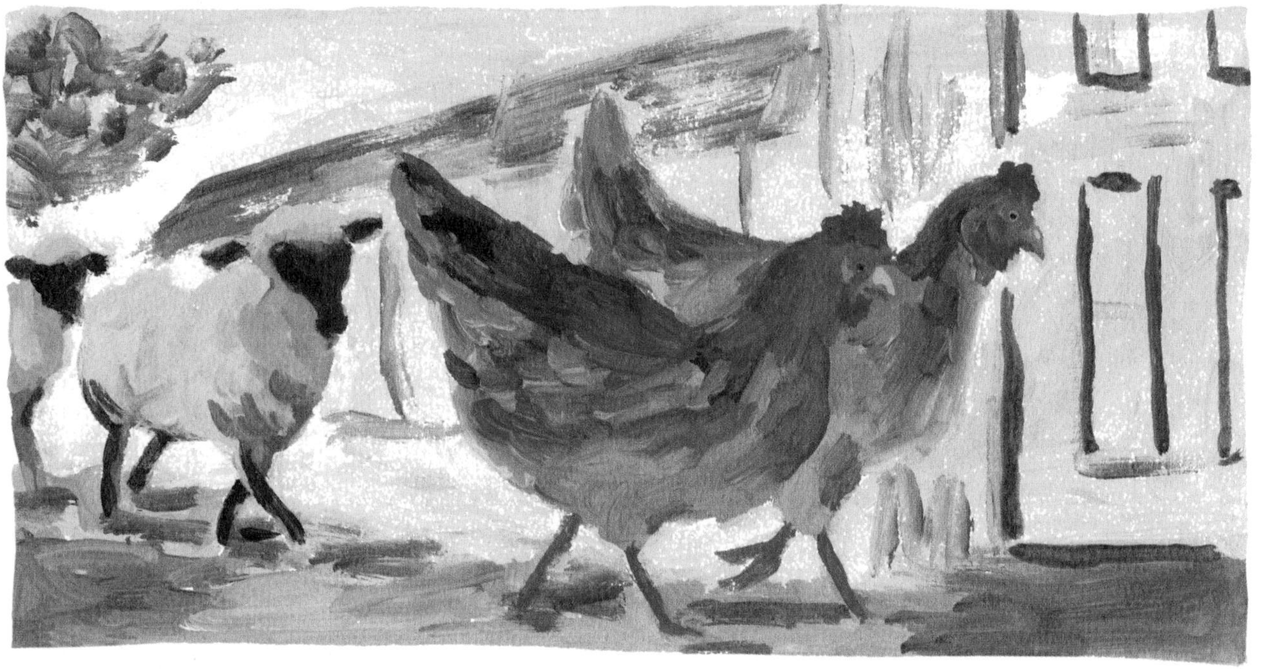

Snowball stood up and, though occasionally interrupted by bleating from the sheep, set forth his reasons for advocating the building of the windmill. Then Napoleon stood up to reply.

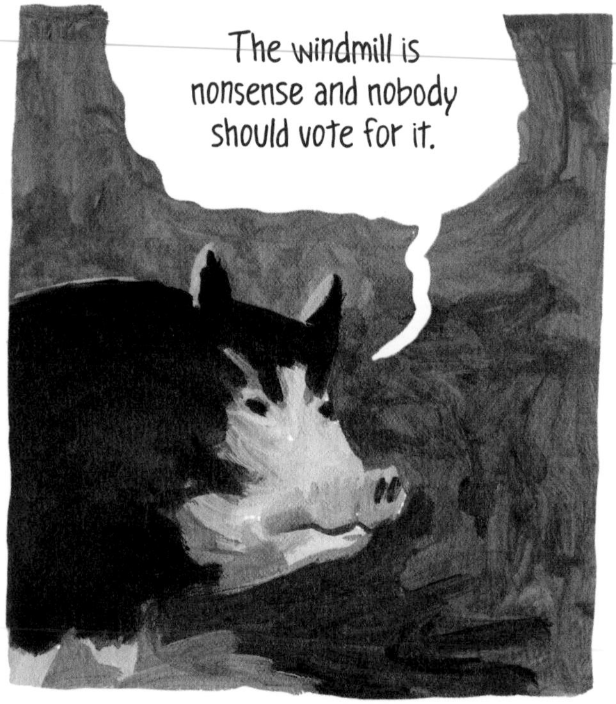
The windmill is nonsense and nobody should vote for it.

He had spoken for barely thirty seconds, and seemed almost indifferent as to the effect he produced.

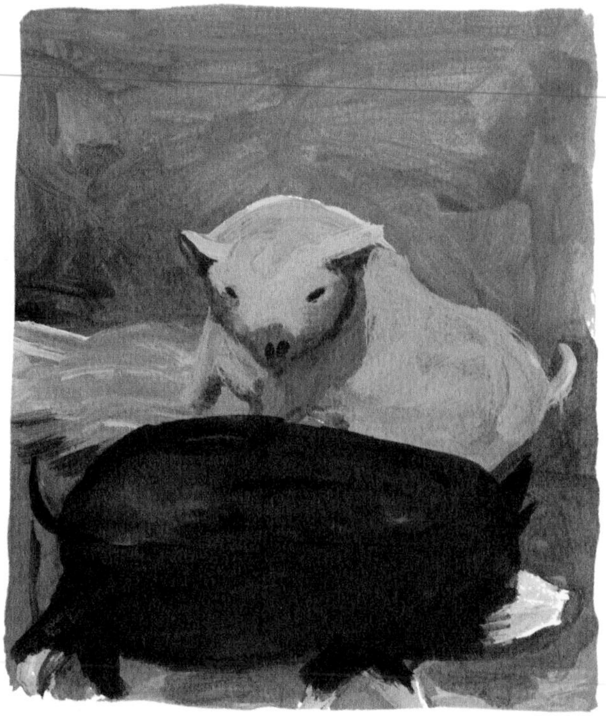

Snowball broke into a passionate appeal in favour of the windmill, and painted a picture of Animal Farm as it might be when sordid labour was lifted from the animals' backs.

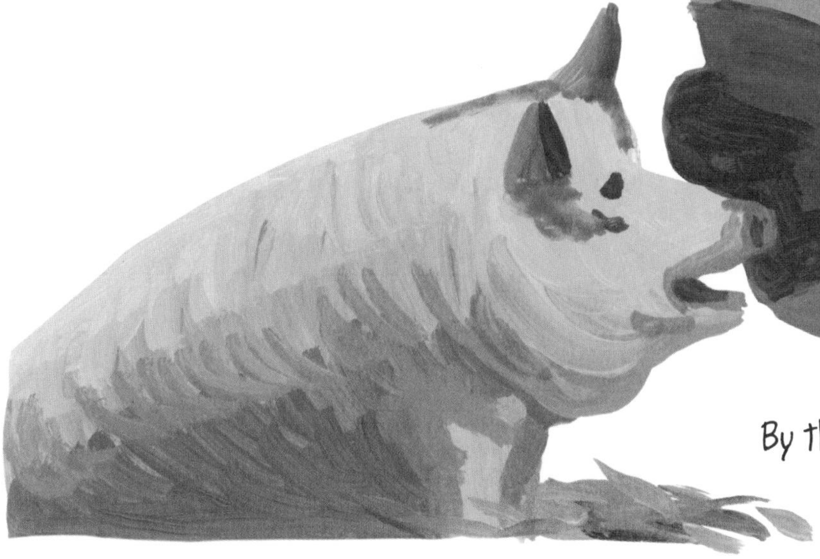

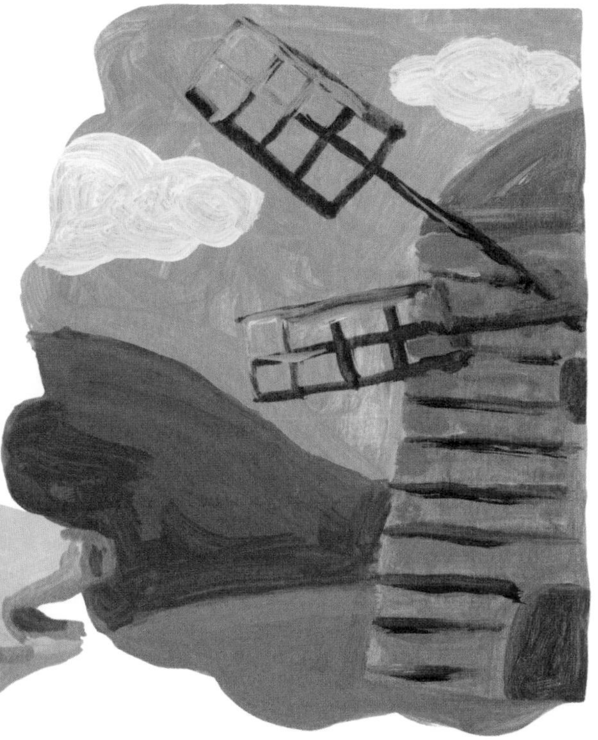

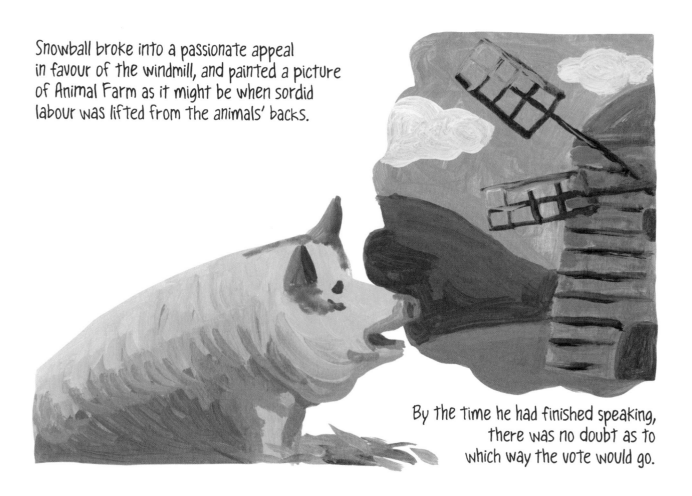

By the time he had finished speaking, there was no doubt as to which way the vote would go.

But just at this moment Napoleon uttered a whimper no one had ever heard him utter before.

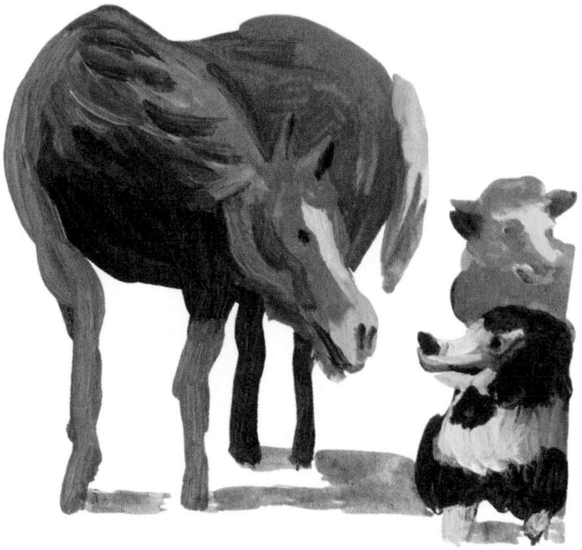

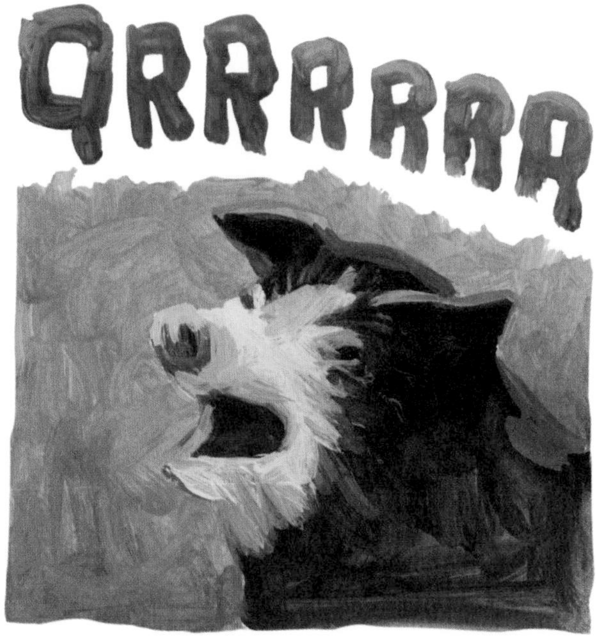
QRRRRRR

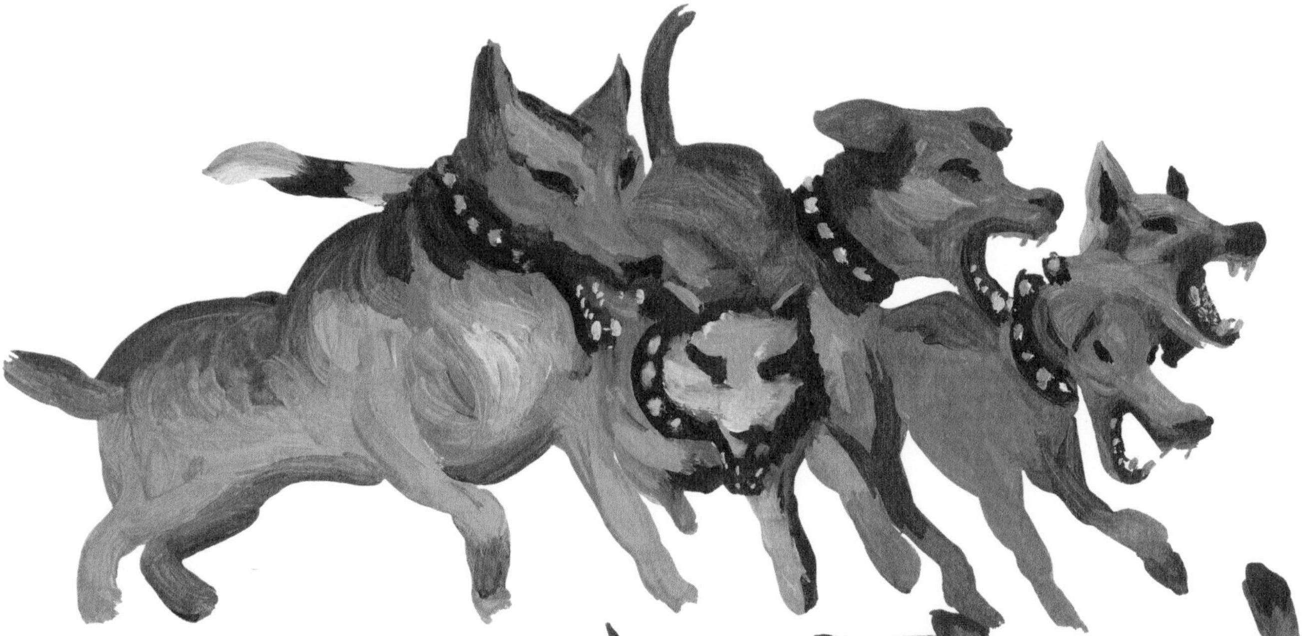

At this there was a terrible baying sound outside, and nine enormous dogs came bounding into the barn.

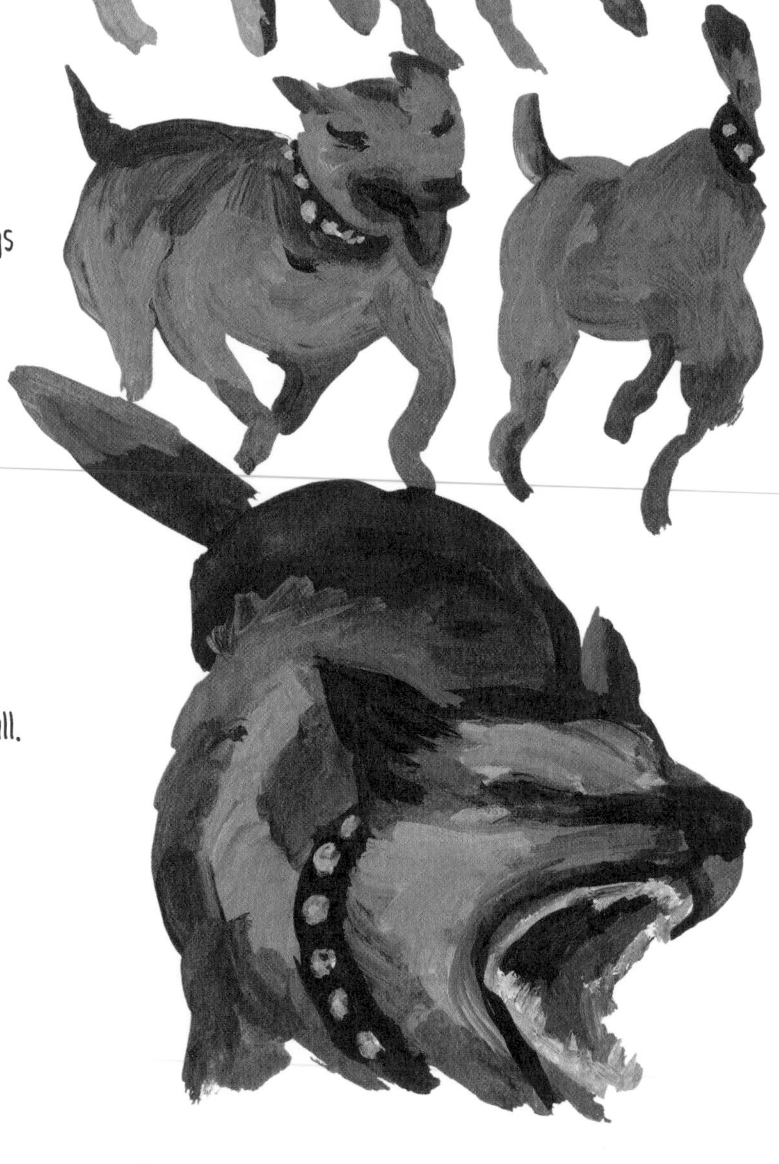

They dashed straight for Snowball.

He sprang from his place just in time
to escape their snapping jaws.

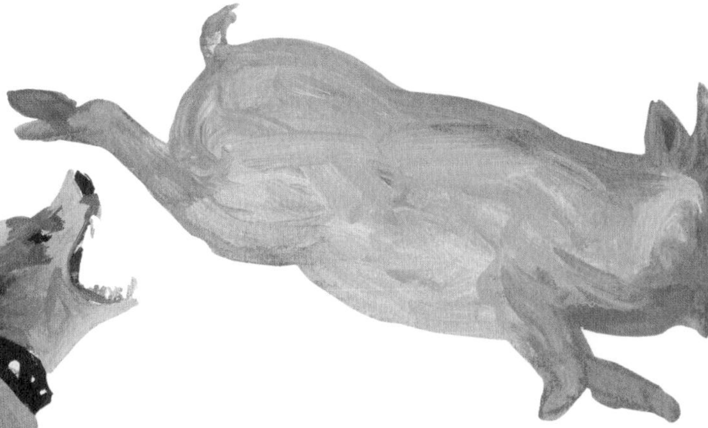

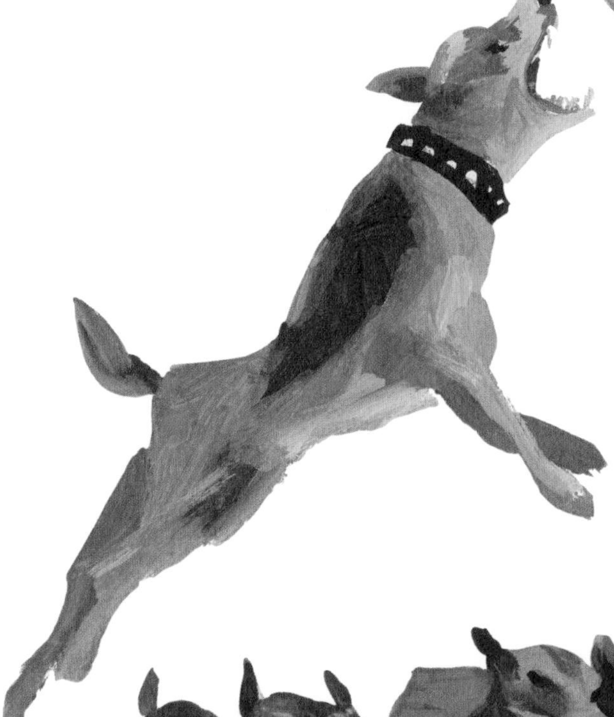

In a moment he was
out of the door and
they were after him.

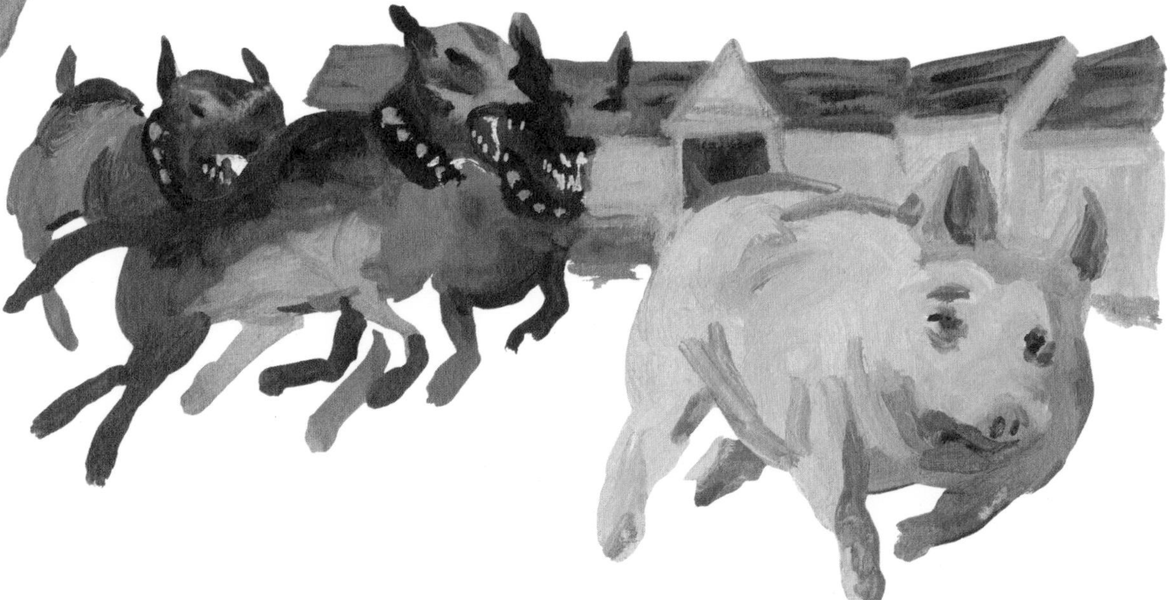

Too amazed and frightened to speak, all the animals crowded through the door to watch the chase. Snowball was racing across the long pasture, slipped through a hole in the hedge, and was seen no more.

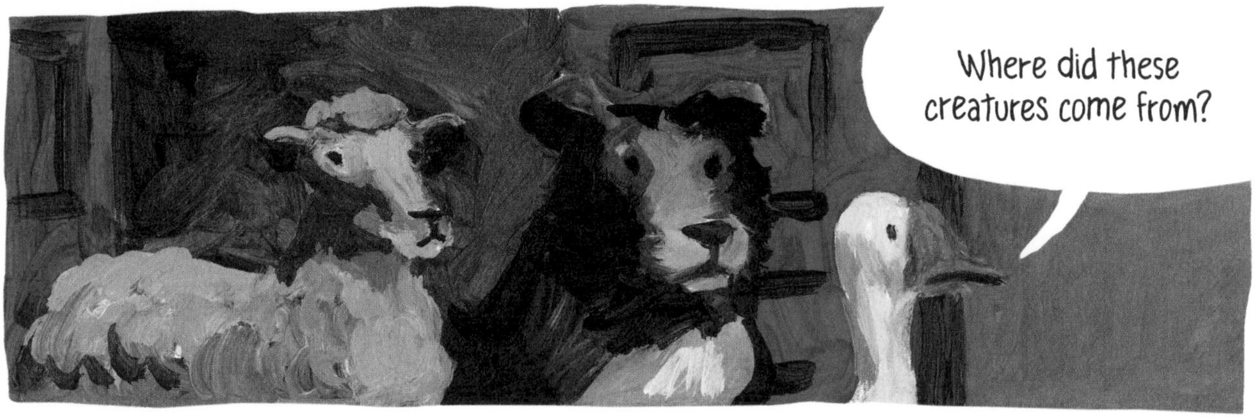
Where did these creatures come from?

The problem was soon solved: they were the puppies whom Napoleon had taken away from their mothers and reared privately.

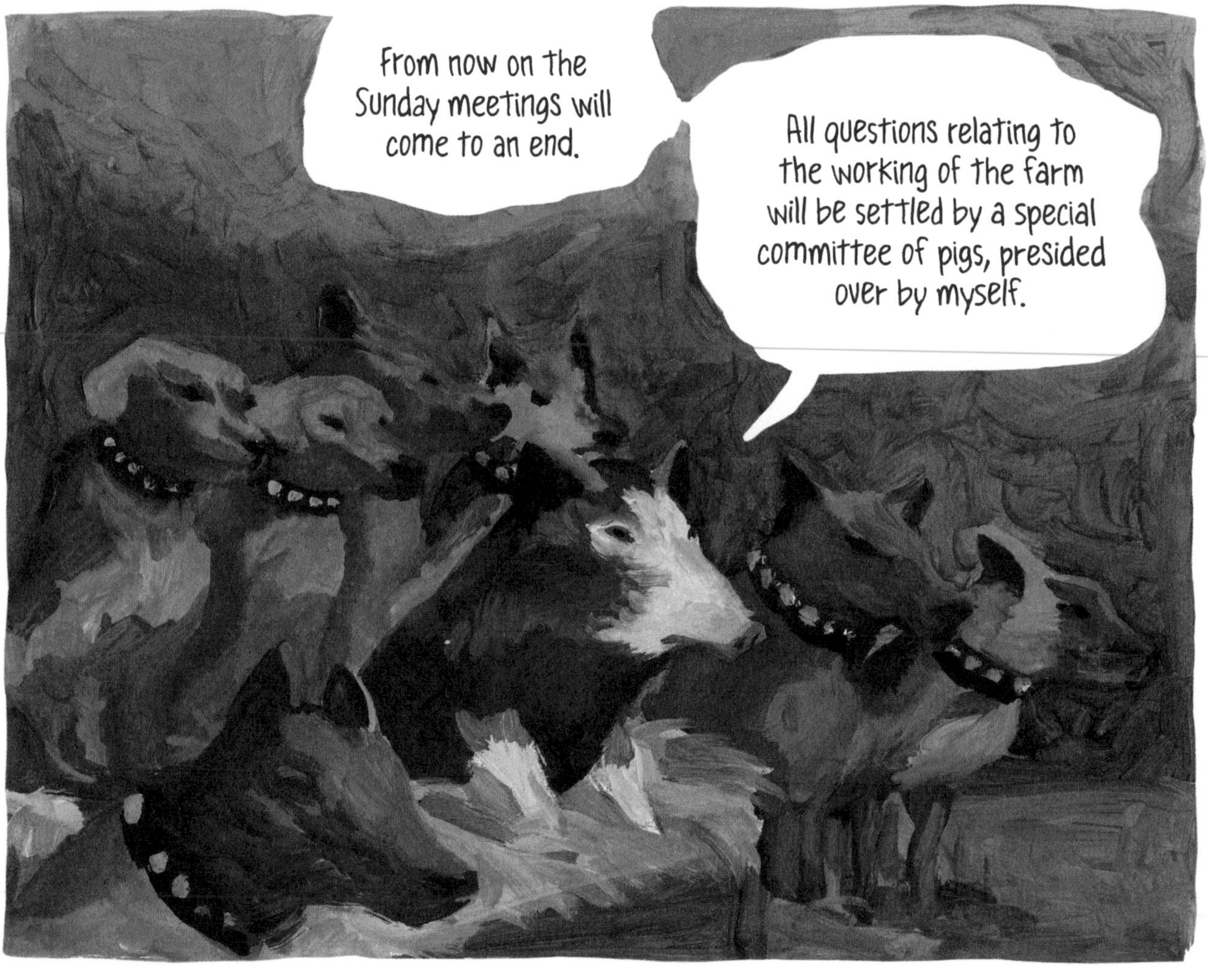
From now on the Sunday meetings will come to an end.
All questions relating to the working of the farm will be settled by a special committee of pigs, presided over by myself.

Afterwards Squealer was sent round the farm to explain the new arrangement to the others.

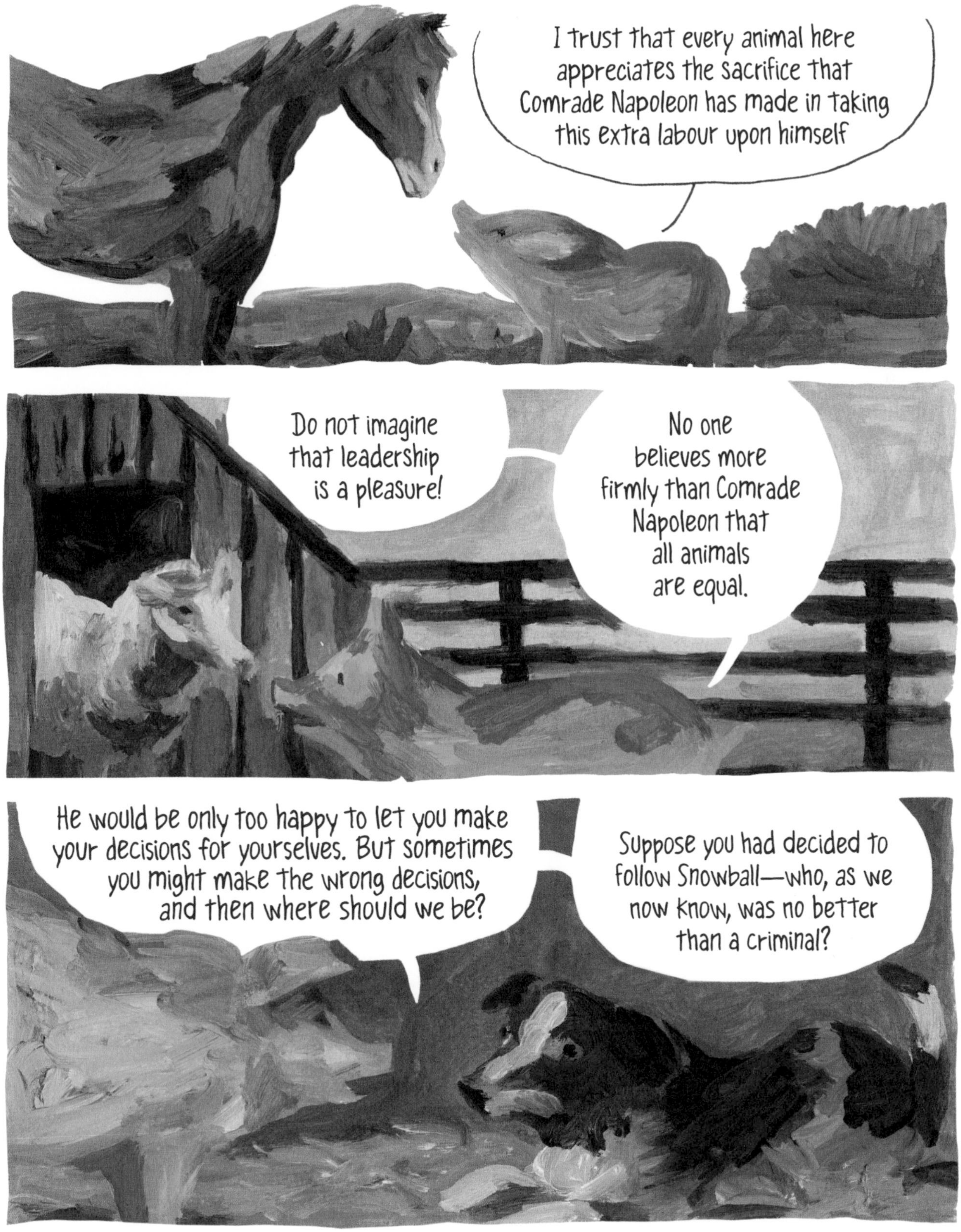
I trust that every animal here appreciates the sacrifice that Comrade Napoleon has made in taking this extra labour upon himself
Do not imagine that leadership is a pleasure!
No one believes more firmly than Comrade Napoleon that all animals are equal.
He would be only too happy to let you make your decisions for yourselves. But sometimes you might make the wrong decisions, and then where should we be?
Suppose you had decided to follow Snowball—who, as we now know, was no better than a criminal?

So every Sunday morning the animals assembled in the big barn to receive their orders for the week.

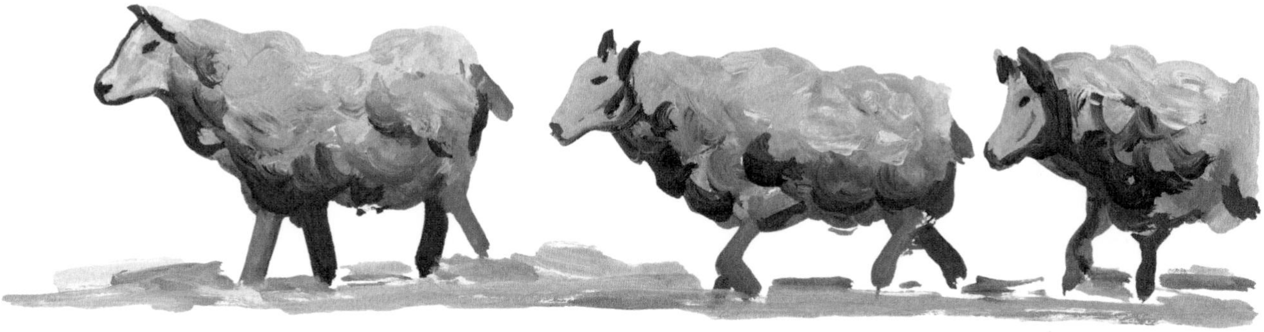

The skull of old Major had been disinterred from the orchard. After the hoisting of the flag, the animals were required to file past the skull in a reverent manner before entering the barn.

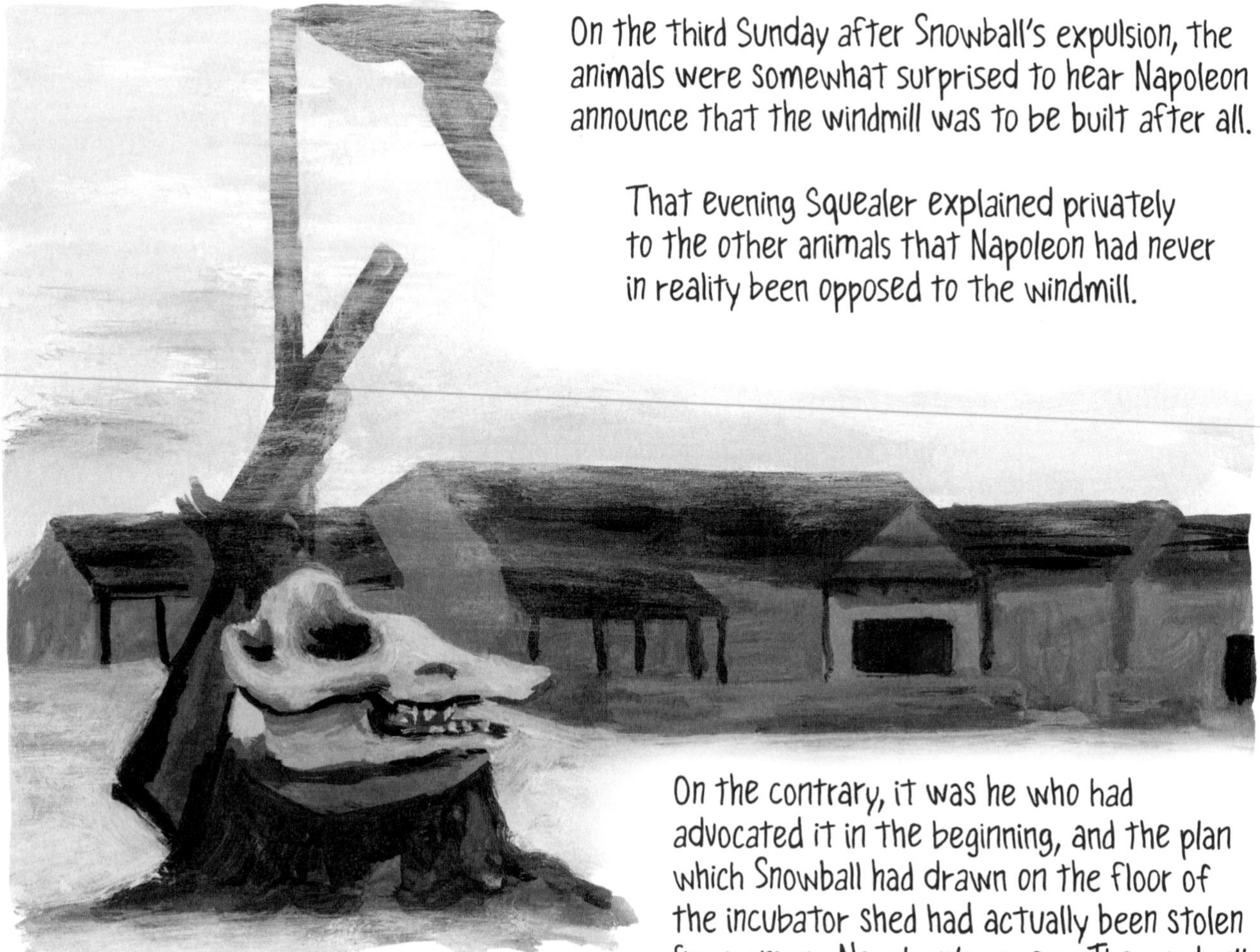

On the third Sunday after Snowball's expulsion, the animals were somewhat surprised to hear Napoleon announce that the windmill was to be built after all.

That evening Squealer explained privately to the other animals that Napoleon had never in reality been opposed to the windmill.

On the contrary, it was he who had advocated it in the beginning, and the plan which Snowball had drawn on the floor of the incubator shed had actually been stolen from among Napoleon's papers. The windmill was, in fact, Napoleon's own creation.

VI

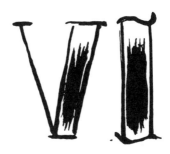

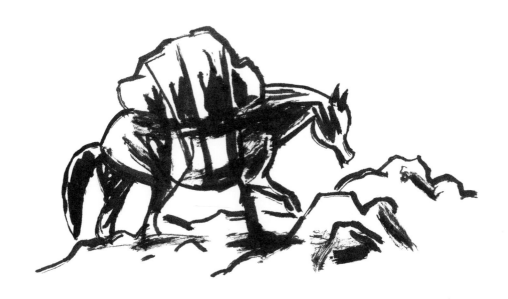

All that year, the animals worked like slaves. But they were happy in their work. They worked a sixty-hour week, and in August Napoleon announced that there would be work on Sunday afternoons as well. This work was strictly voluntary, but any animal who absented himself would have his rations reduced by half.

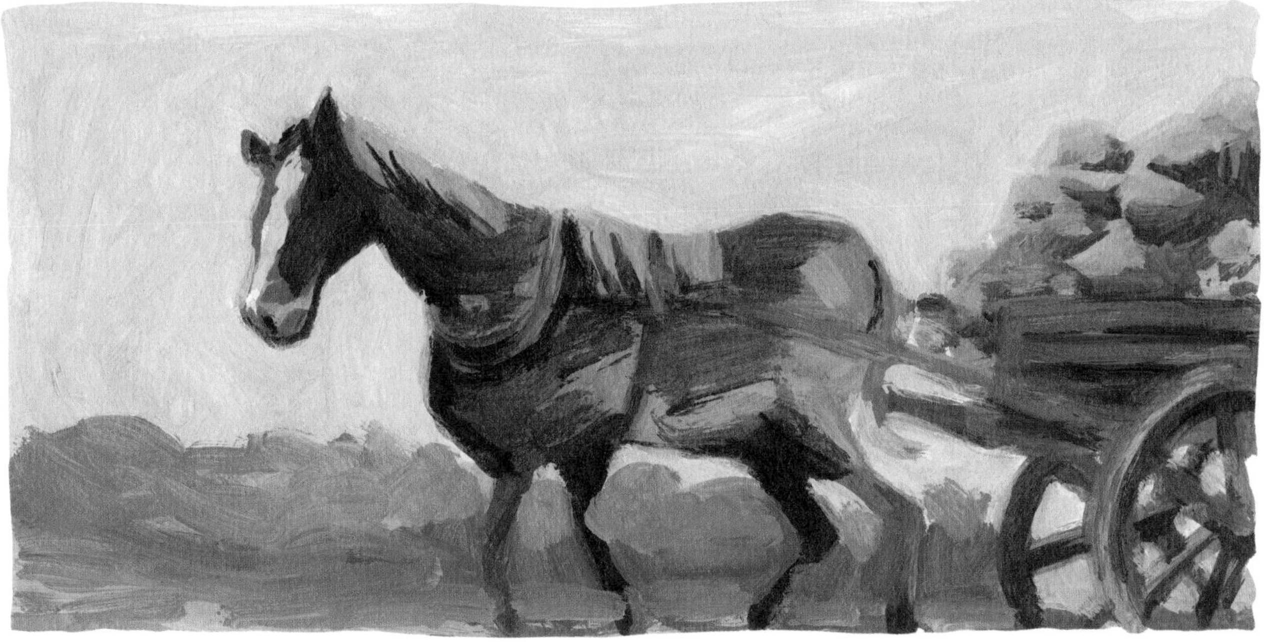

Even so, it was found necessary to leave certain tasks undone. The harvest was a little less successful than in the previous year, and the ploughing had not been completed early enough.

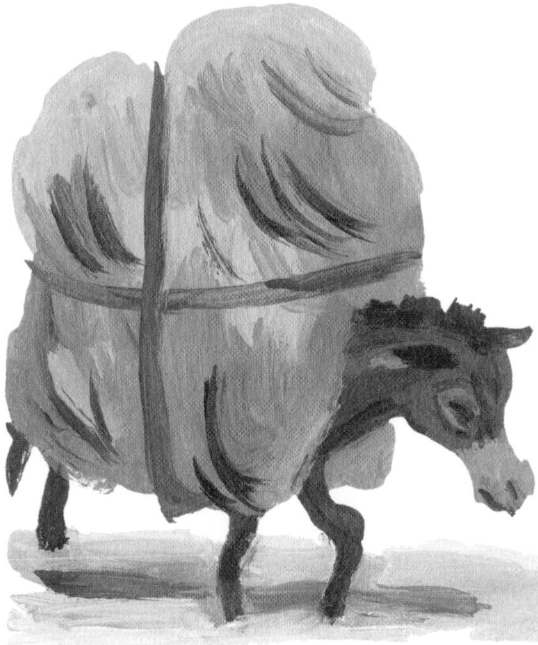

It was possible to foresee that the coming winter would be a hard one.

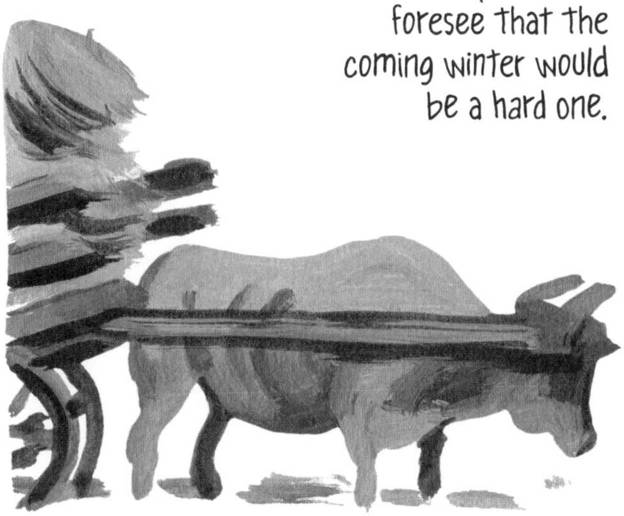

The windmill presented unexpected difficulties.

There was plenty of sand and cement had been found in one of the outhouses, so that all the materials for building were at hand.

But how to break up the stone into pieces of suitable size?

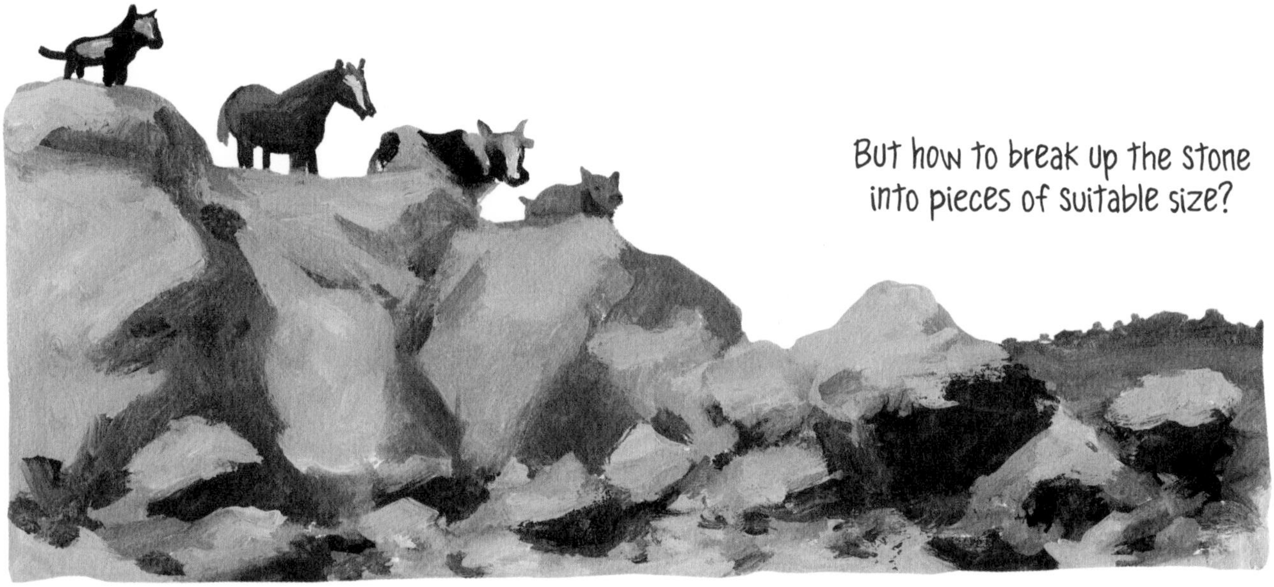

Only after weeks of vain effort did the right idea occur to somebody — namely, to utilise the force of gravity.

Nothing could have been achieved without Boxer.

Huge boulders were dragged to the top of the quarry and toppled over the edge to shatter to pieces.

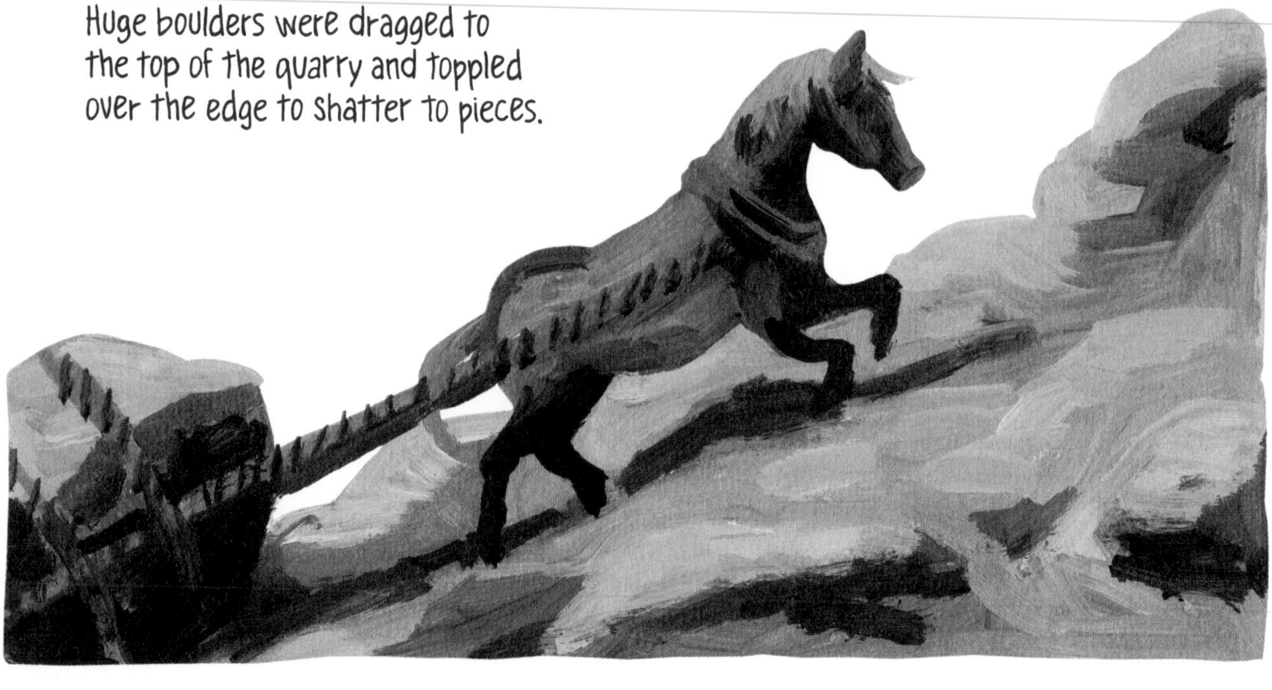

By late summer a sufficient store of stone had accumulated. Nevertheless, as the summer wore on, various unforeseen shortages began to make themselves felt. There was need of paraffin oil, nails, the machinery for the windmill.

Napoleon announced a new policy—Animal Farm would engage in trade with the neighbouring farms: not, of course, for any commercial purpose, with a solicitor as intermediary.

The animals felt a vague uneasiness and watched his coming and going with a kind of dread.

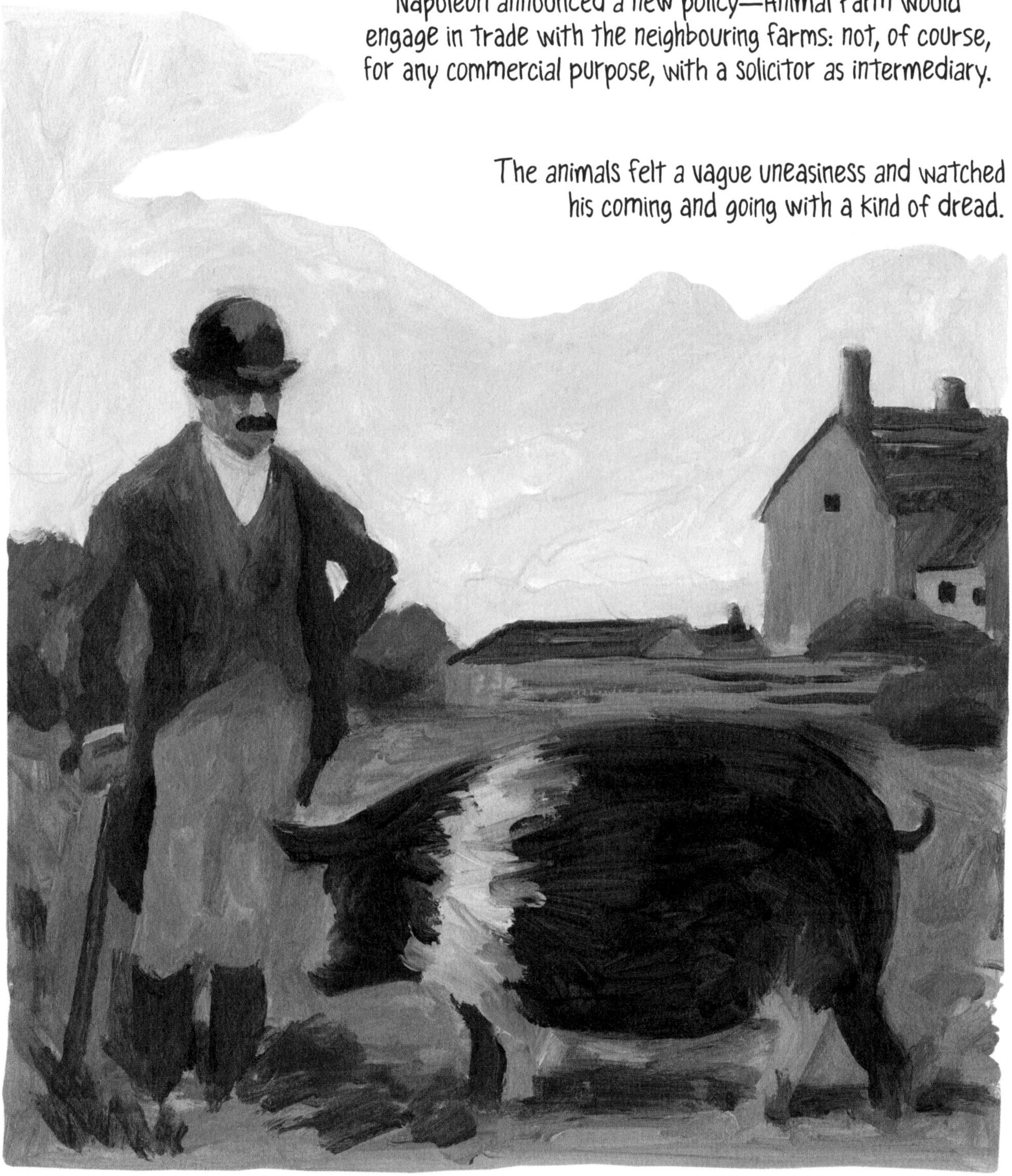

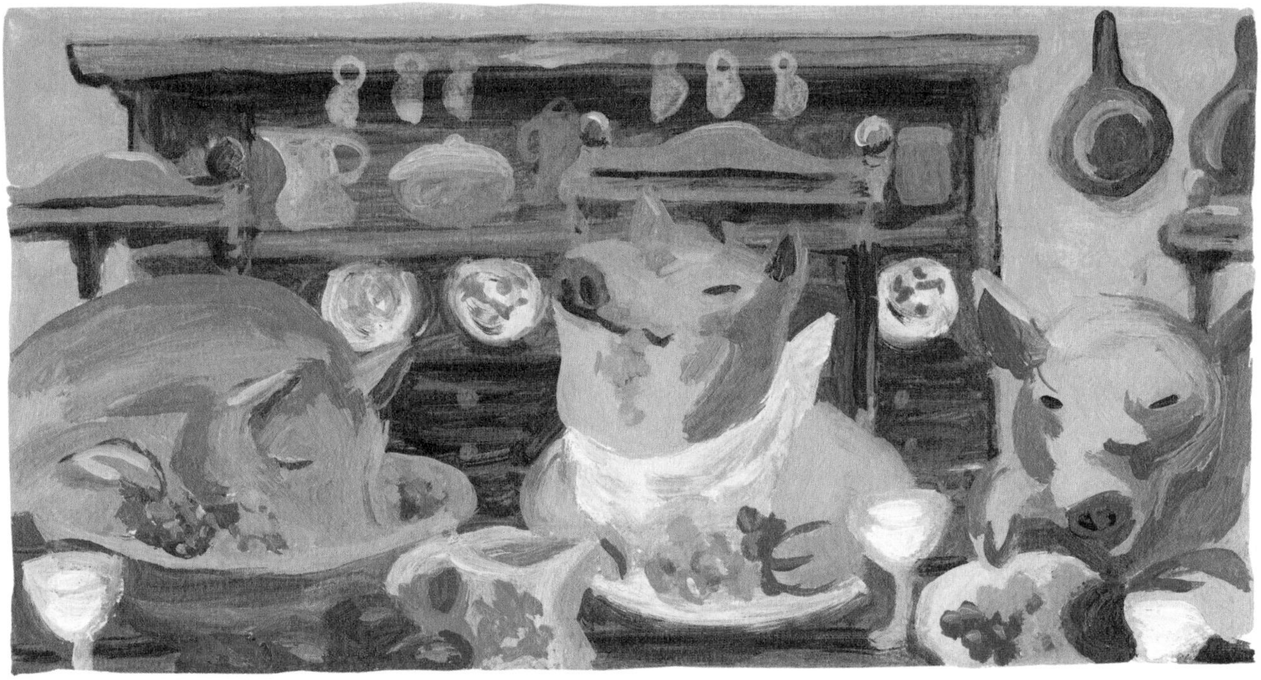

It was about this time that the pigs suddenly moved into the farmhouse and took up their residence there.

Some of the animals were disturbed when they heard that the pigs not only took their meals in the kitchen and used the drawing-room as a recreation room, but also slept in the beds.

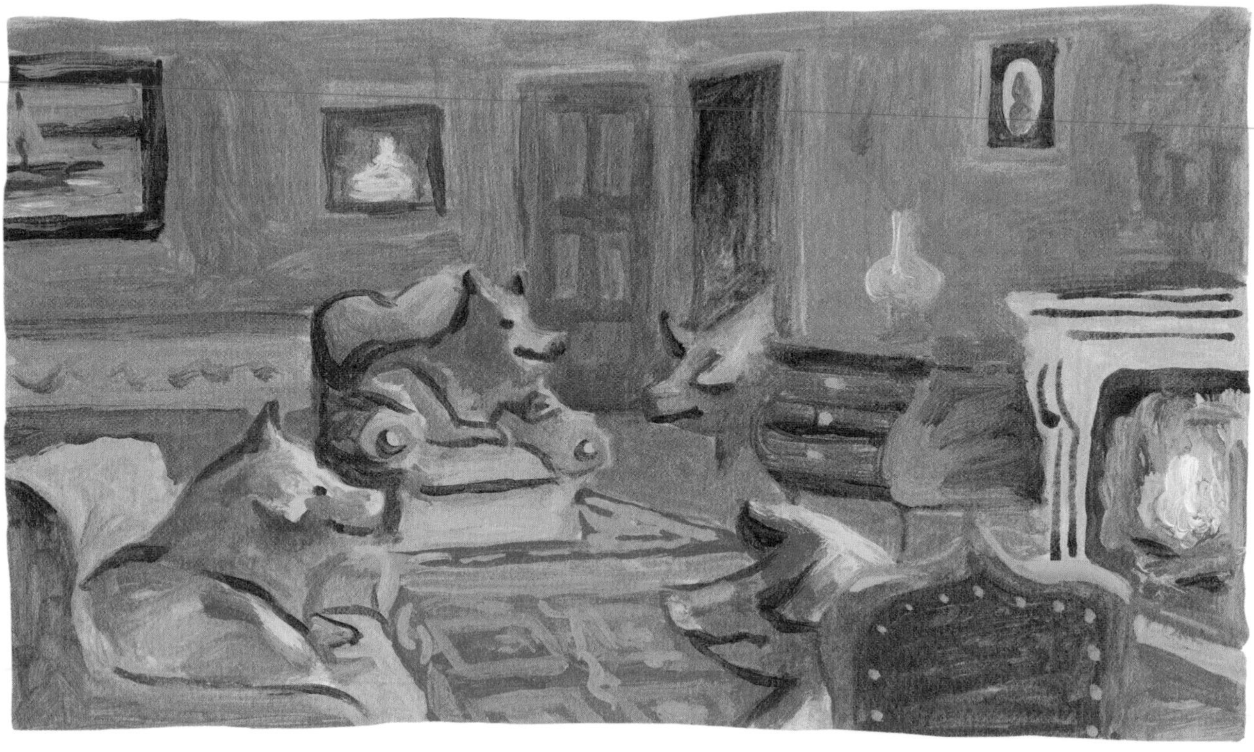

The animals seemed to remember a resolution against this.

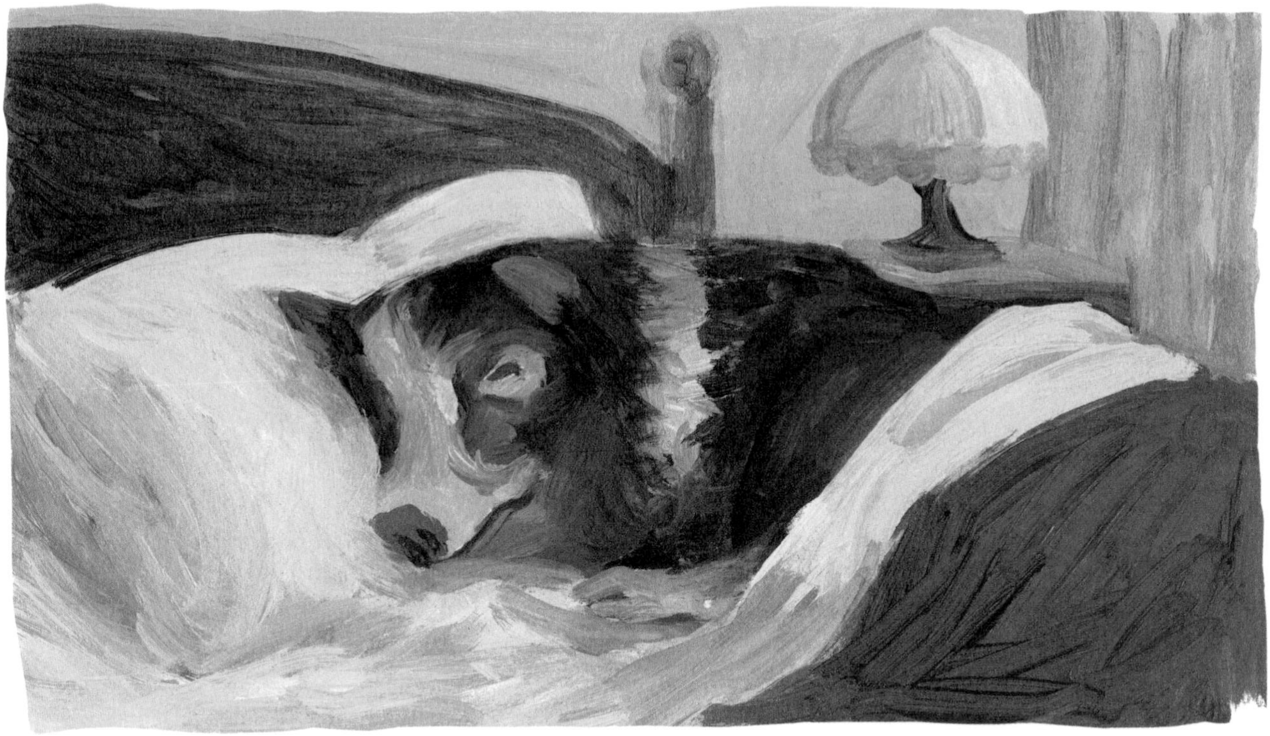

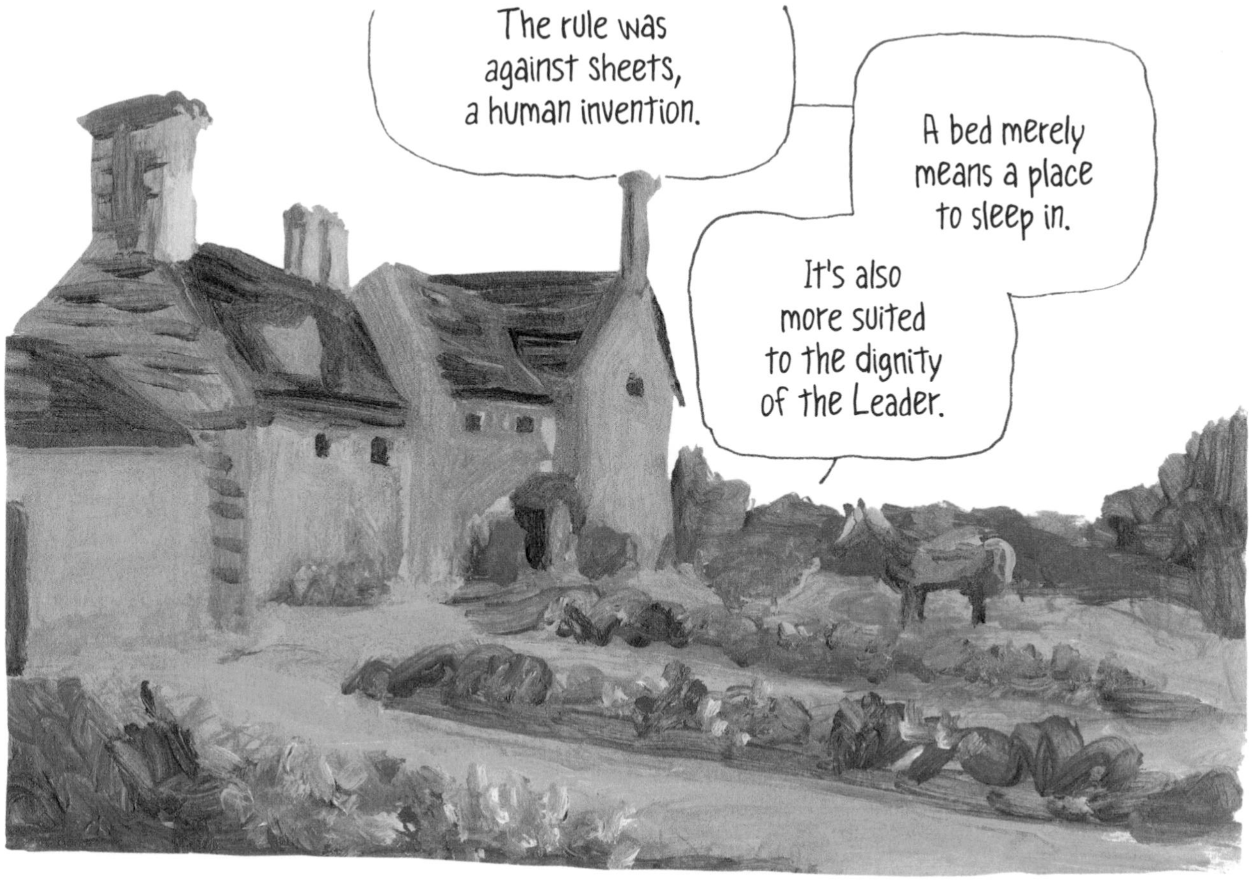
The rule was against sheets, a human invention.
A bed merely means a place to sleep in.
It's also more suited to the dignity of the Leader.

By the autumn the animals were tired but happy.

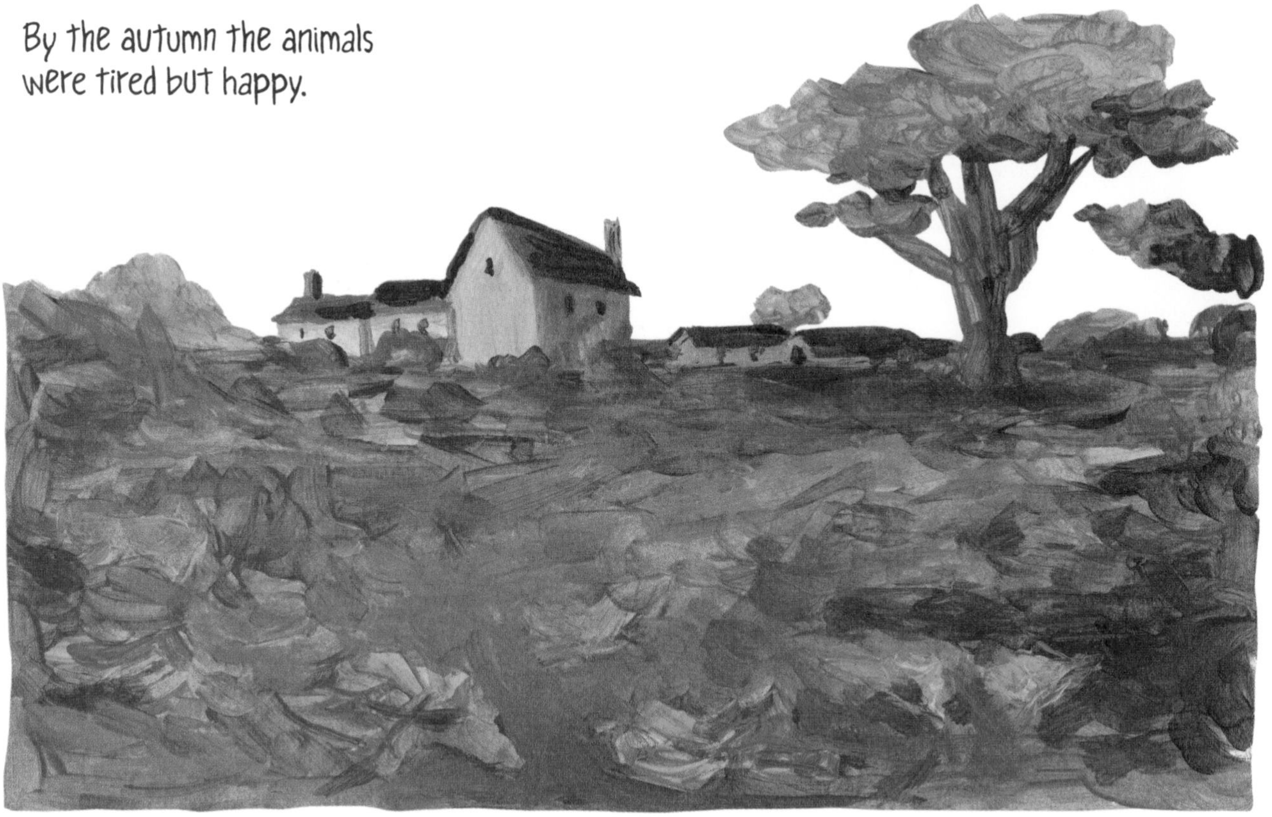

They had had a hard year, and after the sale of part of the hay and corn, the stores of food for the winter were none too plentiful.

But the windmill compensated for everything. It was almost half built now.

In their spare moments the animals would walk round and round the half-finished mill, admiring the strength and perpendicularity of its walls and marvelling that they should ever have been able to build anything so imposing.

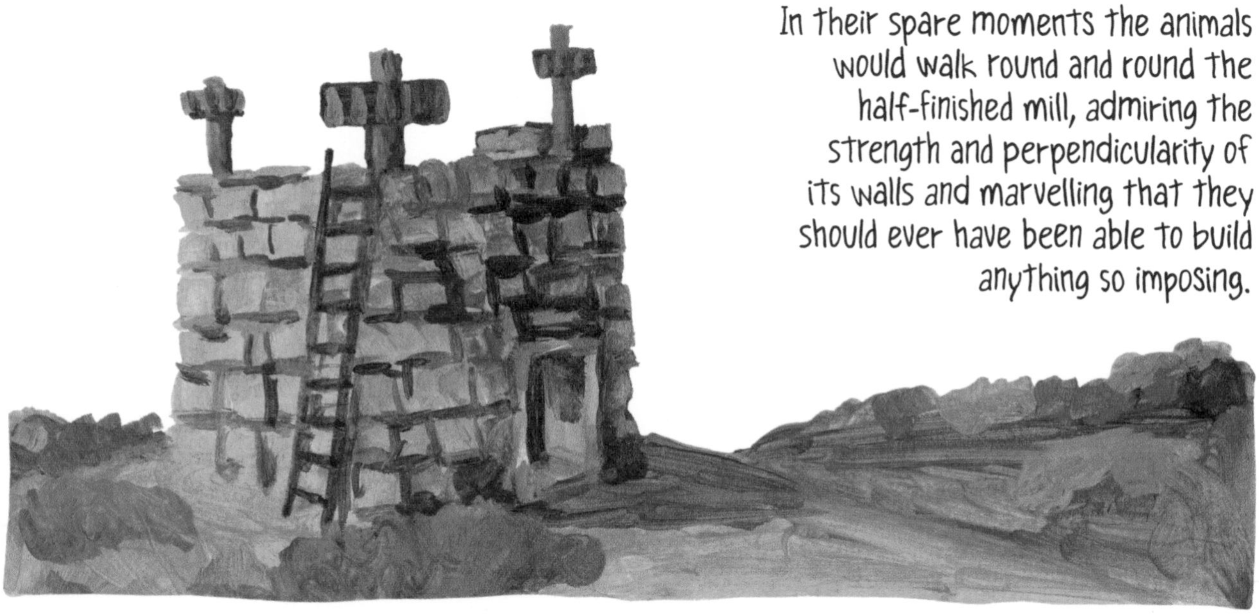

November came, with raging south-west winds. Finally there came a night when the gale was so violent that the farm buildings rocked on their foundations.

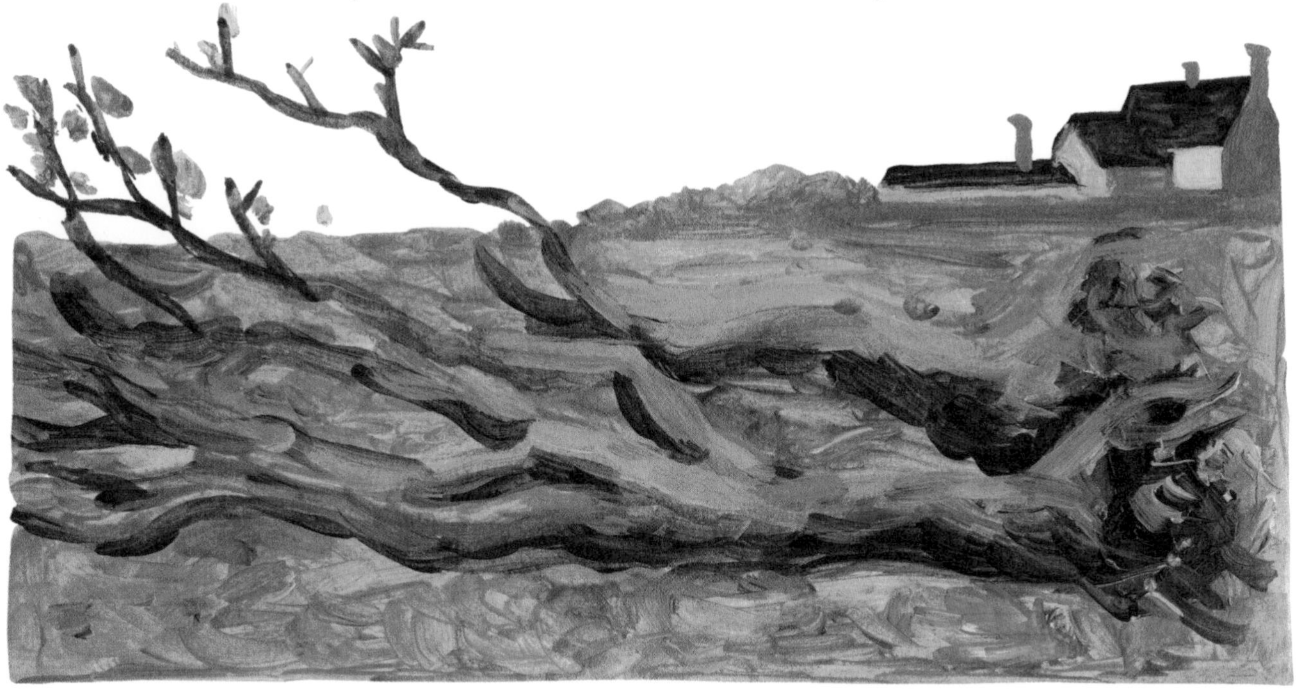

In the morning the animals came out of their stalls. A terrible sight met their eyes. The windmill was in ruins.

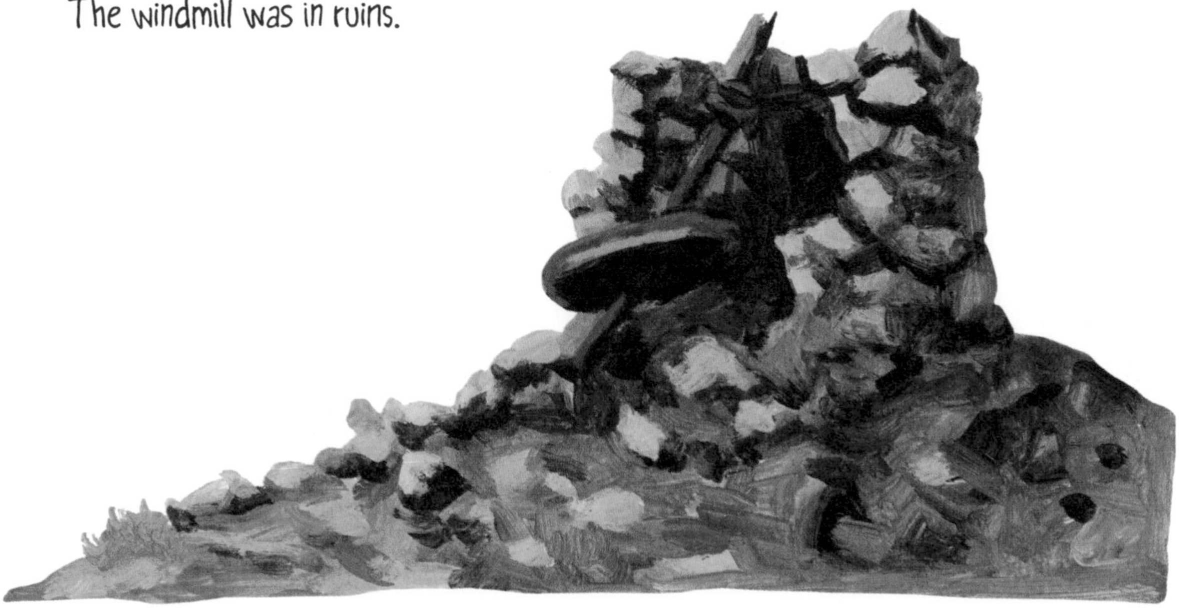

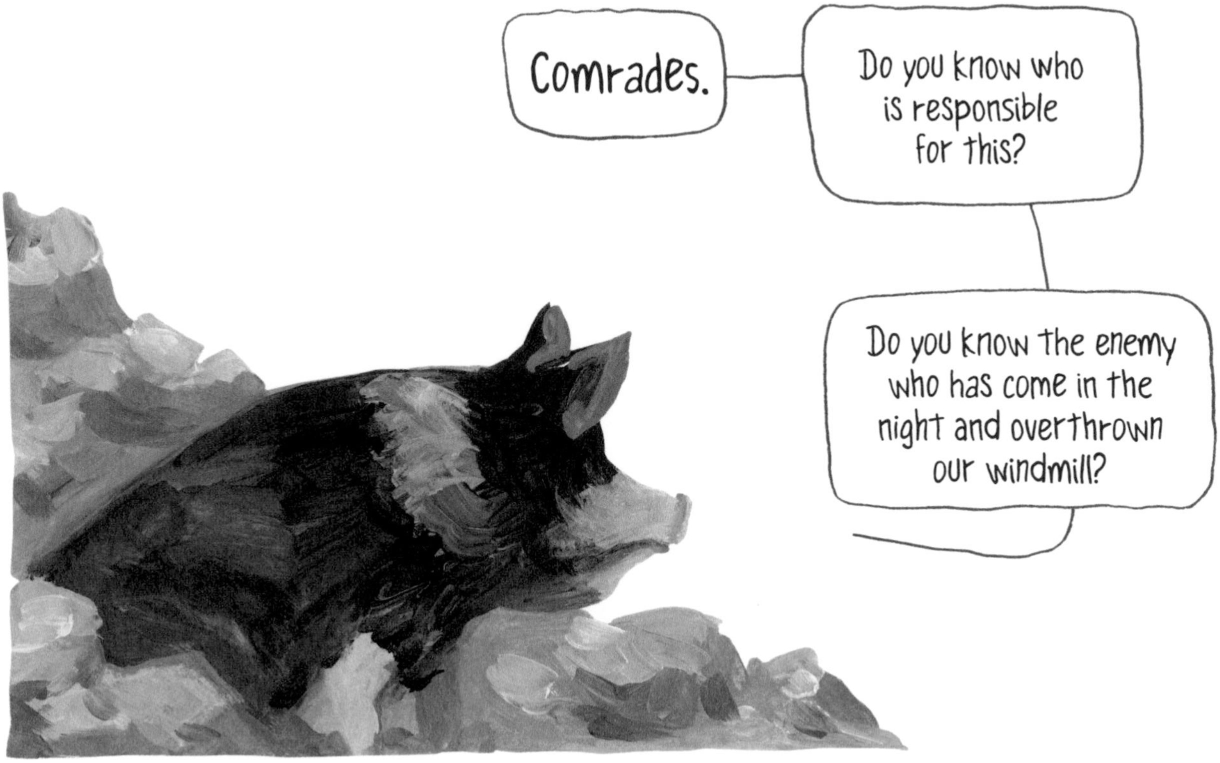
Comrades.
Do you know who is responsible for this?
Do you know the enemy who has come in the night and overthrown our windmill?

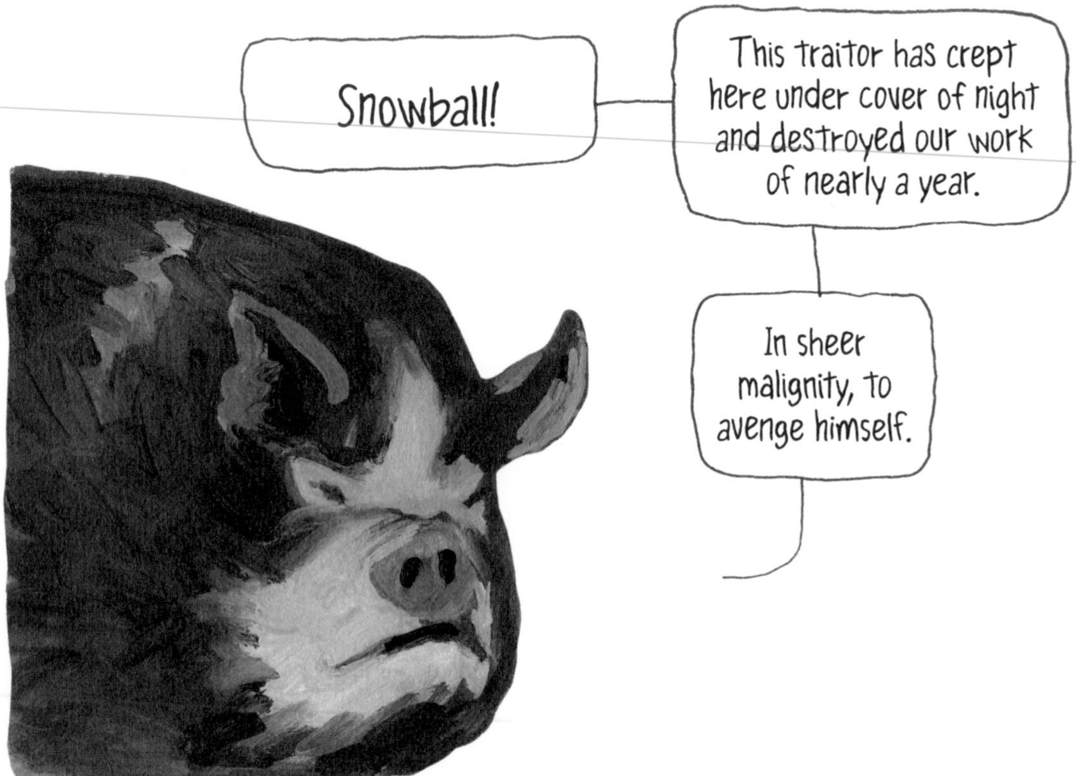
Snowball!
This traitor has crept here under cover of night and destroyed our work of nearly a year.
In sheer malignity, to avenge himself.

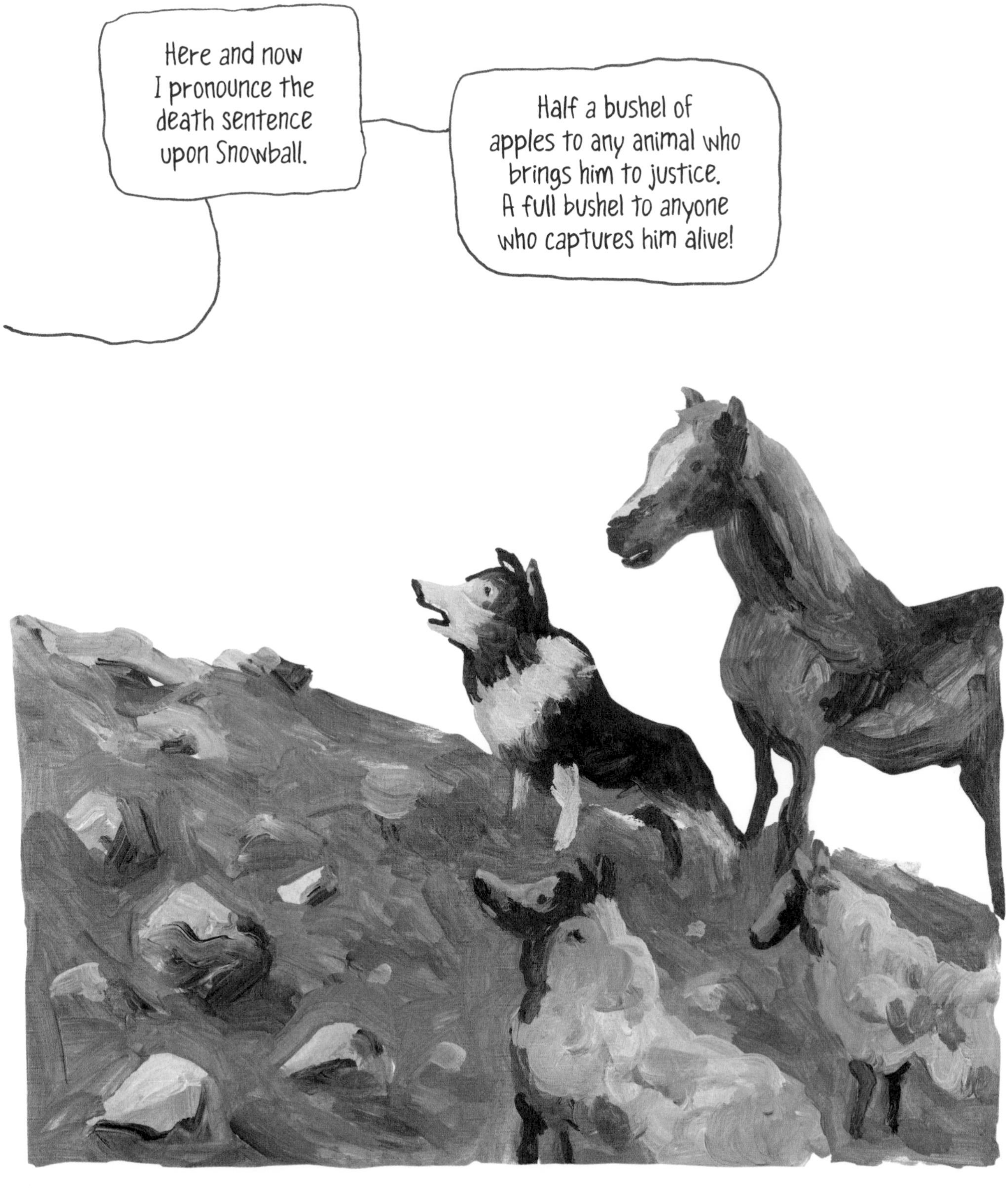
Here and now I pronounce the death sentence upon Snowball.
Half a bushel of apples to any animal who brings him to justice. A full bushel to anyone who captures him alive!

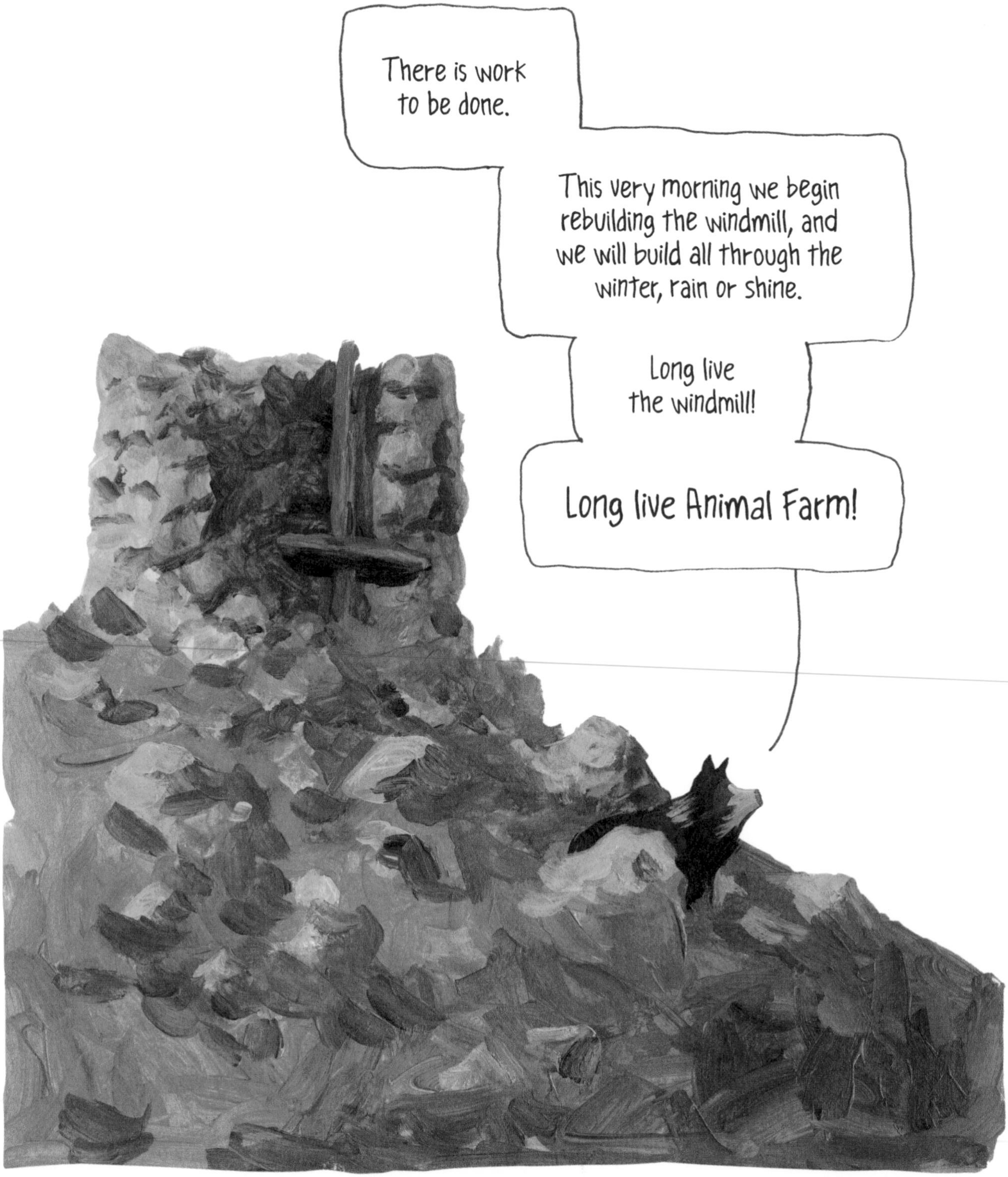
There is work to be done.
This very morning we begin rebuilding the windmill, and we will build all through the winter, rain or shine.
Long live the windmill!
Long live Animal Farm!

VII

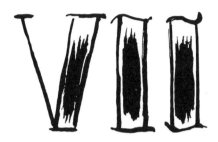

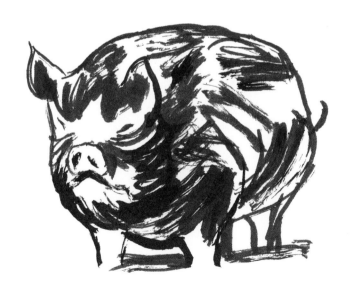

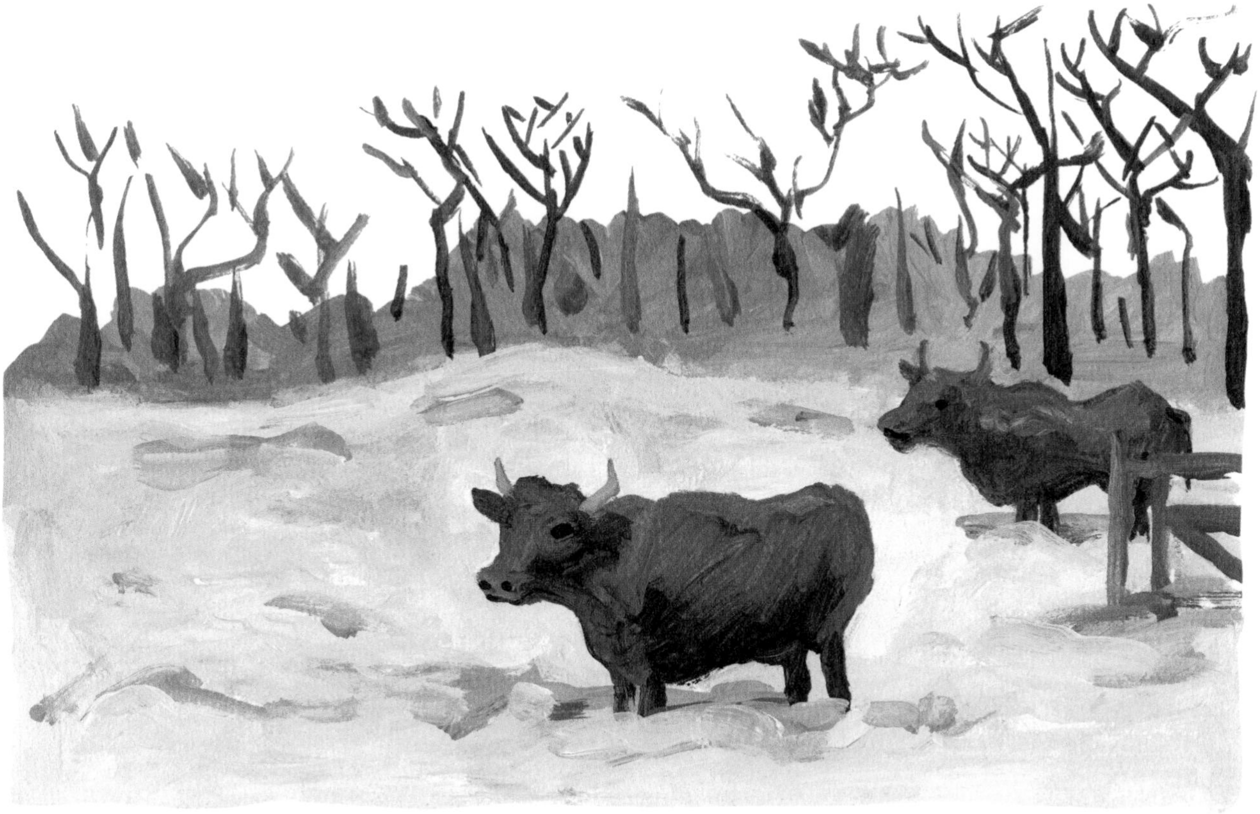

The animals carried on as best they could
with the rebuilding of the windmill.
But it was cruel work.

They were always
cold, and usually
hungry as well.

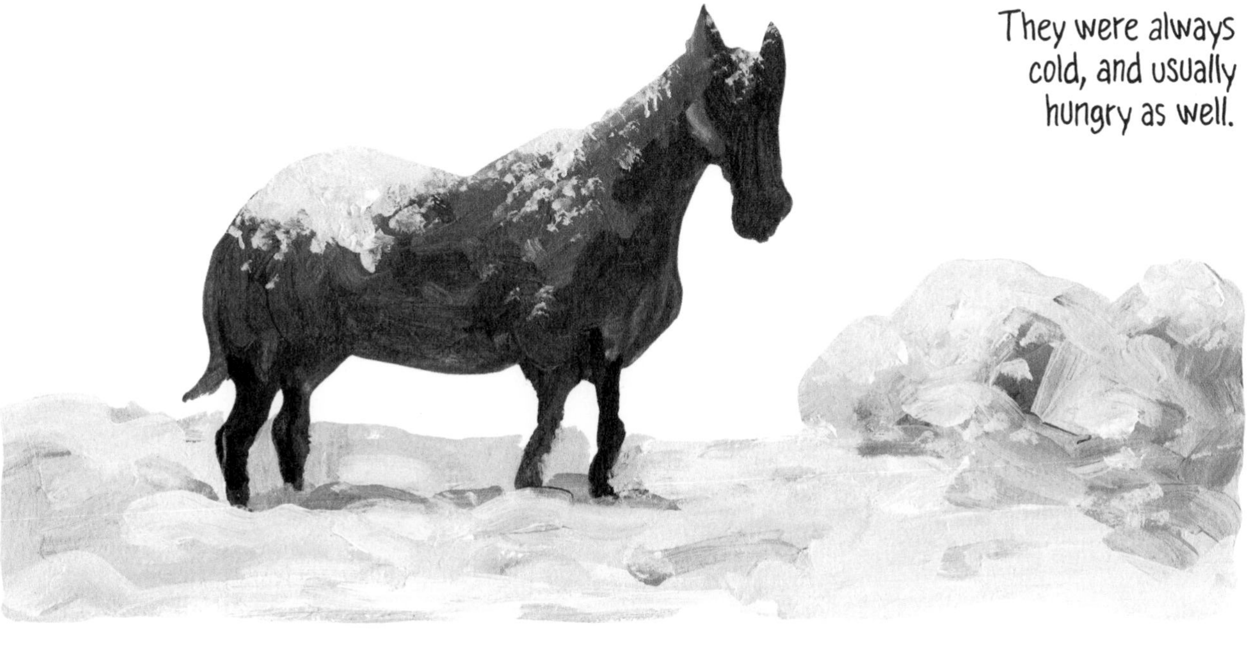

In January the corn ration
was drastically reduced.

For days at a time the animals had nothing
to eat but chaff and mangels.

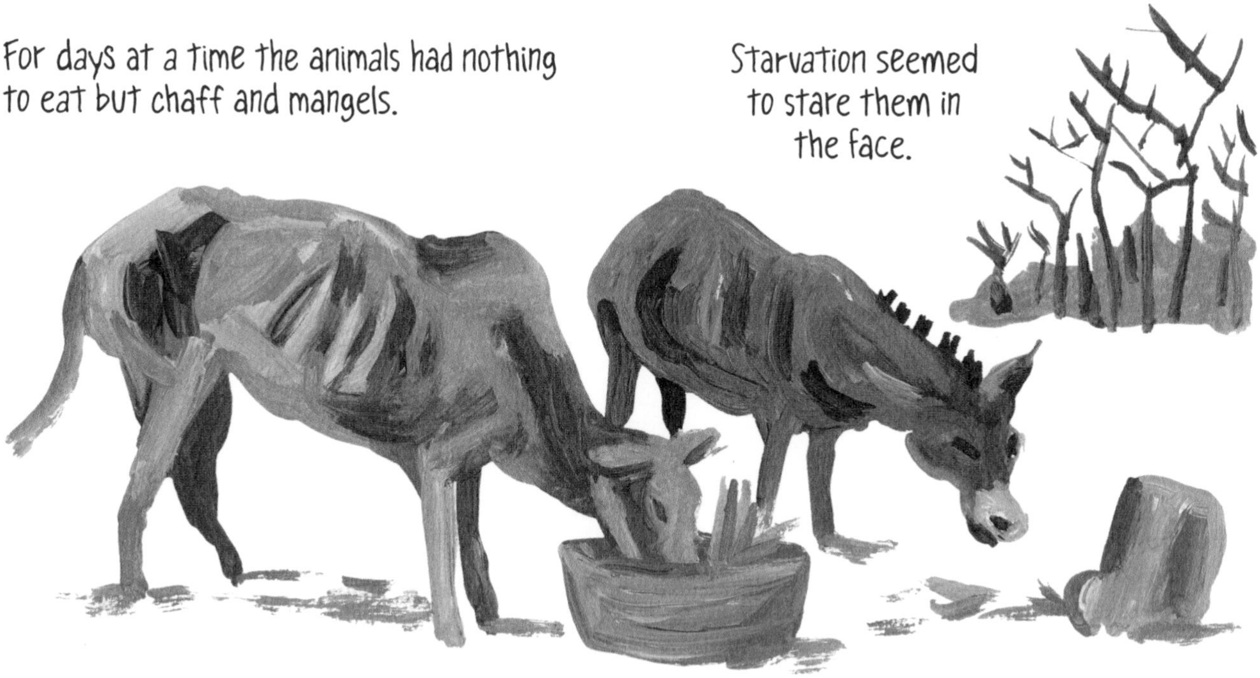
Starvation seemed to stare them in the face.

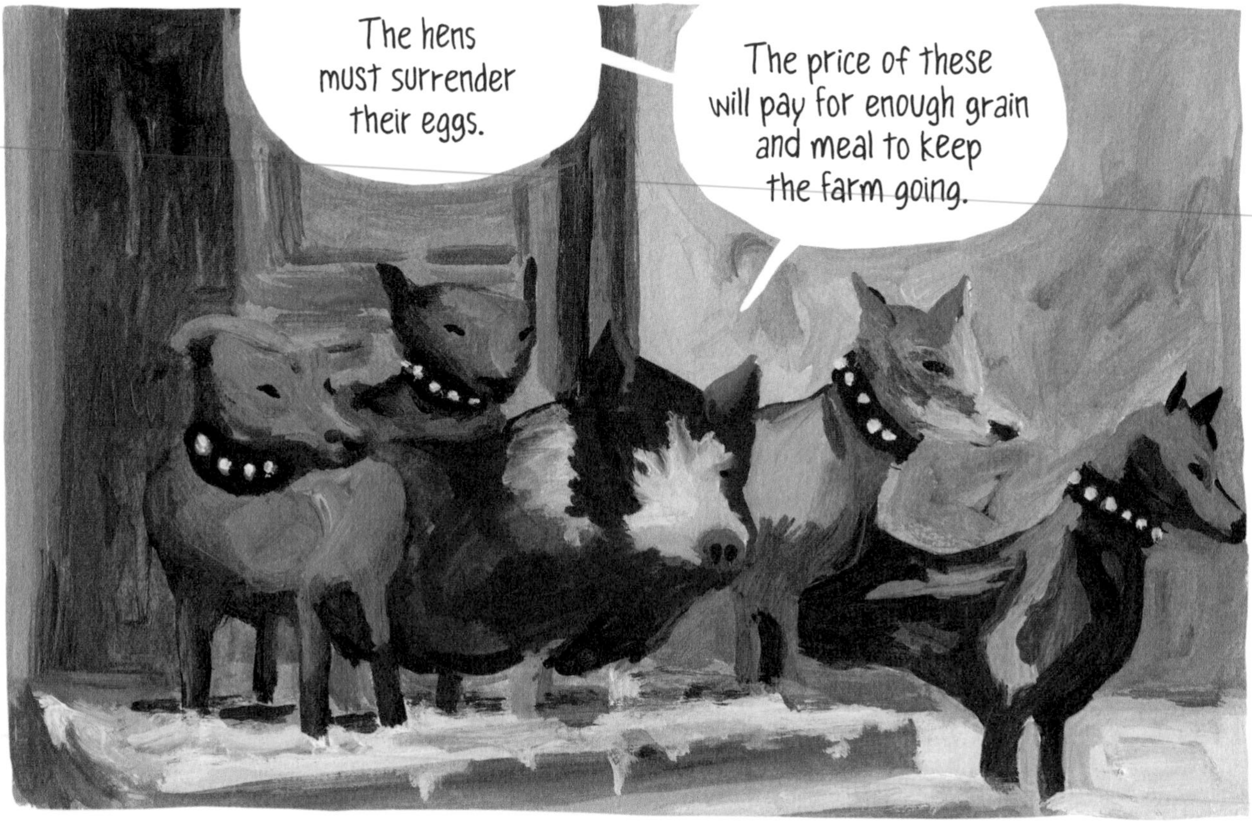
The hens must surrender their eggs.
The price of these will pay for enough grain and meal to keep the farm going.

The hens had not believed that it would really happen.

For the first time since the expulsion of Jones, there was something resembling a rebellion.

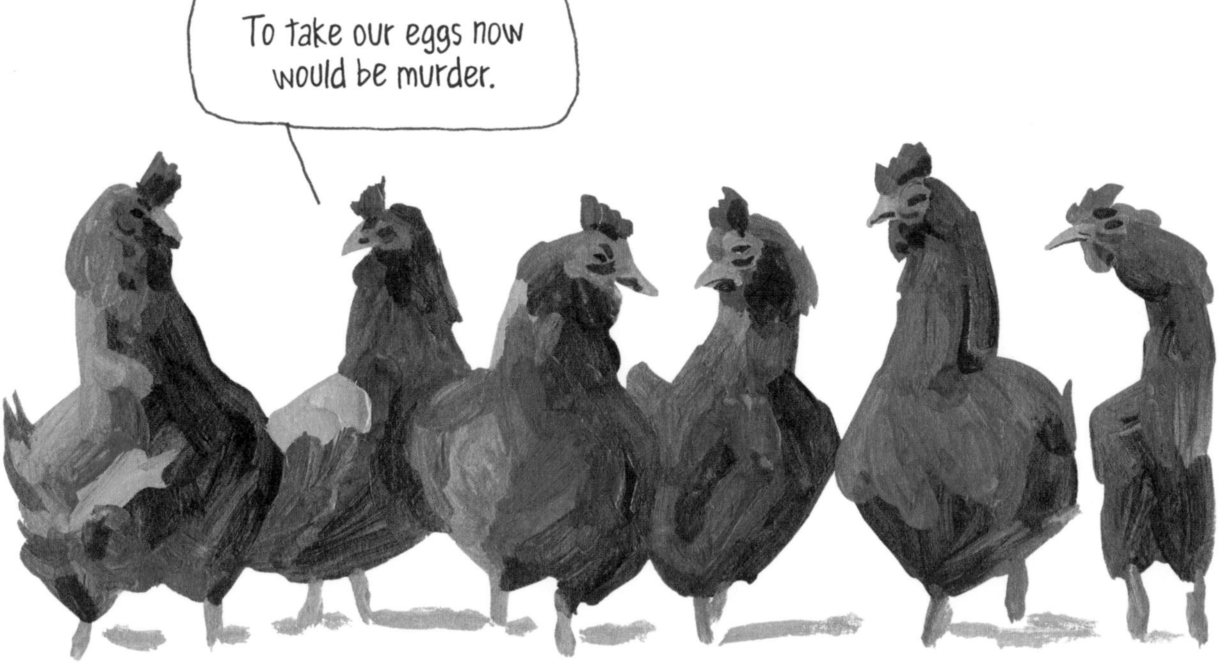
To take our eggs now would be murder.

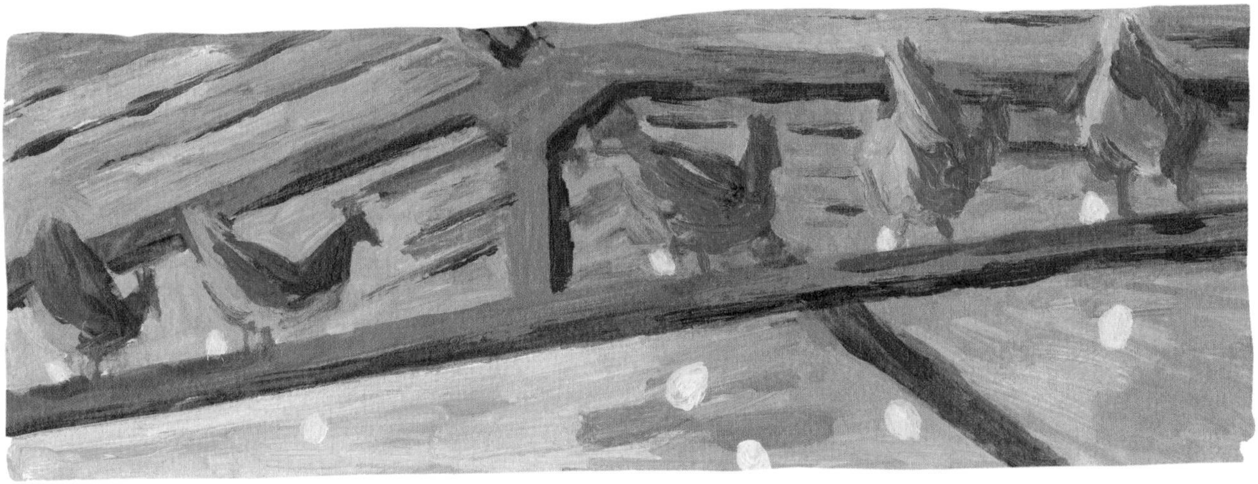

Their method was to fly up to the rafters and there lay their eggs, which smashed on the floor.

Napoleon acted swiftly and ruthlessly. He ordered the hens' rations to be stopped.

For five days the hens held out, then they capitulated and went back to their nesting boxes. Nine hens had died in the meantime.

Early in the spring, an alarming thing was discovered. Snowball was secretly frequenting the farm by night!

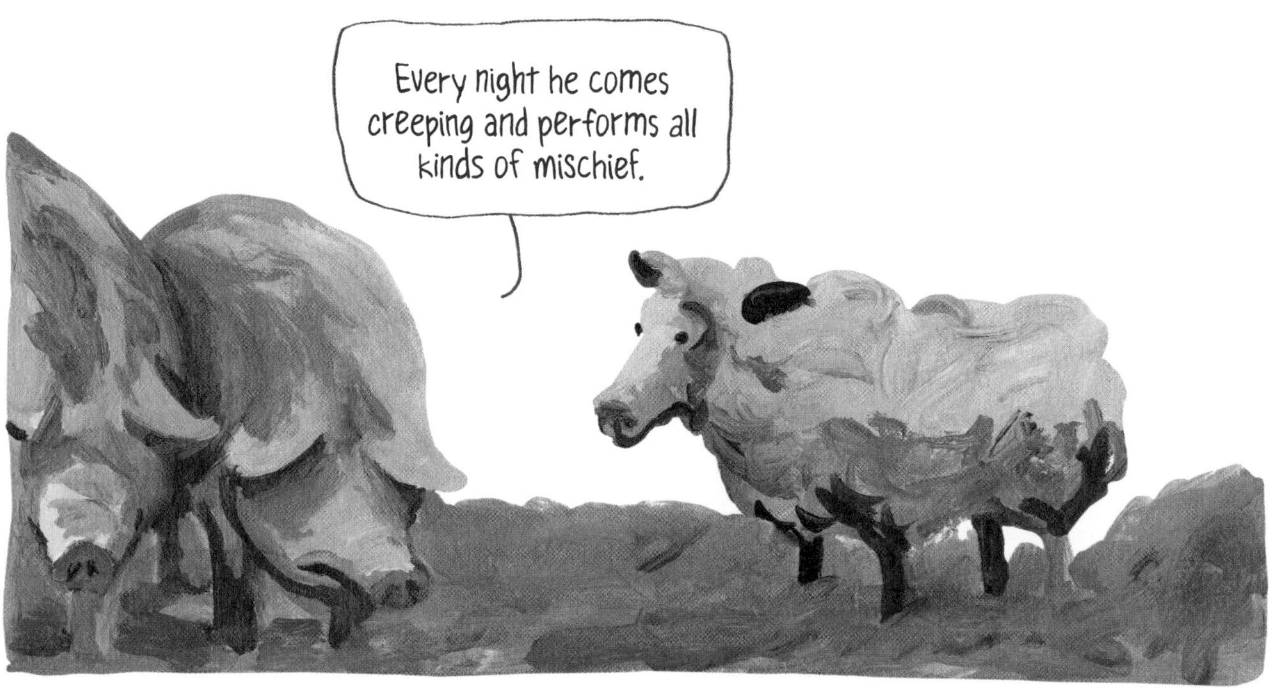
Every night he comes creeping and performs all kinds of mischief.

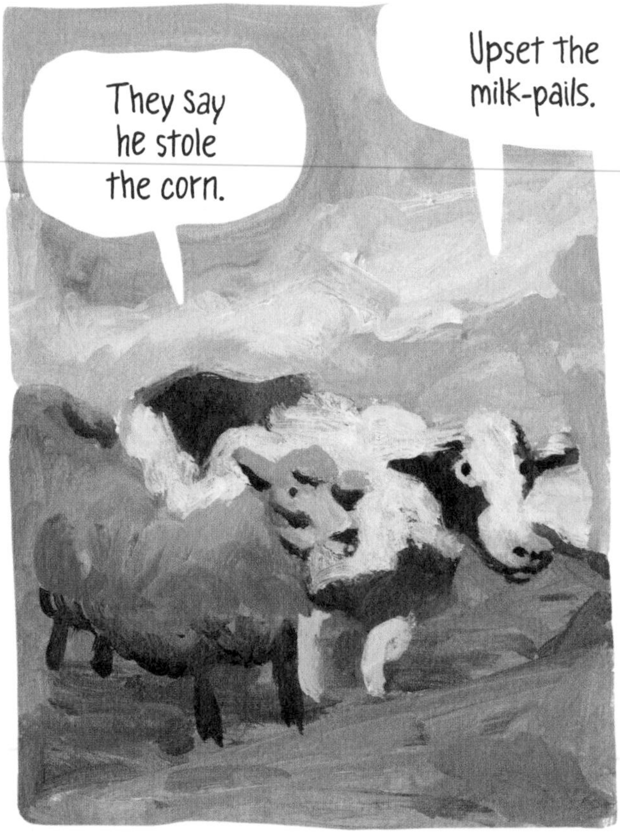
They say he stole the corn.
Upset the milk-pails.

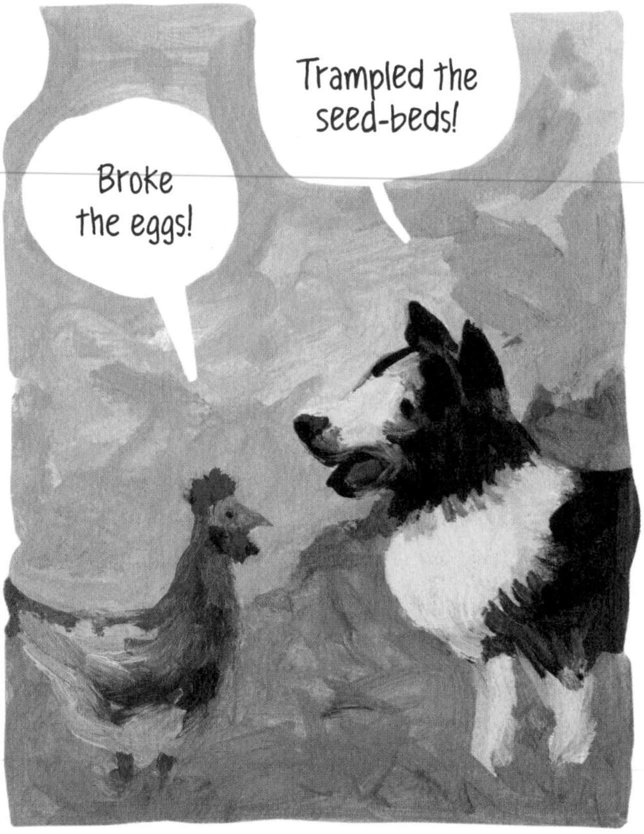
Broke the eggs!
Trampled the seed-beds!

Whenever anything went wrong it became usual to attribute it to Snowball.

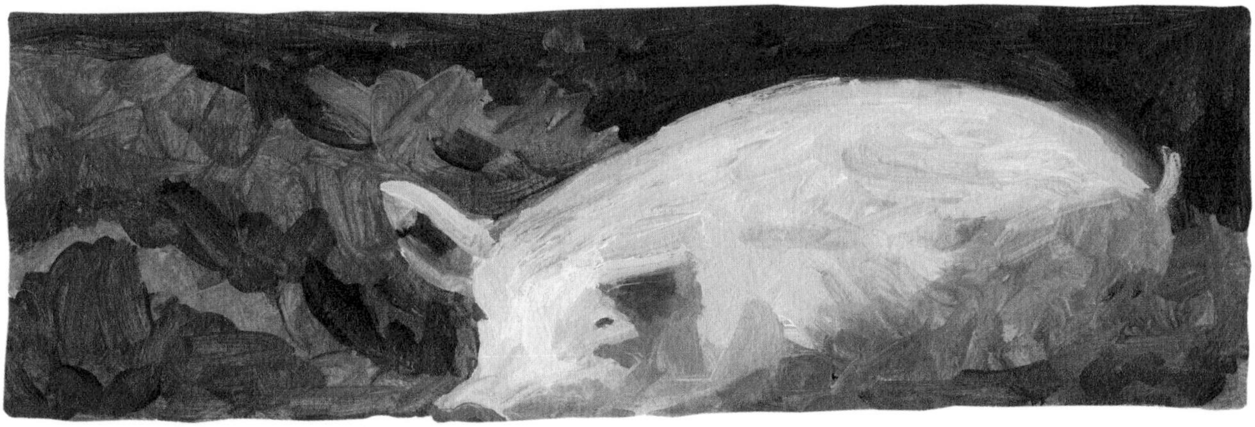

It seemed to them as though Snowball were some kind of invisible influence, pervading the air about them and menacing them with all kinds of dangers.

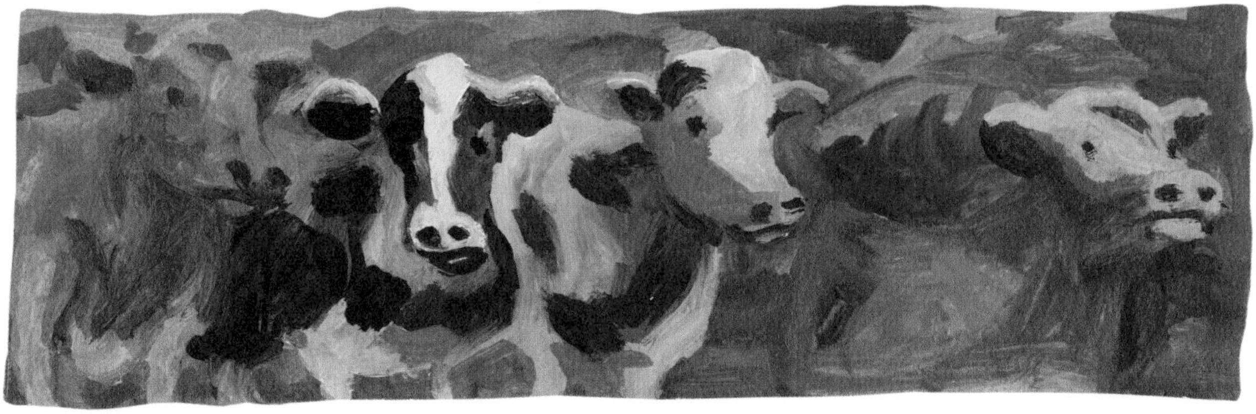

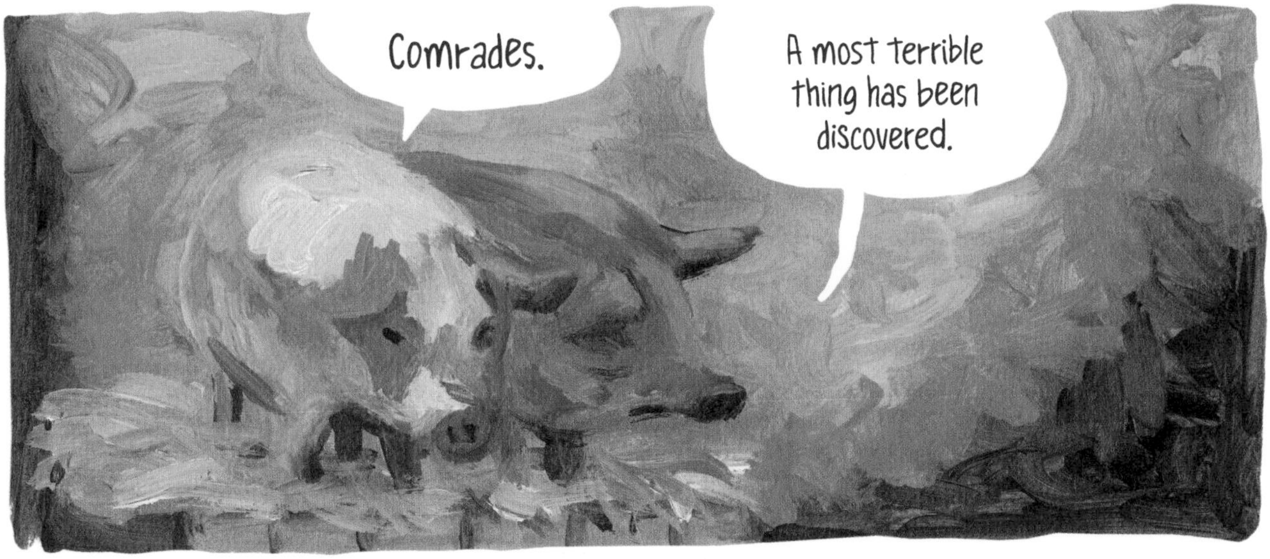
Comrades.
A most terrible thing has been discovered.

Snowball has sold himself to Frederick of Pinchfield Farm,

who is even now plotting to attack us and take our farm away from us!

Snowball is to act as his guide when the attack begins.

But there is worse than that.

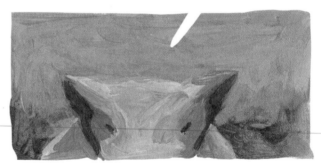

Snowball was in league with Jones from the very start! It has all been proved by documents which he left behind him.

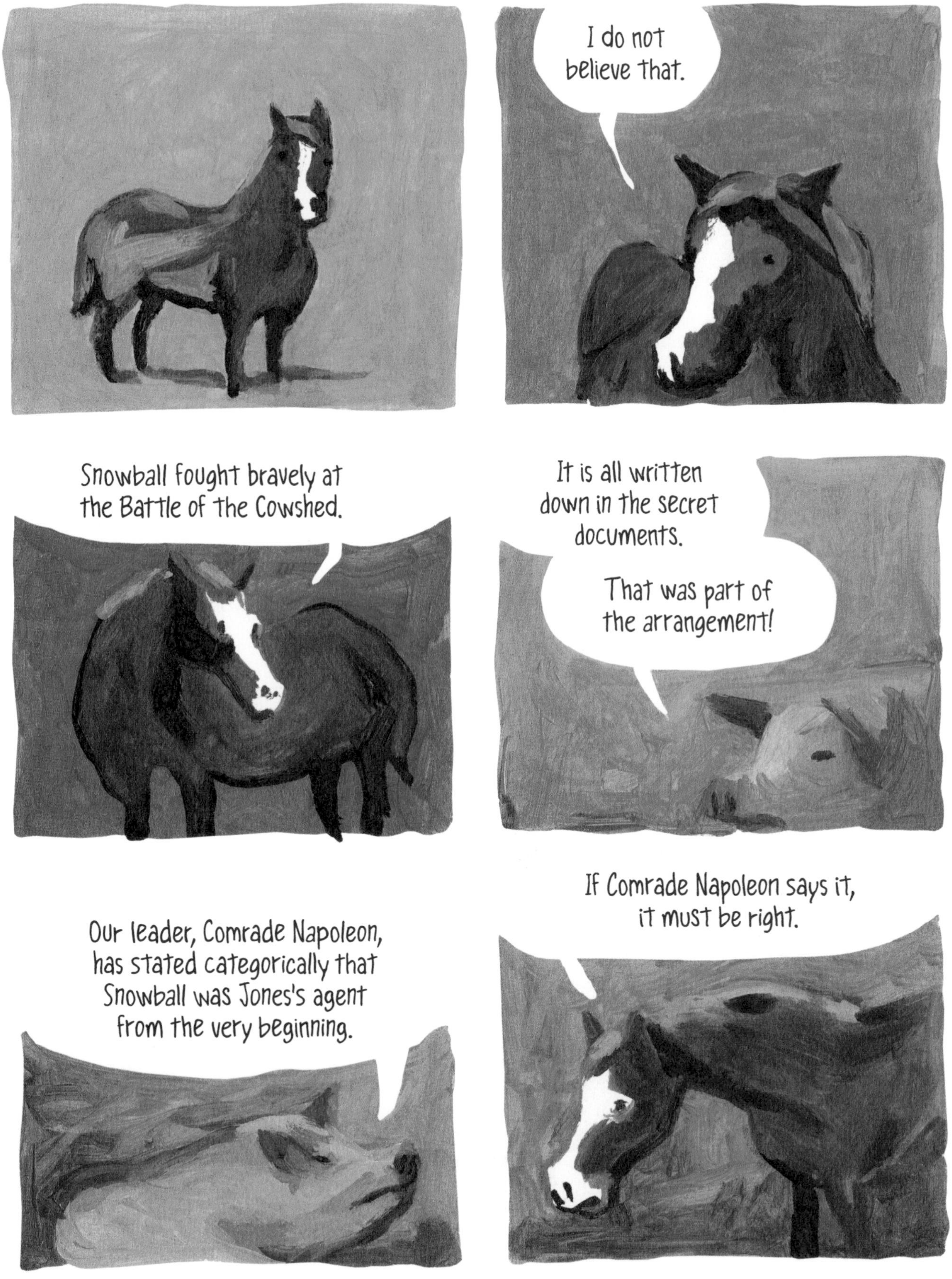
I do not believe that.
Snowball fought bravely at the Battle of the Cowshed.
It is all written down in the secret documents.
That was part of the arrangement!
Our leader, Comrade Napoleon, has stated categorically that Snowball was Jones's agent from the very beginning.
If Comrade Napoleon says it, it must be right.

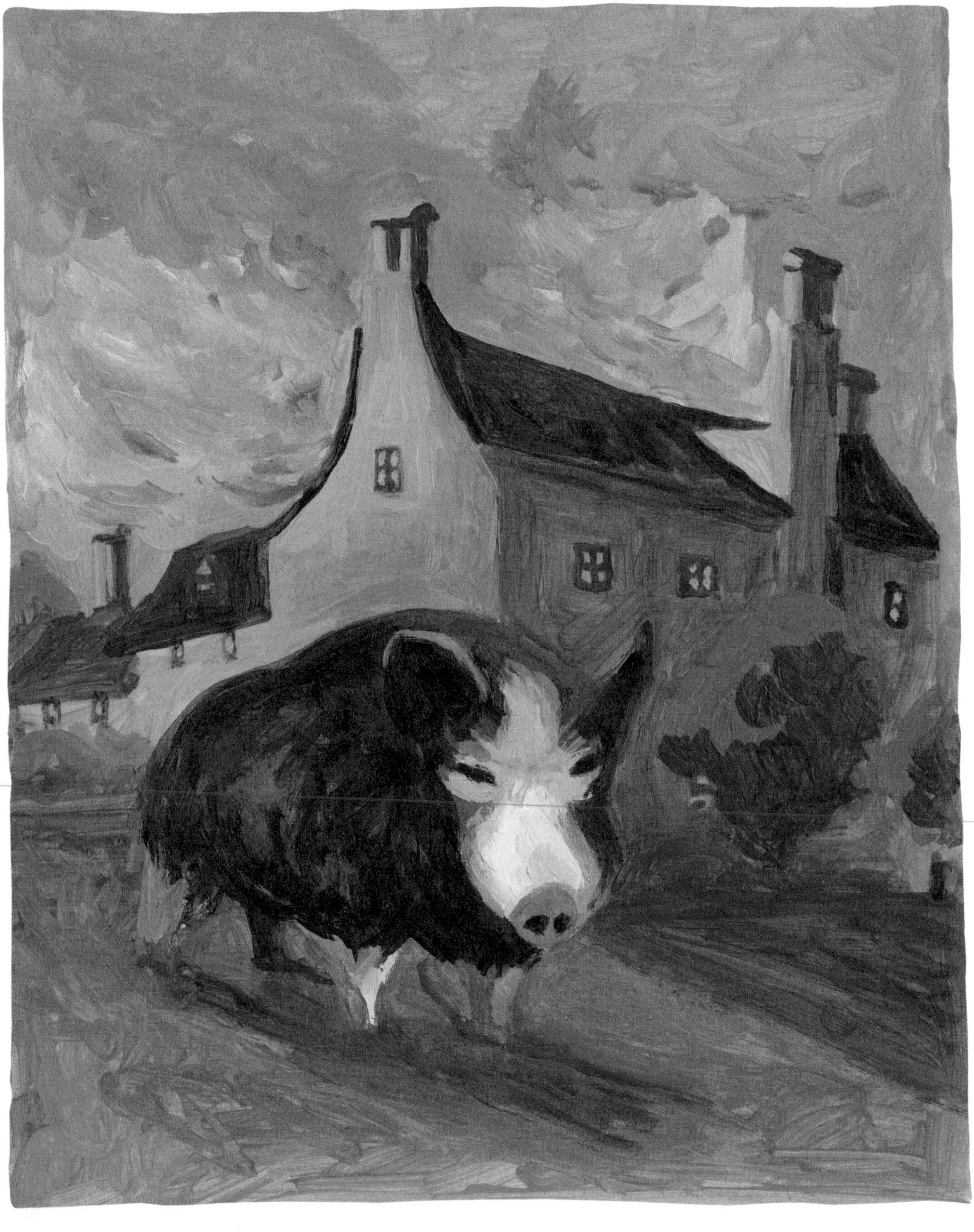

Four days later, in the afternoon, Napoleon ordered all the animals to assemble in the yard.

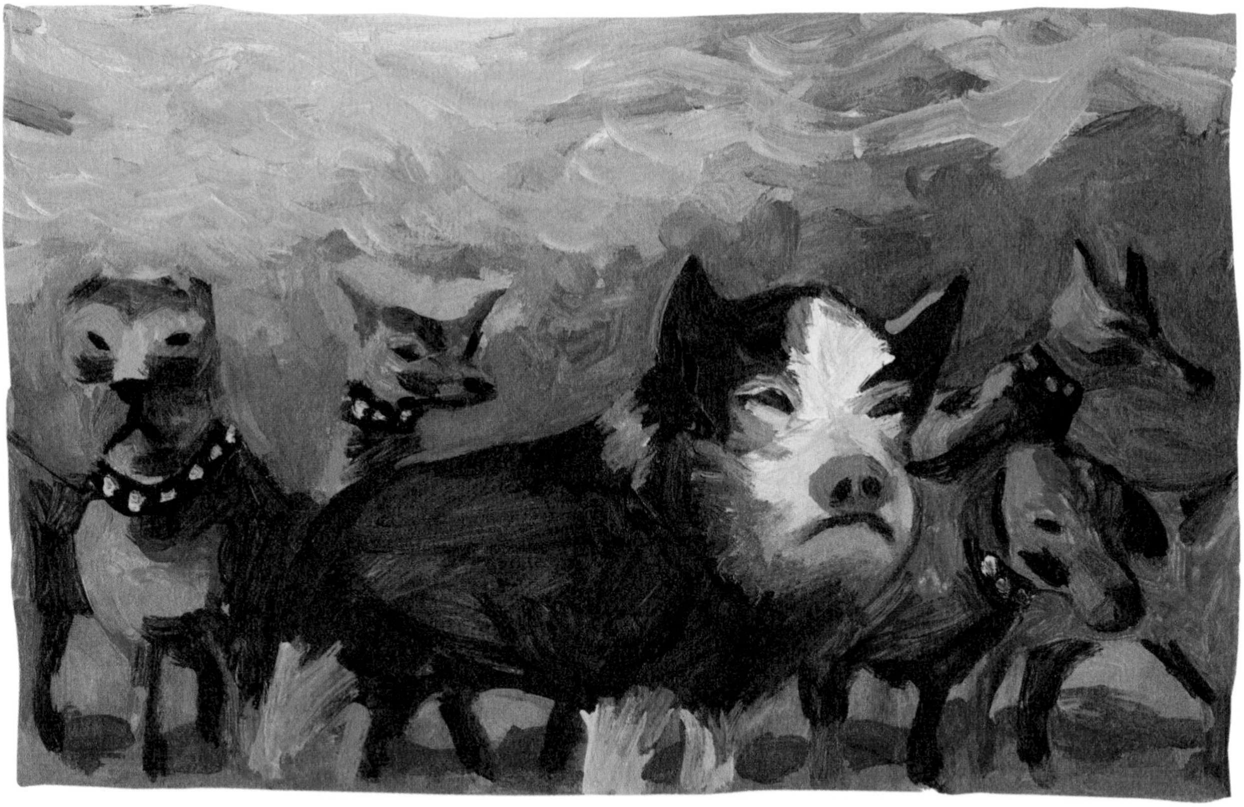

They all cowered silently in their places, seeming to know in advance that some terrible thing was about to happen.

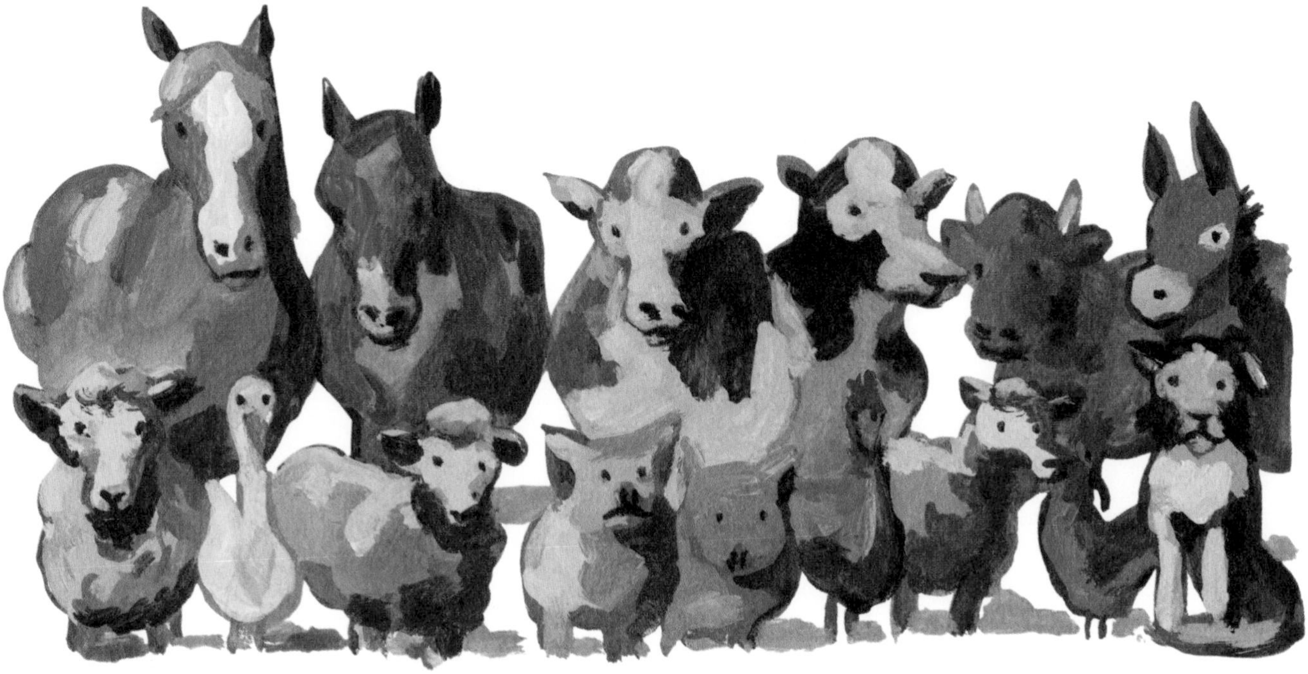

Napoleon uttered a high-pitched whimper.

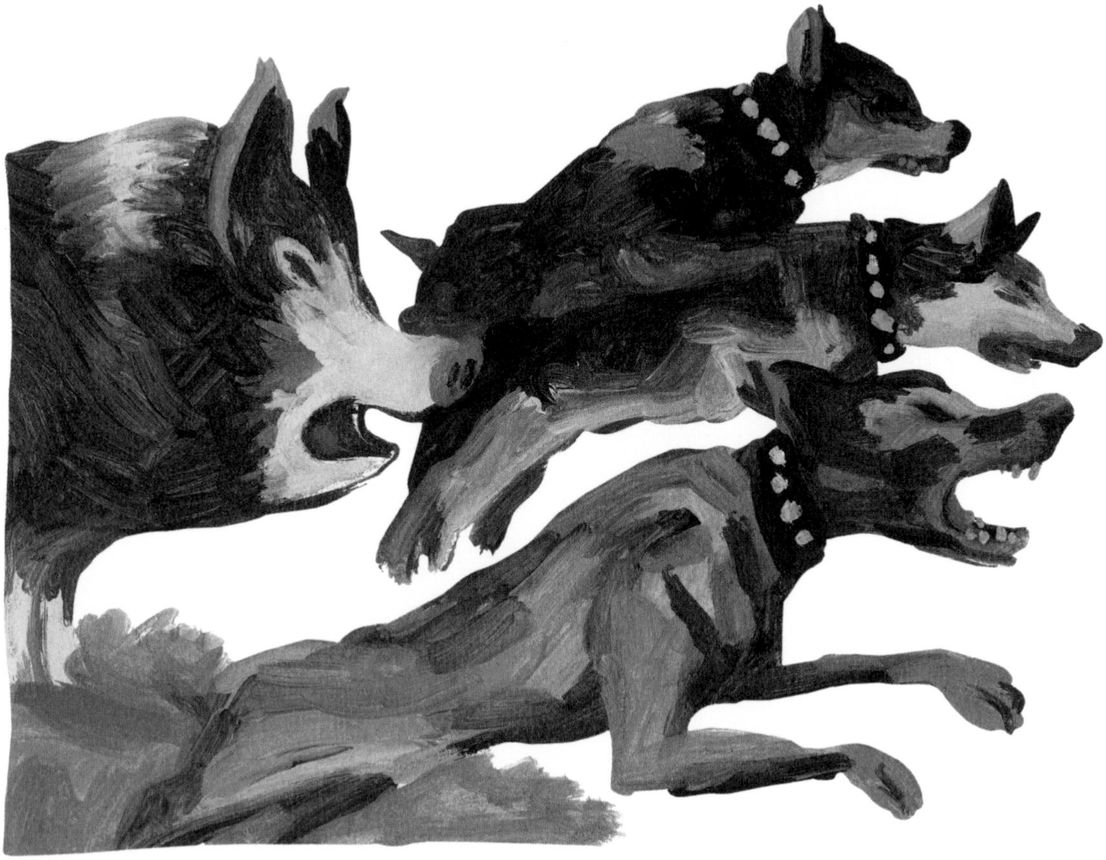

Immediately the dogs bounded forward, seized four of the pigs by the ear and dragged them to Napoleon's feet.

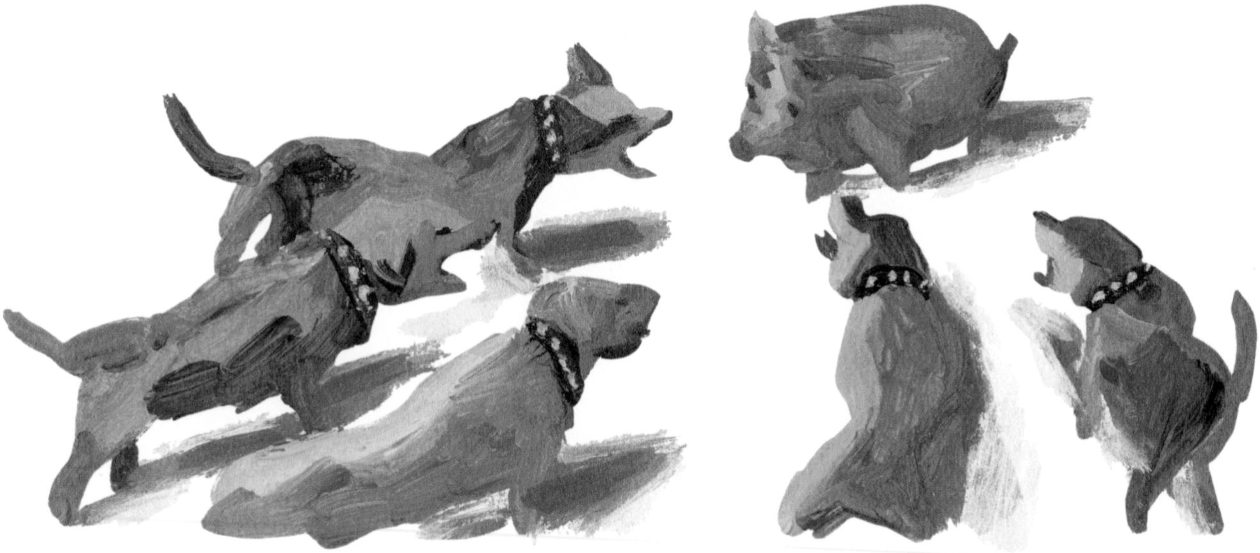

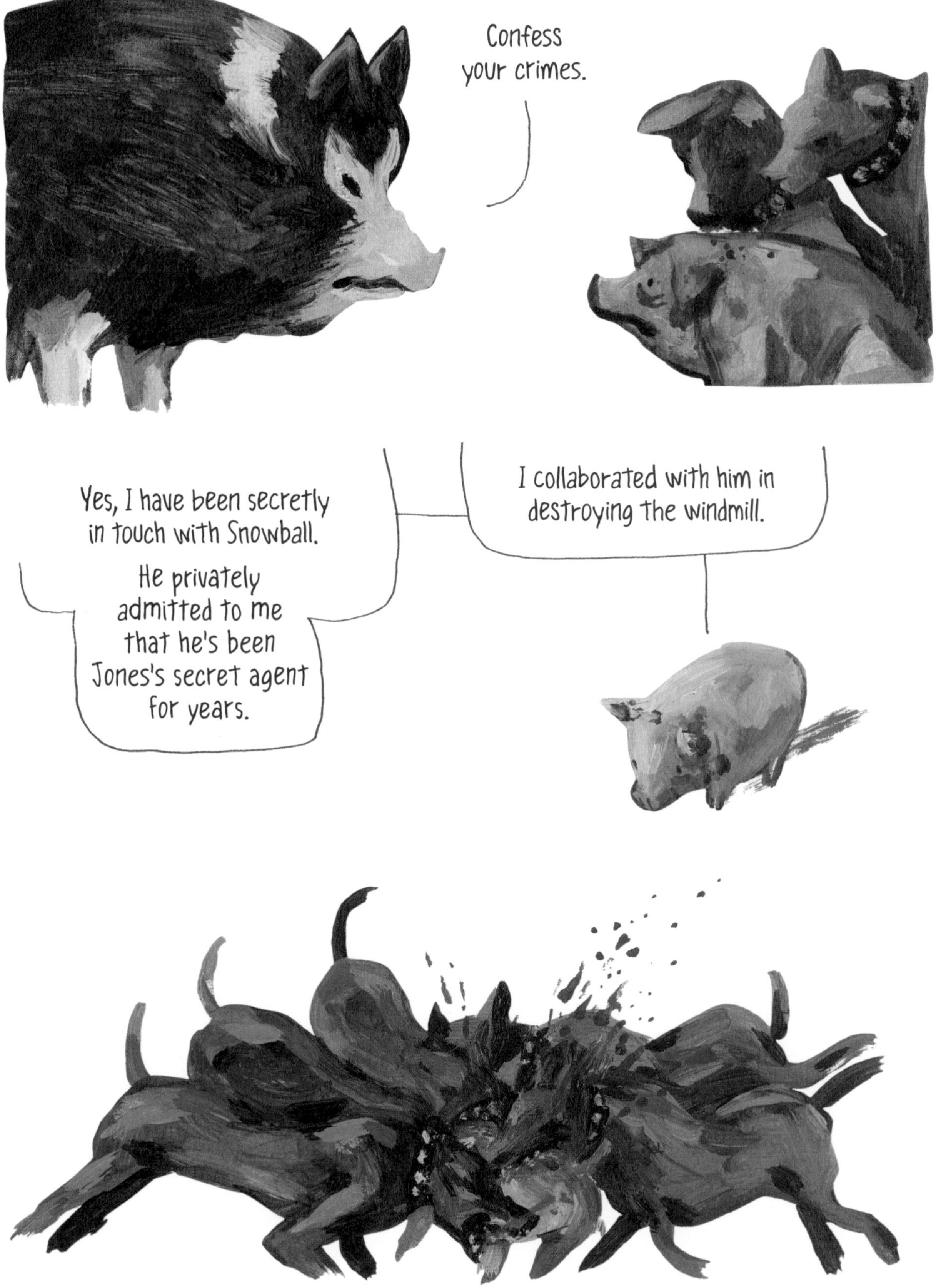
Confess your crimes.
Yes, I have been secretly in touch with Snowball.
He privately admitted to me that he's been Jones's secret agent for years.
I collaborated with him in destroying the windmill.

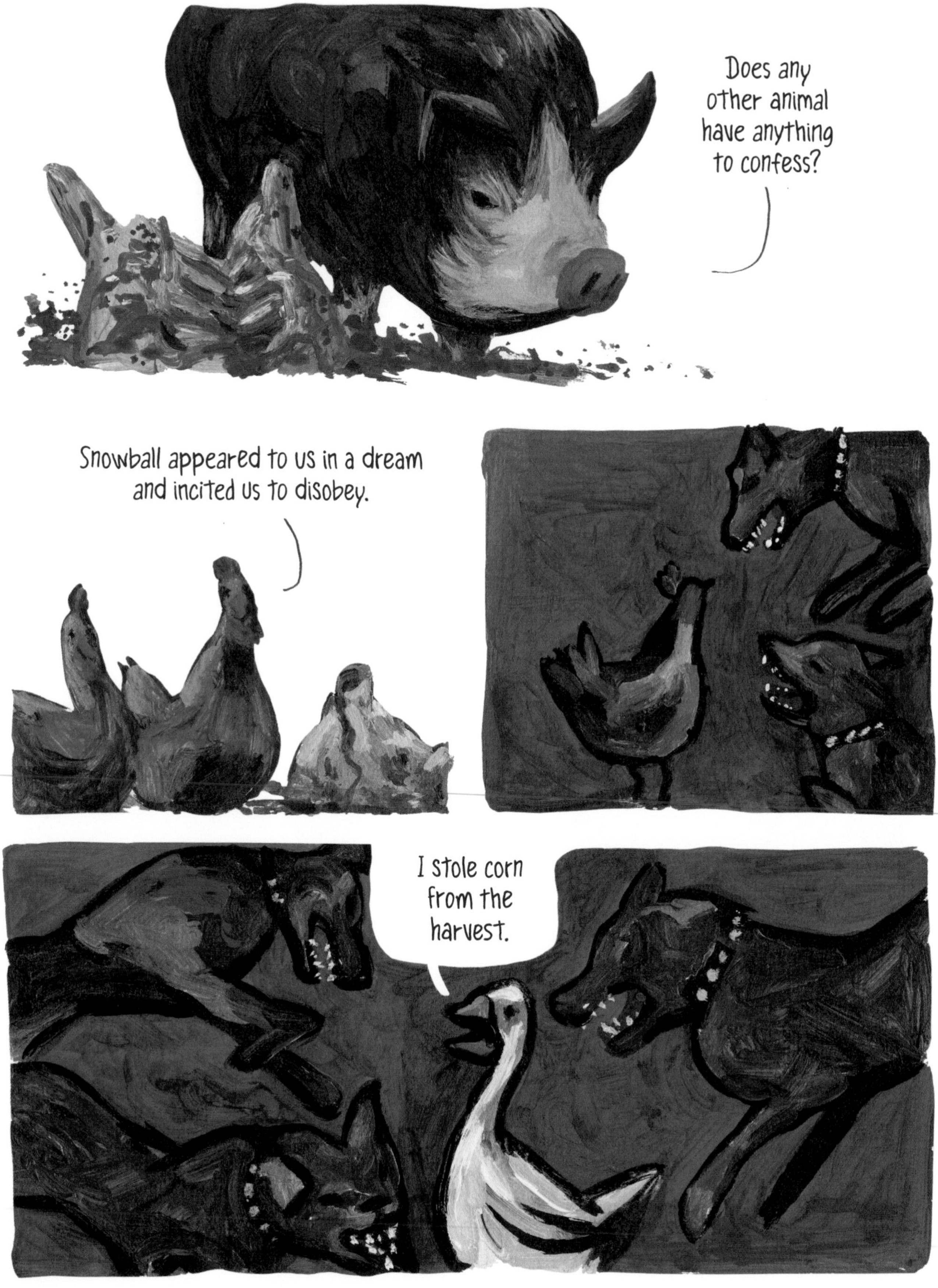
Does any other animal have anything to confess?
Snowball appeared to us in a dream and incited us to disobey.
I stole corn from the harvest.

And so the tale of confessions and executions went on.

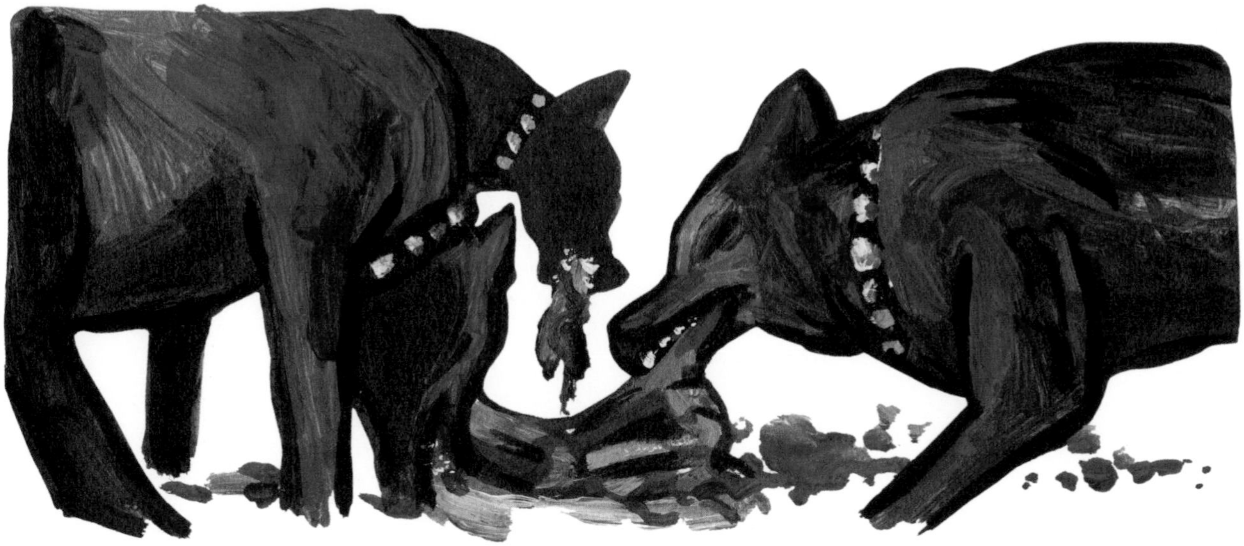

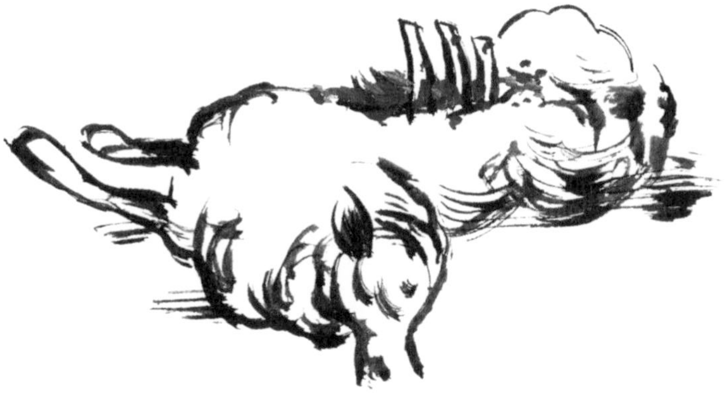

Until there was a pile of corpses lying before Napoleon's feet.

When it was all over, the remaining animals crept away in a body. The air was heavy with the smell of blood.

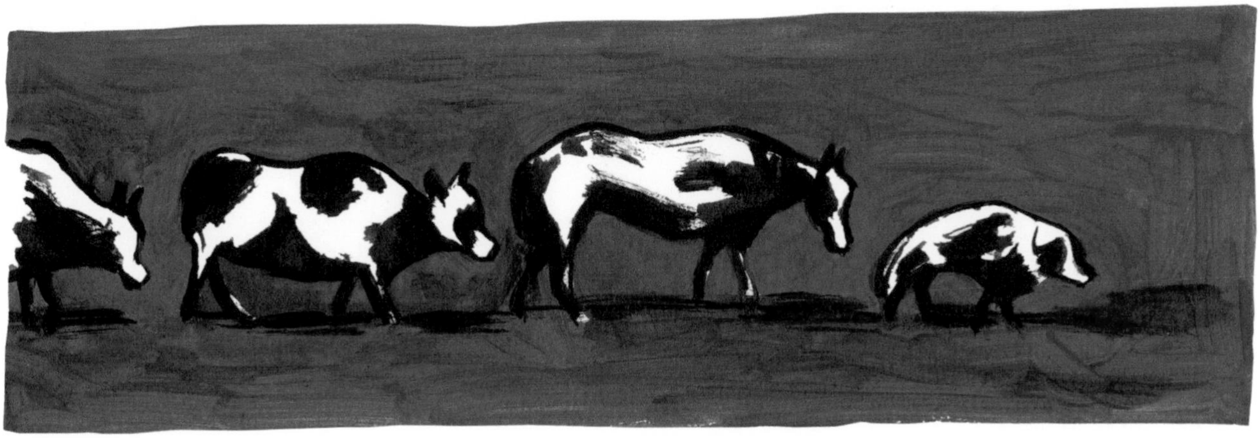

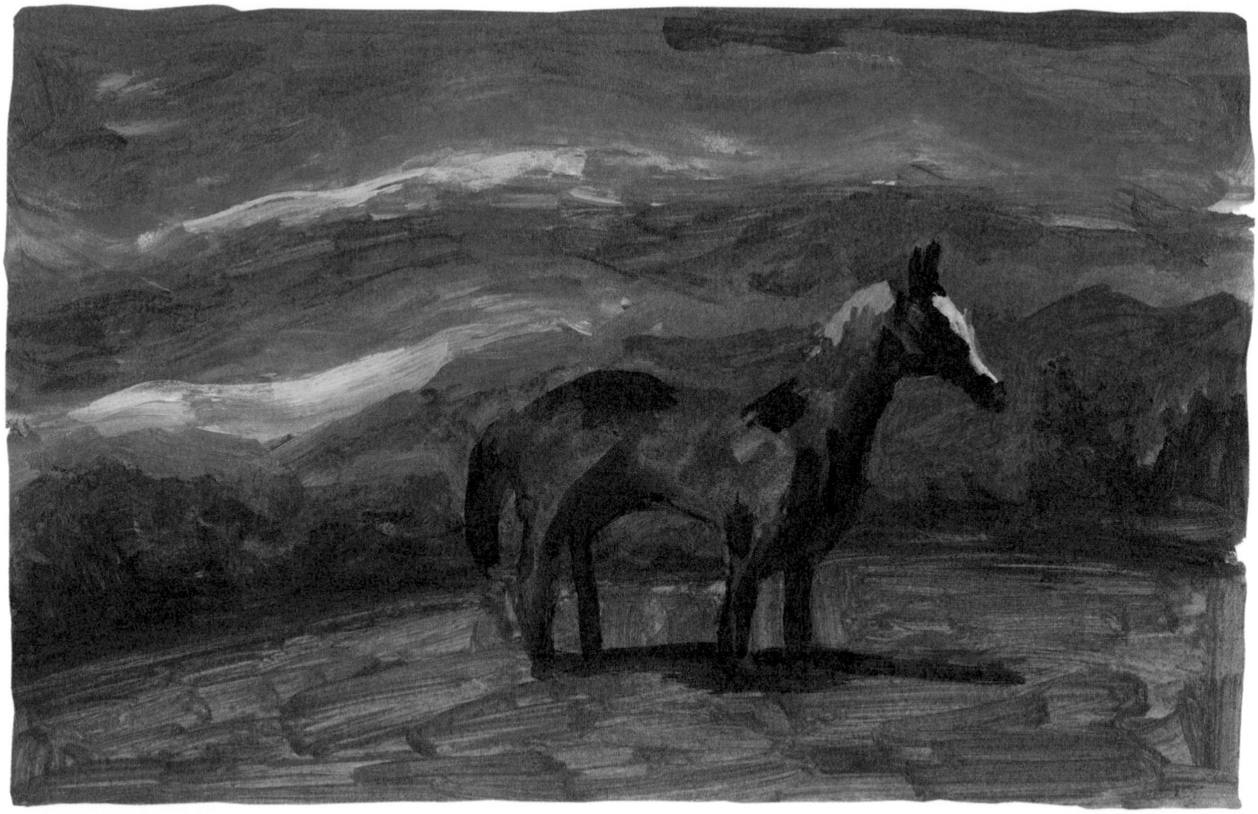

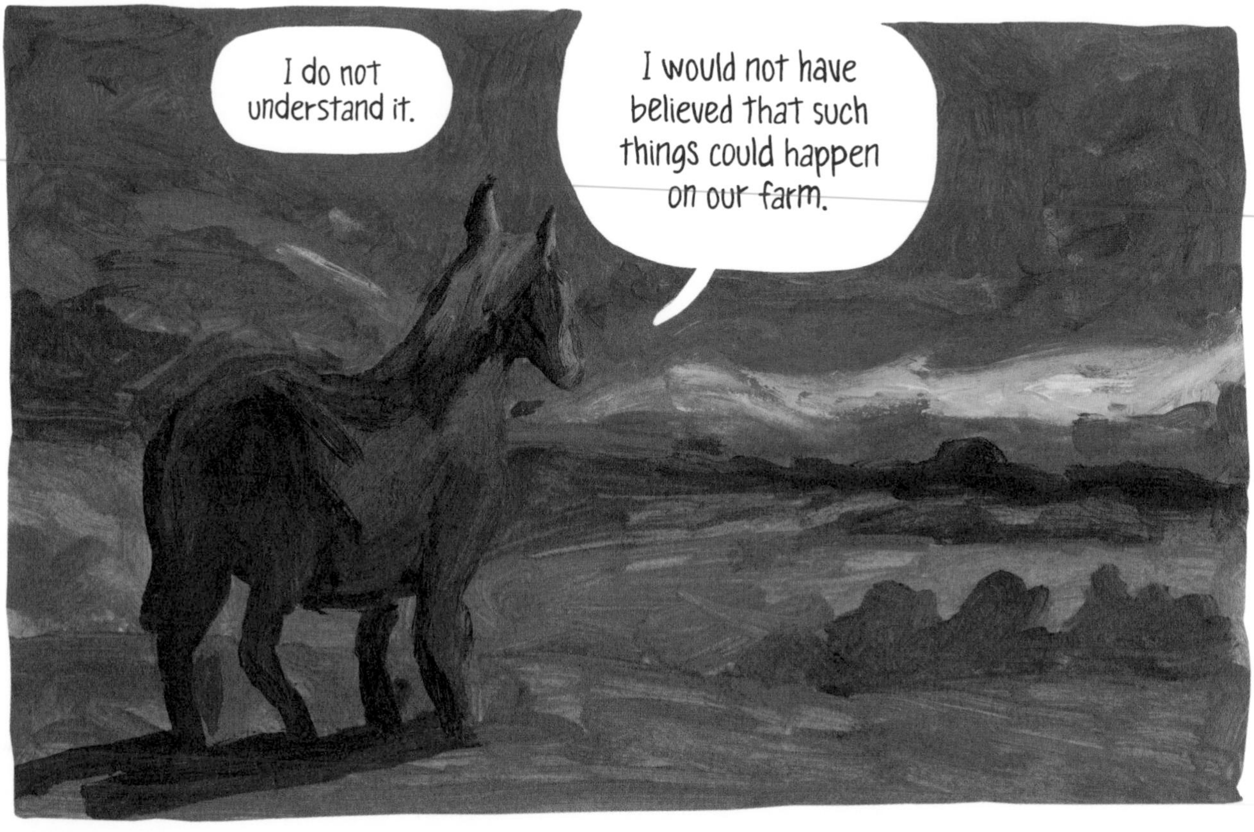
I do not understand it.
I would not have believed that such things could happen on our farm.

VIII

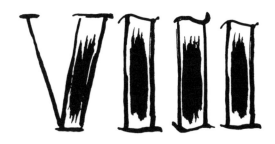

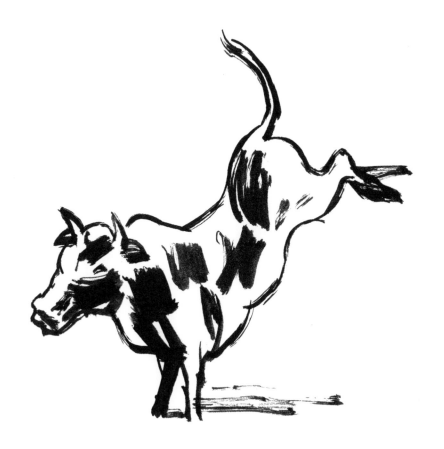

When the terror caused by the executions had died down, the animals worked even harder than they had worked in the previous year to rebuild the windmill.

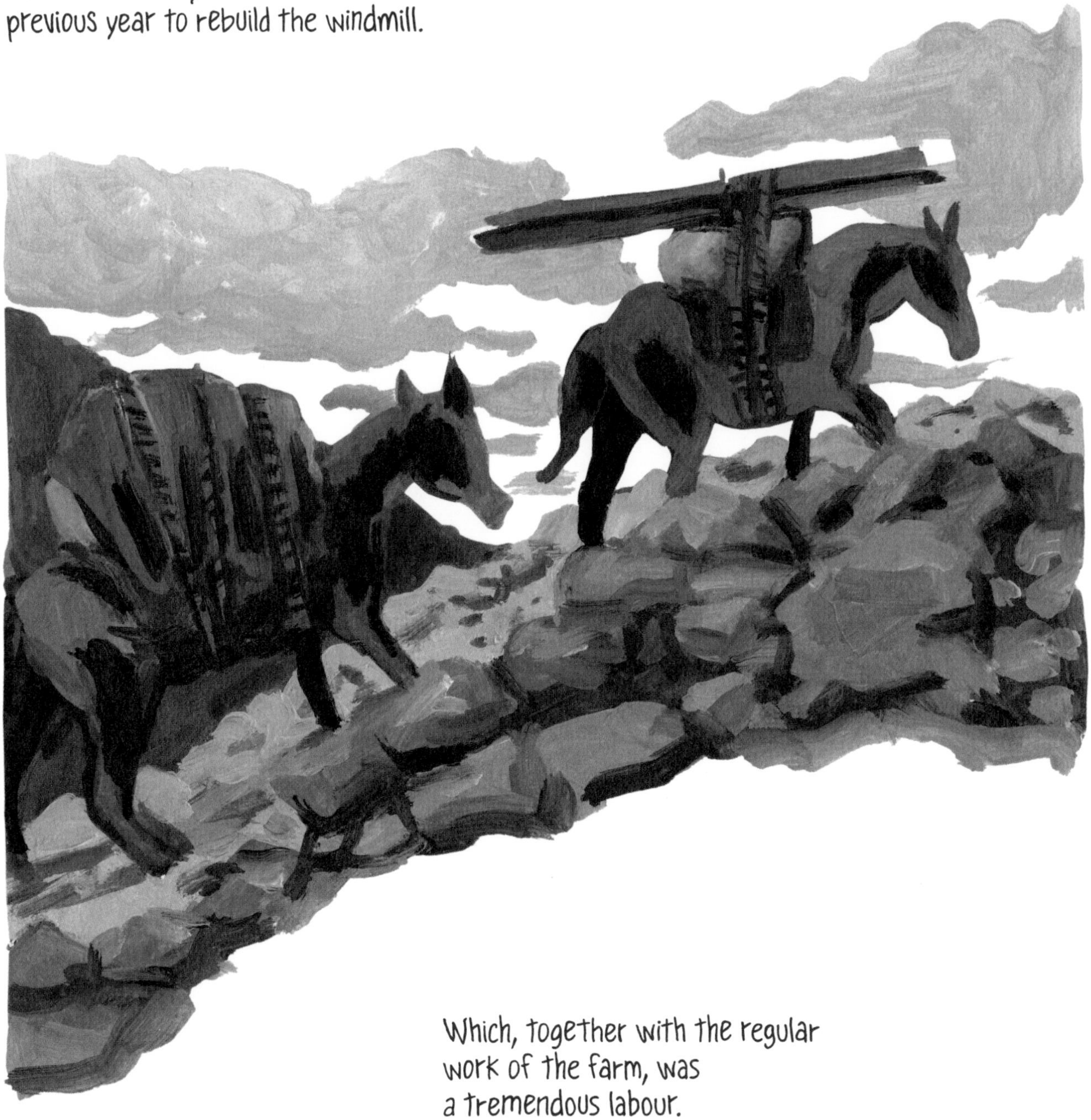

Which, together with the regular work of the farm, was a tremendous labour.

There were times when it seemed to the animals that they worked longer hours and fed no better than they had done in Jones's day.

Napoleon was now never spoken of simply as "Napoleon." He was always referred to in formal style as "our Leader, Comrade Napoleon."

The pigs liked to invent for him such titles as "Father of All Animals" or "Terror of Mankind."

Napoleon was not seen in public as often as once in a fortnight. When he did appear, he was attended not only by his retinue of dogs but by a black cockerel who marched in front of him and acted as a kind of trumpeter.

It had become usual to give Napoleon the credit for every successful achievement and every stroke of good fortune.

In the autumn, by a tremendous, exausting effort, the windmill was finished.

They thought of how they had laboured, what discouragements they had overcome, and the enormous difference that would be made in their lives when the sails were turning and the dynamos running.

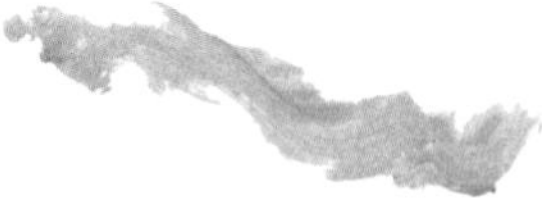

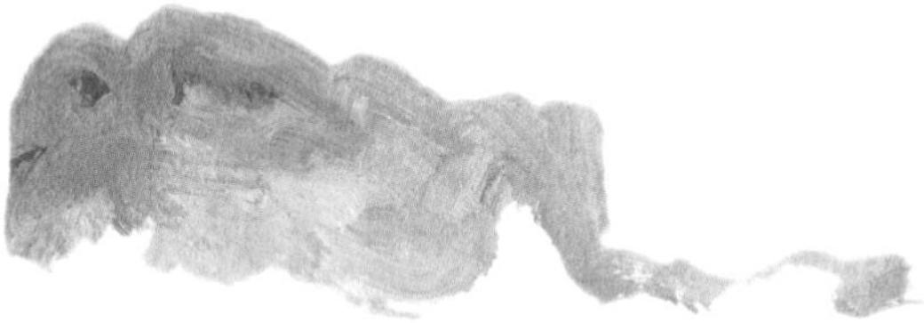

Tired out but proud, the animals walked round and round their masterpiece, which appeared even more beautiful in their eyes than when it had been built the first time.

Moreover, the walls were twice as thick as before.

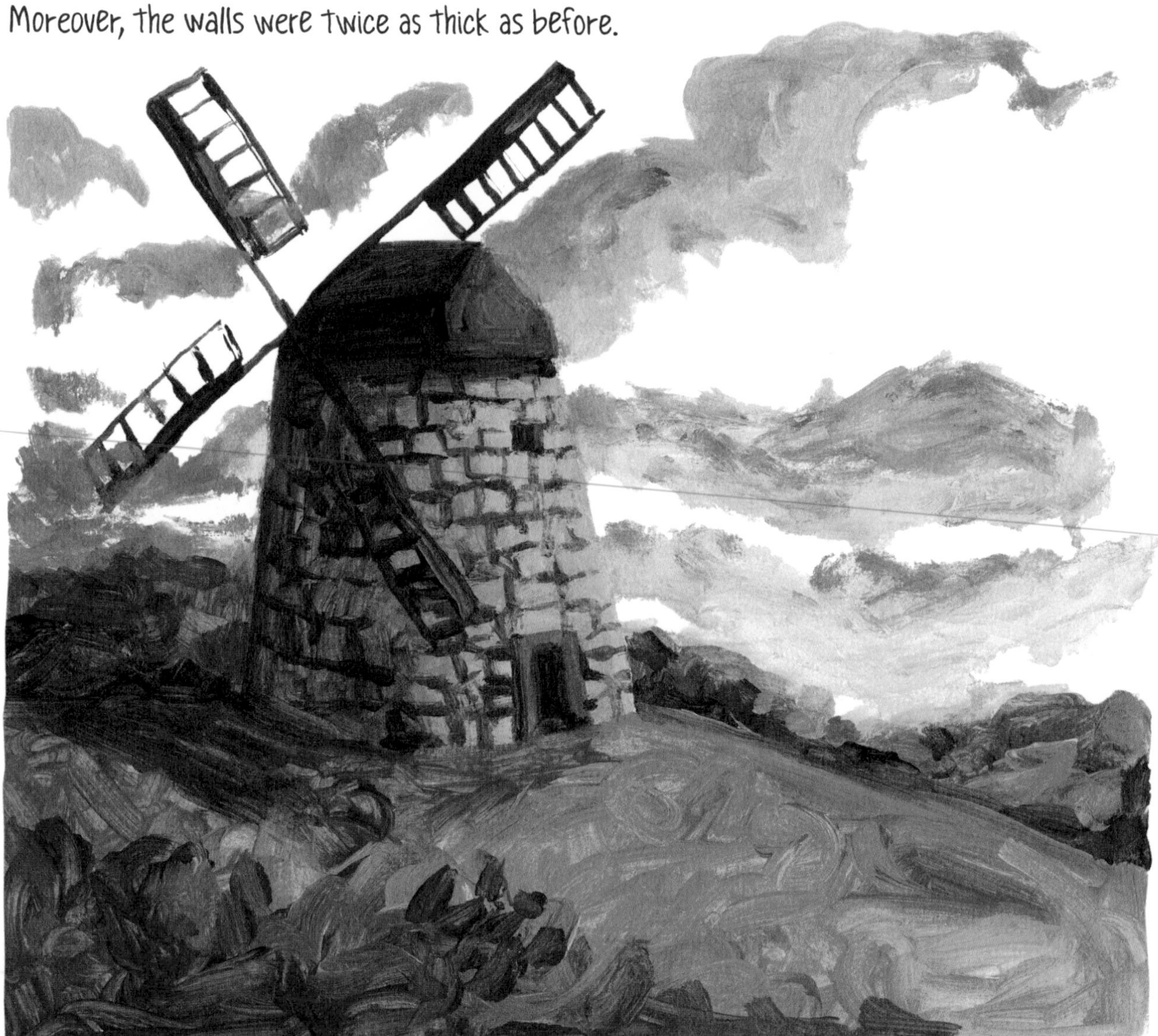

Meanwhile, through his agency of Whymper, Napoleon was engaged in complicated negotiations with Frederick and Pilkington.

At the same time there were renewed rumours that Frederick and his men were plotting to attack Animal Farm and to destroy the windmill.

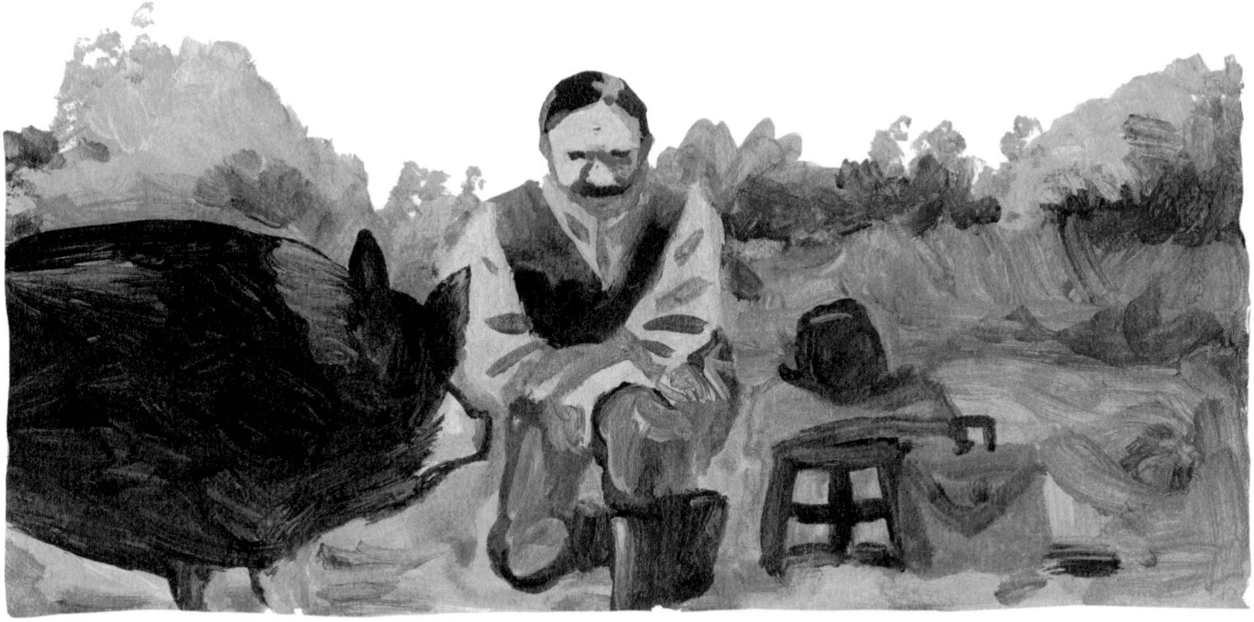

Sentinels were placed at all the approaches to the farm.

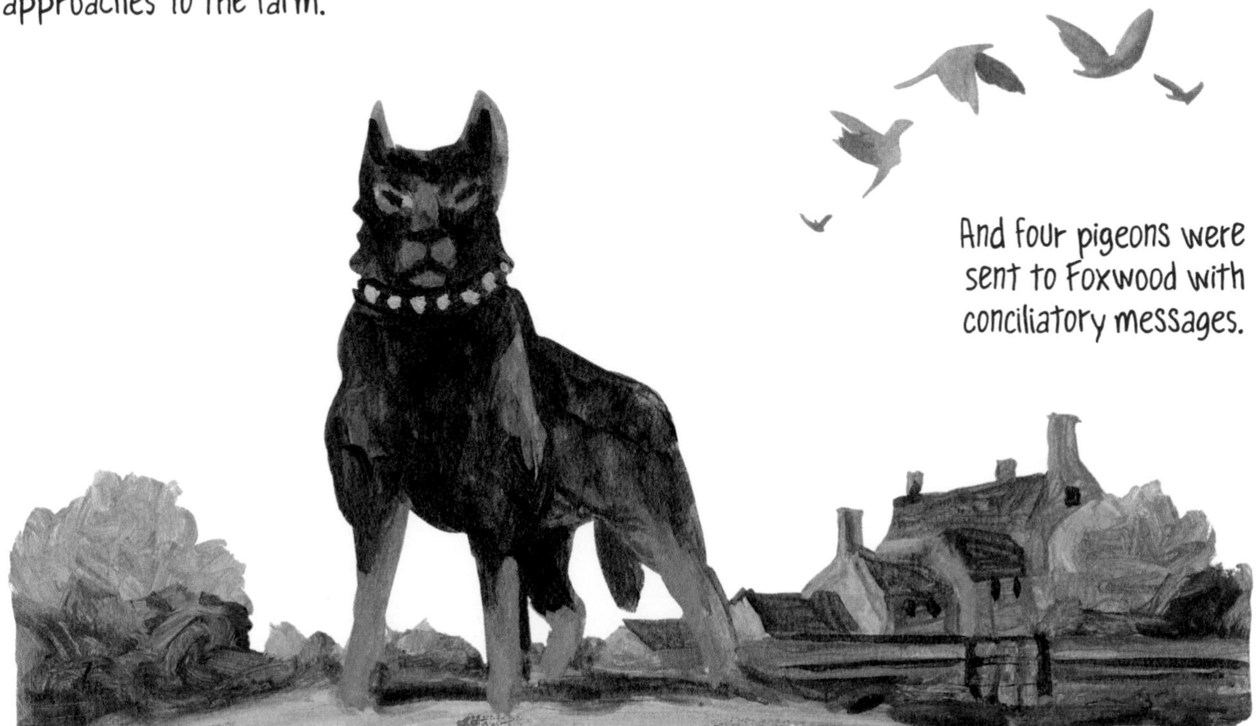

And four pigeons were sent to Foxwood with conciliatory messages.

The very next morning the attack came.

The look-outs came racing in with the news that Frederick and his followers had already come through the five-barred gate.

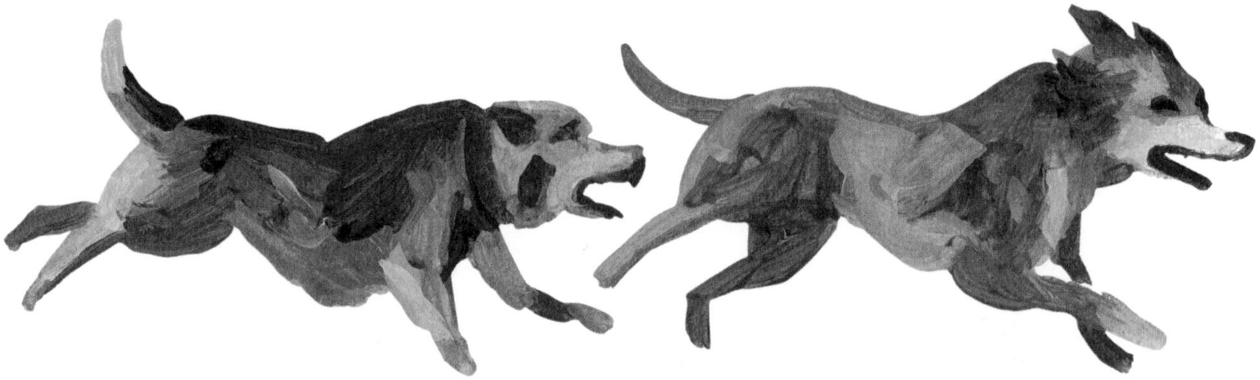

Boldly enough the animals sallied forth to meet them.

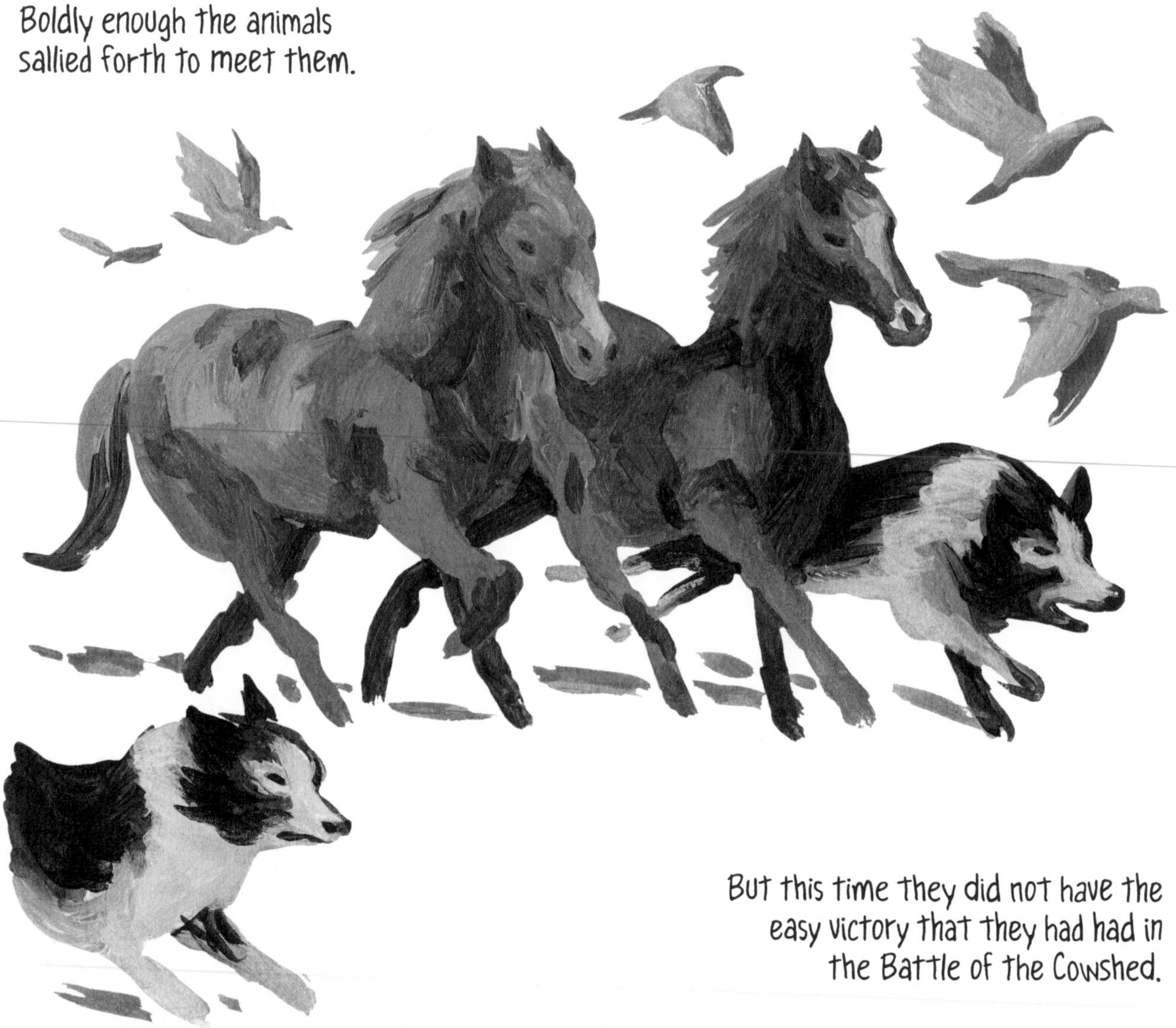

But this time they did not have the easy victory that they had had in the Battle of the Cowshed.

Fifteen men, with half a dozen guns between them, opened fire as soon as they got within fifty yards.

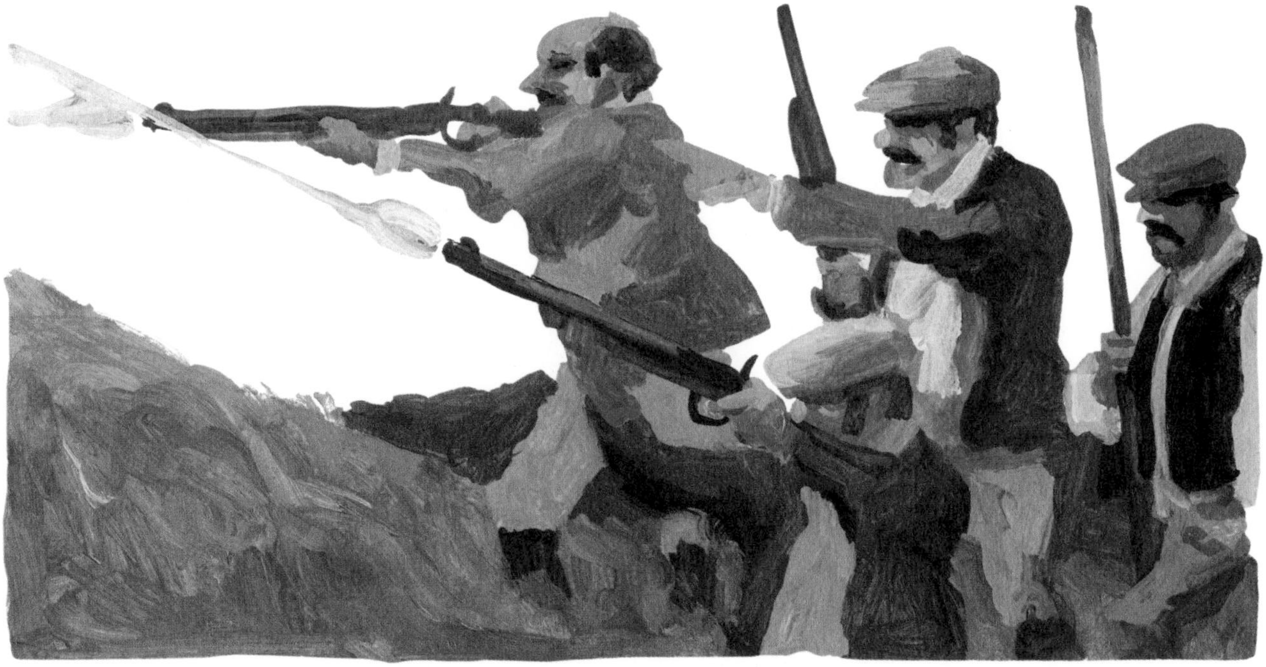

The animals could not face the terrible explosions and the stinging pellets and were soon driven back.

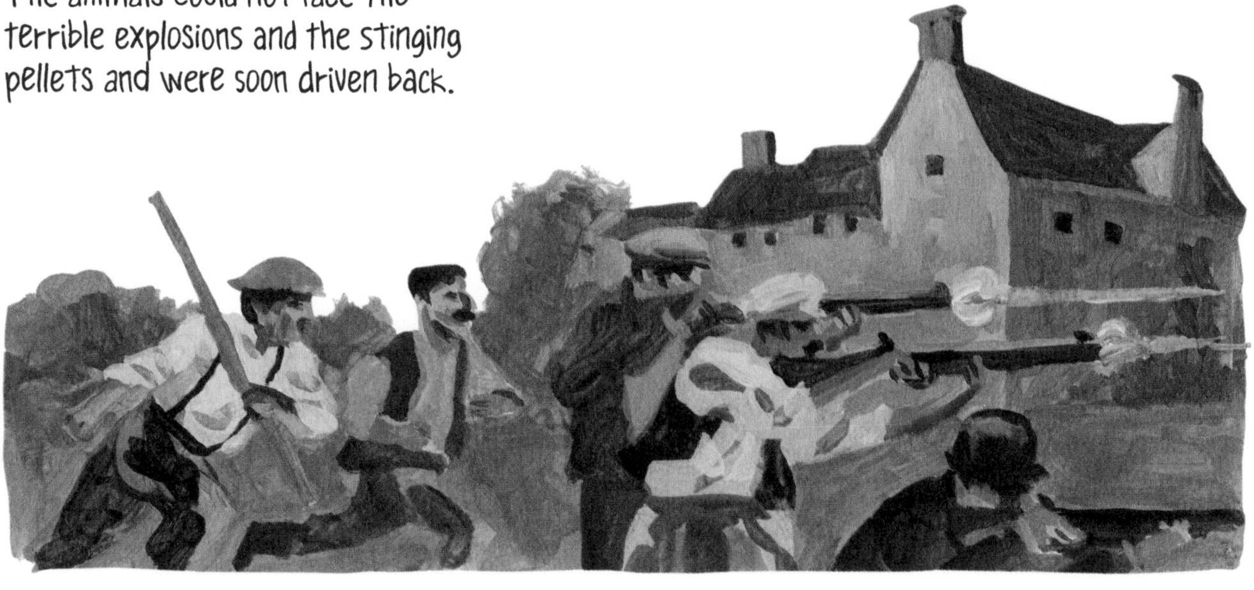

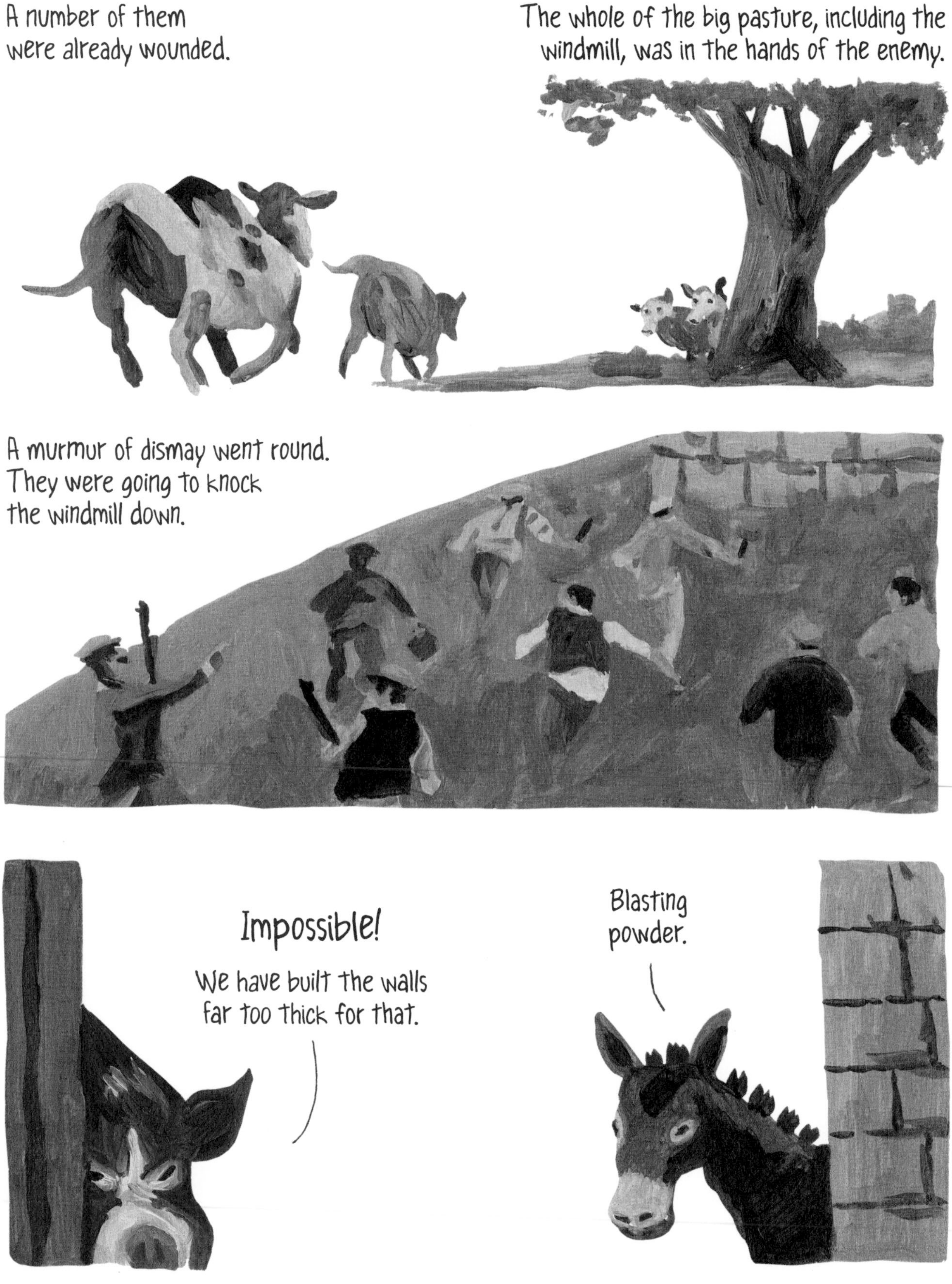
A number of them were already wounded.
The whole of the big pasture, including the windmill, was in the hands of the enemy.
A murmur of dismay went round. They were going to knock the windmill down.
Impossible!
We have built the walls far too thick for that.
Blasting powder.

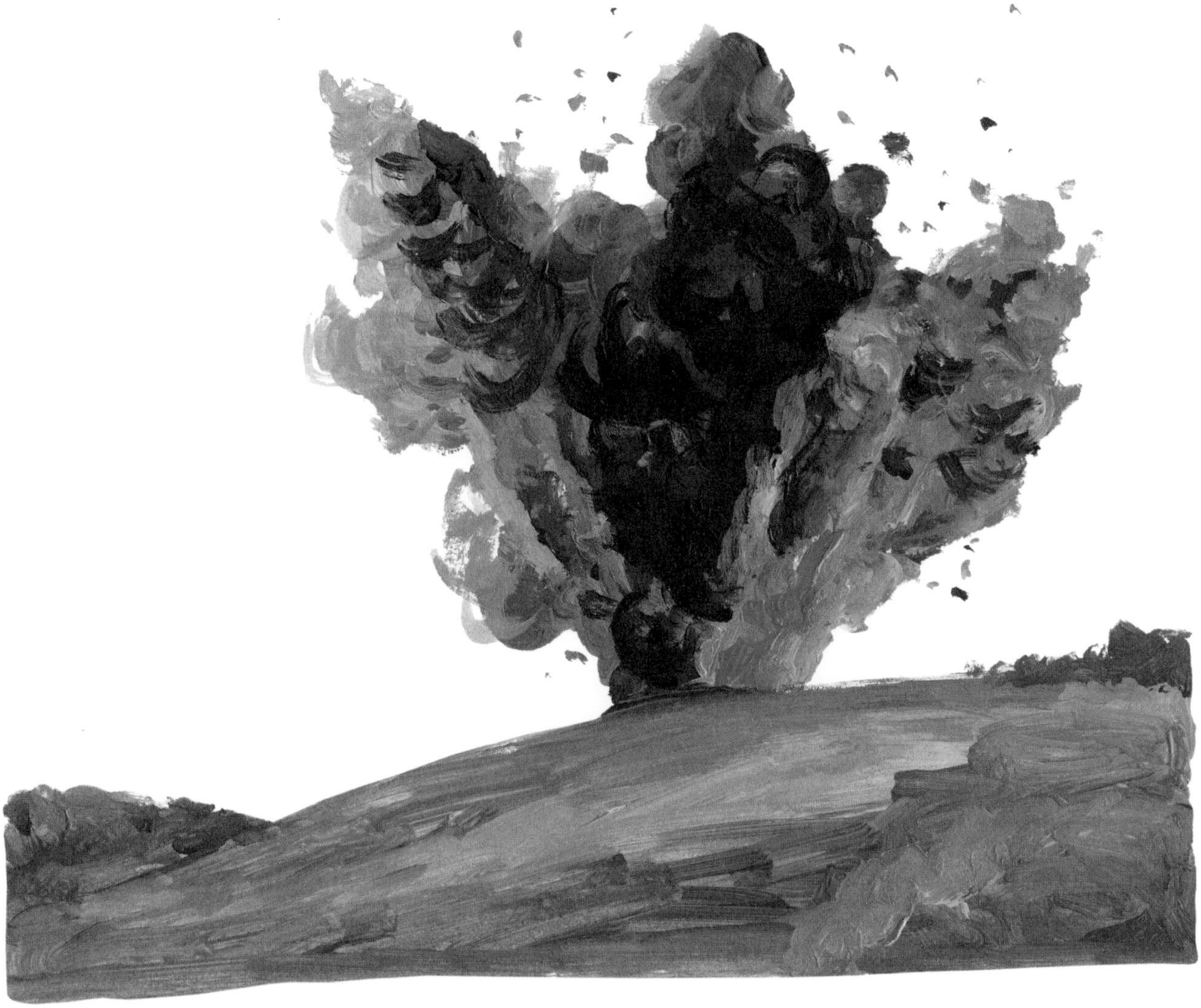

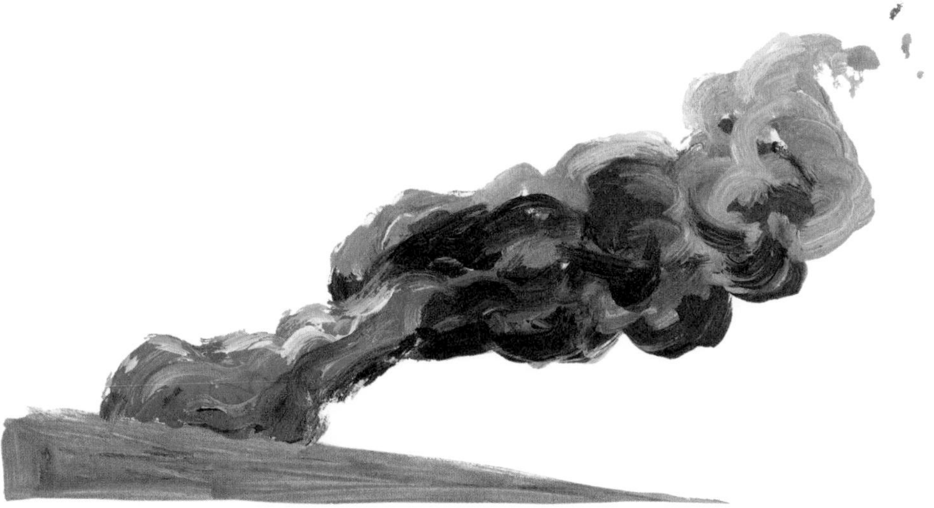

The windmill had
ceased to exist!

At this sight the animals' courage returned to them.

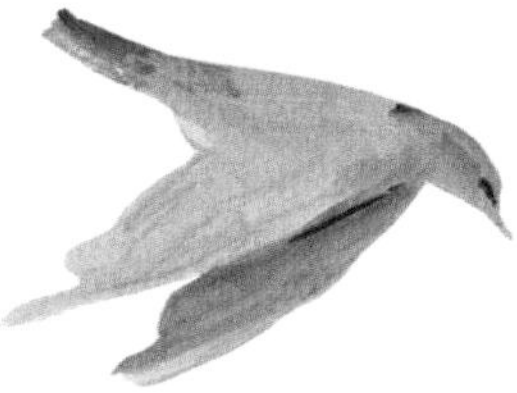

The fear and despair they had felt a moment earlier were drowned in their rage against this vile, contemptible act.

Without waiting for further orders they charged forth in a body and made straight for the enemy.

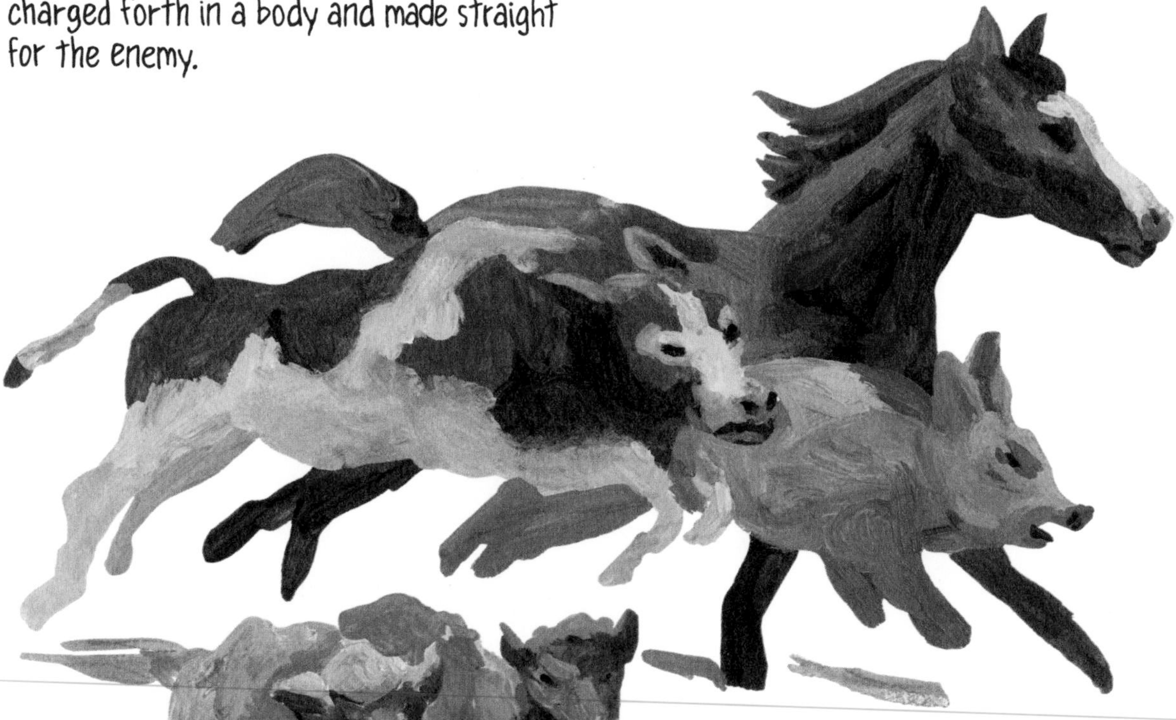

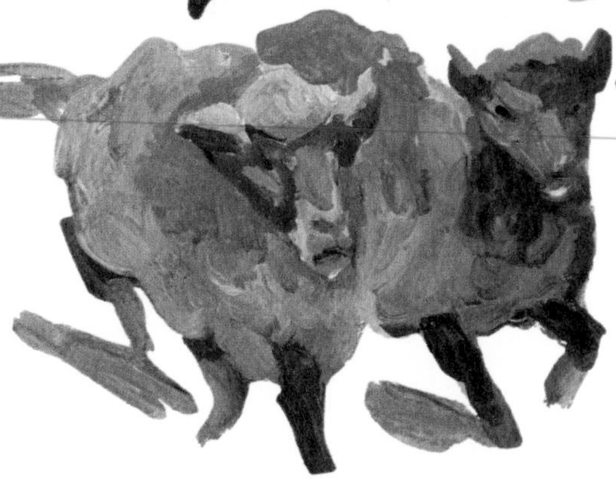

This time they did not heed the cruel pellets that swept over them like hail.

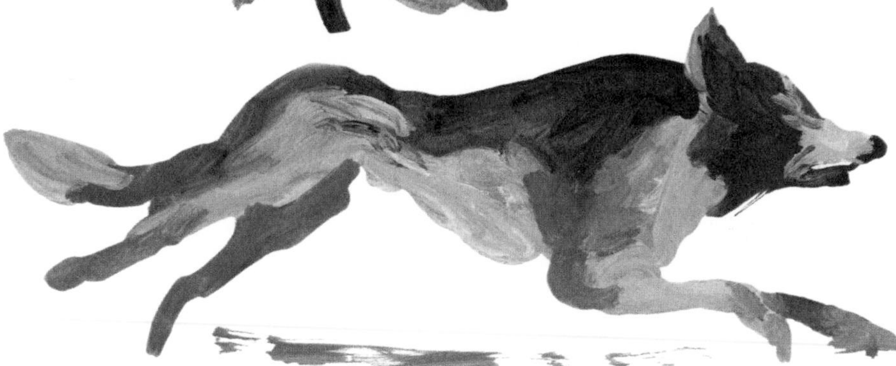

It was a savage, bitter battle.
The men fired again and again.

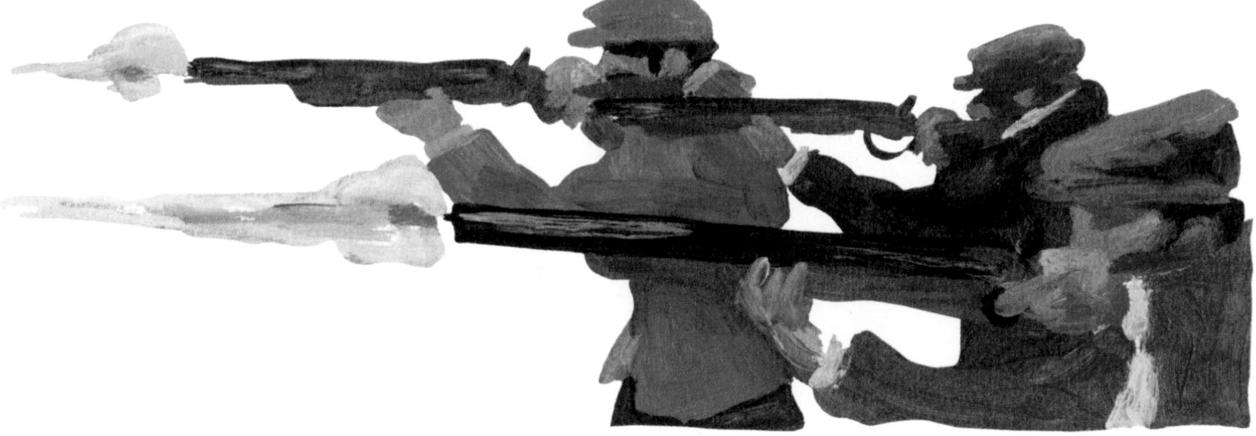

A cow, three sheep, and two geese were killed. Nearly everyone was wounded.

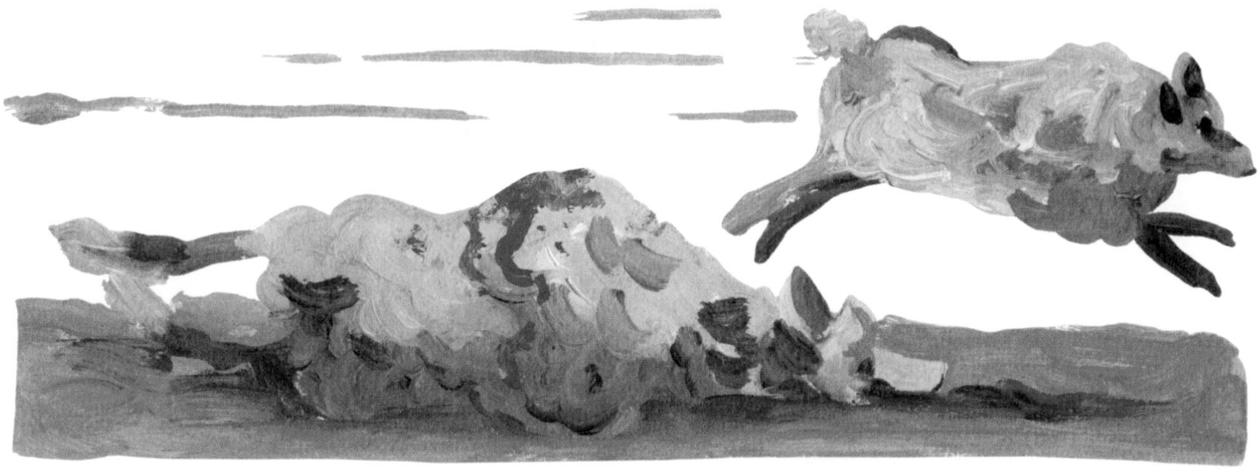

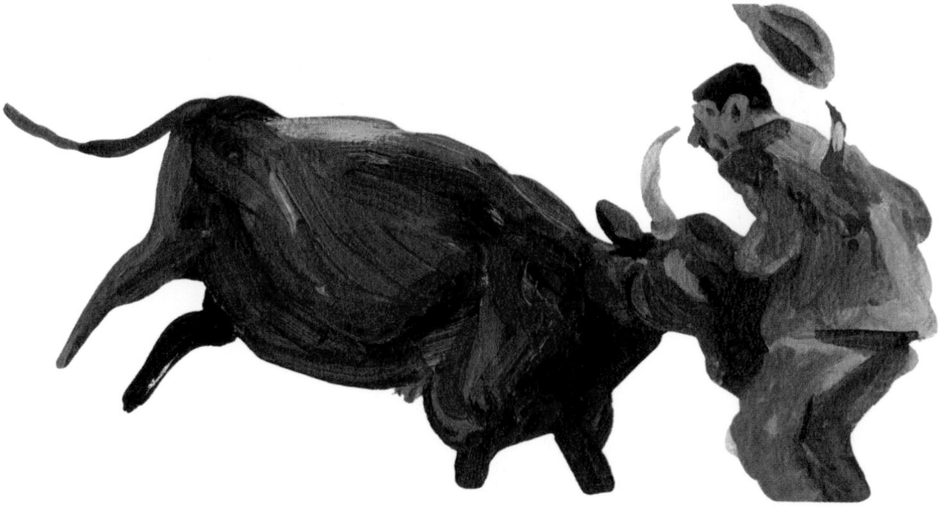

But the men did not go unscathed either.

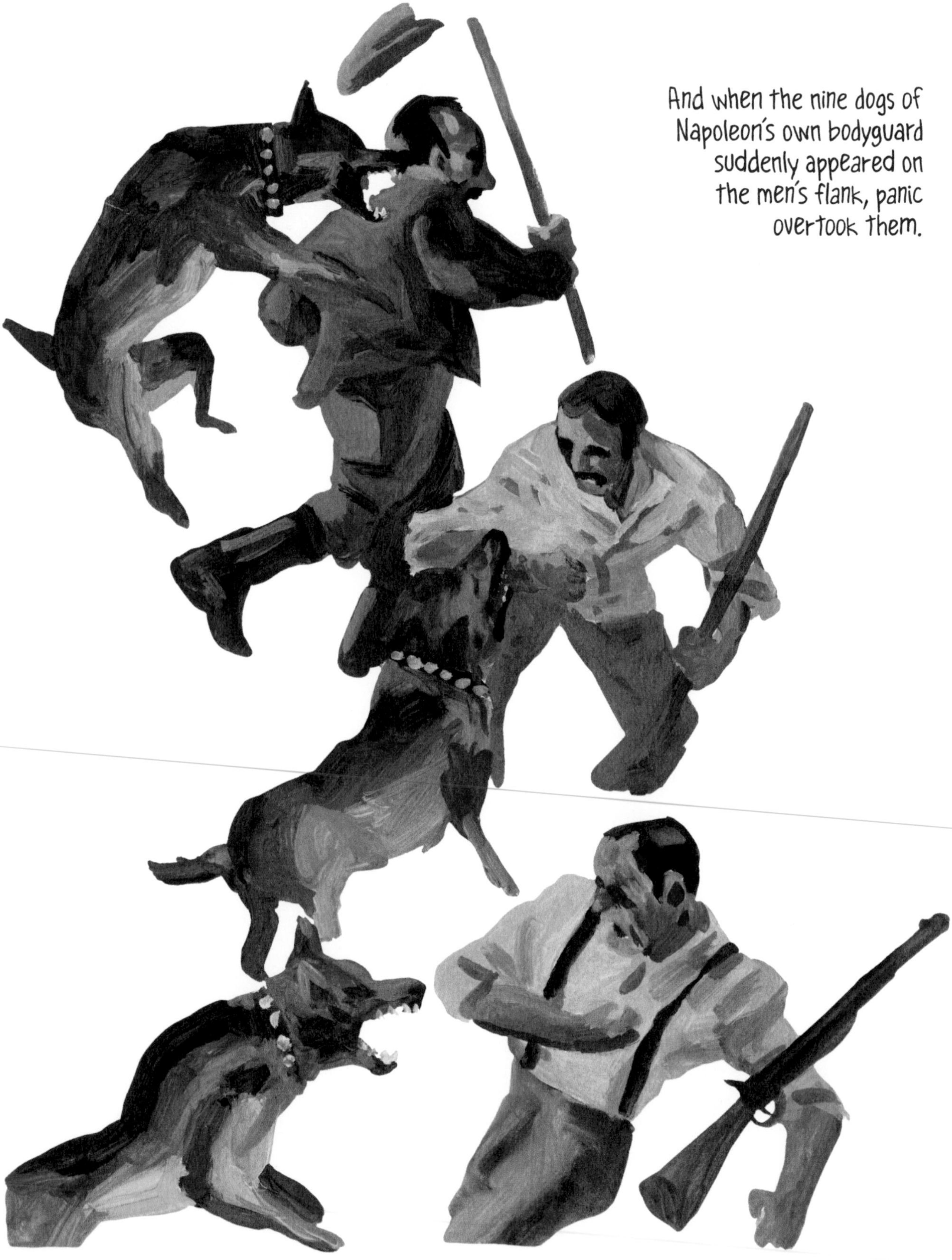
And when the nine dogs of Napoleon's own bodyguard suddenly appeared on the men's flank, panic overtook them.

They saw that they were in danger of being surrounded. Frederick shouted to his men to get out while the going was good, and the next moment the cowardly enemy ran for dear life.

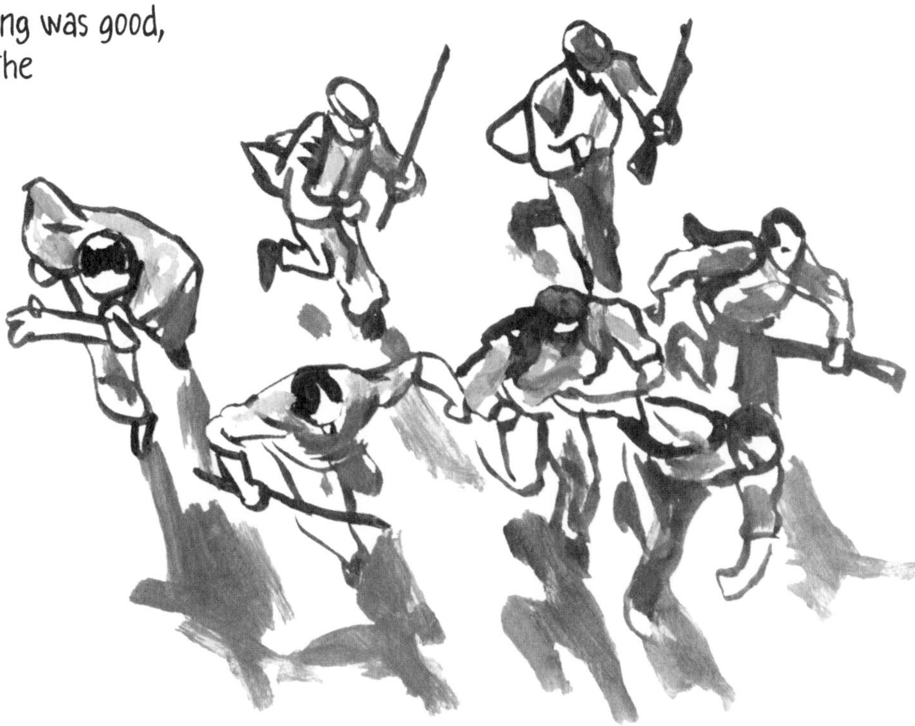

They had won, but they were weary and bleeding.

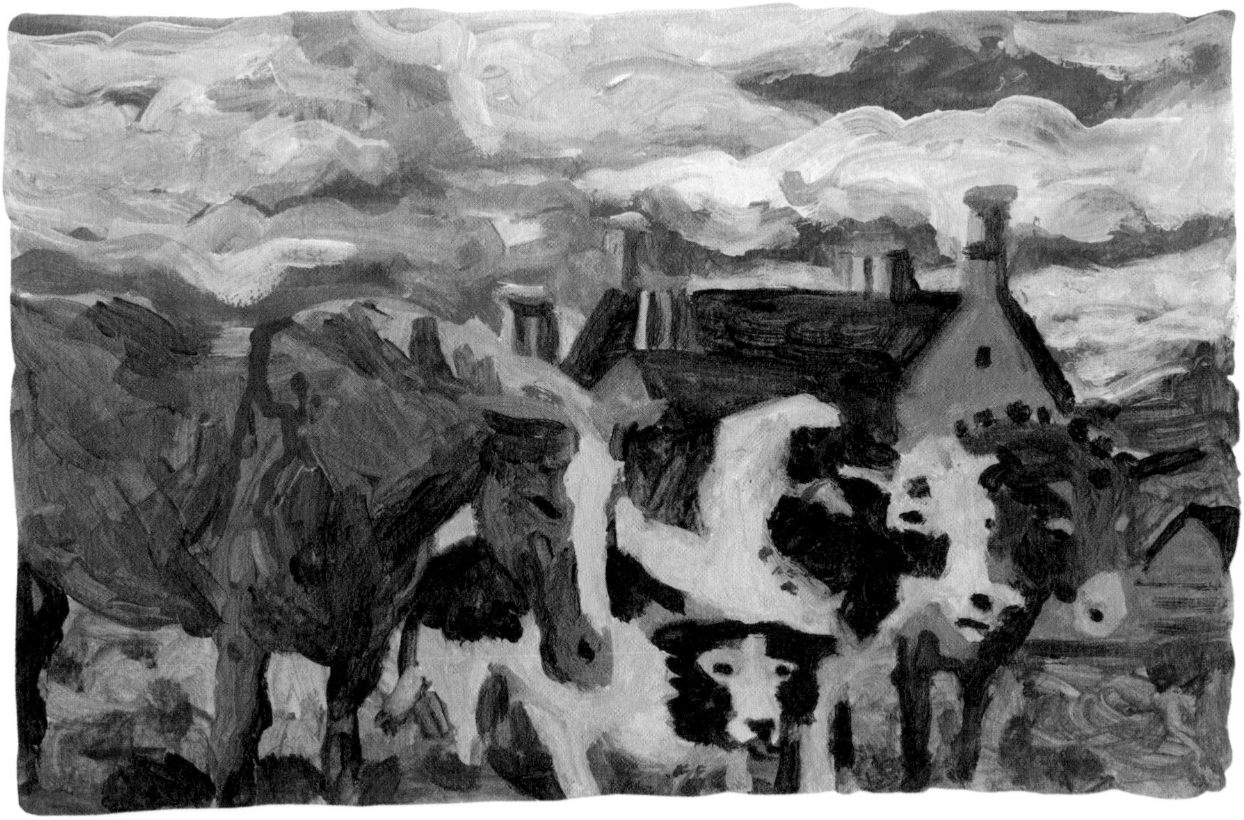

Slowly they began to limp back towards the farm. They heard from the direction of the farm the solemn booming of a gun, to celebrate the victory.

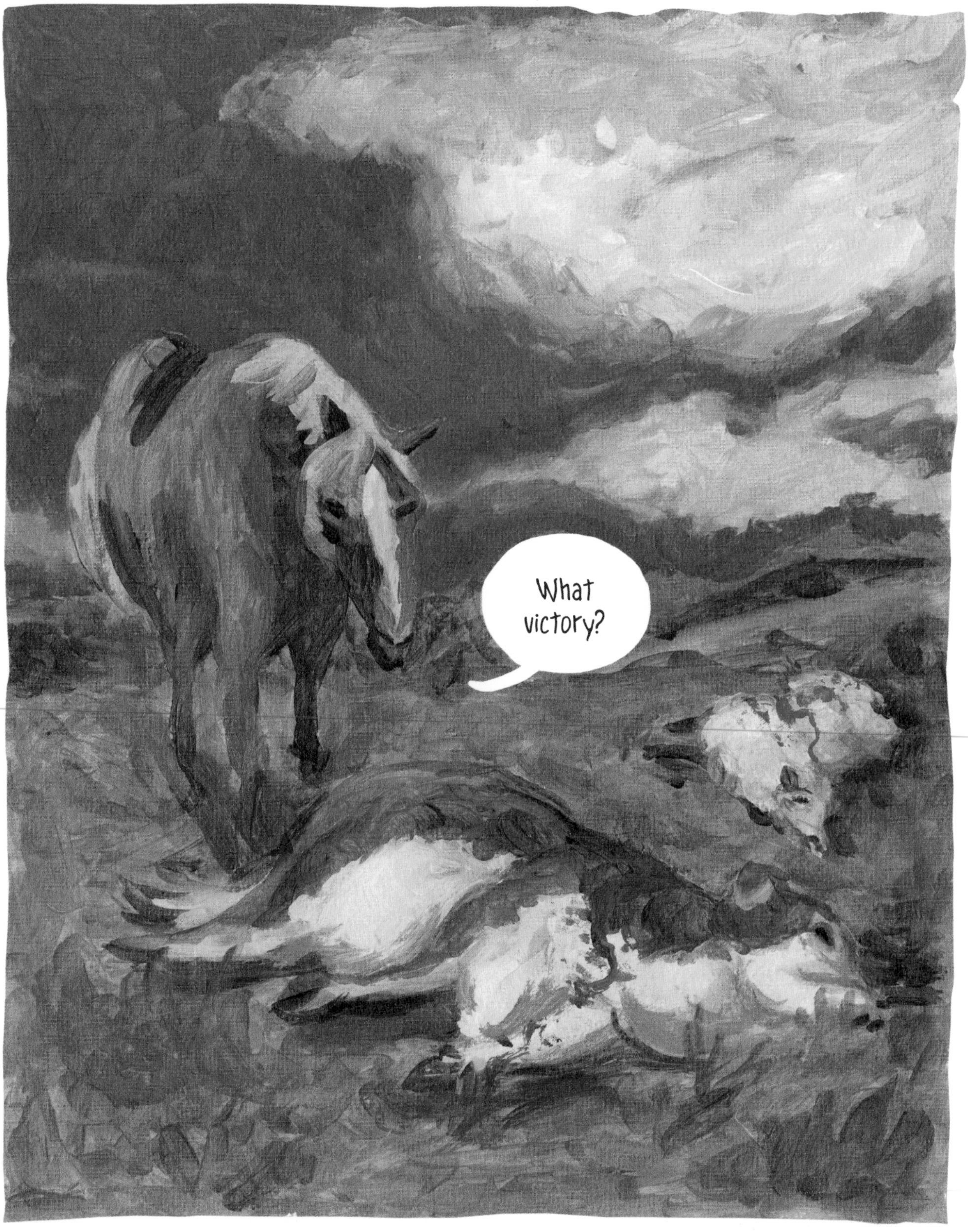
What victory?

But when the animals saw the green flag flying and heard the gun firing again and heard the speech that Napoleon made, congratulating them on their conduct, it did seem to them after all that they had won a great victory.

The animals slain in the battle were given a solemn funeral.

Two whole days were given over to celebrations. There were songs, speeches, and more firing of the gun, and a special gift of an apple was bestowed on every animal.

It was announced that the battle would be called the Battle of the Windmill.

IX

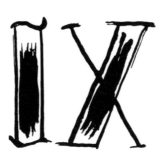

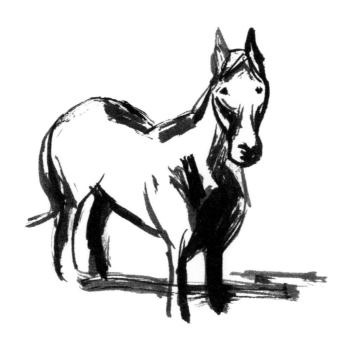

Boxer's split hoof was a long time in healing. They had started the rebuilding of the windmill the day after the victory celebrations were ended. Boxer refused to take even a day off work.

He had only one real ambition left—to see the windmill well under way before he reached the age for retirement fixed for horses and pigs at twelve.

Boxer's twelfth birthday was due in the late summer of the following year.

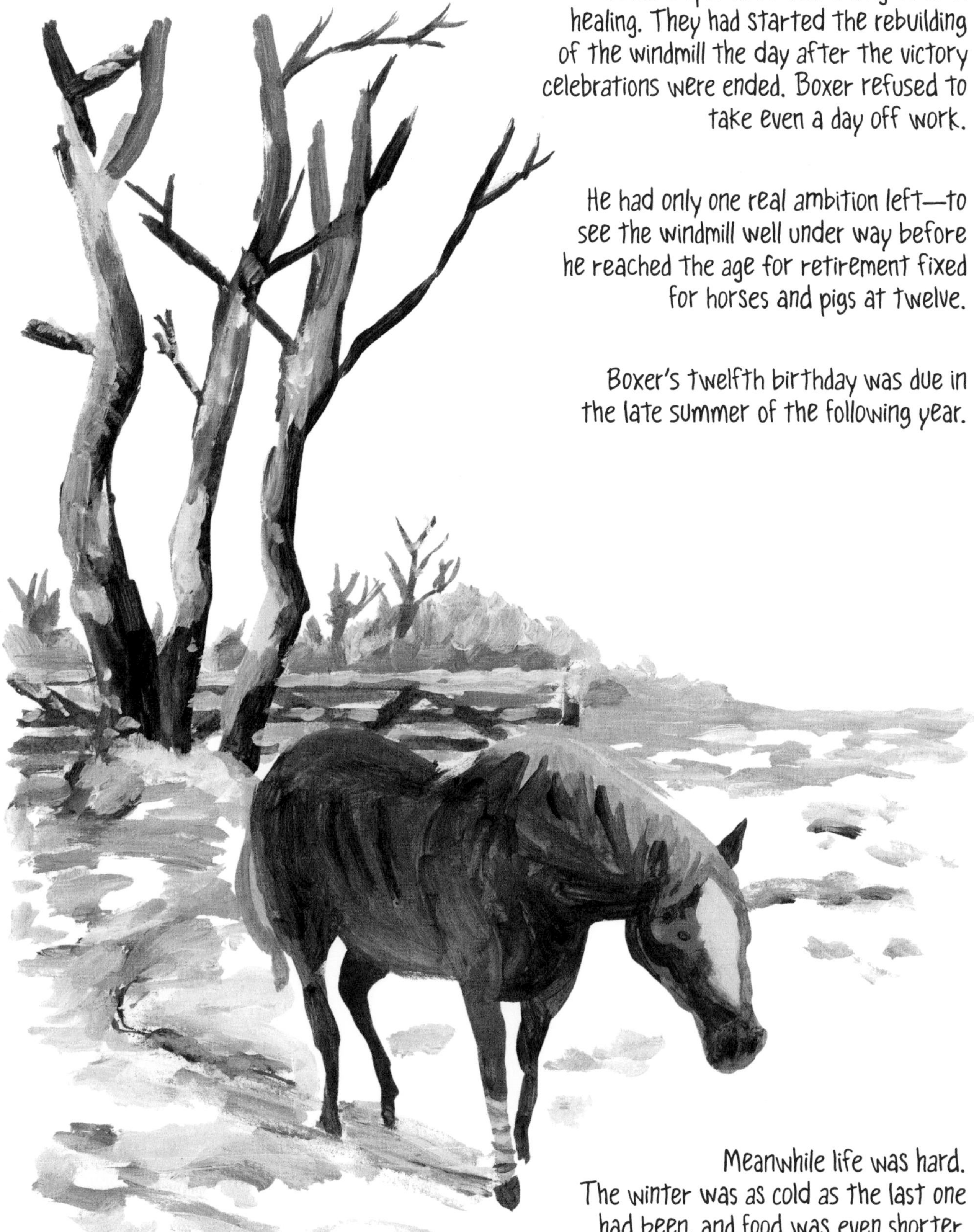

Meanwhile life was hard. The winter was as cold as the last one had been, and food was even shorter.

Once again all rations were reduced, except those of the pigs and dogs.

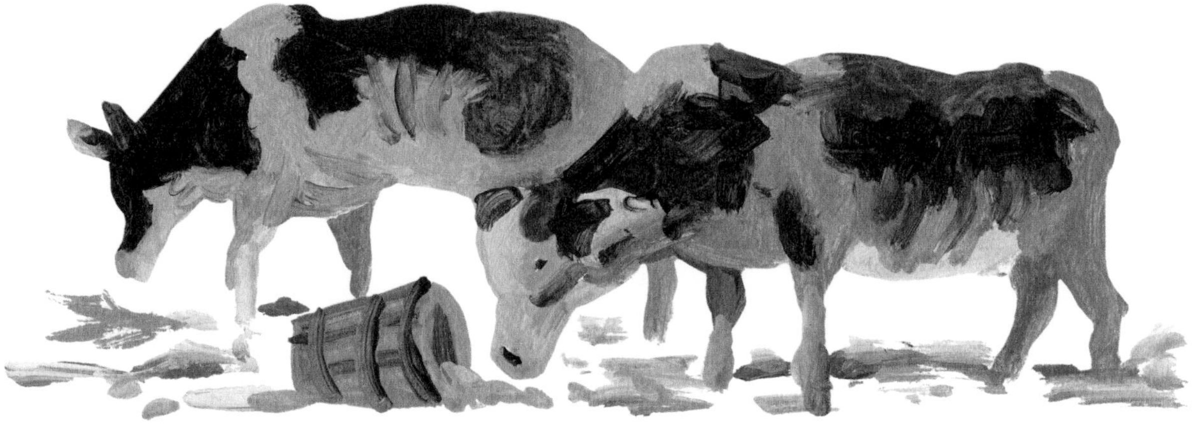

Jones and all he stood for had almost faded out of their memories. They knew that life nowadays was harsh and bare, that they were often hungry and often cold, and that they were usually working when they were not asleep.

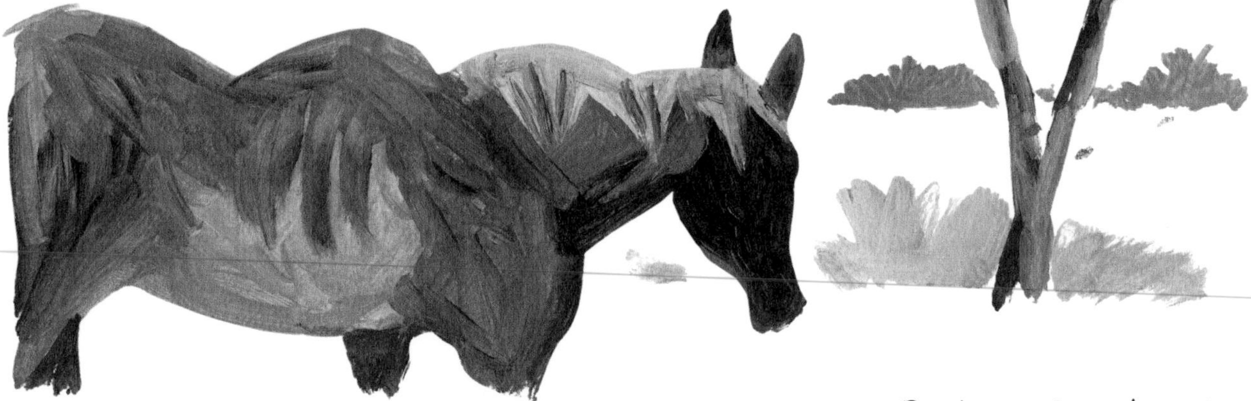

Besides, in those days they had been slaves and now they were free.

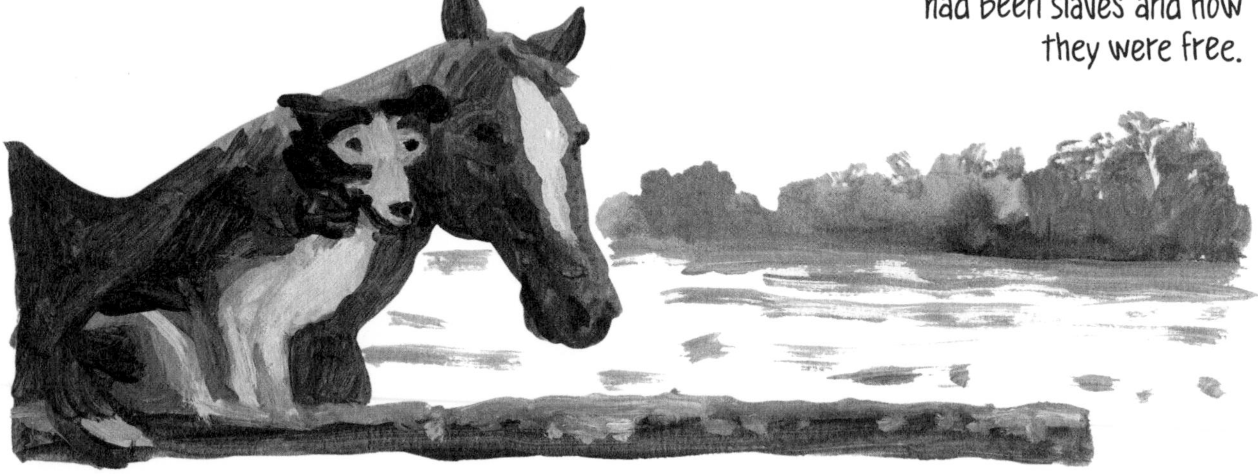

There were many more
mouths to feed now.

Four sows had all littered about simultaneously,
producing thirty-one young pigs between them.
It was possible to guess at their parentage.

They were given their
instruction by Napoleon himself.

And were discouraged from playing
with the other young animals.

It was laid down as a rule that when
a pig and any other animal met on the
path, the other animal must stand aside.

But if there were hardships to be borne, they were partly offset by the fact that life nowadays had a greater dignity.

There were more songs, more speeches, more processions.

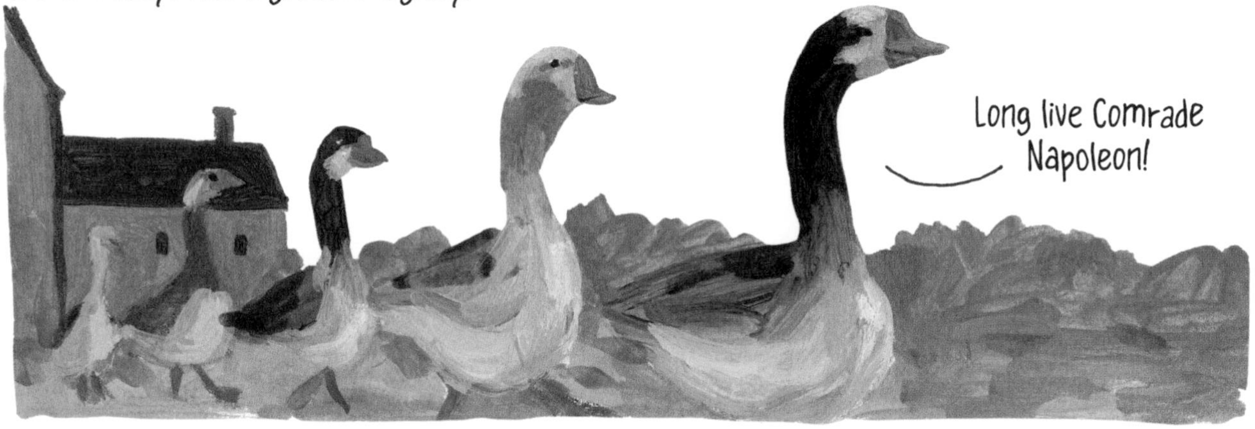
Long live Comrade Napoleon!

The animals enjoyed these celebrations. So that, what with the songs and the processions, they were able to forget that their bellies were empty, at least part of the time.

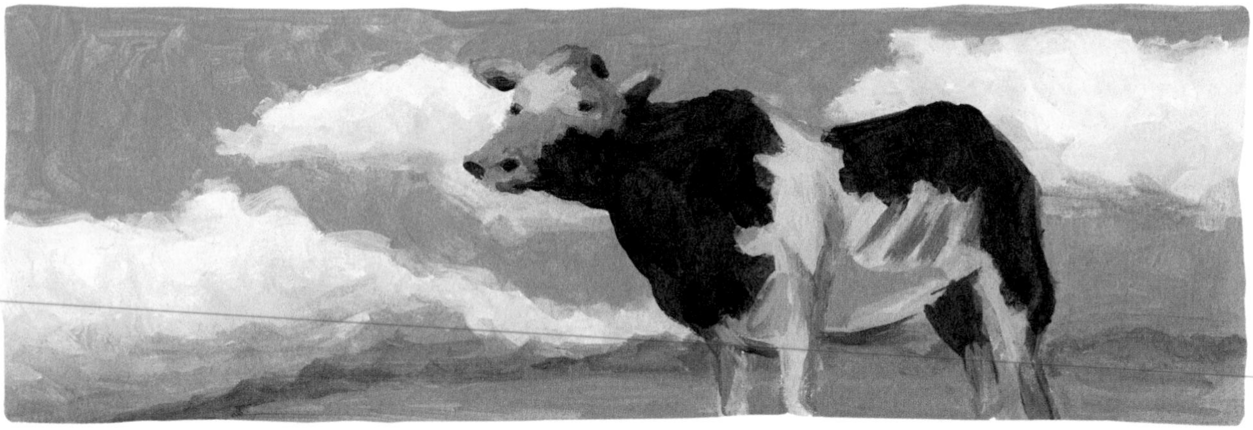

In April, Animal Farm was proclaimed a Republic, and it became necessary to elect a President. There was only one candidate, Napoleon, who was elected unanimously.

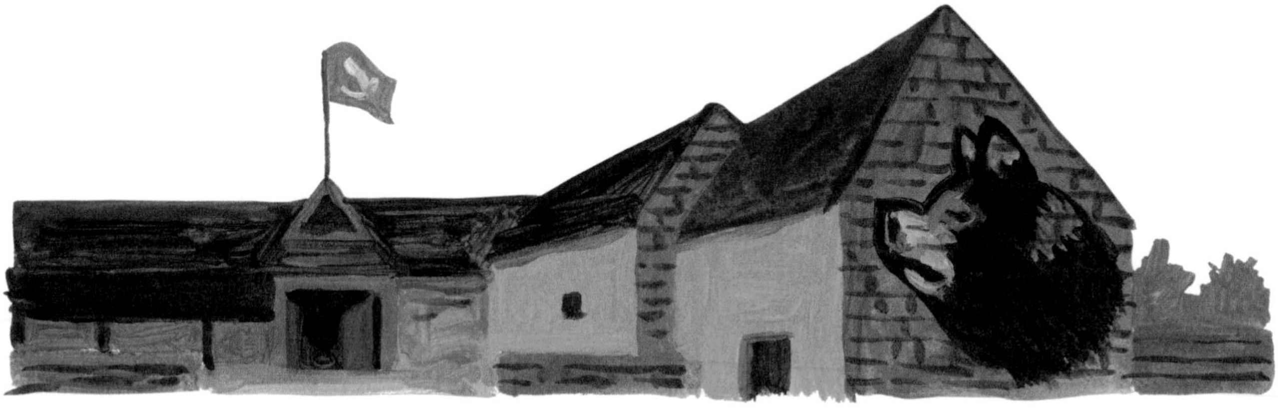

Late one evening in the summer, a sudden rumour ran round the farm.

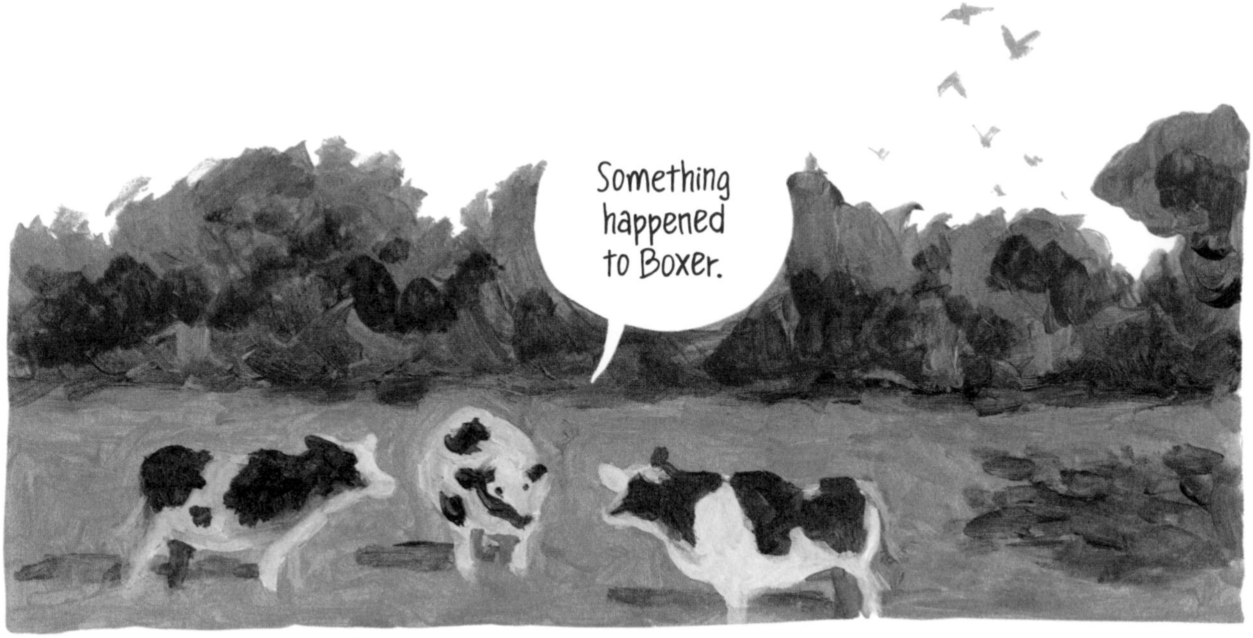
Something happened to Boxer.

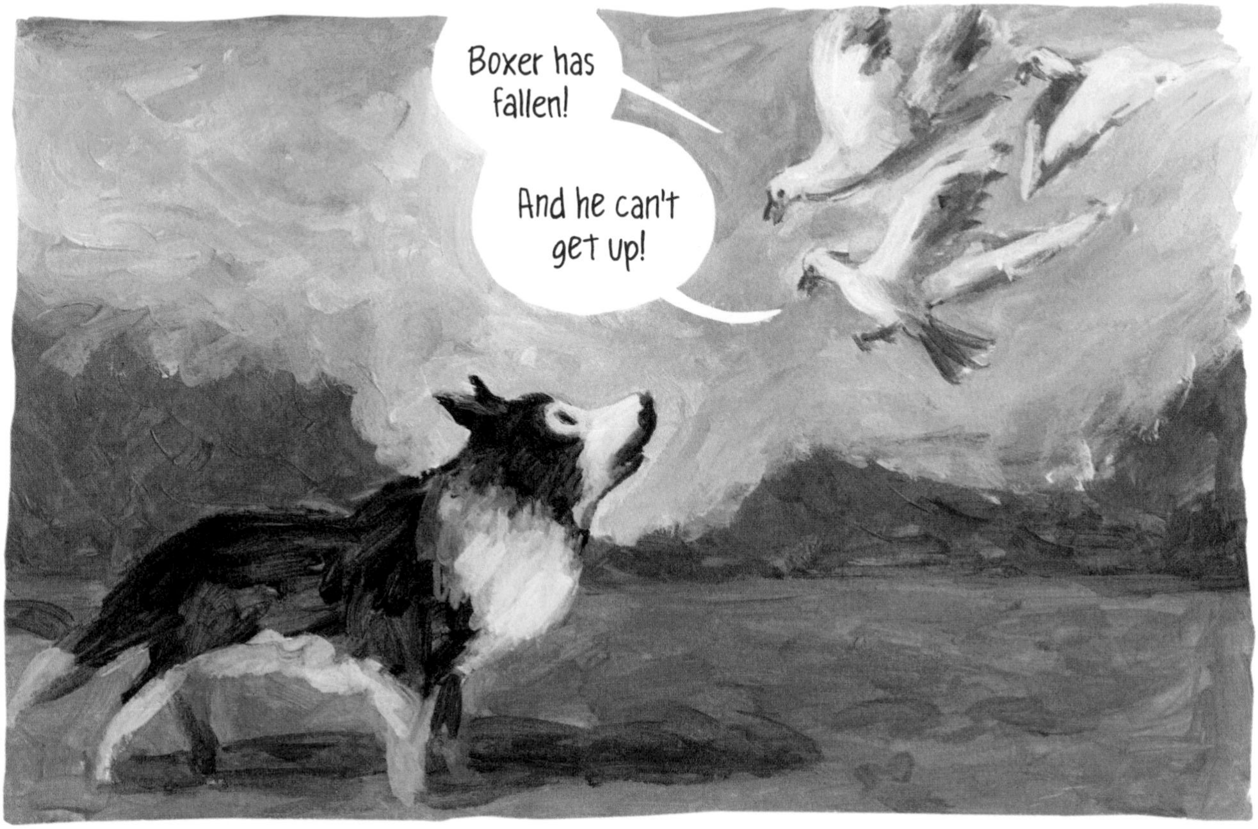
Boxer has fallen!
And he can't get up!

The rumour was true.

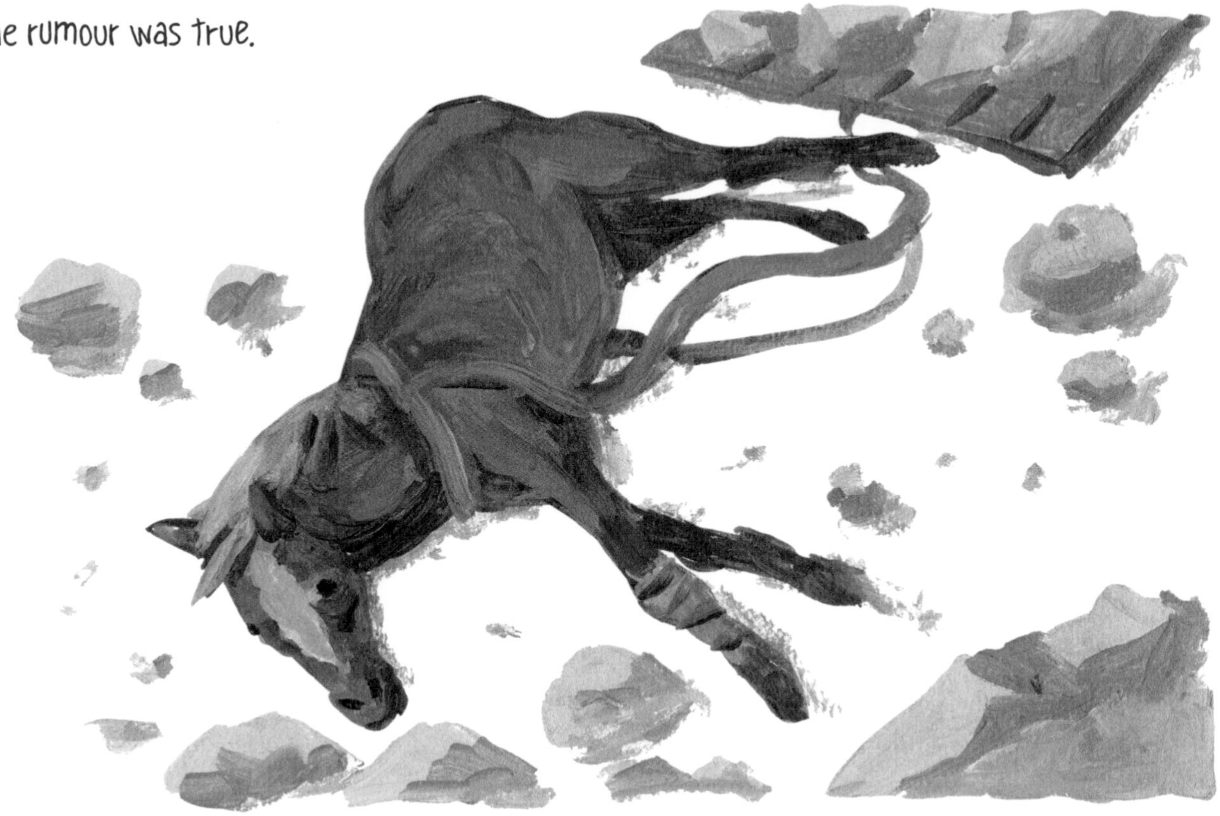

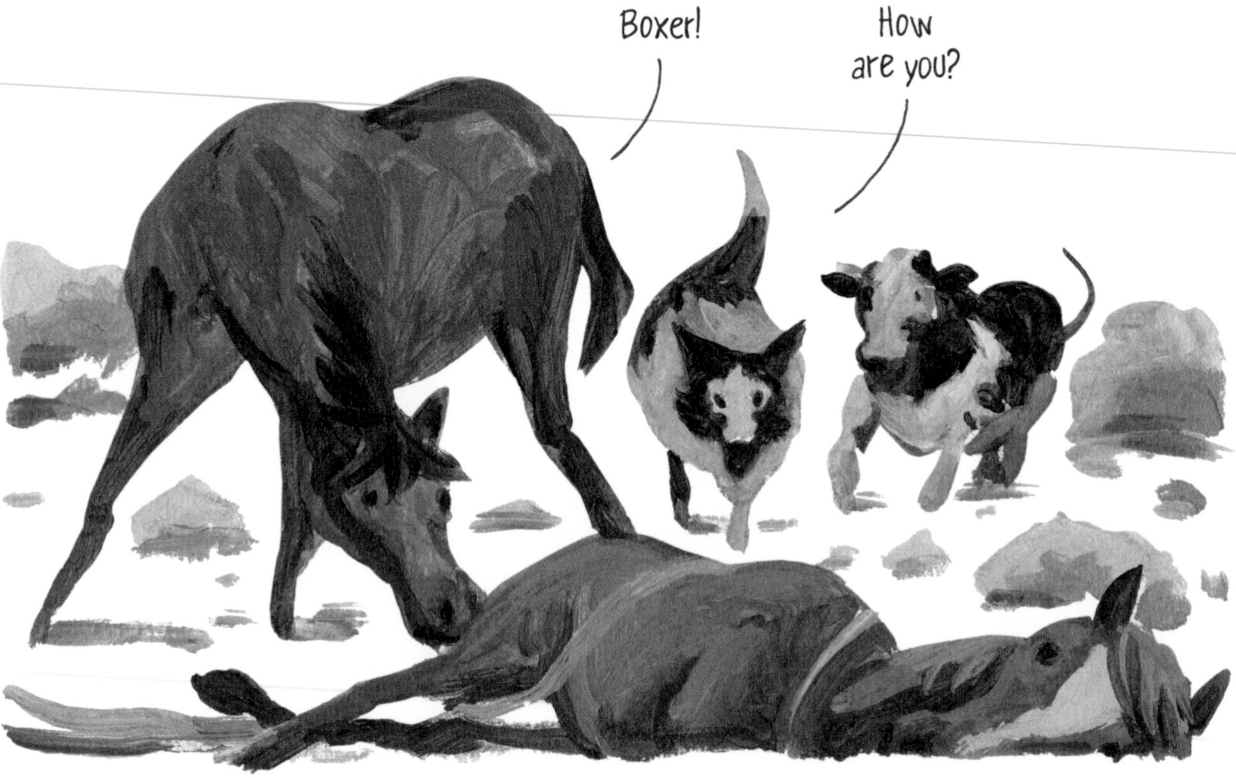
Boxer!
How are you?

It is
my lung.

It
does not
matter.

I think you will
be able to finish
the windmill
without me.

I have been
looking forward
to my retirement.

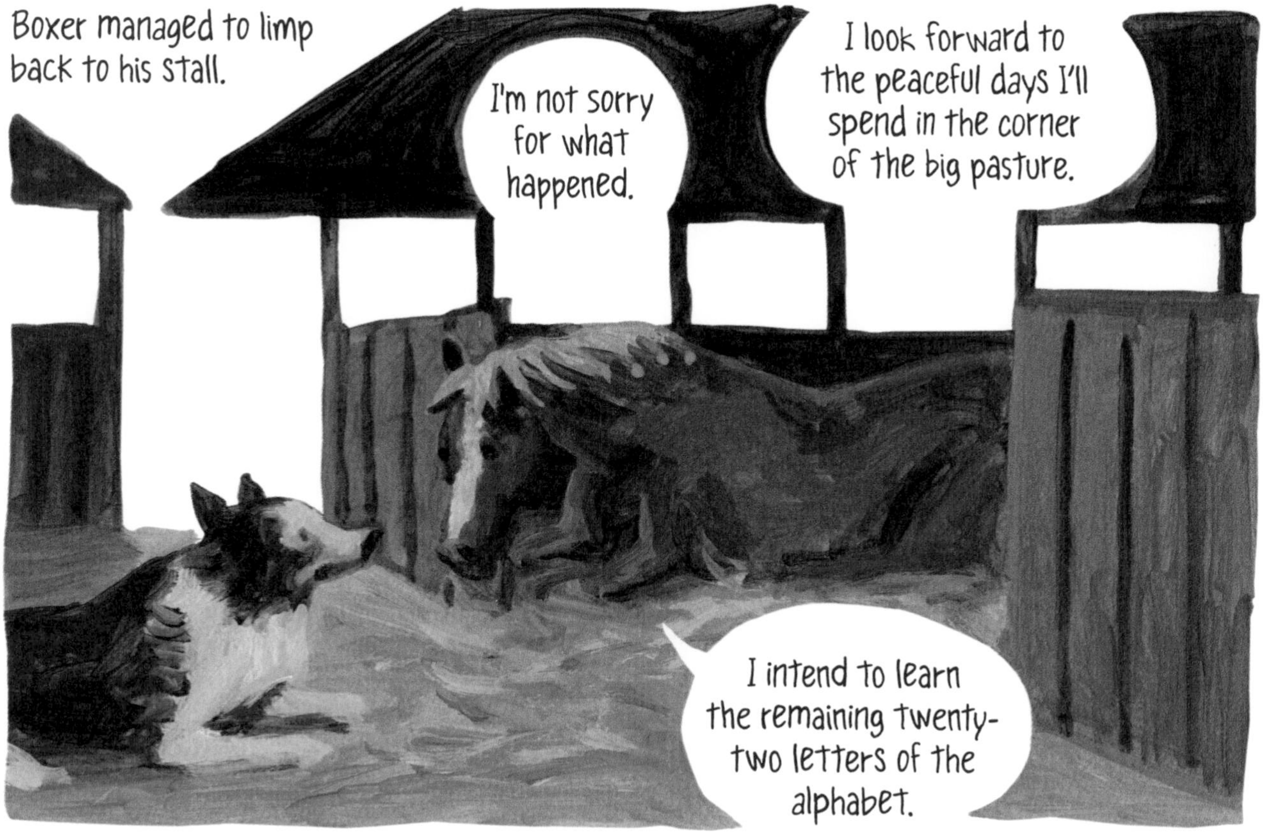
Boxer managed to limp back to his stall.
I'm not sorry for what happened.
I look forward to the peaceful days I'll spend in the corner of the big pasture.
I intend to learn the remaining twenty-two letters of the alphabet.

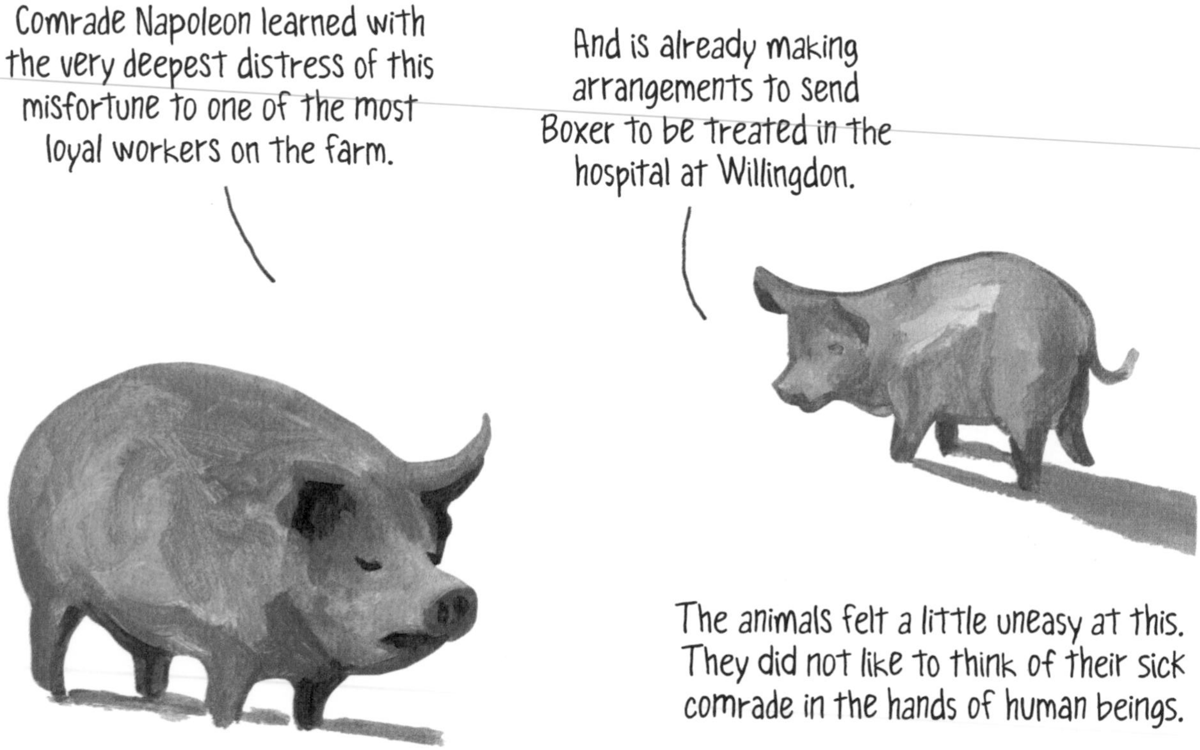
Comrade Napoleon learned with the very deepest distress of this misfortune to one of the most loyal workers on the farm.
And is already making arrangements to send Boxer to be treated in the hospital at Willingdon.
The animals felt a little uneasy at this. They did not like to think of their sick comrade in the hands of human beings.

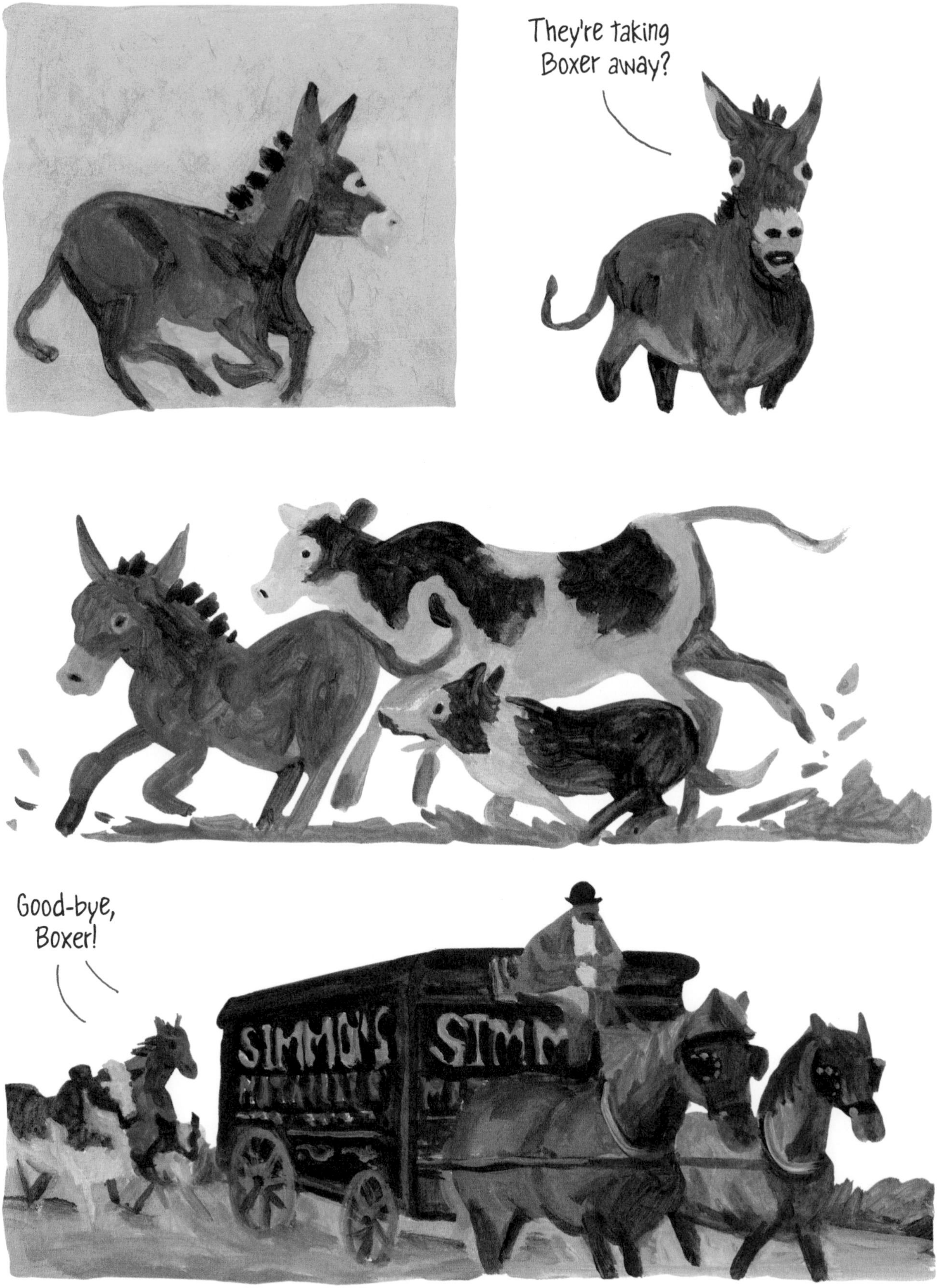
They're taking Boxer away?
Good-bye, Boxer!
SIMMO'S

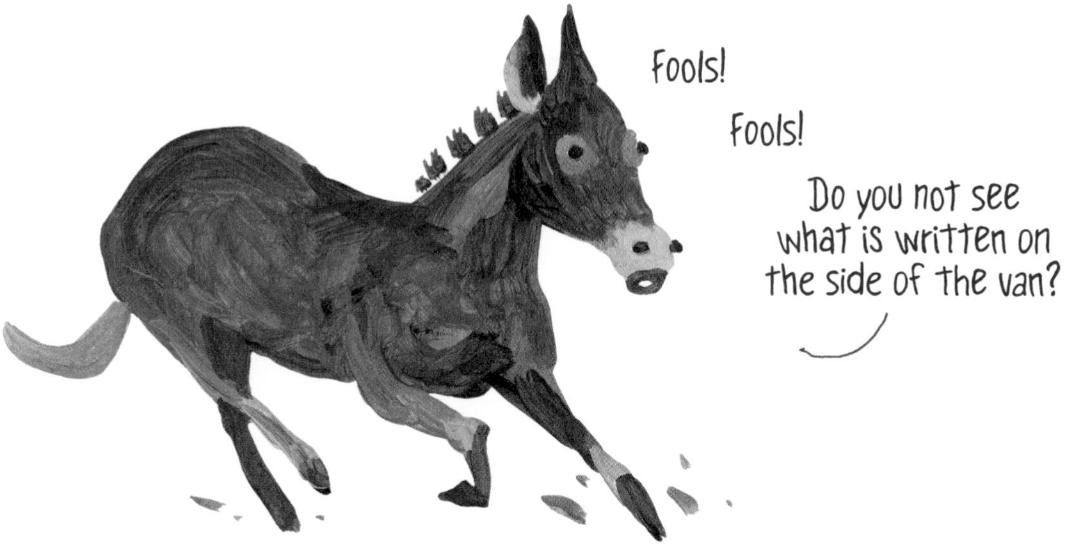
Fools!
Fools!
Do you not see what is written on the side of the van?

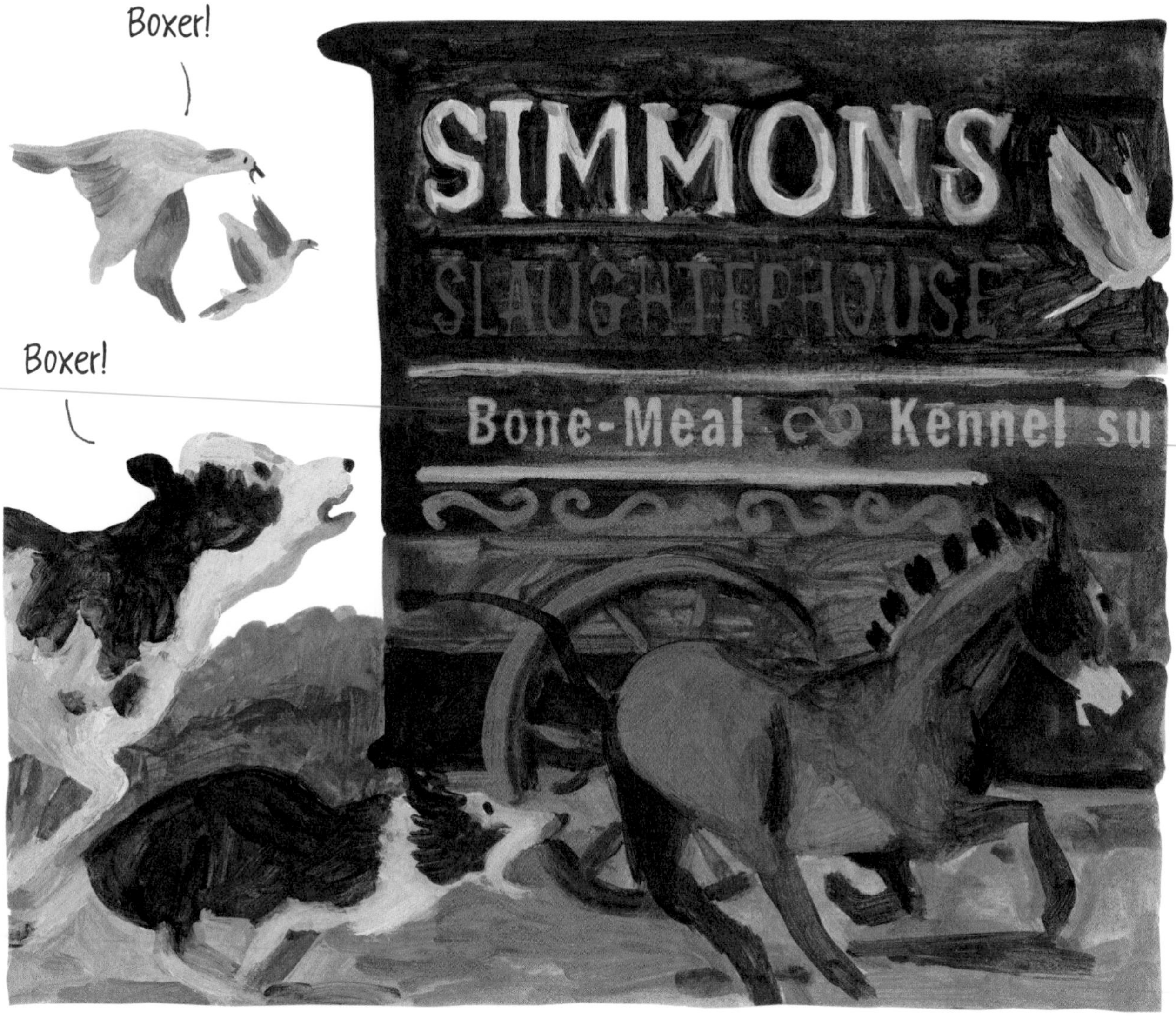
Boxer!
Boxer!
SIMMONS
SLAUGHTERHOUSE
Bone-Meal
Kennel su

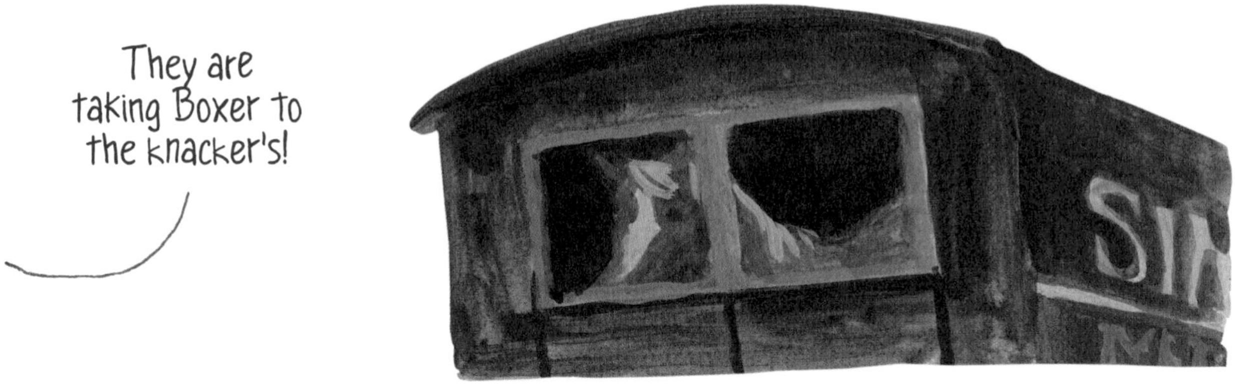
They are taking Boxer to the knacker's!

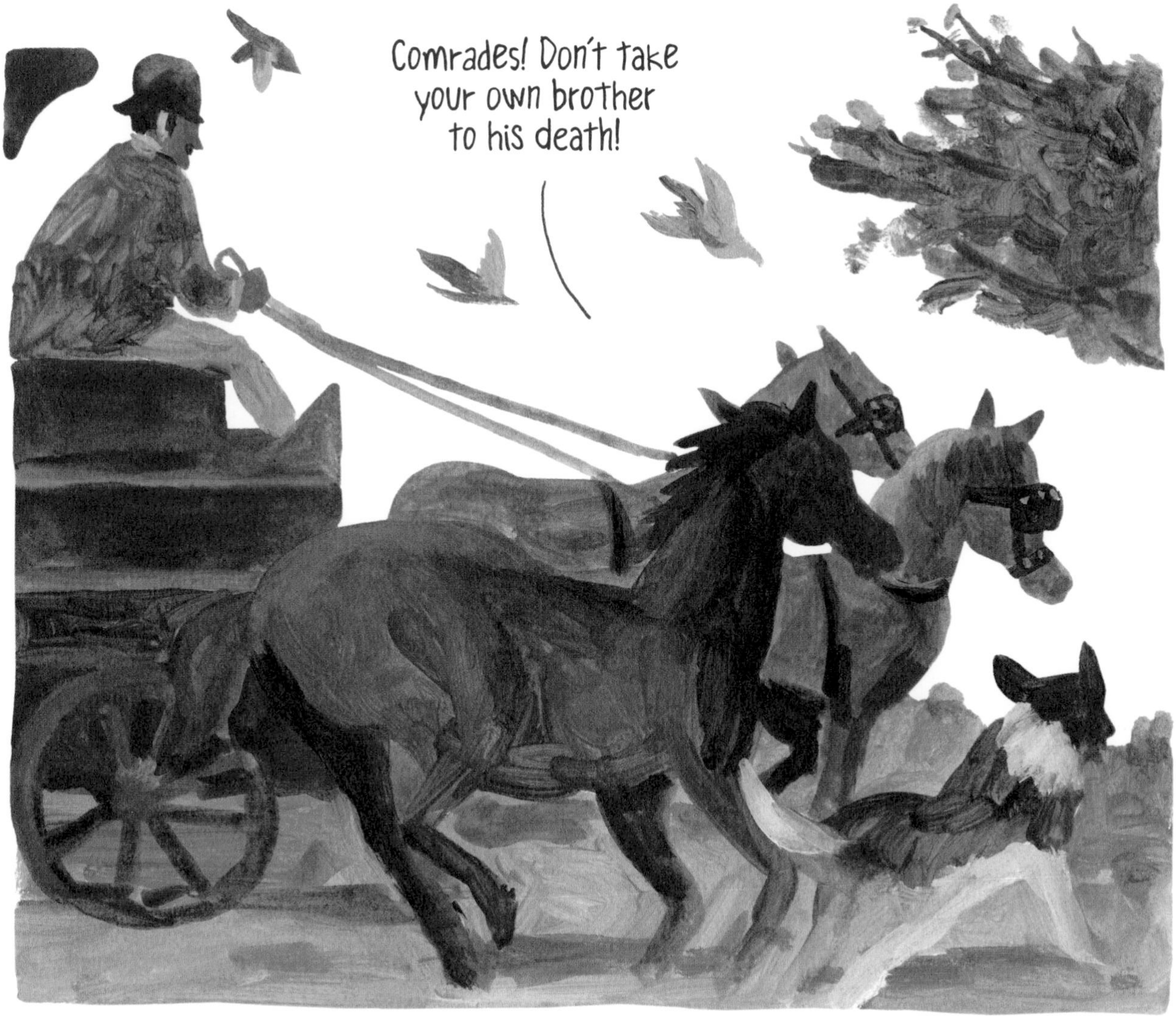
Comrades! Don't take your own brother to his death!

But the stupid brutes, too ignorant to realise what was happening, merely set back their ears and quickened their pace.

Too late, someone thought of racing ahead and shutting the five-barred gate; but in another moment the van was through it and rapidly disappearing down the road.

The explanation was really very simple.

The van had previously been the property of the knacker, and had been bought by the veterinary surgeon.

Boxer was never seen again.

X

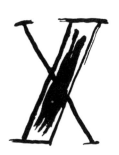

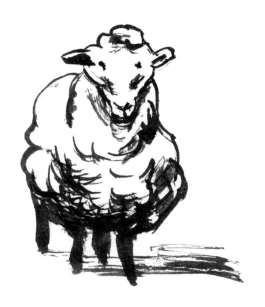

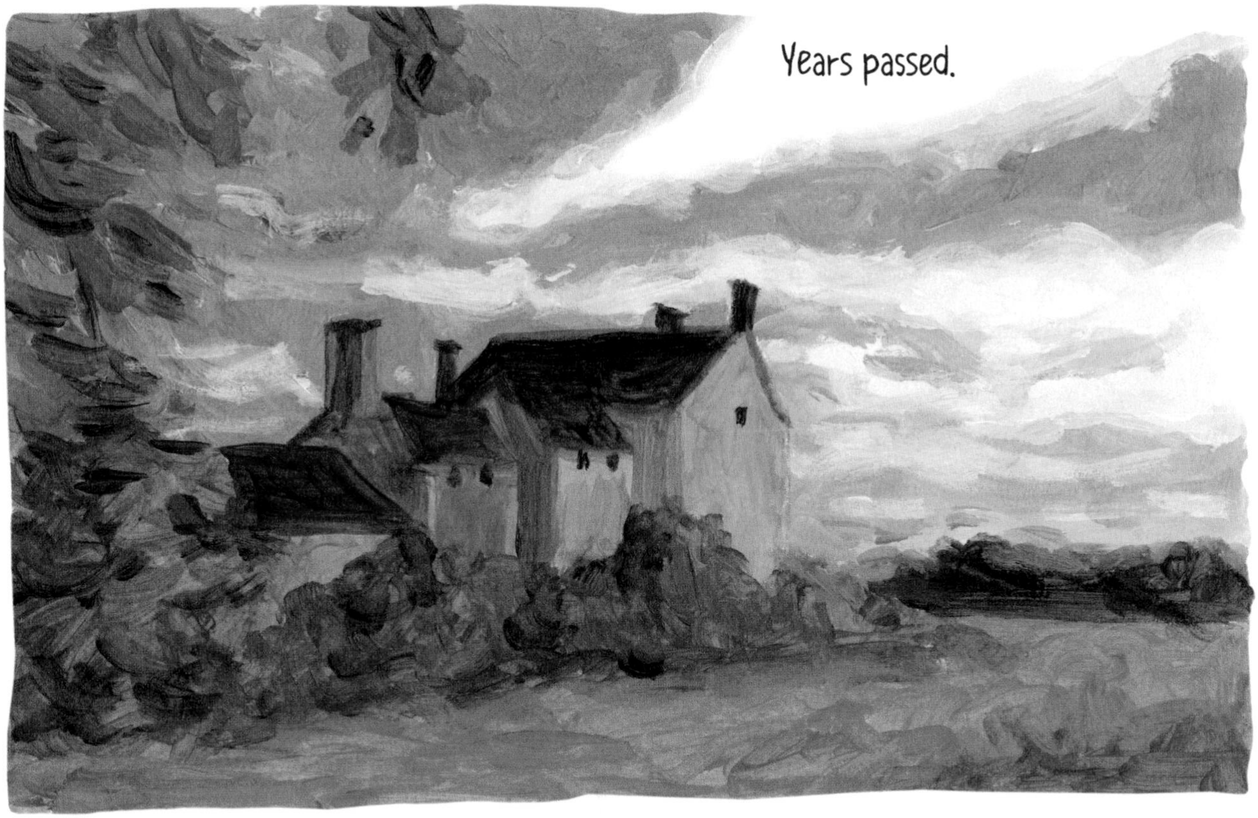
Years passed.

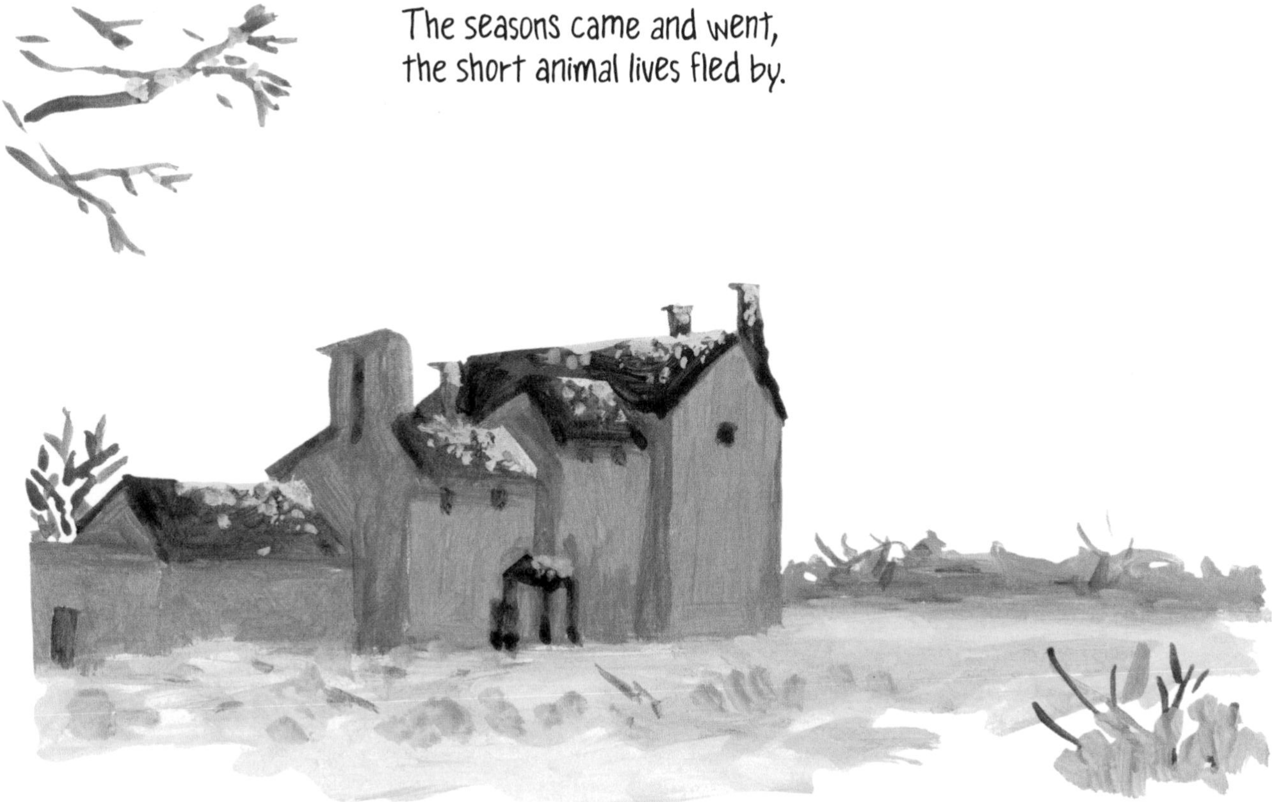
The seasons came and went,
the short animal lives fled by.

A time came when there was no one who remembered the old days before the Rebellion.

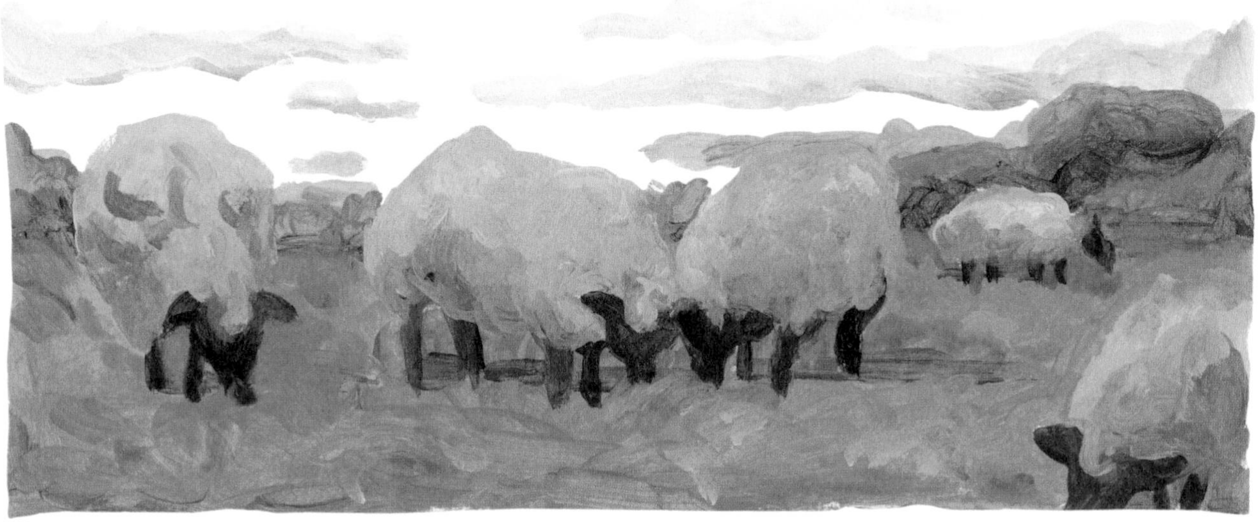

There were many more creatures on the farm, and it was more prosperous now. The windmill had been successfully completed at last.

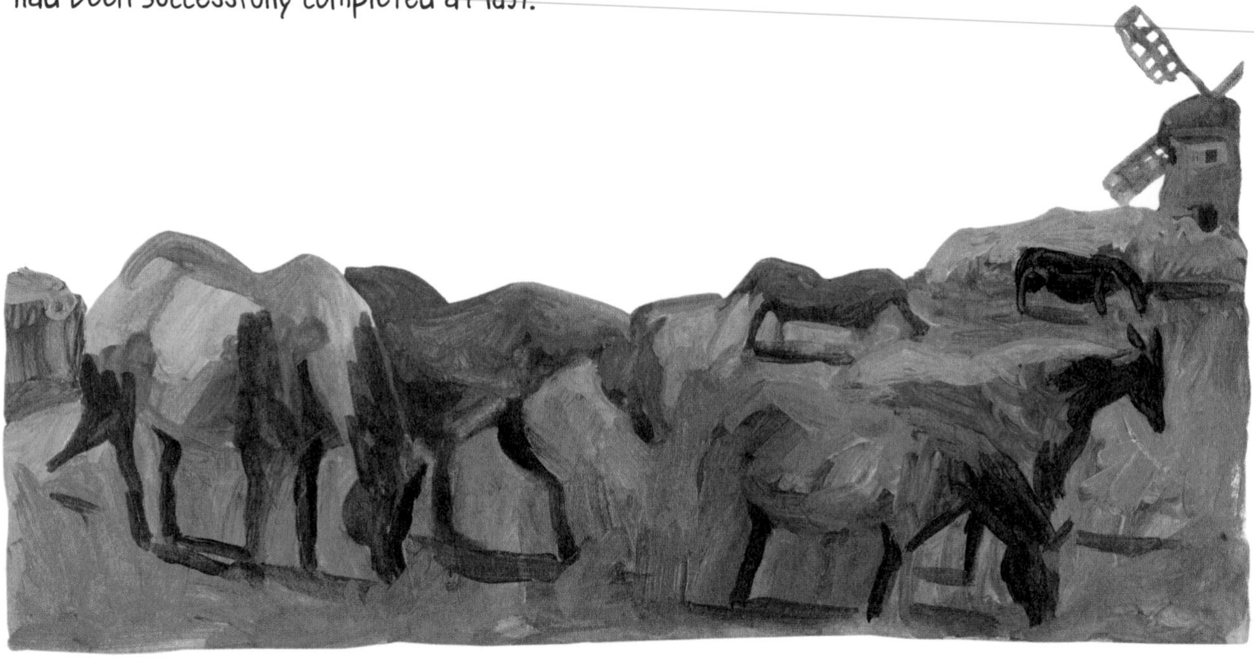

Somehow it seemed as though the farm had grown richer without making the animals themselves any richer.

Except, of course, for the pigs and the dogs.

Perhaps this was partly because there were so many pigs and so many dogs.

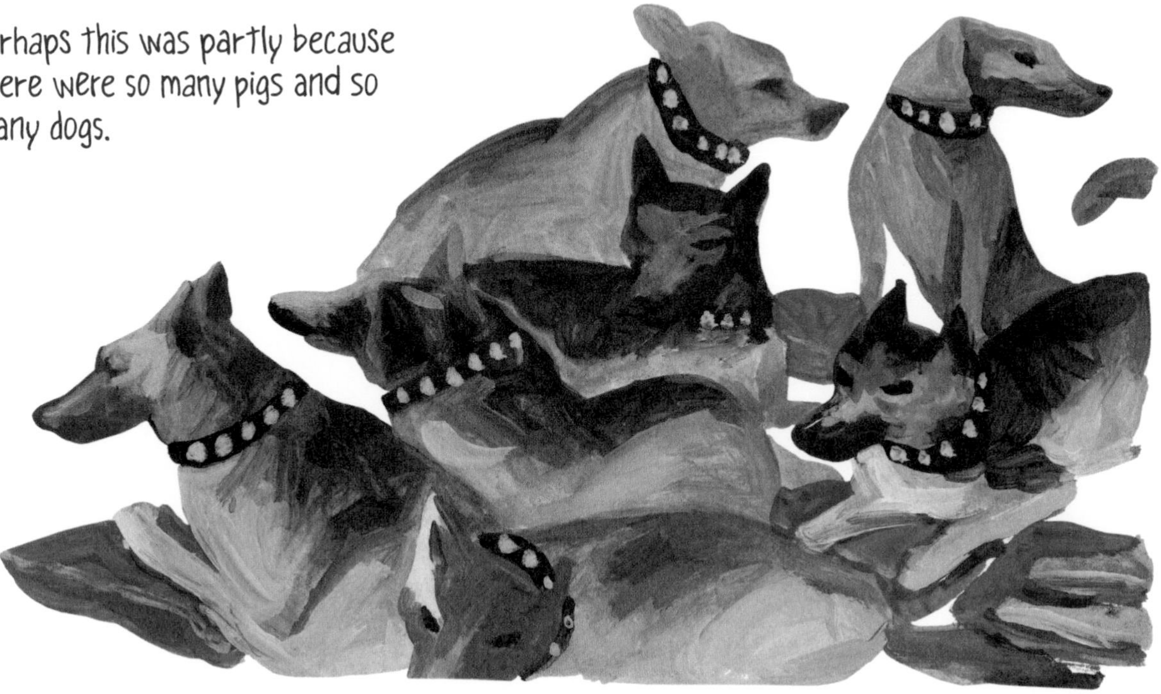

As for the others, their life, so far as they knew, was as it had always been.

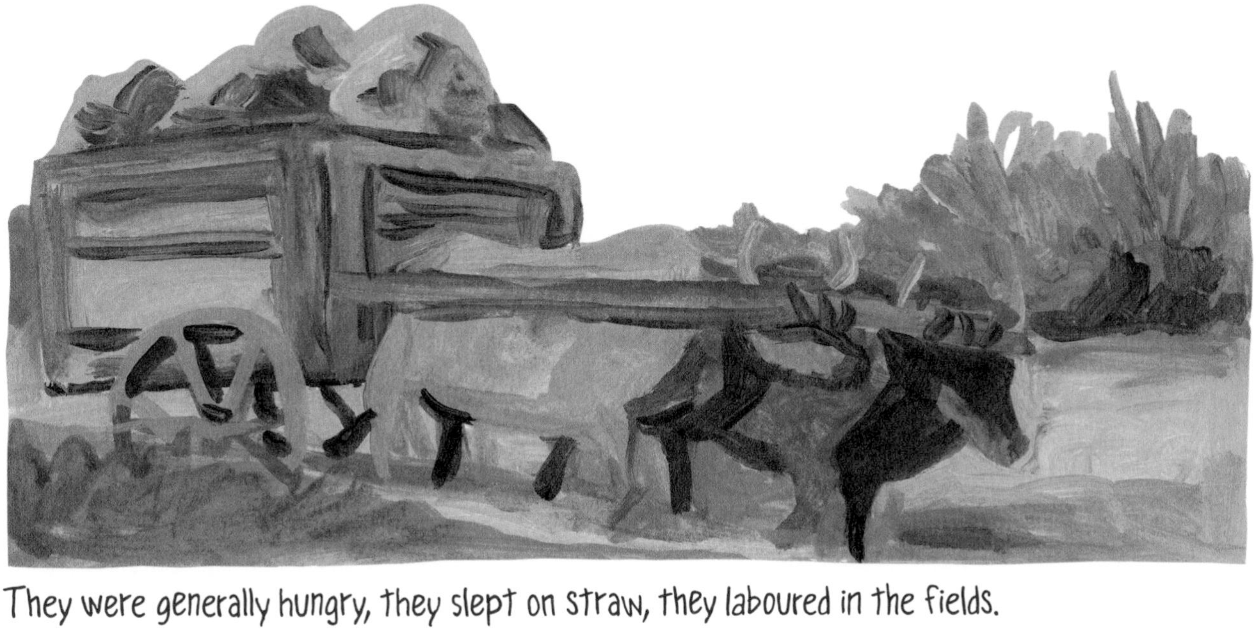

They were generally hungry, they slept on straw, they laboured in the fields.

And yet the animals never gave up hope.

More, they never lost, even for an instant, their sense of honour and privilege in being members of Animal Farm.

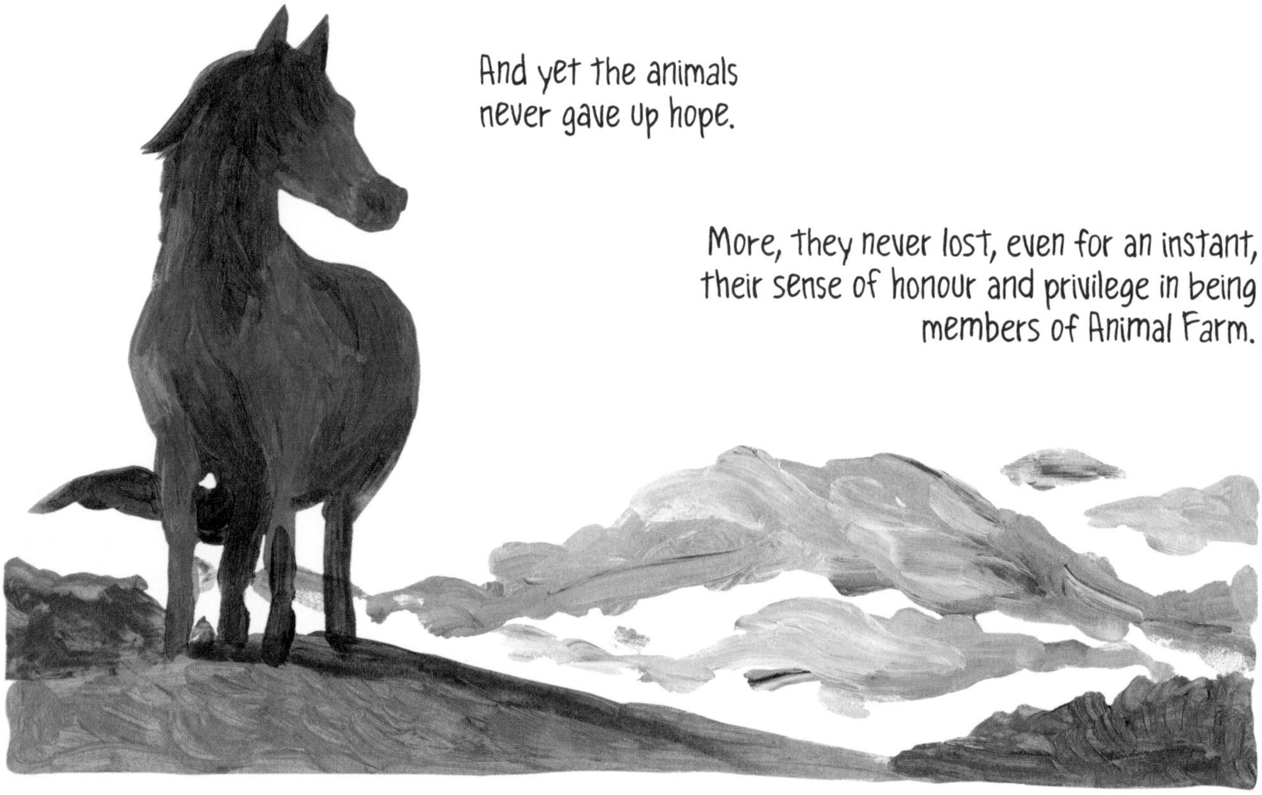

They were still the only farm in the whole county – in all England! – owned and operated by animals.

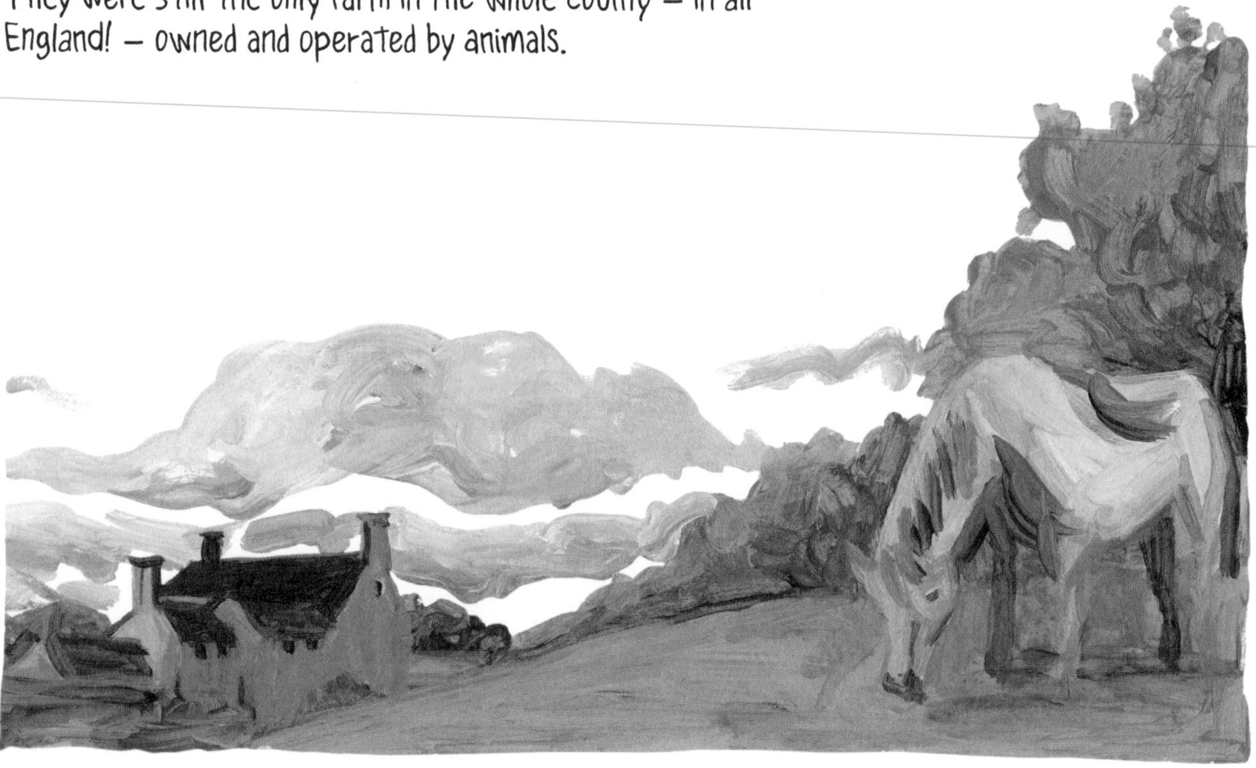

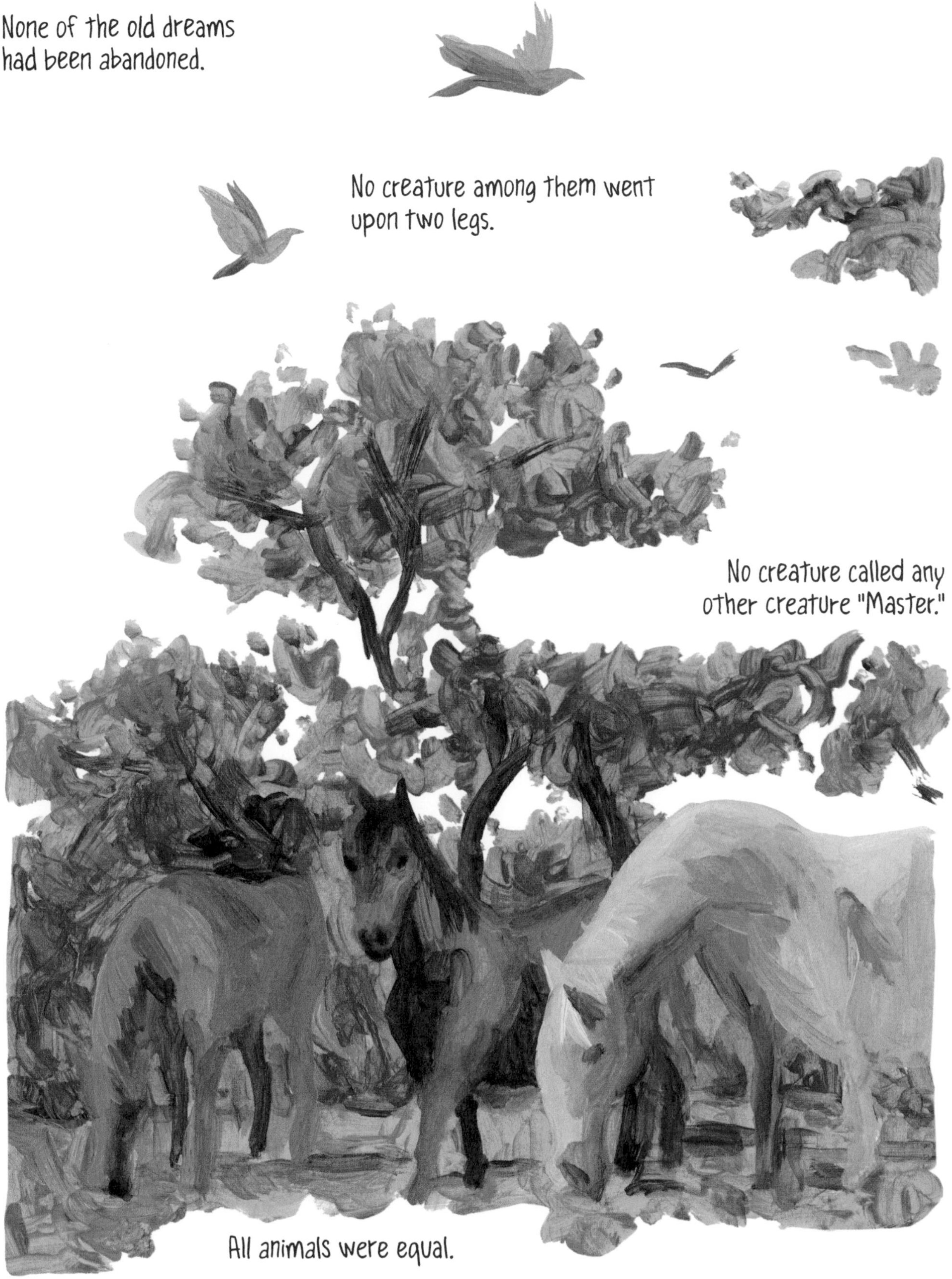
None of the old dreams had been abandoned.
No creature among them went upon two legs.
No creature called any other creature "Master."
All animals were equal.

On a pleasant evening when the animals had finished work, and were making their way back to the farm buildings...

they heard the terrified neighing of a horse. It was Clover's voice.

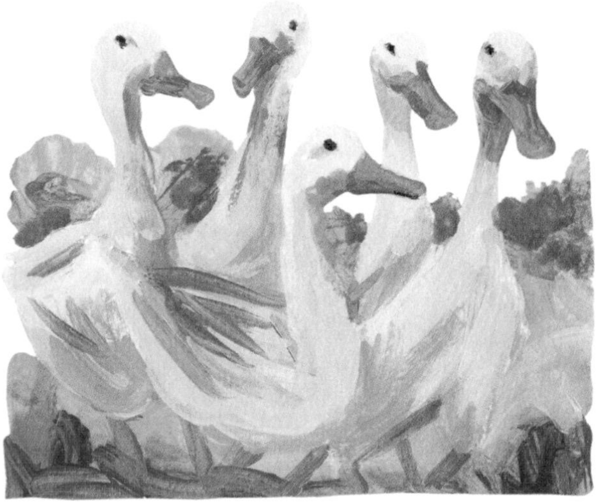

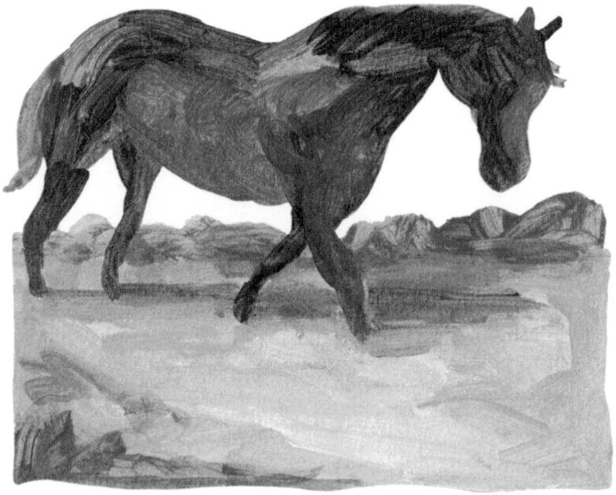

It was a pig walking on his hind legs.

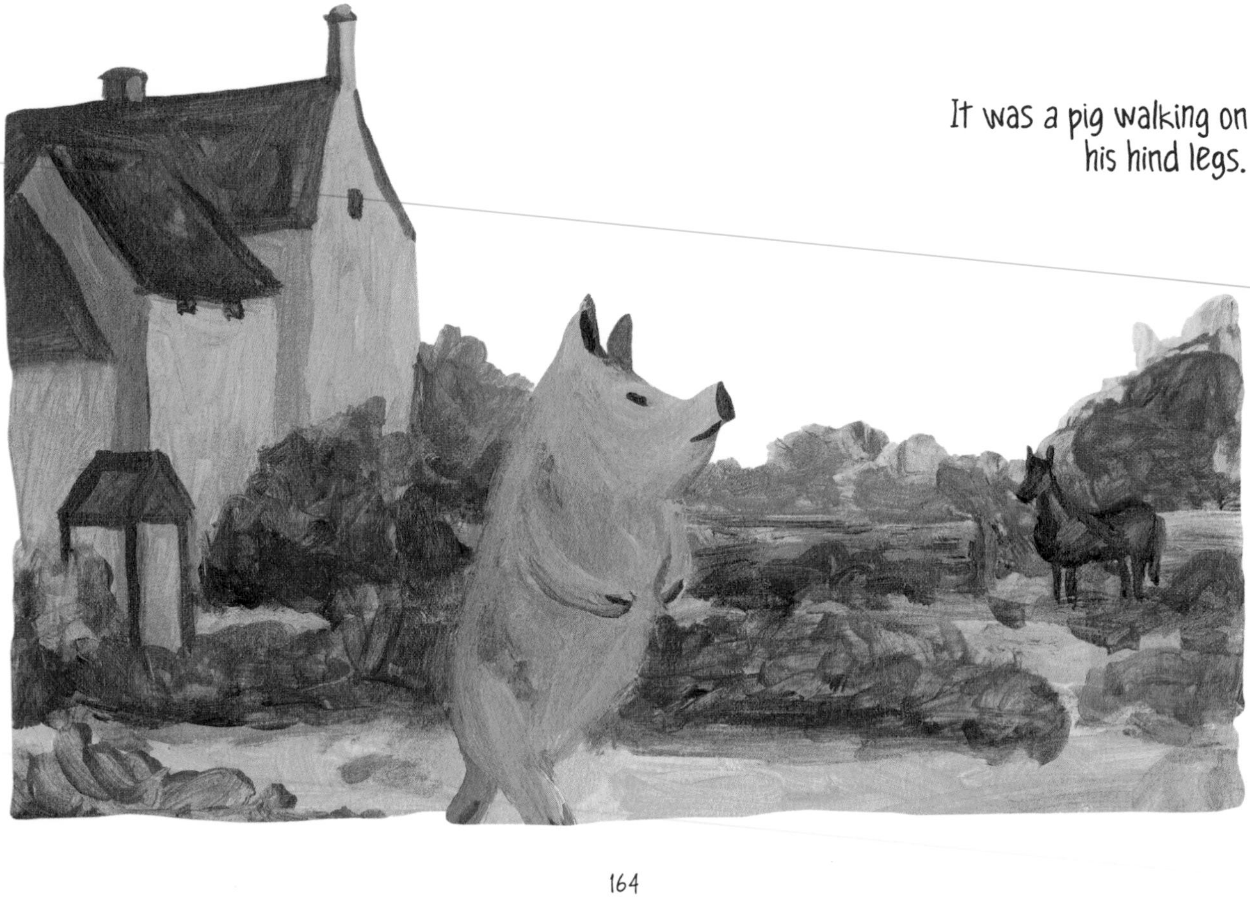

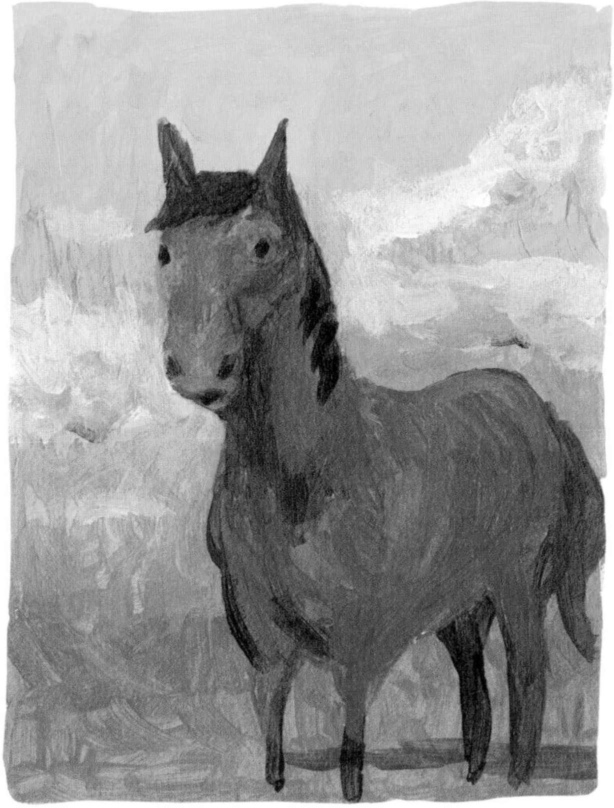

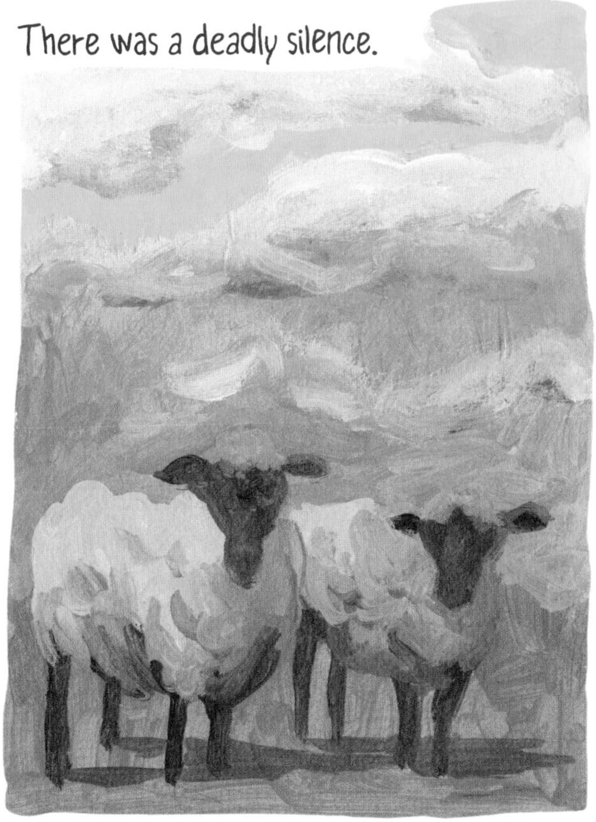
There was a deadly silence.

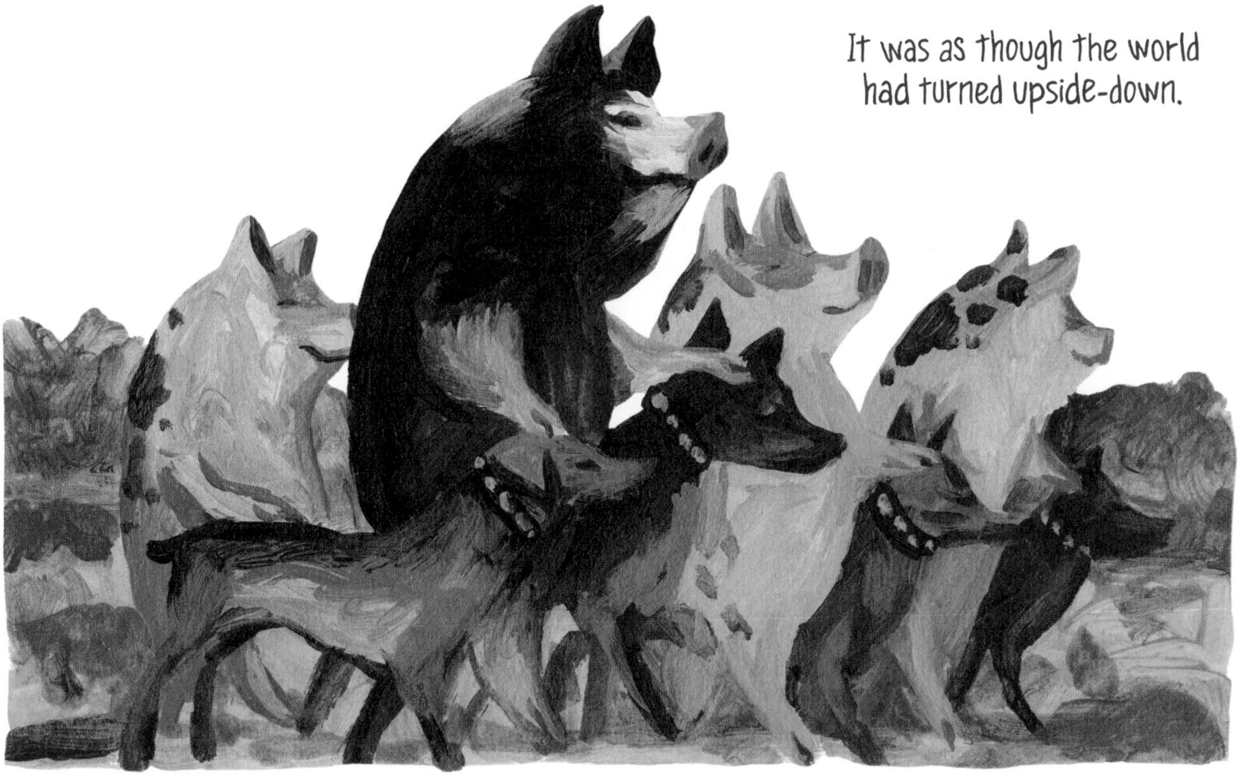
It was as though the world
had turned upside-down.

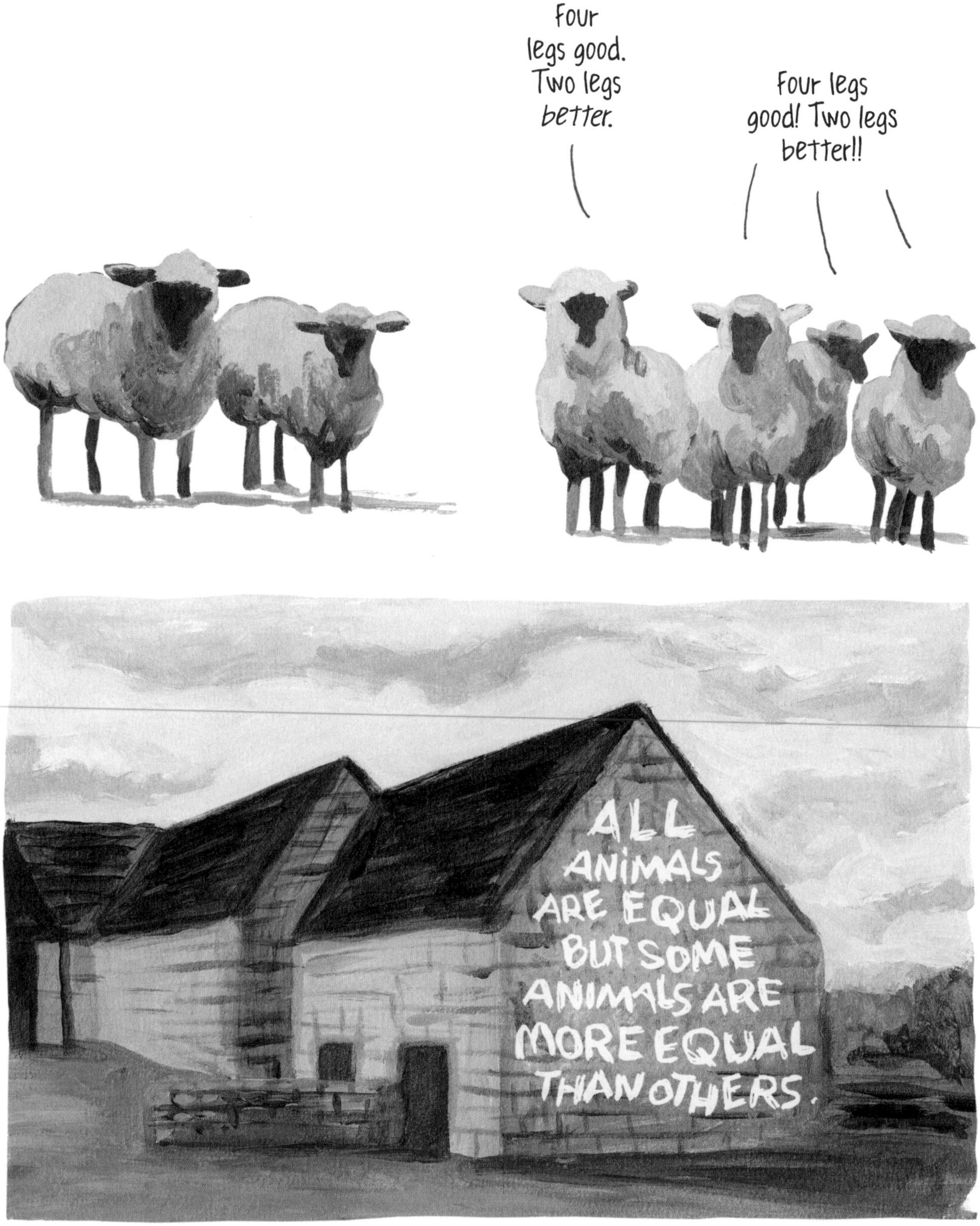
Four legs good. Two legs better.
Four legs good! Two legs better!!
ALL ANIMALS ARE EQUAL BUT SOME ANIMALS ARE MORE EQUAL THAN OTHERS.

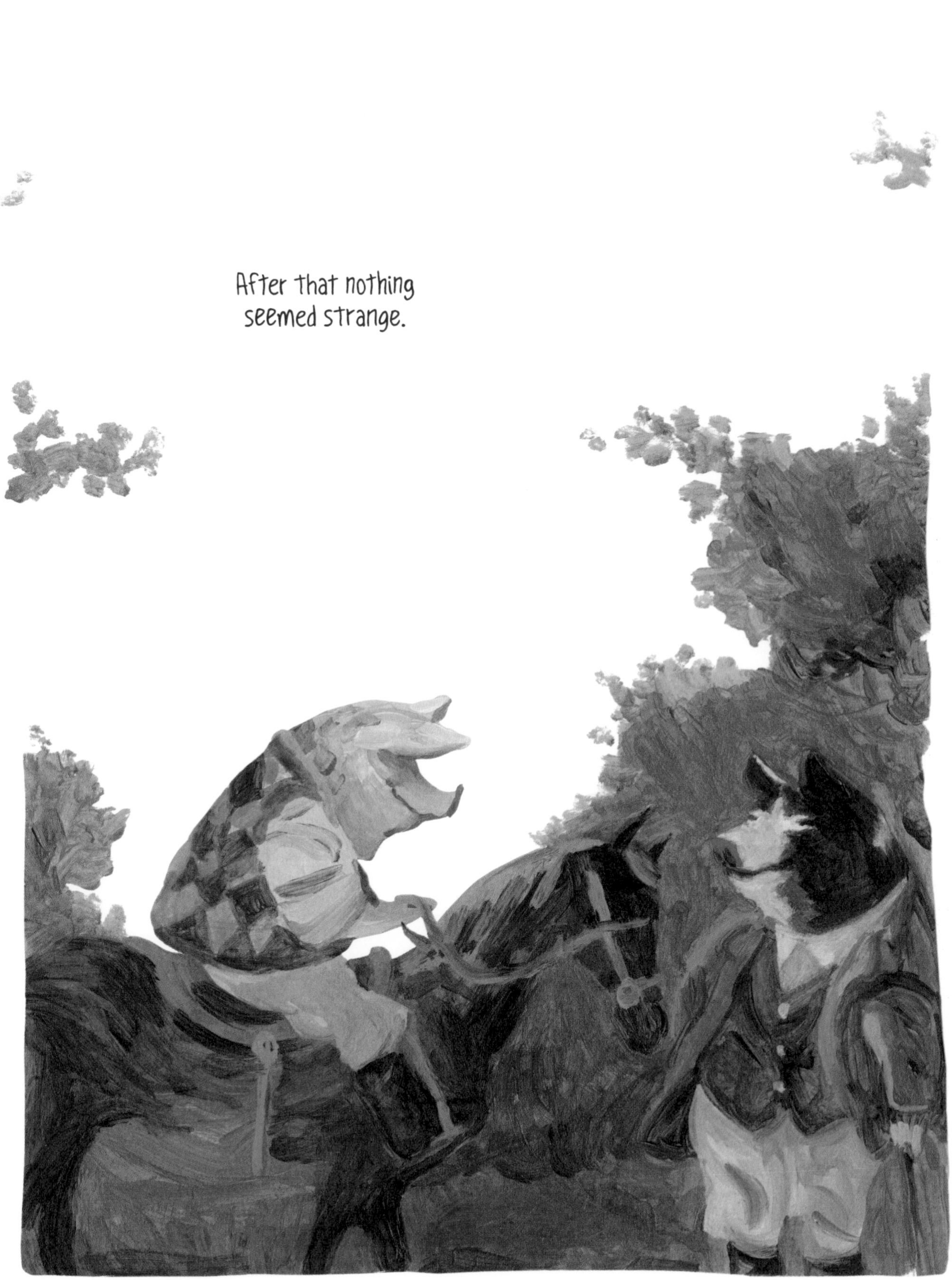
After that nothing
seemed strange.

That evening loud laughter and bursts of singing came from the farmhouse. And suddenly, at the sound of the mingled voices, the animals were stricken with curiosity.

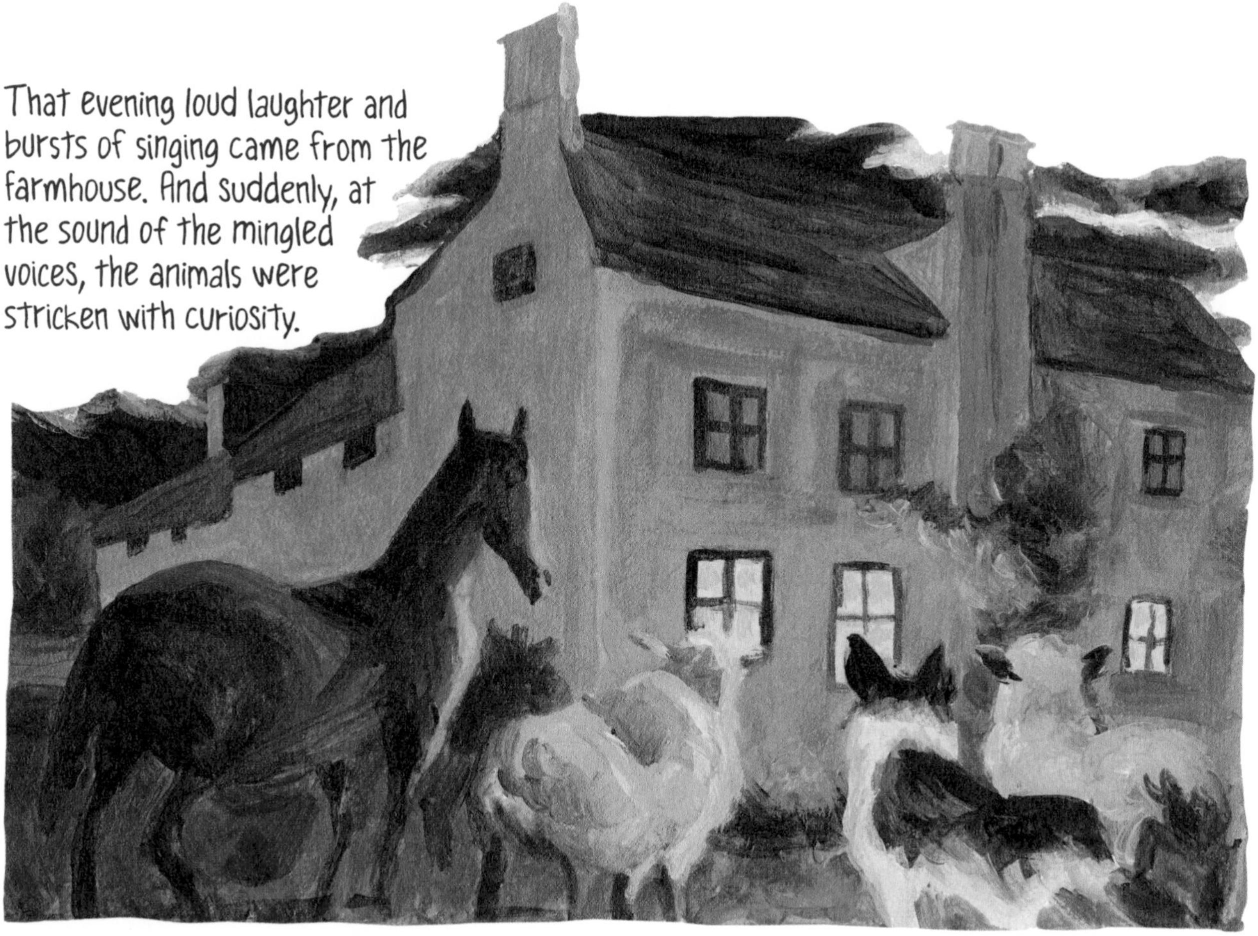

What could be happening in there, now that for the first time animals and human beings were meeting on terms of equality?

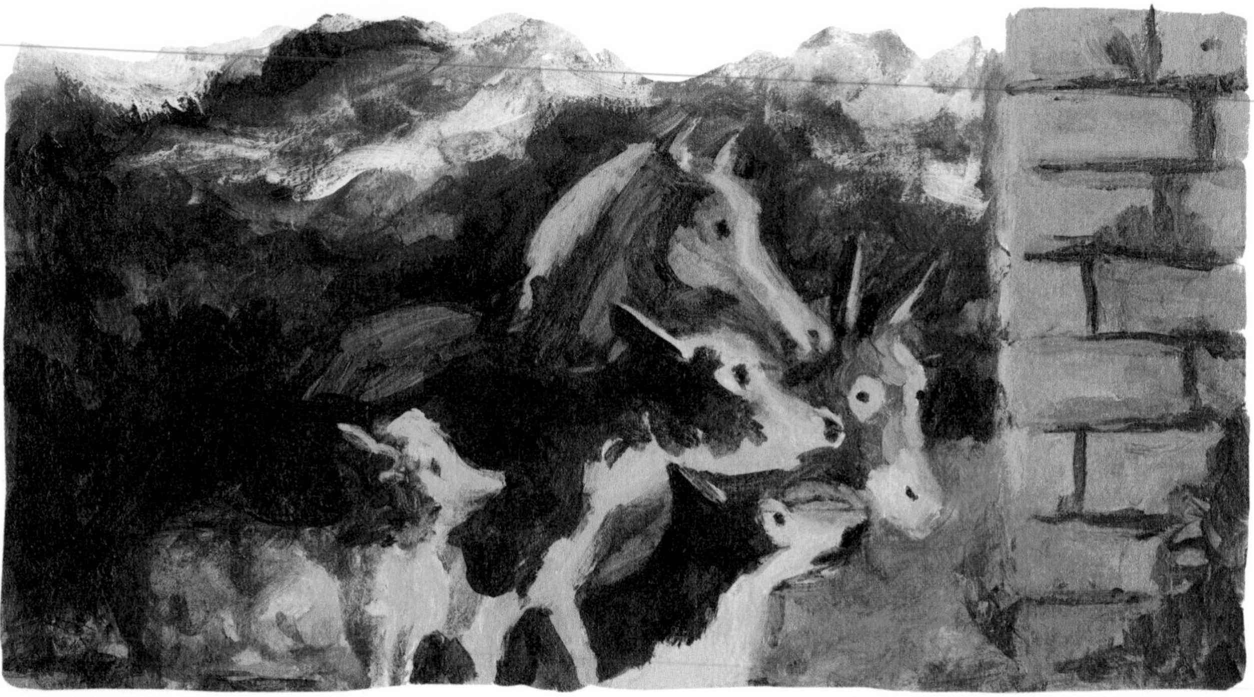

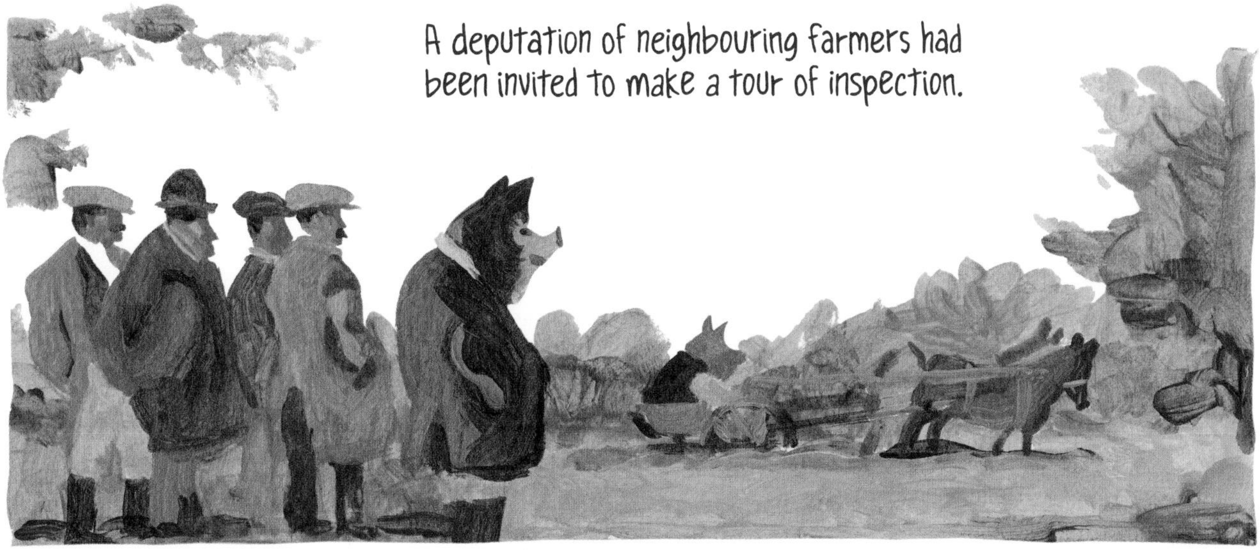
A deputation of neighbouring farmers had been invited to make a tour of inspection.

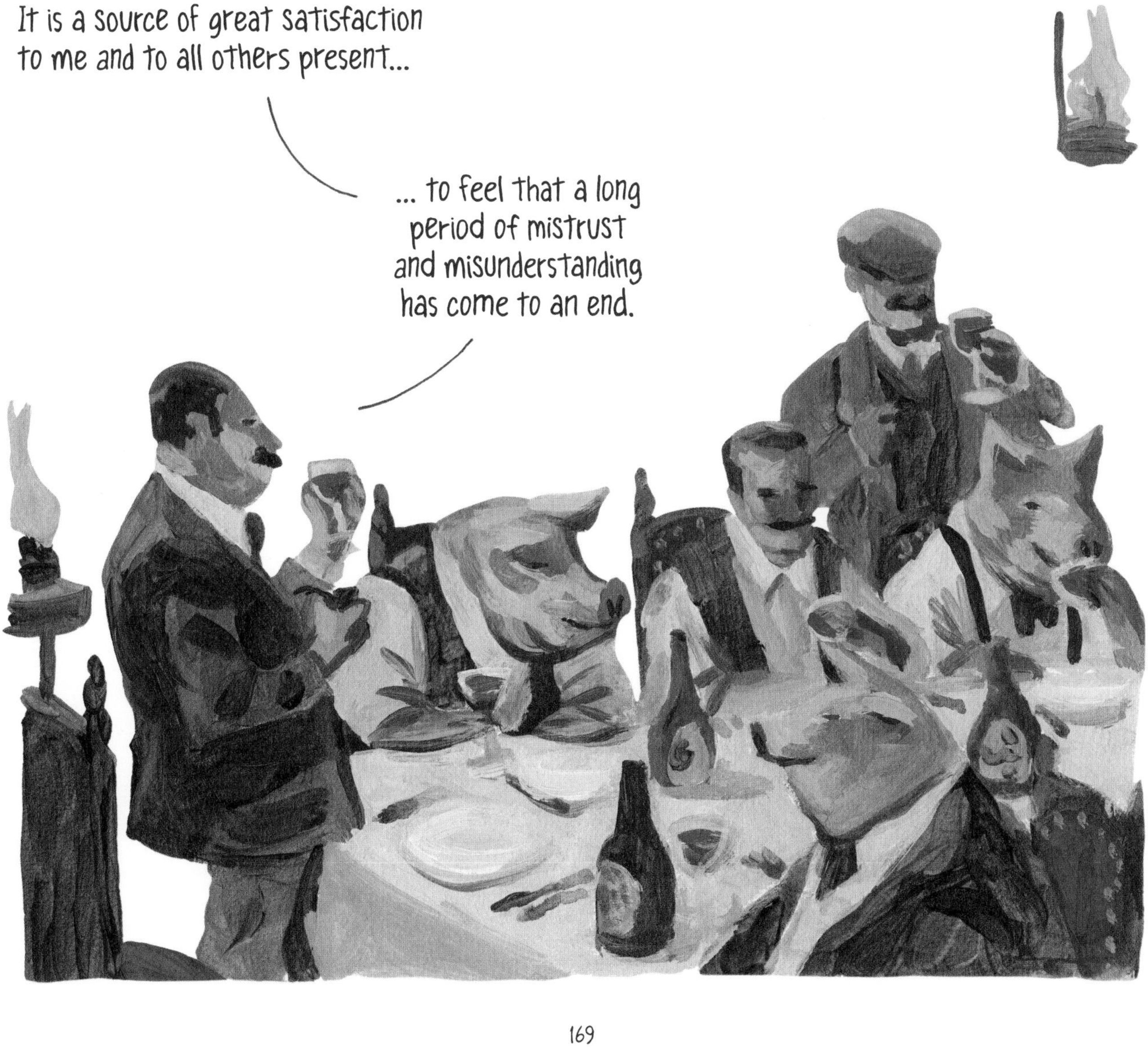
It is a source of great satisfaction to me and to all others present...
... to feel that a long period of mistrust and misunderstanding has come to an end.

They had been nervous about the effects upon their own animals, or even upon their human employees.

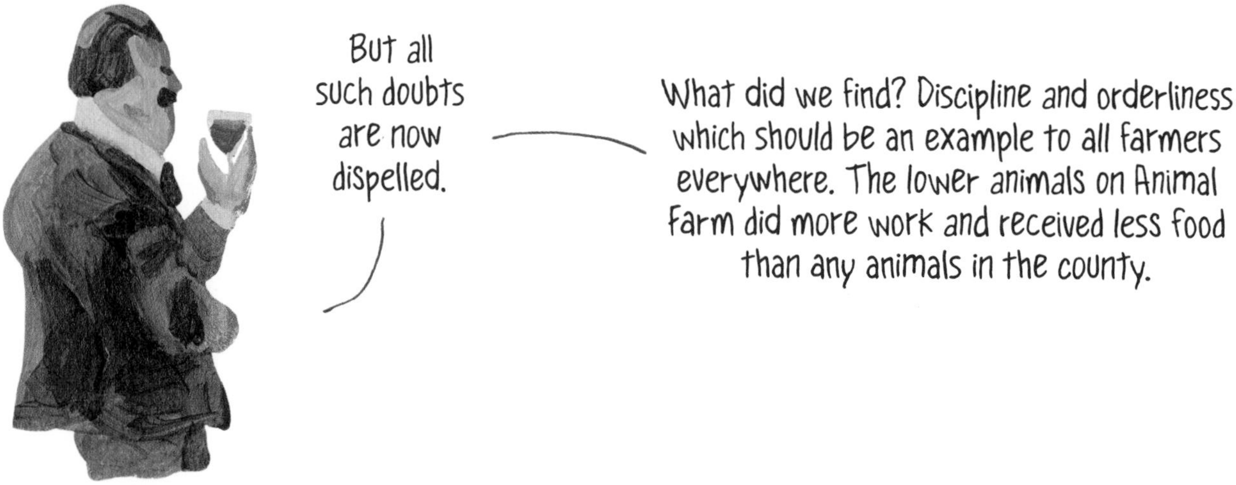
But all such doubts are now dispelled.
What did we find? Discipline and orderliness which should be an example to all farmers everywhere. The lower animals on Animal Farm did more work and received less food than any animals in the county.

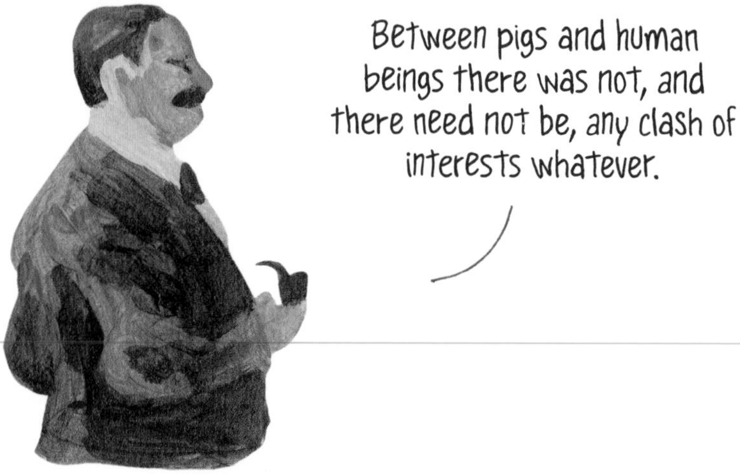
Between pigs and human beings there was not, and there need not be, any clash of interests whatever.

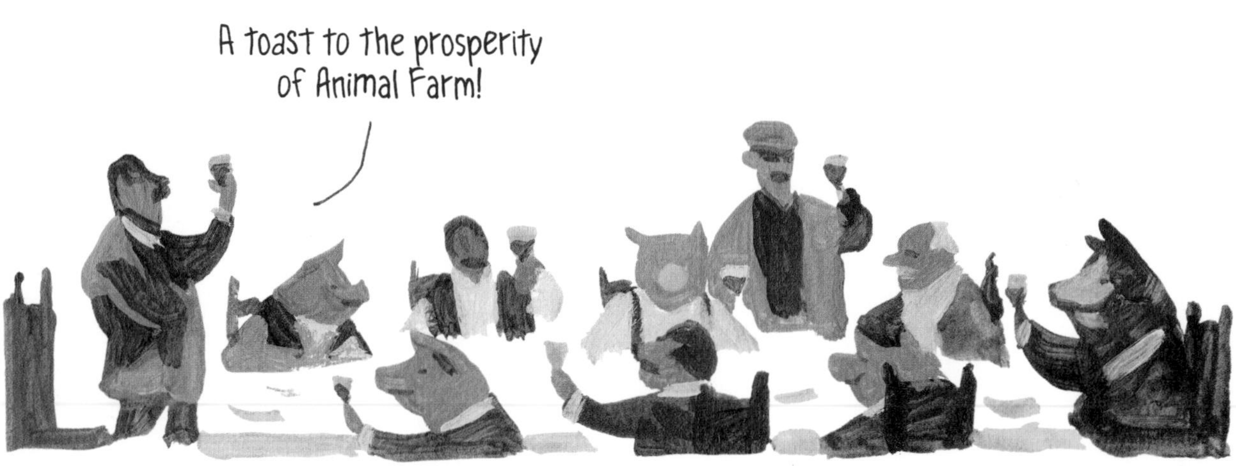
A toast to the prosperity of Animal Farm!

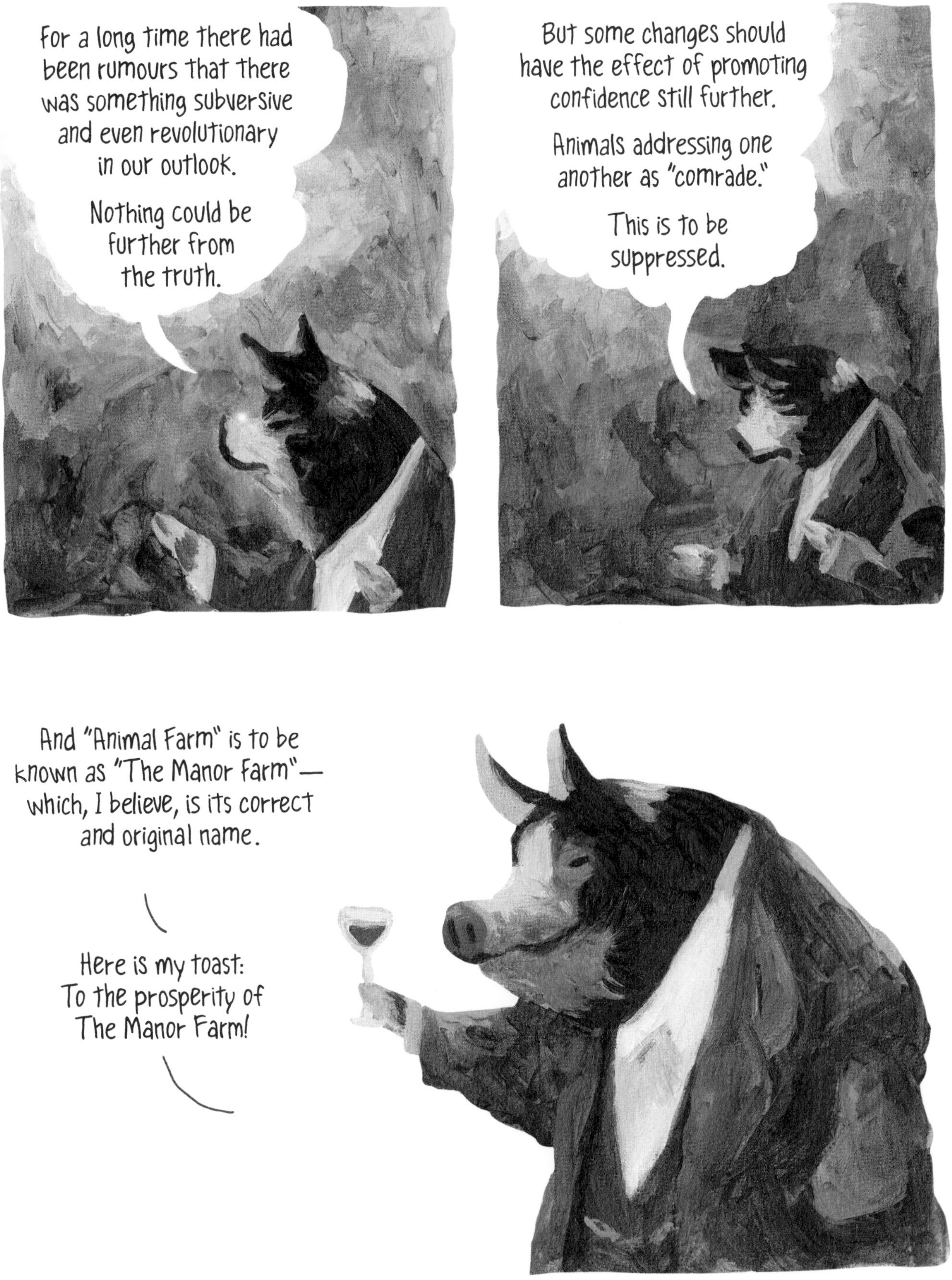

For a long time there had been rumours that there was something subversive and even revolutionary in our outlook.
Nothing could be further from the truth.
But some changes should have the effect of promoting confidence still further.
Animals addressing one another as "comrade."
This is to be suppressed.
And "Animal Farm" is to be known as "The Manor Farm"—which, I believe, is its correct and original name.
Here is my toast: To the prosperity of The Manor Farm!

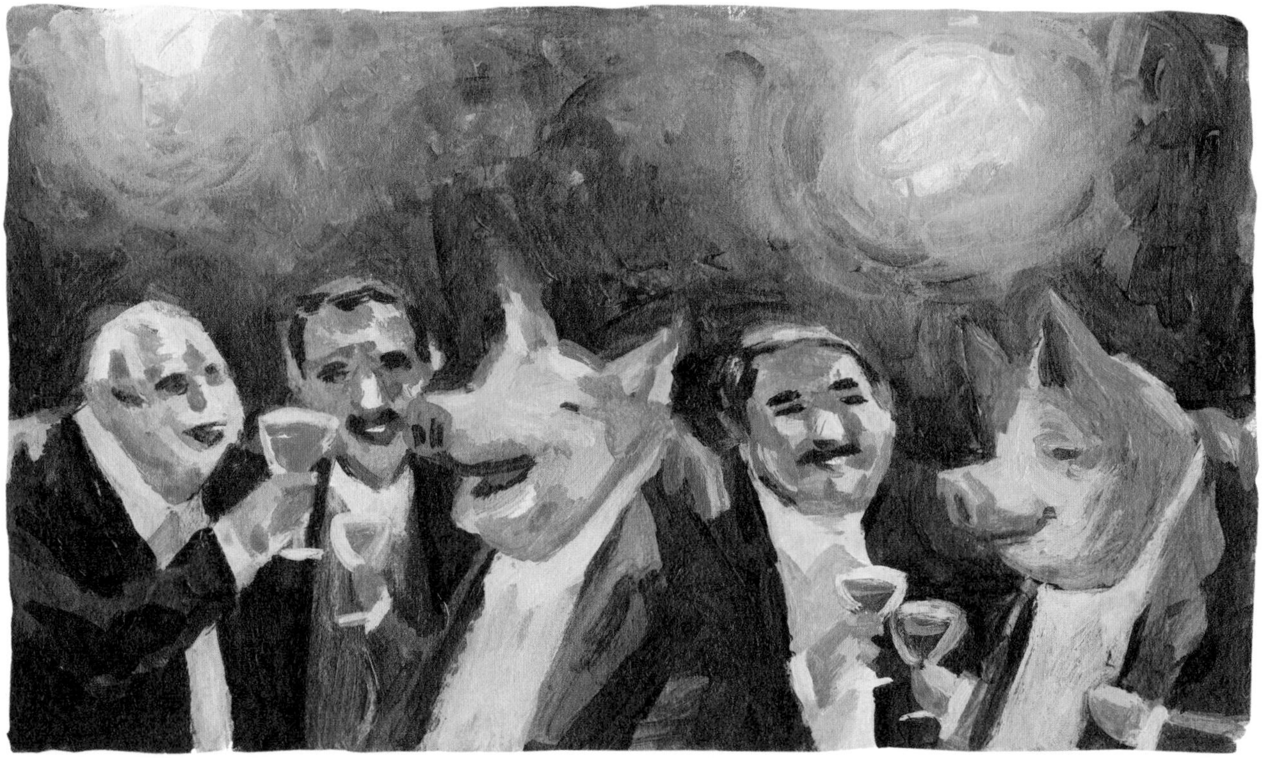

The creatures outside looked from pig to man, and from man to pig, and from pig to man again; but already it was impossible to say which was which.

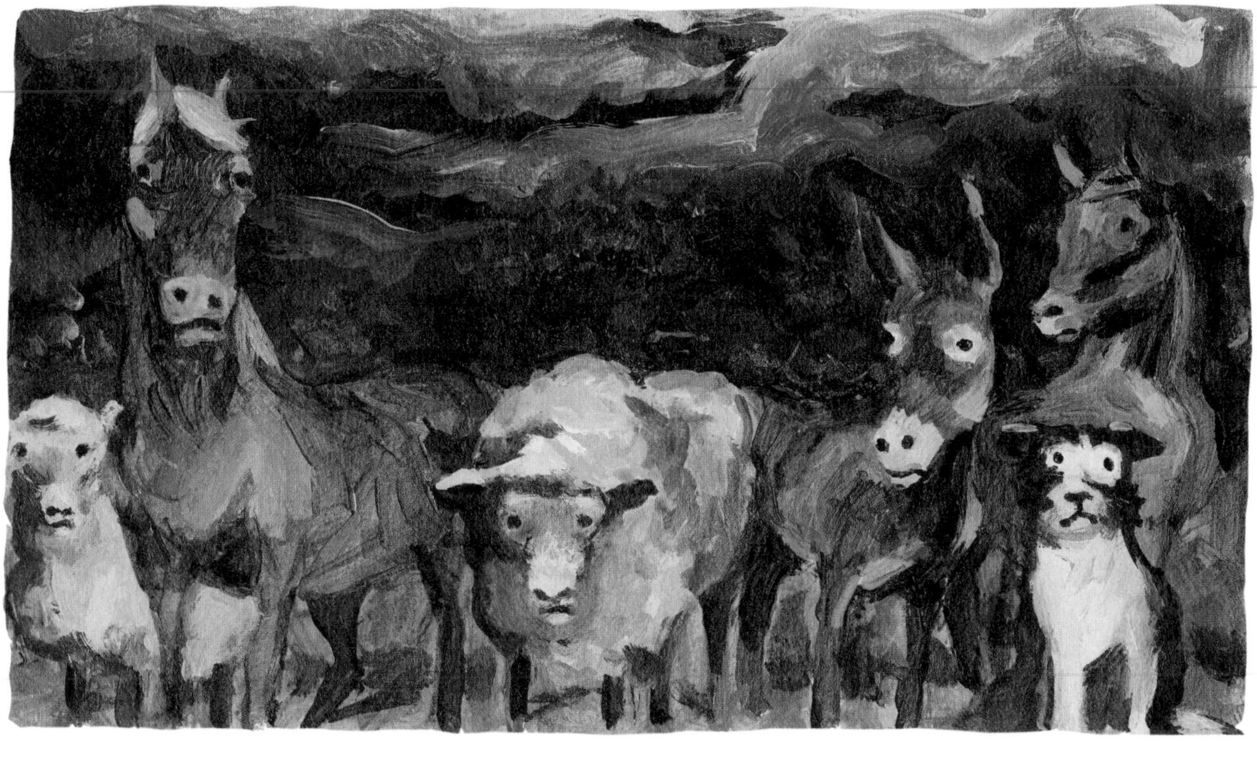

GEORGE ORWELL was born in 1903 in
Motihari, Bengal, India, the son of a British
colonial civil servant. He was educated in Eton
and in 1922 joined the Indian Imperial Police in
Burma, resigning in 1927 to become a writer.
From 1934 to 1949 he published several novels,
essays, and articles. Considered one of the
most important writers of the 20th century,
he is the author of 1984, *Down and Out in
Paris and London*, and *What Is Fascism?* He
died in London, in 1950.

ODYR was born in 1967, in Pelotas, Brazil. He is a comics artist and painter, with two books published – Copacabana, with script by Lobo, and Guadalupe, with script by Angélica Freitas. He participated in several comics anthologies and his short stories and illustrations have been published in Brazilian newspapers and magazines such as *Folha de São Paulo, O Globo, Le Monde Diplomatique Brasil*, among others.